ALSO BY CHARLES TODD

The Ian Rutledge Mysteries

A Test of Wills

A Bitter Truth

LARGE PRINT

ALSO BY CHARLES TODD

A Bitter Truth

Charles Todd

HARPER LUXE

An Imprint of HarperCollins*Publishers*

A BITTER TRUTH. Copyright © 2011 by Charles Todd. All rights reserved. Printed in the United States of America. No part of this book may be used or reproduced in any manner whatsoever without written permission except in the case of brief quotations embodied in critical articles and reviews. For information address HarperCollins Publishers, 10 East 53rd Street, New York, NY 10022.

HarperCollins books may be purchased for educational, business, or sales promotional use. For information please write: Special Markets Department, HarperCollins Publishers, 10 East 53rd Street, New York, NY 10022.

FIRST HARPERLUXE EDITION

HarperLuxe™ is a trademark of HarperCollins Publishers

Library of Congress Cataloging-in-Publication Data is available upon request.

ISBN: 978-0-06-208855-0

11 12 13 14   ID/OPM 10 9 8 7 6 5 4 3 2 1

For Monty,
who won't be there this time.
And for Moses,
who will.
With hugs and much love, as always.

And for Jean, reader, cook, proofreader, friend,
who always does things differently.
With gratitude.

One

A cold rain had followed me from France to England, and an even colder wind greeted me as we
pulled into the railway station in London. As I handed
in my ticket, I looked for my father, who was usually
here to meet me. Or if he couldn't come, he generally
sent Simon Brandon in his place.

But there were no familiar faces among the crowd,
and after waiting nearly fifteen minutes, I decided that
my telegram from Dover must have been delayed. Of
course military traffic was always given priority, but
the telegraph office had assured me that they would do
their best. There was nothing for it but to find a cab for
myself.

Outside Victoria Station, a family with small children was just bespeaking the last one. Well, then, it

would have to be an omnibus. As I walked on to the nearest stop, the wind whipped along the street after me, plucking at my skirts, prodding my back. One going in my direction was already approaching, for which I was grateful, and as we rumbled through the darkness toward my destination, I took stock of the city I hadn't seen for several months.

Even at this hour it was quiet, the streets empty except for a few brave souls going about their business with heads down and coats wrapped tightly against the probing fingers of the wind. Shops were already closing, and everywhere curtains were drawn to keep out the night. In front of a pub we were passing, a few men stood talking for a moment, hands deep in pockets, and even as I watched, they said their farewells and hurried their separate ways toward home. A boy raced up the steps of a church and disappeared through the heavy door, a shaft of light briefly illuminating his worried face. The sound of voices just reached me, a boys' choir, and at a guess, he had nearly missed rehearsal.

We were only three stops from where I usually got down when the omnibus came to a lurching halt.

Just ahead of us, I could see torches flashing this way and that in the street, and someone was shouting at us.

My first thought was that we had struck someone.

I got to my feet, ready to offer whatever aid was needed, just as a middle-aged constable hurried up to the omnibus and spoke to the driver. We couldn't hear what was said, but soon enough the constable had opened the omnibus door and stepped inside. He frowned when he saw me standing there.

"Is anyone hurt?" I asked quickly.

"No, Sister," he said harshly. "Resume your seat."

I did as I was told, and he scanned each of us with a thoroughness that indicated he was intent on finding someone. Finally, apparently satisfied, he was gone, mercifully closing the door behind him and shutting out the wind. But I heard his boots climbing the rear stairs to the upper deck, where no one had had the courage to sit, then pelt down again after several seconds. He and the driver exchanged a few more words, and I saw the driver reluctantly nod. And then the constable was hurrying away, caught for a brief moment in the glare of our headlamps.

A man just behind where I was sitting demanded fretfully, "What's happened? Why did we stop?"

Outside, the driver got down from behind the wheel and opened the door once more, poking his head inside, his face barely visible above a thick blue muffler. "Deserter," he informed us. "We won't be allowed to move on until this street has been cleared. The police have reason to believe he's hiding hereabouts. Or being hidden."

Everyone began asking questions at the same time, but the driver simply shook his head and closed the door. I was looking out the window, clearing the glass with one gloved hand, watching the play of torches against the windows and doors of the houses on my side as the police went on with their search. And then out of the corner of my eye, I saw a figure in black slip down a service passage, disappearing into the deeper shadows cast by the houses on either side. There would be a stout wooden gate at the end leading into a back garden, and with luck, another at the bottom of that, giving onto another garden and another passage to the street beyond. Either a trap—or an escape.

It had happened so fast, I couldn't judge whether it was a man or a woman. Or if I had imagined it altogether. The deserter? Or someone else nearly caught up in the tightening net?

A constable must have seen the figure as well, because he blew his whistle and ran forward. But when he turned his torch into the blackness, it showed only the closed gate. After a moment, he walked halfway to the end of the passage before coming back.

I sat there, trying to come to terms with my duty. As an officer's daughter I understood the need for discipline and order in the Army. To walk away and leave one's fellow soldiers to their fate was, in my view, dishonorable. And yet I'd seen the horror of war, the suffering and the awful cost of doing one's duty. For some men that was insupportable.

There were other reasons too. For all I knew, the hunted man had risked everything to come home to a wife who was desperately ill or to see a newborn child. Even to sit by his mother's deathbed. The Army was not always generous with compassionate leaves, refusing to allow a man torn between love and duty the few days he so badly wanted to comfort those who needed him at home. I'd seen men in despair driven to shooting themselves in the hand or foot in a bid for leave.

Who was I to decide the fate of this man? The constable had already looked closely at the passage, hadn't he? And decided that it was empty?

But this deserter would eventually be found. And shot. The Army was relentless in its determination. It was just a matter of time.

And so I sat there, unable to bring myself to step off the omnibus and speak up. Instead I listened as the hue and cry swirled up one side of the street and then down the other. The shouts of constables, their whistles shrill in the night, were loud at first, then fading as the hunt turned back the way we'd just come.

It was late when the same constable, out of breath now, came to inform the driver that we could go on our way. The driver must have asked the question on all our minds, for I saw the policeman shake his head. And then we were moving, lumbering through the darkness as we continued on our route.

The man behind me said, "I don't envy those constables. It's not a fit night for man nor beast to be out there."

And a woman behind him asked anxiously, "Will he be given a fair trial, when he's caught? The deserter?"

"He'll be found guilty, right enough," an elderly laborer answered her. "It's not the Army's way to be lenient. Mark my words."

And from the last seat, a soldier in the uniform of the discharged wounded said quietly, "God help him."

I could see my corner coming up now, and I dreaded getting down. Even in my boots, my feet were icy cold from the long wait, and my gloved fingers as well, although I'd tried to keep them tucked under my arms.

Stepping down in the lee of the omnibus, I had a moment to catch my breath before it moved on and the full brunt of the wind struck me with such force that I nearly stumbled.

Narrowing my eyes against the bite of it, I walked on briskly, listening to the far-off sounds of police whistles.

Ahead was Mrs. Hennessey's house, where friends—also nursing sisters—and I had taken a flat. As I drew nearer, I saw that there were no lights shining from the windows of the ground floor, and I remembered that this must be Mrs. Hennessey's night for dinner and a cozy gossip with an old friend. Above, on the second storey, the windows of our sitting room were also dark. Tired as I was from two days of traveling, I was just as glad that no one else was in London. I could leave the gifts I'd found for each flatmate with Mrs. Hennessey. She would enjoy playing Father Christmas when next she saw them.

Busy with my own thoughts, I didn't at first notice the dark figure huddled in the shallow outer doorway, pressed so tightly into that pitiful bit of shelter that only a vague outline was distinguishable in the shadows cast by the streetlamp. When I did, my first thought was that the deserter was hiding here. Would he force his way into the empty house when I reached Mrs. Hennessey's door?

And in the same instant, I realized that it wasn't a man, it was a woman.

But what was she doing there? Did she have anything to do with the deserter?

As I slowed, she stirred, murmured, "Sorry!" and moved into the street away from me.

Two things registered as she spoke. Her voice was thick with tears, and she was shivering, as if she'd been out in this wind for a very long time.

I remembered what the man on the omnibus had said, that this was a night not fit for man nor beast.

"No, wait—" I said, putting out a hand to stop her. But she shrugged it off, keeping her face turned away as she made to slip off into the night. It was close on ten o'clock now, and the empty streets were no place for a woman to be walking aimlessly at this hour.

My gloved fingers reached for her sleeve, missed, and then caught in the belt of her coat. "Come inside and warm yourself for a quarter of an hour." I added quickly, "It will do no harm."

I could see that she was tempted—but she was also desperate to get away, on the point of pulling free when a gust of wind, stronger than before, buffeted both of us. I realized that her coat—unlike mine, which was meant to keep me warm—was well cut and fashionably thin, not designed for walking on a night like this one. It was intended for stepping out of a cab to enter a restaurant or theater. I wondered, fleetingly, if it was hers or if she had been given it by a mistress or found it in a charity shop. It was even possible that she'd been sacked, with nowhere to stay.

"Thank you, I'll be all right," she said, still keeping her face in the shadows. "Let me go. *Please.*"

I hadn't been wrong about the tears. And to my surprise her voice matched the coat, well bred and well educated. I had no choice but to release her belt.

"No, you won't be all right," I told her bluntly, before she could hurry away. "You'll make yourself ill. Pneumonia. Pleurisy. I'm a nursing sister, I've just returned from France. I know what I'm talking about." I hesitated. "I won't ask questions. Or try to stop you when you wish to leave. Warm yourself, have a cup of tea. There's no one else about. I promise you."

I had the outer door open now, and there was a lamp burning on the small table under the stairs. It must have seemed a haven in this weather. She hesitated an instant too long, and I touched her sleeve again, urging her inside. I myself was shivering with the cold now, and I knew she must be chilled to the bone. Even for a London December, it was unbearably wretched.

With an anxious glance over her shoulder, she preceded me through the door, then stood there in the small entry as if she couldn't think what else to do.

"I live up the stairs. This way," I went on, not looking at her as I started to climb. "There's no one here but me. My flatmates are all in France." I prayed it was true as I heard her follow reluctantly in my wake. After all, I realized, no lamplight could mean that someone was there but already asleep.

"Only for a few minutes," she said as we reached the landing. "I'd be grateful for that tea." Her voice was still husky with tears, but cultured, polite.

We reached the door of the flat, and I took out my key, unlocking it and fumbling for the lamp just inside. As a rule I could light it in the dark or even with my eyes closed, I'd done it so often, but now my fingers were stiff with cold. Finally brightness bloomed, illuminating the flat, picking out the small area we called our kitchen, our sitting room, and the closed doors to our five bedrooms.

I breathed a sigh of relief. There was no luggage piled in a corner or coats thrown over the tall walnut clothes tree. We were alone.

"Here," I said, pulling out a chair for her. "Let me take off my coat and in a moment I'll have that tea for us. I can tell you, I long for a cup myself."

I'd made a point not to look her in the face, knowing she'd be embarrassed for anyone to see she'd been crying. But now as I came back from my own bedroom and caught her staring around the flat, I could see the mark across her cheek, the swollen eye rimmed with black, and the deep bruising.

Someone had struck her, hard and fairly recently because the redness was only just giving way to a darker blue. I immediately looked away. I couldn't help but wonder if she'd been attacked on the street—or in her own home. Was this why the deserter had come to England? To catch his wife in an infidelity? He wouldn't be the first—nor the last—to suspect that all was not right in his marriage. She *was* married. I'd seen the handsome rings on her left hand when she pulled off her gloves.

I didn't hold with men who struck women. I'd never seen my father raise his hand to my mother, and I regarded men who did as despicable.

She hastily put up her hand to hide that side of her face, turning as if she intended to rush out the door and down the stairs before I could ask questions. I had glimpsed the stark alarm in her eyes when she saw me looking.

"I told you I wouldn't pry," I said quickly. "But I'm not blind. Let me put the kettle on, and I'll give you a cool cloth to help bring down the swelling."

She was a very attractive woman, and I put her age down as midtwenties, perhaps twenty-five or twenty-six. Certainly no more than that. And I'd been right, her clothes were stylishly cut, and of good cloth, although from before the war. But then very little was available in the shops these days. I made the tea, ignoring her while I worked, and then while it steeped, I went to find a cloth for her face and wring it out in cold water. She took it gratefully and held it as a shield. When the tea was ready, I set a cup down before her with the bowl of honey. "I'm sorry, there's no milk. One of my flatmates must have used the last tin."

"No, this is lovely. Thank you very much."

I let her drink it in peace, then said as offhandedly as possible, indicating the other doors, "There are five bedrooms here. One of them is mine, and the others are empty just now. Won't you stay the night, what's left of it, and wait until the morning to go on your way? I know I'm a stranger to you, and you to me, but there is a lock on the bedroom doors, if you feel the need."

"I must go—" she began, but I didn't let her finish.

"Where? If you had a place of your own, you wouldn't have been sheltered in Mrs. Hennessey's doorway. I don't know your reason for being there, that's your affair. It's just that I wouldn't send a dog back out into this weather. And I think you must know that you aren't dressed for spending the night in the street."

She looked down at her clothes, smiling ruefully. "I was in something of a hurry."

"There's another cup in the pot," I urged. "And I believe there are some biscuits in the cupboard. Have you had any dinner?"

"I don't remember. When I last ate, that is. Yesterday?" She accepted the second cup of tea and even one of the biscuits.

I had set my satchel down at the door, and I went to fetch it and put it in my own room. Opening the door to Diana's, I said, "This should do. The sheets are clean. Mrs. Hennessey sees to that for us. The bed's quite comfortable, and a good night's rest makes sense. Tomorrow . . ." I shrugged. "Everything looks better in the daylight, doesn't it?"

Biting back tears, she said, "Yes, all right. Thank you very much. I don't like to be a burden, but I dread going back outside. You're very kind."

I smiled. "You would have done the same for me, I think, if you had found me on your doorstep with nowhere to go."

She nearly laughed at that. "My doorstep?" she began, then broke off, shaking her head. "I live in the country," she added after a moment. "We seldom find strangers at our door."

Then she was not from London. What had brought her here? Or perhaps I should say, who had brought her here? I waited, hoping she might tell me more, but the moment had passed.

I went to fetch soap and towels, setting them on the table beside her. "You'll find a fresh nightdress in the tall chest, middle drawer. You and Diana must be of a size. If not, we'll look for one in Mary's room."

I busied myself clearing away the cups and filling the pot for tomorrow morning. I knew what my father and Simon would have to say about taking in a stranger, most particularly one who might be hiding from the police, but my mother would have understood that leaving her to the streets on a night like this was unconscionable. There was no way this woman could have guessed that I would be coming home tonight. She had simply chosen a doorway in which she could find a little respite from the wind. And perhaps, as well, shelter from whoever had struck her such a blow.

She took the towels and after a moment, pulled off her coat and hung it on the rack by the door, as if to be handy if she had to leave in a rush. Her clothing was of the same quality as the coat and her hat.

In the street below, I heard the sharp blast of a constable's whistle. Was the hunt still on? My guest heard it as well. Crossing quickly to the window, she pulled the curtain aside just far enough to look out. Down in the street someone burst into a drunken song, breaking off as the constable ordered him to move along. Relieved, the woman let the curtain drop, then flushed as she turned to find me watching her. But she didn't explain her anxiety, ducking her head and moving past me without a word.

I felt a moment's unease, but it was forgotten as she reached the door to Diana's room and swayed, suddenly dizzy. From worry? Not eating properly? Bad as it was, I couldn't quite believe that the blow to her face had been that severe.

The dizziness passed, and I said nothing.

Sitting on the bed in Diana's room, she allowed me to bring her a fresh cloth for her face, and then gently shut the door behind me with another murmured word of gratitude. I could hear her moving about as she prepared for bed, but I had a feeling she hadn't looked for a nightgown. Would she leave, once she was warm enough to face the cold again?

I blew out the lamp, went into my own room, and when I had undressed, lay down on the bed to keep watch. But in spite of good intentions, I went soundly to sleep, and when I awoke, it was late morning. I sat up, wondering if my orphan of the storm had left while I slept. I hoped she hadn't; I could hear the patter of a steady rain. I hastily threw on some clothes and went to see.

To my surprise, I saw that her coat was still there on the tree, and I suspected she was even more tired than I had been. Emotionally as well as physically.

It was close on ten o'clock when I heard her stir, and then she came frantically through the door, still trying to button her jumper, as if somehow believing I'd discovered her name and sent for whoever it was she'd run from. When she found me sitting there with a cup of tea in my hands, looking out the window at the rain, she stopped, suddenly shy.

"I was dreaming," she said. "I thought—I didn't recognize my surroundings when I woke up."

A nightmare, I reckoned, rather than a dream.

"Let me make you a fresh cup." The bruise was darker today, and there was heavier blackness around her left eye as well. It would be a week—ten days— before it faded completely.

"No, this will do nicely," she told me, coming forward to pour her own tea. With her back to me, she said, "You must be wondering how I got this—this—" Not able to find the right word, she gestured in the general direction of her face. "You'll forgive me if I don't wish to speak of it?"

"Someone struck you." I let the words fall between us. "I told you, I'm a nurse. I can't help but know that much," I went on. "As I said, it's your affair, of course it is. But if for a while you need sanctuary . . ." I let my voice trail away.

She was torn. I could see that. At a guess, she'd dashed out of the house in the clothes she stood up in, too shocked or frightened to think beyond the need to get away. It would only have occurred to her later to give any thought to where she was going and what she would do when she got there. In fact, I wondered if perhaps she had very little money with her, unprepared to pay for food or hotels or other clothing.

If she was telling the truth about living in the country, perhaps even reaching the train to London had seemed an impossible task. I wouldn't have wanted to walk from my parents' house in Somerset to the nearest railway station. Yet when I glanced at her shoes, I could see that they hadn't seen hard use on a country lane in winter.

She didn't answer my suggestion directly. Instead she confessed, "I thought—I thought he might follow me. After leaving the railway station, I walked and walked. For hours. First this direction and then that. Until I was completely lost. And there was nowhere to turn, no one I could trust. Not even the constables I passed from time to time. But they must have seen me, because suddenly they were hunting me. He must have given them my description. And I didn't know what they would do with me, if they caught me. I've heard—the suffragettes. They were treated cruelly in prison."

"The police last evening weren't hunting you," I said gently. "They were searching for a deserter. I was on an omnibus. They stopped it and told us why."

"A deserter?" She stared blankly at me. "I— Are you sure?"

"Quite sure. Unless, of course, the man you speak of is wanted by the police."

"No, of course he isn't." She seemed shocked that I should think such a thing.

I realized then that a guilty conscience had led her to believe the worst.

"He. Your husband?"

"No. Yes." She came to take the chair across from me, staring at the window. "I wouldn't want you to think ill of him. That he's brutal. It was as much my fault as it was his. I—I taunted him. I said things I shouldn't have. When he struck me, he was as shocked as I was. But I couldn't stay, you see. Not after that. We can't take back our actions, can we? However much we may wish to."

She was taking the blame for what had happened. But I kept an open mind on that issue, having been accustomed to hearing battered women in hospital claim that their drunken husbands hadn't meant to strike them, that it was their own fault. Their excuses were infinite. Dinner was late, or their husband's trousers hadn't been pressed properly, or the children were noisy. I had been a junior sister on a women's ward where broken bones and bruised bodies were common, and the husband, once sober, came to beg forgiveness. I knew, as the women in the ward had known, that the words were hollow, the promises too. But almost invariably, the wife returned to her home, because she had nowhere else to go.

I thought it best to change the subject before she had talked herself into a deeper sense of guilt. I said, "We weren't properly introduced last evening. My name is Elizabeth. Elizabeth Crawford. Most of my friends call me Bess. What would you like me to call you?"

Startled, she said quickly, "I'd rather not—"

I smiled. "It's rather awkward not to know what to call you. I don't mind if it's not your true name."

At that she gave me a faint smile in return. "Yes, all right. My mother's name was Lydia."

I went about clearing away the tea things, my back to her, giving her a little privacy. After a few minutes I said, "I must leave to do a little marketing. You must be as ravenous as I am. But you'll be safe enough here. No one will come, I promise you. And the shops are just a few streets away. I shan't be long."

She made no comment. But after a little time had passed, she said, regret in her voice, "I was terribly foolish. I can't think what came over me. But he'd never struck me before. I was mortified. And angry. And frightened. And so I ran away."

I could see that in the light of day she was beginning to have very cold feet indeed. I wondered where that would lead her. At the moment she appeared to be convincing herself that the best course open to her was to return to her home. But that could change. I wondered if it was true, that he'd never struck her before this, or if she was concealing other occasions of lashing out in anger. And I still wasn't convinced that her husband wasn't in some trouble or other. She wouldn't betray him. Whatever he had done, whatever they had quarreled about.

I put on my coat and took an umbrella from the stand. "You'll be here when I return?" I asked. "It's only that I need to know what to buy."

She looked at the window, listening to the cold rain pelting down. "I haven't the courage to leave," she said in a very small voice.

And so I went out to do my marketing, finding the shops dismally short of everything, but in the end I managed to find half a roast chicken for our dinner, a loaf of bread, and some dried apples as well as a little poppy seed cake for our tea. Walking back to the flat, I wondered if I would find it empty, after all. Without an umbrella, she would be wet to the skin in ten minutes. Even with one, I was hard-pressed to keep my skirts dry.

I came through the door, calling her name softly, but our kitchen cum sitting room was empty. Then the door to Diana's room opened, and she came out to meet me, looking a little sheepish.

"I heard someone on the stairs," she said, "and took fright."

"You needn't worry. No man—not even my father—escapes the sharp eye of Mrs. Hennessey, who lives on the ground floor." I hung up my damp coat to dry, returned the umbrella to its stand, then began putting away my purchases. "Even if by some incredible bit of luck your husband discovered you were here, she wouldn't let him trouble you if you didn't wish it."

I could see she didn't quite believe me, and I wondered just how persuasive her husband might be. Not that it would matter to Mrs. Hennessey, who took pride in protecting the young women she'd accepted as lodgers. Neither cajoling nor bribes would get him anywhere.

A few minutes later, Lydia said out of the blue, as if it had been on her mind all morning and she couldn't hold it in any longer, "I shouldn't have brought up Juliana. It was wrong of me."

Who was Juliana? A member of the family? Her husband's former sweetheart? His mother? It could be anyone, of course, and yet I could tell from the way she spoke the name that this was someone who mattered a great deal.

I brought out my mending to repair a tear in one of my stockings, giving Lydia an opening to go on talking to me if that eased her mind a little, because it was clear she was wrestling now with whatever was troubling her. A silence fell. As I finished my work, I glanced in her direction. Her thoughts were far away, and I realized that she had herself under control again and was unlikely to blurt out anything more. After putting away my needle and the spool of black thread, I paused by the window, opening the curtains as I tried to think of a way to persuade Lydia to confide in me without seeming to press her. If I could help her to look clearly at whatever had caused the quarrel with her husband, she might be better prepared to consider the future.

"Oh, no," I said involuntarily, glancing down at the street below.

Instantly she was on her feet, the bruises garish against her pale face, as she all but ran across the room to peer over my shoulder. I could see that she was trembling. "Who is it? Is it Roger?" She was searching the street below, panic in her eyes. "So soon? I'm not ready to face him yet."

"It's—a member of my family," I said, watching Simon Brandon stride toward the door of the house, his motorcar standing just under our window. "My mother must have got the telegram about my Christmas leave."

"I must go—" Lydia said, hardly listening to me as she turned to look for her coat and hat. "I've stayed too long as it is. I couldn't bear to have anyone else see me now. Not looking like this."

"He won't come up," I told her. "Mrs. Hennessey's rules? Remember? She'll inform me that he's here. And I'll go down. You needn't worry."

"She'll want to know who I am—why I'm here in your flat. I can't blame her—this is her house. I'll leave. It's best."

"And where will you go then?"

She stopped in midstride, staring at me. "I—I don't know."

"Then stay here. I'll hurry down and speak to Simon before Mrs. Hennessey comes to our door. Will that be all right? There's nothing to fear from him, by the way. He's traveled here from Somerset, and he'll want to ask what my plans are."

That seemed to reassure her. She dropped her headlong dash for her coat and hat, sitting down in the nearest chair as if her limbs suddenly refused to hold her upright any longer. I could see that touch of dizziness returning as she closed her eyes against it.

"You're very kind. I don't like to take advantage . . ." Her voice trailed away.

I went to the door, smiled at her, and then closed it behind me.

Simon was standing in the entry, a tall, handsome man with that air of confidence about him that had always marked him and my father, the Colonel. My mother told me once when I was young that it was the badge of command. Simon had served with my father, rising through the ranks to Regimental Sergeant-Major, and leaving the Army when the Colonel Sahib, as my mother and I called him behind his back, retired. He'd been a part of our lives since I could remember, and I trusted him implicitly. But how to explain that to my nervous guest? It was better to leave it that he was a member of my family.

He greeted me and then said apologetically, "We only received your telegram early this morning. Or I'd have met you at Victoria Station. Your mother has sent me to collect you. The Colonel is away."

My father, though retired, was often summoned to give his opinion and offer his experience to the War Office. As was Simon. I never knew what they did, nor did my mother, but they would sometimes leave rather abruptly and return looking as if they hadn't slept in days, telling us nothing about where they'd been or why. I did know that my father had once been sent to Scotland for a week, because he brought my mother a lovely brooch to make up for missing her birthday.

"Simon—" I glanced over my shoulder. "I'm so sorry. I can't come with you just now. Let me walk with you to the motorcar."

He was used to my ways. He said, "Bess," in that tone of voice I'd heard so many times.

"Not here," I replied and stepped out into the raw, cold morning air. The rain had become a damp drizzle, but the clouds were still dark enough to promise a downpour sooner rather than later. He took off his coat and settled it around my shoulders.

I huddled gratefully into its warmth, and when we were out of hearing of the woman up in my flat, I said quickly, "There was someone in the doorway last night, when I came home. A woman. She had nowhere to go, and her face was badly bruised. I took her in, and she's still upstairs, very frightened. I can't leave London until I've sorted out what brought her here last night."

"And her husband will come looking for her, mark my words," he warned. "This is not a very good idea, Bess."

"Even if he does, he can't have any idea where to begin. You see, she took a train to London and then just walked aimlessly for hours. It's a wonder she hasn't made herself ill. She wasn't dressed for the weather." I sighed. "What was I to do, Simon, leave her standing there in the cold wind? And what should I have done this morning, let her walk out into that pelting rain, and consider myself well out of it? Even Mother would agree I didn't have a choice."

"Your mother is as tenderhearted as you are. Yes, all right, I take your point. What is this woman's name? Where does she come from?"

"She hasn't told me yet," I admitted. "At the moment she's trying to convince herself that she made a mistake, leaving. She feels her husband is just as unhappy that this happened."

"Men who take their own fury out on women always repent what was done. Until the next time."

"Oddly enough, I'm beginning to think this isn't the usual case. I think it may be true that Lydia was shocked by the blow."

"I thought you didn't know her name."

"Well, no, it's her mother's name. I told her I had to call her something."

He took a deep breath. "Very well. If she decides to leave in the next few hours, we'll drive Lydia to the railway station and put her on the next train going in her direction. Will that do?"

"Simon, she has nowhere else to go. I can't walk away, knowing that, and I can't rush her into making a decision that could be wrong. What's more, I have a feeling she left in such a rush that she has little or no money with her. And she doesn't even have a change of clothing. For all intents and purposes, she's destitute."

Simon had to agree with me, however reluctantly. But he reminded me, "It's also possible her husband keeps her deliberately short of money. All right, shall I take the two of you out to a restaurant? I'd like to form my own opinion of your Lydia."

"It's very kind of you to suggest that, but I don't believe she'll want to be seen in public. She's terribly embarrassed by her appearance. The bruising really is quite stark. There's no way to hide it with a little powder."

"Fair enough. I won't choose a restaurant where she might be recognized. Tell her that."

I wanted to look up at the window, to see if Lydia was watching us. But that would have given away the fact that we were discussing her. "There's one other thing." I hesitated. "The police were searching for a deserter last night. Not on this street, but still, it was just east of here. She thought her husband had sent them to find *her*. This morning she's afraid that her husband is going to appear before she's prepared to face him again. But what if that's just wishful thinking on her part? What if Lydia's husband doesn't want her to come back? For instance, there's someone called Juliana who is involved."

"My dear girl, you can't fight her battles for her."

"No, I understand that. But since I can't abandon her, it may be necessary to take her to Somerset with me until this is sorted out."

"See if you can discover her true name, and I'll find out what I can about her background. Meanwhile, persuade her if you can to join us."

I could tell that Simon was afraid I might have been led down the primrose path, that Lydia was lying to me or taking advantage of my sympathy for her own ends.

The best way to prove him wrong was to do as he asked.

"I'll try, I promise you."

I handed Simon his coat and went back into the house. Mrs. Hennessey came out to greet me, asking about France, and I told her that I was fortunate enough to have Christmas leave.

"How lovely for your mother and father," she said. "Did I see Sergeant-Major Brandon pass my window just now?"

"Yes, I came down to speak to him. I thought you might be resting."

She nodded. Simon was quite her favorite, and had been since the summer when he'd all but saved her life. And mine. She asked about my family, and about Somerset, and finally after telling me that she would be happy to bring up anything I needed, she went back into her own flat.

I hurried up the stairs and found Lydia listening at the door. "I overheard. You're expected in Somerset," she said. "And here I am, keeping you from leaving. I've trespassed long enough on your kindness."

"As a matter of fact," I told her, "Simon has come to take me out to dine. Would you like to go? Somewhere you aren't known, of course." I added cheerfully, "It will be all right."

"No, I couldn't possibly consider it."

"Well, it's rather early, at that," I said, sweeping aside her refusal. "I believe he has some business to see to first, but he'll come again at one o'clock. There's time to reconsider."

I hurried out the door, as if Simon was waiting for my answer. He was standing at the foot of the stairs, and I asked him to collect me at one o'clock, and he reluctantly agreed.

"I may bring a friend along," I said, for Lydia's benefit. "Do you mind?"

"Not at all," he answered, and then with a gleam in his eye that told me he was getting his own back, he added, "Is it Diana? I've missed her."

"I think she's in Alexandria," I told him, making a face.

Then I set about convincing Lydia that she would be safe with us.

It was an uphill struggle. She wavered between worrying that she had already been away too long, that Roger might believe she wasn't coming back, and the certainty that all would be well once she could see him face-to-face and tell him she'd been wrong.

Watching that inner battle, I was well aware that it wasn't wise to pry. But I was beginning to think that knowing who Juliana was might help me understand why Lydia had fled to London. She couldn't have known how badly her face would be bruised. She must have needed to put distance between her and something—or someone. And where were the other members of her family—or Roger's—to let her go without making certain she was properly clothed and had the money to support herself for a few days?

I waited for an opening to ask questions, but it was clear that she wasn't ready to talk to me or anyone else.

In the end I don't think it was my persuasion that convinced Lydia to let Simon take us to lunch as much as it was her own need to escape from the torment in her head. All the same, she went down the stairs warily, as if she expected this to be a trap. I wouldn't have been surprised if she'd suddenly dashed away as soon as she reached the street.

Instead, just as we arrived at the door and were about to open it, she put her hand to her cheek and said, "No. I'd forgot. I can't go out like this. I can't face the stares. On the train it was awful, people would look at me and then look away. I was mortified."

"Natural curiosity," I said bracingly. "Here in London they're more likely to assume you were in an accident of some sort. Or fell."

But she refused to go. And then Simon was there, at his most charming, and the next thing I knew we were walking toward the motorcar and she was listening to him, her face turned toward his.

Even then I would have given much to ask him what his impression of Lydia was, but of course that was impossible. Still, I'd caught the fleeting glance he'd given me as he closed her door and turned to hold mine for me. He was not happy that I'd been unable to find out the information he'd asked for.

The restaurant was not one where Lydia or her husband were likely to meet anyone they knew. For one thing, it was well outside of London, on a narrow turning from the main road. For another, it was a country inn, more comfortable than elegant, the paneling old and the wide hearth decorated with horse brasses and coaching horns. But the food was very good, consisting of vegetables from the owner's own cold cellar, and meat from his farm, and the service was impeccable. We sat at a table where the bruised side of her face was turned away from the other guests, although from time to time she raised a hand to shield it, so conscious of it was she. Still, before very long, she was telling Simon about growing up in Suffolk.

He said, "Were you sad to leave Suffolk when you married?"

To my surprise, she answered him readily. "I'd seen my new home first in high summer. It was winter that I found almost unbearable. Have you ever lived at the edge of a heath? It's extraordinary, and each season is so different." She realized then what she was saying and changed the subject almost at once. "My brother inherited the house in Suffolk, but he's dead now, killed in the war. His widow and two sons live there. I've visited sometimes, but it isn't the same without him."

Which told me she couldn't turn to them in her distress.

The meal went well, and I did justice to the slice of ham that I'd ordered, small by comparison to the generous portions we were used to before the war. We had cabbage and steamed apples, and onions stewed in a cheese sauce, with a flan to follow. Lydia ate with an appetite but afterward seemed to be a little pale, as if the food sat heavily in her stomach.

We took our tea in the lounge, and then there was no excuse to linger. Simon went to find the motorcar.

Lydia said, "He's a very nice man, isn't he?"

"Yes, he is," I agreed. Turning to look out the windows, I added, "It will be dark before very long. And another cold night, I expect."

Lydia was silent, and then, pressing her fingers to her swollen face, she said, "Bess, you've been so kind. In spite of the fact that you know nothing about me."

"How could I turn you away?" I asked. "But I wish there was something I could do to make whatever is troubling you easier to face."

"Do you mean that?"

"Of course I do."

I hadn't seen the request coming. I was totally unprepared.

"Would you consider going with me to Vixen Hill? I think it would be easier to face Roger and his family if I had moral support. You're stronger than I am, Bess.

I could take my courage from you. Besides, it will be easier to explain to Roger and his family that I had come to London to stay with a friend. What I did would seem less—rash, ill-considered." She made a deprecating face. "It would only be a small lie. No one would know that it was."

"My parents are waiting for me in Somerset," I began, and then realized that it was the wrong thing to say. "Lydia. Perhaps if you told me why you quarreled and how it was that your husband struck you—if I understood the circumstances a little better, perhaps I could help you see your way more clearly."

She shook her head. "I shouldn't have asked. It's presumptuous of me even to think you could come with me."

"Lydia—"

But Simon was walking through the restaurant door to fetch us, and we followed him out to the motorcar without speaking.

The drive back to London began in silence. Simon, concentrating on the road as the rain began again in earnest, was taciturn. Glancing over my shoulder, I could see that Lydia was anxiously smoothing her gloves, as if regretting broaching the subject of my traveling with her to her home.

Finally, as the rain let up a little, I said to Simon, "Lydia has asked if I'd go with her to Vixen Hill. That's her home."

"Where is Vixen Hill?" he asked, raising his voice a little so that she could hear him.

"It's in Sussex," she replied after a moment, her voice reluctant in the darkness.

"Tomorrow we'll drive you there, shall we?" he suggested. "It will be no trouble."

"No—that's lovely of you to ask, but I think—I'd rather not take you so far out of your way," she answered him, trying to refuse him as politely as she could.

"On the contrary," he said, "Bess would like to see you safely home."

"I couldn't consider it," she told him. "Please. No."

And that was the end of that.

I could see Simon's profile in the dim reflection of the headlamps and could almost read what was going through his mind—that her refusal struck him as odd, given the fact that she'd just asked me to accompany her to Sussex. But I thought I understood her. My presence wouldn't appear especially threatening. Arriving with someone like Simon as well could send a very different message—that she felt the need of protection.

I said, trying to cast a little oil on troubled waters, "There's no hurry, Lydia. Truly there isn't."

"I must mend this quarrel somehow. It can't go on—Roger is leaving for France on Boxing Day. I don't know what to do."

I thought of offering to let her stay in the flat after I left for Somerset, but I had a feeling she would refuse. And even if she accepted, without money, how would she feed herself, or buy warmer clothing to see her through?

Simon asked, "I know a Roger Markham from Sussex. Royal Engineers. Is he by any chance your husband?"

"Oh, no. No. His name is Ellis. Roger Ellis." She added his rank and regiment.

How simply Simon had discovered that!

"He's home on compassionate leave," she went on when Simon said nothing more. "His brother Alan died a fortnight ago. Alan is—was—a Navy man, torpedoed off Ireland. He was severely wounded, but there was hope for a time. And then the doctors could do no more, and we brought him home to Vixen Hill. It was rather awful. I shouldn't have quarreled with Roger, under the circumstances. It was foolish of me."

We were coming down the street to Mrs. Hennessey's house now, and Lydia added wistfully, "We were all so fond of Alan."

We thanked Simon as he walked with us to Mrs. Hennessey's door, and Lydia preceded me up the stairs, giving me a moment alone with him.

I could say very little—she was within hearing—but I asked, "You'll stay over in London tonight?"

"Yes, of course," he answered. "I'll come in the morning."

Just then, Lydia paused on the stairs, and I turned quickly to see her leaning against the banister, her head down.

"I'm so sorry," she said, seeing my alarm. "I seem to have hurried too much and given myself a headache." She went on up the stairs more slowly, and I heard the door to the flat open.

"Go ahead, make sure she's all right," Simon told me, and then he was gone.

I followed her up the stairs and into the flat. "When did your head begin to ache?" I asked.

"It was a sharp pain, catching me off guard. It isn't as bad now."

"Lydia. Sit down and let me have a look."

Removing her coat and hanging it on the tree, she did as I'd asked. With the light from the lamp trained on her face, I examined the bruising and the swelling around her eye. "Where was the sharp pain?" She pointed to the side of her head just above and a little behind her ear. I carefully ran my fingers over the area, and she winced just as I touched what appeared to be a raised wound. Parting her thick, fair hair, I saw that it was actually an open cut that had bled a little and then clotted.

"How did you come by this?" I asked, letting her hair fall back into place.

"After Roger struck me, I ran up the stairs to our room to find my coat. I tripped in my haste and fell forward, hitting my head against the edge of the newel post. I saw stars, I can tell you," she added with a smile. "But I was all right after a moment. I got up and went on to our room." She pointed to her knee. "There's a bruise here as well. Rather a colorful one."

"Did you know it was bleeding? Where you fell against the newel post?"

"Not until last night, as I was preparing for bed. I really hadn't given it much thought until then." She grimaced. "I just knew that it hurt—my face and all that side of my head."

I pressed my fingers carefully on either side of the wound, but as far as I could tell there was no indication that the skull had been fractured. Still . . . "You ought to see a doctor," I began, but she cut me short.

"Oh, no, I couldn't. I don't like Dr. Tilton. He gossips, and he'll want to know how I got this bruise."

"It isn't the bruise that worries me. There are doctors here in London."

She wouldn't hear of it. But I thought, remembering her dizzy spells, and now the headache, that she must have a concussion. "Have you felt sick? Nauseated?"

"Only when I ate too much at the restaurant," she replied wryly. "I hadn't realized just how hungry I was."

I made her a compress for her face, then said, "Will you go with me to Somerset for a few days, Lydia? I think it would do you good to rest before you go home." And she could see our doctor.

She refused outright. "If I go anywhere, it will be to Vixen Hill," she told me. "I'll leave tomorrow."

I wasn't sure I believed her. And the thought of her wandering about London, alone and with a concussion, was worrying.

"Why won't you let Simon drive us to Vixen Hill?"

"I don't believe it would make it easier for me to face Roger," she said earnestly.

"Lydia. Is that your real name?"

She flushed. "I'm so sorry. Actually it is. And it was also my mother's name."

"If I agree to go home with you—tomorrow, let us say, or the day after—and deliver you safely to your family, will you promise to see a doctor? Just as a precaution."

"You must stay the night," she told me, trying to keep her hope from showing in her face. "There's only the one train a day, coming north, and by the time we reach Vixen Hill, you'll have missed it."

"Yes, all right. One night. As long as you agree to see that doctor."

"Bess, you won't regret it. I promise you. And the sooner the better. I shan't be able to sleep now, thinking about tomorrow. Are you quite sure?"

It was the only solution that I could see to the problem of what to do about Lydia. It set me free to go on to Somerset, and I could leave her in Sussex, secure in the knowledge that she had returned safely to her family. I was sure Simon wouldn't approve, but tomorrow morning I could explain to him why I'd made this decision, and arrange to have him meet me in London on my return. After all, Lydia had told him who her husband was, and where she lived. It wasn't as if I were going off with a complete stranger to an unknown destination.

And if I had any reason to believe that Lydia had made the wrong choice, if her husband refused to take her back, then she could come with me to Somerset until she could decide what she ought to do next.

Her happiness at having the decision to return to Vixen Hill taken out of her hands was obvious. For her sake, I hoped that her faith in Roger Ellis was justified.

I said, "There's one thing I'd like to ask you, if you don't mind. Who is Juliana?"

At first I didn't think she was going to tell me. And then she said, "Juliana? She's Roger's sister."

Two

The next morning, I looked for Simon to return, but as the time sped on, I realized that it was likely I'd miss him. But where was he? What had held him up?

I wrote a hasty note and left it with Mrs. Hennessey, and then there was nothing for it but to find a cab to take us to the railway station. I even looked over my shoulder before we turned the corner, to see if Simon's motorcar was in sight.

The train was crowded, as usual, and Lydia and I had difficulty finding two seats together. She was embarrassed that I had to pay for her ticket, but she promised to see that I was recompensed as soon as she reached Vixen Hill.

I said as we pulled out of the station into the misting rain, "Won't it be awkward—a guest arriving without any warning? Perhaps we should have sent a telegram. After all, your family is in mourning."

"I'd considered that, but I think it will be best just to walk in without fanfare. And Roger will very likely be as grateful as I am for your presence. There's the awkwardness, you see, of meeting for the first time. I have no idea what to say—or what he'll do. It's so difficult to know, isn't it?"

She'd persuaded herself that my presence would make all well again. But I had my doubts. Quarrels were not always settled so easily—or so amicably. Roger Ellis could see her flight to London as a more serious infraction than his blow. I was beginning to see that Simon was right, this was a more complicated business than I'd foreseen. Mainly because Lydia herself was far more uncertain than I'd realized.

"Are you sure," I asked, "that this is the right thing to do? Perhaps we should have waited another day until you're more comfortable with returning. It would be simple enough to get down at the next stop."

"Oh, no, I want to put it behind me as quickly as possible."

We talked for some time after that, exchanging information to make it appear more likely that she'd known me for some time.

"Wasn't it difficult," she asked at one point, "to work with badly wounded men? I know how distressing it was to care for Alan in his last days. Roger was wounded, you know. In the shoulder. He never told us, and it mustn't have been severe, because he wasn't sent back to England." She bit her lip. "It was George who mentioned it. He's a friend of the family. He'd run into Roger in France. But I hadn't seen Roger for three years. Not until he came home because of Alan. And he treated me like a stranger. As if he couldn't remember those months before the war when we were so happy."

"War does change people," I pointed out. "And of course there was his brother."

"Yes, I know," she said wistfully. "I shouldn't have pressed. But I wanted so badly to have a child. Someone to love, if—if the worst happens. That's what we quarreled about, you see." She touched her face. "The hurt went deeper than the blow. That's why I couldn't stay at Vixen Hill."

This was the truth, finally.

"We are a house of widows," she went on. "For all intents and purposes these last three years, I have been one as well. Roger's mother and his grandmother live with us, and I could see that their children have been their salvation. He may never come back from France, once he leaves. This could be our only chance."

"Was Alan married? Did he have children?"

"He was married, yes. But he and Eleanor had no children. And neither do Margaret and Henry. She's Roger's sister, she lives near Canterbury."

"And Juliana?"

"No. Of course not."

She was silent for a time. Then she said, "Sometimes I think they're cursed. Margaret and Alan and Roger. Mama Ellis told me once that Juliana's death was devastating. It scarred all of them. Roger's father couldn't accept it. He tried, but in the end he went out into the heath and shot himself."

I was shocked. "She's dead?" It was all I could manage to say.

"She died when she was only six years old. Of a mastoid tumor. Roger won't speak her name. It's as if she never existed. He was closer to her in age than Margaret and Alan. Alan, when he came of age, turned Vixen Hill over to Roger. He felt he couldn't live there, and he bought a house in Portsmouth before joining the Navy as a career officer. Margaret married young. I think to escape. Although it turned out well enough. She and Henry have been very happy."

"Did you—were you told these things before you married Roger Ellis?" I asked.

"I told myself I'd make Roger forget Juliana. But you can't really change people, can you? We took a house in London for the first six months, and then I could tell that he missed Vixen Hill. Alan could walk away, you see, but Roger couldn't. And so we returned to Sussex." Putting a hand to her head, she said, "I wish this pounding would stop."

I didn't remind her about her promise.

We pulled into a station at that juncture, and in the flurry of people getting down or settling into seats, conversation was impossible. Lydia closed her eyes, and I thought she slept for a quarter of an hour or so.

We reached the station just outside of Hartfield in the early afternoon. I was glad, for the train was stuffy and so crowded we could hardly hear ourselves think. I said, as Lydia and I stepped down into a small station hardly worthy of the name, "How far is it to Vixen Hill?"

"Not far, as the crow flies," she said, handing in our tickets. "There's a carriage we can hire to take us there. I was so fortunate the day I left—a neighbor was on her way to Hartfield to do her marketing, and she was willing to take me to the station. I wouldn't have wanted to walk—I'd have missed my train for one thing. But I would have walked, you know. I was that desperate to get away."

We found the carriage without any trouble, and the driver, an elderly man with a foul-smelling pipe, was more than willing to take us to Vixen Hill. We were soon on our way through the village of Hartfield. It was prosperous enough, with cottages and houses leading into a street of shops and an inn. I could see the tower of a church up a side street, and farther along, I glimpsed the doctor's shingle on a house facing a small shop selling dry goods.

Several people turned to stare, but I thought that had more to do with the fact that I was a stranger than with Lydia's bruised face and blackened eye. Still, she kept her gloved hand raised, as if to keep her hat from blowing off.

I heard her murmur, "I knew this would be an ordeal."

"It will be over soon. There's the end of town in sight already."

We came to a slight bend in the road just before the outskirts, and I turned to my left, aware of someone watching us. My gaze met that of the village constable standing there.

I was used to the constable who walked past Mrs. Hennessey's house each evening and paused to pass the time of day with her. And to the constable in Somerset whose children brought us fresh strawberries from his garden every spring. Comfortable figures who kept order and were a part of the fabric of our lives.

This man was cut from a different cloth, and I thought perhaps he'd been in the war, wounded and discharged, for his face was hard, his eyes cold, as if he remembered too much and had no way of forgetting.

And then Hartsfield was behind us, and the heath, encroaching on the outskirts, as if lying in wait, quickly surrounded us. I was used to the moors in Devon and Cornwall. But this was dramatically different, low, black twisted branches of stunted heather and gorse filling the horizon now as far as the eye could see.

The land was sour, bare in places, in others dotted with blighted shrubs and what appeared to be the struggling remnants of grasses and other vegetation that had given up long ago.

"This is where you live?" I asked, surprised. I'd been to Sussex before, lovely villages and a countryside that was inviting. This was quite different.

"Ashdown Forest," Lydia murmured. "I hate it. In winter it sucks the life out of you, leaving you as twisted and dead as it is. Winter bleak, that's what it is."

Apparently, from what she was telling me as we held on tightly on the now bumpy ride over winter-rutted tracks that bore little resemblance to roads, Ashdown Forest had been a hunting preserve of kings. A ditch had surrounded it to keep the animals in and the peasant poachers out.

"You can still find bits of the ditch if you know where to look. But the forest has long since disappeared. There are stands of trees here and there, mere remnants of what used to be."

I could see why she called it winter bleak.

The day was overcast now, and that did little to make the drab brown and black landscape more appealing. In the far distance I glimpsed sheep grazing, which must have meant that this wiry and unappealing growth was nourishing. But there was so little color to this palette. Even the moors in the West Country were greener and more inviting.

I said, "Is it always so dreary?"

"To be fair, in the spring when the gorse blooms, it's touched with green and gold. And in summer the ling—the heather—flowers. A carpet of lavender, and it comes right to the edge of the lawns. But I know winter is coming when I see the ling blooming, and that's depressing. Winter seems to last longer than any other season. When my brother was alive, I'd find an excuse to go to Suffolk for a week or so. We were close, he and I, and while I like his wife well enough, sadly we have very little in common. After he was killed, I began to feel like a guest there on sufferance."

Roger, I thought, sounded rather selfish. And so did her brother's widow, for that matter.

She fell silent, as if bracing herself for what was to come.

As we moved deeper into Ashdown Forest, the landscape became even more bleak, if that was possible. The occasional sheep or cows, the handful of horses, seemed overwhelmed by the silence. From time to time we moved into the shadow of trees, their bare branches arching over our heads like the high ribbed ceiling of a cathedral nave. Occasionally I saw narrow, overgrown paths leading off into denser growth, mysterious, almost secretive.

I was hard-pressed to tell one featureless track from the other as we made our way across the heath. I found it difficult to imagine that this was once a great forest, with deer and whatever else a king chose to hunt confined here awaiting his pleasure. That was a chilling thought, that the animals were all but penned here, until he and his cronies came again to slaughter them. I was beginning to feel rather vulnerable myself in this strange world, and I compared it to the blighted landscape of France where war had destroyed every vestige of grass and trees and fields. Very different—and yet in some way, very much the same. I couldn't quite put my finger on the similarity until I realized that no one seemed to live here either. A wasteland of man's making. No Man's Land. Just then I saw the distant broken arms of a windmill, but the house attached to it was not visible.

We turned off the track into a lane, bordered by a line of ash trees, that led in turn to a red brick house whose lawns ended abruptly at the edge of the gorse and heather. As if a line had been drawn, and the wildness told not to cross it. Or had the wildness told the grass to encroach no farther?

I wondered if the house had begun life as a hunting lodge, because there was a tall central block that appeared to be older than the wings to either side, the brick a mellow rose. High above the door, an oriel window broke the plainness of the facade, the panes dark and lifeless under the dull sky. Gardens graced the lawns where the lane became a drive looping back on itself. But at this time of year the gardens too were dead, bare beds with no promise of spring, not even a brave bit of green from a tulip or daffodil poking tentatively up.

I thought of the old legends of cursed land. Or Mr. Conan Doyle's tale of great black hounds haunting the moors. One could believe in them in such a place. I couldn't help but remember the comfortable drowsiness of Somerset, a soft green countryside where I would be now if I'd gone home with Simon.

"Vixen Hill," Lydia said. "Home." There was a hint of melancholy in the words.

As we came out of the looping drive, I could see the pair of holly trees standing guard on either side of the doorway, their tough, glossy leaves like armor in the pale light, the rich red berries bright against the brick. Whoever had planted those hollies, I thought, must have been hungry for even a small bit of color.

The carriage drew to a halt before the massive door, arched and faced with stone, barred with iron. It was either very old or a Victorian replica that had weathered well. I looked up at the long oriel window, and thought I saw a flicker of movement there. But it was only a trick of the light as the clouds scudded overhead.

Lydia gripped my hand like a drowning woman reaching for a lifeline. I could see, glancing at her face, that she was more likely to turn around and leave than get down and walk to the door. "I feel sick," she whispered.

But it was too late to walk away. She would have to face whatever lay beyond that door. I wondered what role Roger's mother and grandmother might play in this reunion. I hadn't thought to ask Lydia about that.

"I'm here," I said quietly. "Chin up, and take your courage in both hands. You've come home of your own free will."

She smiled, a shaky one at best, but a smile nonetheless. "Is that what you tell your patients when you send them back to their regiments?"

"Of course," I lied, paying the driver and grateful to be seeing the end of that pipe. What I told my patients was very different. *Take care. And God go with you.* Only I never spoke that last aloud. It was a silent prayer that they would survive another week, another month, another year. So many of them didn't.

The horses moved restlessly, steaming in the cold air. Lydia got down and marched to the door like a man walking to the gallows, upheld by pride alone. I followed her. The carriage was on the point of turning in the drive, and as she realized it, she called to the elderly man who had brought us here, "No, wait."

At that moment, the door swung open, and it was a middle-aged woman in a dark blue uniform who greeted Lydia with relief, staring anywhere except at that bruise as she said, "I thought I heard the carriage. Mrs. Roger? You're all right then?"

"Hello, Daisy. Is Mr. Ellis at home?"

"I was told by Molly that he'd gone out again to search for you. He's been that worried." Her gaze moved from her mistress to me, politely curious.

"I've brought a guest with me. Miss Crawford, from London." Lydia's voice was steady, but I heard the undercurrent of nervousness. I hoped Daisy didn't.

Daisy swept me an old-fashioned curtsey and welcomed me to the house, then took my valise and led me inside.

If I'd thought this was once a hunting lodge, I was proved right as I entered the hall. The ceiling was high, there was a massive stone hearth on one side, and displayed on the walls were an array of weapons and the mounted heads of game staring down at me.

Lydia, noticing my appraisal, said, "When the house was rebuilt in the late seventeen hundreds, this room was kept. The rest is more comfortable, I promise you." Turning to Daisy, she asked, "Where is everyone?"

"Your grandmother is resting. Mrs. Matthew is putting together the menus for the guests she's expecting. And Miss Margaret has gone out for a walk."

Lydia said contritely, "Oh, dear, I'd forgot we're to have guests. It completely slipped my mind. Mama Ellis will be wondering what on earth I was thinking of! Could you put Miss Crawford's things in the room overlooking the knot garden?" And to me she added, "You'll like that room. It looks away from the Forest. Nowhere near as gloomy as most of the other rooms. And you won't mind, will you, Bess, if we speak to my mother-in-law before we go up?"

We crossed the hall, passing the stairs built into the wall on one side, and Lydia opened a door at the far end of the room. Beyond was a passage that branched left and right, leading to the two wings of the house. Lydia turned to her left and opened another door into a very pleasant, very feminine little room. She said tentatively said, "Mama?"

Over her shoulder I saw the woman seated at the desk by the window look up and stare for a moment, then rise to embrace Lydia.

"My dear. Your poor face!" she exclaimed. I remembered that the blow must have been just a red splotch the last time she'd seen Lydia, and that the bruising must have come as something of a shock. "Can nothing be done for it? Are you in any pain?"

"It's all right, Mama. I promise you. I've been in London—visiting a friend. She's come home with me. Elizabeth Crawford. She's a nursing sister, just back from France."

Mrs. Ellis smiled at me. "Welcome to Vixen Hill, Miss Crawford. I'm Amelia Ellis, Roger's mother. I hope you'll be comfortable here. Has Lydia shown you to your room?"

"Not yet," I said, taking the hand she offered me. "I look forward to my stay. It's a lovely house."

"Yes, it is," she said, not with arrogance but with pride in her home. "I've been happy here." But even as she spoke the words a shadow crossed her face, as if this was not the whole truth. "You must be in need of tea, after that cold drive from the station. I need a bit of distraction myself. I've spent all morning on menus and arrangements."

Lydia said contritely, "And I was not here to help."

"Never mind," Mrs. Ellis said cheerfully. "There's still much to be done."

She led us from her small sanctuary to the sitting room next door. There were long windows letting in what light there was, and a tall music box in a beautiful mahogany cabinet stood between them, the sort of music box that played large steel discs. The rest of the furnishings were a little shabby, as if this room was used often. The chair I was offered was covered in a pretty chintz patterned with pansies faded to a pale lavender and rose, each bunch tied by a white ribbon. Mrs. Ellis crossed to the hearth and rang the bell beside it.

As she turned back to us, she said, gesturing to my uniform, "You're only just returned from France? What is it like out there? My son won't tell me the truth. He says that the casualty lists are exaggerated."

A sop to his mother's fears?

"I only know how busy we are when there's a push on," I said, trying not to make her son out as a liar. "As you'd expect. But my father has high hopes, now that the Americans are coming over. He says their General Pershing knows what he's about." He'd also said that we badly needed fresh viewpoints at HQ, but I thought it best not to mention that.

"Crawford," she murmured thoughtfully. "Not related to Colonel Crawford, by any chance, are you?"

"He's my father."

"My dear! How wonderful," she exclaimed. "My husband met him briefly in India. Oh, years ago. Matthew had gone out on one of the mapping expeditions, and he hoped to do a little exploring while in the north. Your father—he was a captain then—was his contact in Peshawar. They got on well and corresponded until Matthew's death. I wonder if Colonel Crawford remembers him."

"I'm sure he will. I look forward to asking him."

Another middle-aged maid appeared in the doorway and then stepped aside as a tall, vigorous woman with very white hair came in. "What's this I hear about Lydia coming back?" She turned her sharp gaze on her granddaughter-in-law, but before she could say anything more, Mrs. Ellis asked for tea to be brought. The woman, whose name was Molly, quietly shut the door as she left.

"How did you come by that nasty bruise?" the elder Mrs. Ellis was demanding. "And don't tell me that Roger inflicted it. I won't believe it."

"It's true, Gran," Amelia Ellis replied quickly, before Lydia could answer.

"Nonsense. The Ellis men don't strike their women. Surely a little powder will make you more presentable? I don't hold with powder as a rule, but in this case, it's necessary. Regrettably."

Lydia said, "It was my fault, Gran. Truly it was." She gestured toward me. "May I present my friend, Miss Crawford? Matthew knew her father in India."

"Indeed. Don't change the subject, my girl. What will our guests think, to see you looking like that?"

"I'll try powder, Gran, I promise."

Her grandmother turned to me then. "A nursing sister, are you? I hope you've brought some other clothing with you. It won't do to be the skeleton at the feast at dinner tonight."

"Perhaps I can borrow something suitable from Lydia," I answered politely. I'd brought one pretty dress with me, expecting to dine tonight, but it appeared that no one contradicted Gran.

Molly came in just then with the tea tray, and Gran inspected it with a frown on her face. "We've hit a new low, Amelia," she said to Mrs. Ellis. "There are no cakes for our tea."

"Yes, dear, I know. Cook has been holding back eggs and honey and flour for our guests. I hope you don't mind."

"I shall write to my MP and demand to know what England is coming to," she said, taking the first cup of tea and moving to a chair by the fire. "We had no wars in the old Queen's day. I don't see why we must put up with them now."

Mrs. Ellis smiled at me as she passed me my cup. "Yes, Gran, dear, I should think that would be a very good idea."

"Don't patronize me, Amelia," the older woman snapped. "I'm not in my dotage."

"I wouldn't think of it, Gran. There are some biscuits here. Would you care for one?"

The elder Mrs. Ellis grudgingly accepted one, and then said, "It's not what I'm accustomed to. Where's Roger? He ought to be here. It's already getting dark. He knows I don't care for him to wander about on the heath after dark. That shoulder can't be fully healed, whatever he tries to tell himself."

"It's been nearly two years. He'll be in shortly—"

At that moment the sitting room door opened again, and a tall, fair man entered. He was wearing country clothing rather than his uniform. "Here you are," he began, and then he saw Lydia. She set her cup aside and rose, unable to speak. But I could see the tears glistening now in her eyes.

He stared at her, several emotions flitting across his face. First surprise, then relief, and finally anger.

But he came quickly across the room to his wife and put his hands on her shoulders. She flinched in spite of herself, and he dropped his hands at once. "My dear" was all he said, and she nodded, as if she understood without the need for words. He touched her face gently with one finger, and added, "I'm so very sorry."

"No, it was my fault," she said tremulously.

Gran, watching them, interjected, "Do have some tea, Roger. You must be frozen."

The emotional moment between husband and wife was broken, and he stepped back, took the cup his mother handed him with a wry smile, and said, "I was worried. We looked everywhere."

"I went to London," Lydia said. "To think, actually. Bess, out of kindness, took me in."

He turned to me, and I felt the power of his gaze as he thanked me for being such a good friend. My first thought was, *He doesn't believe her.* Then where did he think she'd gone? And was that why he wasn't in London, scouring the city for her? I remembered too her refusal to let Simon bring us here comfortably in his motorcar.

"We ran into each other unexpectedly. I was glad, we hadn't seen each other in several years."

"Indeed."

I looked him in the eye. "I'm glad to meet you at last," I said, to give him something to think about. "Lydia has told me so much about you." It was a common enough remark when meeting someone related to a friend, but I gave it the slightest emphasis, on purpose.

He had the grace to flush at that. He knew exactly what I meant, that she had confided in me about the bruises. And I suspect he understood as well why she had brought me home with her. A buffer, in the event he was still angry.

"Welcome to Vixen Hill," he said, and I knew we had a sound grasp of where each of us stood now.

He accepted a biscuit from the plate his mother held out to him, then went to sit down next to Lydia.

Gran said, "You were careful with that shoulder, I hope."

"Yes, of course," he answered impatiently. "But the doctor instructed me to exercise it to bring it back to full strength. You know that."

"Exercise and walking off a black mood are two very different things," she retorted, and reached for another biscuit.

Mrs. Ellis mentioned the guests they were expecting, and Roger said, "Are you sure you want to go through with this, Mother?"

"Yes, why not? Eleanor will wish to see Alan's stone in its proper place, and Margaret is already here. What's more, I think it will be good for George. He wasn't able to stay when Alan was so ill."

"I doubt it will be good for him," Roger argued. "He's changed, Mother, whether you wish to admit it or not. First Malcolm's death, and then Alan's. I'm surprised he hasn't killed himself, to tell you the truth."

Her son's bluntness made her wince.

"He was best man at your wedding. Your oldest friend," Mrs. Ellis reminded him. "Have a little charity, Roger. He needs patience and understanding."

"He's moody and unpredictable these days. He'll cast a pall over the entire event. I hope he'll change his mind and stay in Hampshire."

"You have also been moody and unpredictable, my dear." Her voice was very gentle. "I think Sister Crawford will agree with me that it's what war does to one's spirit."

Roger said nothing, but I could see that he felt otherwise. It struck me that I'd been right about his selfishness.

"It's starting to rain harder," Gran reported, rising to walk to the window. "I hope it won't last for days the way it usually does. The tracks will be nearly impassable. The ceremony spoiled."

I looked toward the windows and could see that indeed it was raining, the wind picking up to blow it in sheets against the glass. I could just make out the lawns, and the dark line of heath beyond, visible as if through a veil. I was glad we weren't traveling in an open carriage from the station just now.

Lydia rose. "Bess, I'll show you the house, shall I? So that you can find your way."

I thanked Mrs. Ellis for the tea, and went with her. Out in the passage she sighed. "It wasn't as difficult as I'd expected. I thought—well, never mind what I thought. But I was very glad you were there, all the same. My backbone, as it were." She smiled, but there was still a touch of anxiety behind it. "My head was thundering in there. It's better now. The passage is so much cooler."

But it wasn't aching from the heat of the fire on the hearth. I said, "You should rest. It's been a very tiring day."

"No, I'm fine. And there's so much to do."

I said only, "Lydia, if your mother-in-law is expecting a family gathering, I shall only be in the way. Meanwhile, will you at least speak to your family's physician? It will set my mind at rest."

She wouldn't hear of it. I persisted.

"It wouldn't do if you had problems with a house full of guests. What's more," I added, "the blame would fall on Roger, wouldn't it? I mean to say, that's the most conspicuous injury, your hair covers the other."

She stopped in the passage and regarded me for a moment. "What could I say, that wouldn't be a reflection on Roger? You don't know Dr. Tilton."

"Tell him you slipped on the stairs. It's true."

"Will you go with me?"

"Of course."

"Then tomorrow. Before your train leaves."

With that out of the way, Lydia seemed to be as relieved as I was. We went first to my room, and on the landing I could see for myself the sharp edge of the square mahogany newel post. The cut in her scalp was proof enough of how hard she'd struck it. Hard enough indeed for a concussion.

A fire had been lit on the hearth, taking away the damp chill of the day, and the drapes had been drawn against the rain. I went to the window anyway, and pulling them aside, looked out. The knot garden lay spread out below, an intricate design of boxwoods and flower beds that seemed at odds with a house on the edge of a heath. Around the garden were planted tall evergreens as a shield against the wind and also, I thought, to shut out the landscape beyond.

"It's my favorite view," Lydia said, coming to stand beside me. "And in high summer, it's beautiful. It was put in for Gran, you know. A wedding gift from her husband, Roger's grandfather. Her room overlooks it too." We returned to the hall by the main stairs, and Lydia said, "Everything starts here. Those stairs along the wall lead up to the oriel window above. You saw it as we came up the drive. The formal rooms are in the right wing, and the family rooms are in the left. Go through the door—the one over there, that we used when we first arrived—and turn to your right in the passage and you come to the drawing room. Well, we call it that, although it's not all that splendid these days. After we were married, Roger's mother told me I could redecorate it to suit my tastes, which was very kind of her. Before I could really set about it, the war began." We were walking through the door and following the passage now. "That door is the dining room, this one the drawing room, and beyond it is a small library. Across from the library is Roger's grandfather's study. Gran uses it sometimes, when she isn't in the mood to sit with the family." We retraced our steps, and she opened the door into the formal dining room. It was elegant in dark green upholstery that set off the well-polished wood, and the tall, handsome sideboard. Long dark green velvet drapes trimmed in cream framed the double windows. The carpet was a paler green and cream in a floral pattern.

Lydia pointed to the fox mask carved above the sideboard. The chairs at the head and foot of the table had smaller versions at the ends of the arms. "The house is said to have been built originally over a vixen's den. That's where the name comes from. But one story has it that Roger's ancestor used the lodge for assignations, and when his wife found out, she killed him and blamed his death on a rabid fox."

"How charming," I said with a smile.

"Yes, I felt the same when I first came here. Sadly, the room is used very seldom now. With just the three of us, Gran and Mama Ellis and me, we usually take our meals in the sitting room."

I could see why. The table would seat twenty comfortably, and with only one hearth, it must be very cold in winter. I noticed the paintings hanging on the walls, mostly landscapes from Italy and Switzerland and by a very accomplished hand.

"Gran painted them. On her honeymoon. Roger's grandfather had them framed and hung as a surprise for her after their first child—Matthew, Roger's father— was born."

She closed that door and turned to the one across the passage, opening it into the drawing room. It faced the drive, and even on such a dreary afternoon, it was well lit and very pleasant. Stepping inside, the first thing that drew my eyes was the lovely hearth of Portland stone—and above it the most astonishing portrait.

The child was beautiful, fair haired and sweet faced, with an impish gleam in her blue eyes, and she had been captured in an informal pose, glancing toward the artist over one shoulder, her smile so touching I stood there in amazement.

"That's Juliana," Lydia was saying in a flat voice.

Three

"How sad!" I replied, meaning it. I couldn't take my eyes from the painting. Juliana appeared to be on the verge of laughter, and I almost held my breath listening for it. If the living child was anything like this portrayal in oils, I could understand why her memory was so vivid in the minds of her grieving family.

"We use this room only when we have guests. I suggested once to Roger that we move the portrait. And he was furious. He said she belonged here, in a tone of voice that told me I didn't. It was our first quarrel."

As she closed the drawing room door, she went on, "He worshipped her, you know. Roger. He took her death so hard that he didn't speak for months.

They feared for his sanity, Gran said. Margaret and Alan were older, they understood death a little better, although that didn't make hers easier for them."

I thought about what it would have been like, watching helplessly as the little girl slowly weakened and died.

We walked back to the great hall, and Lydia pointed to one of the chairs in front of the fire. "Let's sit here for a bit, shall we? Before dressing for dinner."

What she meant was, she wasn't ready to face Roger alone in their bedroom.

We sat down, feeling the draft at our backs as the rain beat against the door and the walls. It sounded like distant drums or even muted gunfire.

"What am I to do, Bess?" she said at last, staring into the heart of the fire. "I love Roger. In spite of this. How long will this war go on? What if he's killed—or horribly wounded? What if he's like George, bitter and hurtful, and I can't bear to have him touch me?"

"Yours isn't the only family asking these questions tonight," I replied after a moment. "Love isn't a certainty, Lydia."

But she shook her head. "You aren't married. You don't know what it's like to love someone and want to have a part of them for your very own."

It occurred to me that one of the reasons Lydia was so insistent on children was that she had lived these past three years with two widowed women. She could already see what the future held if Roger was killed. In India some wives preferred to throw themselves on the funeral pyre and be immolated with their husbands. Sometimes it was true grief—sometimes it was knowing what a bleak empty life lay ahead of them, especially if they were dependent on the charity of a family that didn't want them. Death was sometimes preferable to living. The British had done their best to outlaw suttee, but it hadn't been completely abolished.

I said gently, "Then I'm the wrong person to ask."

Sighing, she said, "Well. Roger's leave will be up soon enough. I have until then to change his mind. Somehow."

I looked across at her bruised face. If Juliana died of a mastoid tumor, it was no one's fault. Unlike some tragic accident where guilt couldn't be avoided. Why had her death affected her brother so deeply? Was it the shock of loss, unacceptable to a child's mind? Had Margaret and Alan also been haunted by their little sister's death? They too were childless.

"You said you shouldn't have mentioned Juliana when you quarreled. Did you blame her for your husband's refusal to have children?"

"Yes, I told him he was afraid he'd lose a child, the way his family had lost Juliana, and it was time now to let her rest in peace and begin to live in the present."

We sat there in silence for a time, and then Lydia reluctantly got to her feet. "It's nearly time for dinner. I'm glad you came, Bess," she said. "It was terribly kind of you—"

She clutched at the back of her chair, suddenly dizzy. But by the time I reached her, it seemed to have passed. "Don't fuss. I'm all right, I assure you."

But she wasn't. I was certain of that now.

After dinner, I quietly asked Mrs. Ellis if it would be possible to take Lydia to Dr. Tilton's surgery at this late hour, explaining my concern.

"I didn't know," she said. "About the fall on the stairs. Yes, of course, I'll drive you myself. I think Roger's a little tired."

He didn't appear to be tired, but I said nothing. She rose and went to speak to Lydia. "Will you come with me, my dear?"

Surprised, Lydia said, "Yes, of course," and followed her mother-in-law out of the room. I went with them, leaving Roger Ellis and his grandmother to their own devices.

In the passage, Mrs. Ellis said, "Miss Crawford feels you ought to see Dr. Tilton. Shall I fetch your coat? I wish I'd known sooner about the fall, my dear, I would have suggested speaking to him straightaway."

Lydia was angry with me, as I'd expected. "I'm all right, Mama, I truly am. Bess was wrong to worry you."

But Mrs. Ellis had the last word. "You must do as I ask, Lydia. Tomorrow will be a very busy day, and I can't have you ill on my hands." The unspoken reminder that Lydia had already been away for two days when she could have been helping with preparations precluded any argument. Still, she cast a reproachful glance in my direction as she went to fetch her coat.

I brought down my own from my comfortable, warm room, dreading the thought of traveling in a motorcar through the cold and dark night. Still, it was the right thing to do. Lydia was waiting for me by the door, and Mrs. Ellis was just bringing the motorcar around. We dashed through the rain to climb quickly inside. The little heater hardly made a difference where I sat in the rear, and I was glad of my gloves and a scarf. There was nothing to be done about my cold feet as we followed the looping drive and went down the avenue of ash trees.

Mrs. Ellis was saying, "I hope this weather passes before the service. I'd so counted on everything going well."

"It will be all right, Mama," Lydia assured her.

The rest of the drive was made in silence, and I watched the headlamps bounce across the dark landscape, touching first this patch of heather and then a taller, twisted stand of gorse. We passed horses standing head down just off the road, and I saw the bright eyes of a fox or a dog before whatever it was scurried into the safety of the shadows. I could hardly see the next turning, but Mrs. Ellis was familiar with the roads and drove with care.

Dr. Tilton's surgery was dark when we reached Hartfield, and we pulled up instead in front of the house. It was two storeys, looming above us in the now misting rain.

"Thank goodness, there are lights still on downstairs," Mrs. Ellis said as she set the brake.

"I'll go to the door," Lydia told her, getting down and dashing through the puddles to the house, before we could stop her. The high roof of the porch offered little shelter, and she huddled there for nearly a minute before someone answered her summons. She stepped inside the entrance, and the door was swung shut behind her.

Mrs. Ellis started to call her name, then broke off. "I don't know what's troubling her," she said after a moment. "I don't know why she and my son are so at odds."

"You weren't there when he struck her?" I asked.

"No. But I saw her as she ran out of the room, and I asked Roger what had happened. He answered that she was upset. The next thing I knew, she was gone. I thought perhaps she'd just taken a walk, cold as it was. Later, when I tapped at her door, she didn't answer, and it wasn't until Roger went up to dress for dinner that we realized she hadn't come back. I thought perhaps she'd got into trouble somewhere on the heath. Roger went out to look for her. He came back, his face like a thundercloud and took the motorcar. He was gone for some time, and when he came home again, he told me he couldn't find her. I stayed up most of the night, thinking she might come back. But she never did. I didn't know what to think and was all for summoning the police. But Roger was adamant. He believed she'd come home when she was ready. I don't think any of us dreamed she'd gone to London." She was silent for a time, watching the doctor's door. Then she asked, "Did Lydia confide in you, Miss Crawford? Did she tell you why she wouldn't come home?"

"She was afraid of your son," I told her. "It was difficult for her to make the decision to return."

"And when she did, she brought you with her. It was very kind of you to, Bess. May I call you Bess? You are a very strong friend. I just wish I knew what the quarrel was about. Roger wouldn't tell me anything. I wouldn't have known he'd struck her if I hadn't seen her face as she passed me. I couldn't believe my eyes. But then Roger has been very tense, you know. I expect the war takes a greater toll than we can imagine."

"It's very difficult," I said carefully, "to be killing people one day and the next to be standing in your own doorway, trying to remember what it's like to be a part of a family again, if only for a short time."

"I hadn't thought of it in that light. Yes, I take your point. He brought the war home with him, then, and we none of us recognized it."

I believed it went deeper than that, but I said nothing. Just then the door opened, and a man stuck his head out, calling for Mrs. Ellis. We got out together. Inside the entrance hall, Dr. Tilton, a balding man with a paunch, led us to his study, a room filled with medical books and—to my surprise—several shelves of biographies of famous men.

Lydia was sitting in a chair by the hearth, looking rather chastened. Nodding to me, Dr. Tilton said to Mrs. Ellis, "I have every reason to believe that your daughter-in-law has suffered a concussion. The wound is still open, but I hesitate to sew it up because that would require some shaving of the head." He turned to glance at Lydia. "She appears to be under great stress as well. I can't give her a mild sedative, under the circumstances. But she should rest for several days. Body and mind. Will you see to it? I've told her that she should have come to me at once, and to make up for that, she must pay the piper, as it were, and let herself heal." He turned to me. "If symptoms persist, you'll send for me immediately."

"Yes, Doctor," I replied.

"Have there been periods when she slept and you couldn't rouse her? She told me she had been with you since the accident."

So that was why Lydia had gone in alone. She must have left the impression that her fall had occurred in London!

"Not to my knowledge. Headaches, some dizziness. A little nausea."

"Yes, that's a good sign, then. Take her home and put her to bed. Miss Crawford, I'd like you to sit with her. In a day or two, if the symptoms disappear, we can assume that Lydia will be all right. If the symptoms persist, then I'll keep her in my surgery for observation."

"Rather than impose on a guest, Roger can keep an eye on her," Mrs. Ellis began, but the doctor shook his head.

"Miss Crawford knows what to look for. I've already explained that to Lydia."

"Thank you, Dr. Tilton," Mrs. Ellis said. "I'm so sorry to disturb you this late, but Miss Crawford was most insistent."

"As she should have been." He helped Lydia put on her coat and saw us to the door. As I turned to allow Lydia to precede me, I noticed a woman at the head of the stairs, and wondered if she'd been listening. I thought perhaps she was the doctor's wife. She moved out of sight almost at once.

As Mrs. Ellis started the motorcar, Lydia said anxiously over her shoulder to me, "Bess, do you mind? I told him I'd fallen in London. That you'd brought me home. I couldn't tell him—not when he's coming to dinner!"

"Yes, I understand," I replied, trying to keep her calm. "Put it out of your mind tonight."

"I'm so sorry. But could you stay another day? Just one more?"

It dawned on me then. That I was the excuse why she couldn't share a room with her husband. If I was to look in on her throughout the night, she must sleep elsewhere. Coming home was one thing. Facing Roger Ellis in the seclusion of their bedroom was another. I couldn't be sure whether it was because she was still afraid of him—or because she didn't want to answer his questions.

I had hoped that Lydia would spend a quiet night and that my return to London the next afternoon would still be possible.

Instead at two o'clock in the morning when I looked in on her in the guest room where she was sleeping, she was pacing the floor.

"I can't sleep," she told me at once. "I ought to be tired to the bone, and instead every time I shut my eyes, they fly open again."

Pulling my dressing gown closer about me in the chill of the room—the fire had burned down to ashes—I asked, "What's worrying you, Lydia? Your husband seemed to be glad to see you. He was very pleasant during dinner. Your sister-in-law, Margaret, was very solicitous. She likes you, that's obvious even to me."

Margaret was very like her mother, a tall, slender woman with a very pretty face and a nature to match.

Touching her bruises, Lydia said, "They'll be here this afternoon. Everyone. George, Eleanor, even Henry, if his leave comes through. And then there's Dr. Tilton and his wife. The rector and his sister. It's one thing to

tell Dr. Tilton that I fell in London. I can't lie to everyone else. Roger will be angry with me. But I can hardly
tell them the truth, can I?"

"Just say that you had an accident. You needn't go
into details."

"Roger told me he was sorry, but I couldn't tell if he
meant it."

"You've hardly given him a chance to speak to you
alone. Have you thought about that?"

She walked to the window, then turned and came
back again. "I'm afraid."

"Don't you trust him?"

"I don't trust myself, Bess. I'll start to cry. Besides,
he hasn't shown any softness toward me. He was just as
pleasant to you, if you think about it."

I disagreed. But it was clear that Lydia was still uncertain of her welcome.

"Lydia, I must go to Somerset. I've been looking
forward to seeing my family."

"Another day. Two. They'll arrive tomorrow, and
the service will be the next day. Friday. Sunday they'll
leave. George can drive you back to London. He won't
mind at all. I know what Roger said, but George lost
his brother and then Alan, after being wounded himself. It hasn't been easy."

"Lydia, I've promised. My family—I—"

"I know. Dear God, I know." She put her hands to her head, one on either side. "I can't think for it hurting. Could I have something for it?"

"No, it isn't wise to take a sedative when concussion is suspected."

With a sigh she nodded. "All right. I'll try to sleep again."

I left her then, and went back to my own bed. When I came again at four, she was sleeping, but restlessly, without dreaming. I stood in the doorway, watching her toss and turn, then went again to my own room.

The next morning Lydia came down to breakfast looking pale and anxious. Mrs. Ellis hovered, asking me if all was well. Roger, watching his wife, made no comment. I thought perhaps Mrs. Ellis had told him the doctor's diagnosis, and I wondered if he'd taken it with a grain of salt. But Gran had something to say.

"This is ridiculous, Lydia. Brace up, and let's get on with the work that needs to be done before anyone sets foot through our door. You can feel sorry for yourself when they've all gone again."

"Gran—Dr. Tilton was worried about her."

"Yes, Amelia, no doubt he was. But what are we to do? It's Lydia's fault, after all, that we're behind as we are."

Roger said, "Gran—"

But she interrupted him. "Roger, dear, you have enough to do. We'll manage, somehow."

"I'll help," I volunteered. After all, it was several hours until my train left. And so I found myself swept up in the last-minute preparations.

There were linens still in need of airing, and beds needing to be made up. Margaret and I worked together, and she told me how she was counting on Henry receiving leave.

"I tell myself not to hope, but I can't help it. He and Alan were close, you know. It would mean so much to him to be here."

The weather had cleared marginally, but fires had to be built in all the guest rooms. While Lydia was given the task of polishing the silver, I set the table in the dining room. Mrs. Ellis, looking in on me, apologized again for putting a guest to work, but I was reminded by the strain in her eyes that her son's death was still fresh, and I said only, "It's all right, truly it is."

"I know you're looking forward to Christmas with your family. But could I prevail upon you to stay until Sunday? You've been so good to Lydia, I hesitate to ask more of you, but I'll feel so much better if you're here to keep an eye on her. I'll have my hands full, and I'm not sure she'll take proper care of herself. I'll ask

Roger to drive you directly to Somerset. He'll be glad to do it."

I didn't think he would.

And where was Simon? Had he got my message? I'd thought he might come to fetch me, rather than leave me to take today's train.

"Could you at least speak to your mother, and ask her to let us keep you a little longer?"

What could I say to that plea?

"If someone could drive me into Hartfield, to find a telephone?" I said.

"Of course! Roger has a list of things Mrs. Long requires for the kitchen. There's a telephone at the The King's Head," Then she asked, frowning, "Will she mind terribly? Your mother?"

I thought very likely my mother would. But she would not make a fuss.

Roger Ellis came to collect me shortly before eleven and drove me into Hartfield.

He was, he said, glad to escape the madhouse that Vixen Hill had become. But I thought he actually wanted to ask me some questions.

I was right.

The clouds were heavy with moisture, dark and threatening, but no rain had fallen. As we reached the track that carried us through this part of Ashdown

Forest, Roger swore under his breath as a small herd of some twenty sheep blocked our way. Their thick coats seemed to be impervious to the rain, just as they were impervious to the motorcar's horn. Finally, managing to drive around them without peril to man nor beast, Roger said to me, "How did you meet Lydia?"

I considered what to answer, then said, "In London. I think she told you as much." Did it really matter to him? Because if it did, if this wasn't simply a polite opening to a pleasant conversation, I needed to be on my guard. I didn't think he would strike me, but there was still that well of anger in him I'd sensed the instant he'd come into the sitting room shortly after I'd arrived yesterday. It had been most noticeable when he'd argued with his mother over George's presence. I had no idea what might set it off again in an explosion of violence.

"I'd like to know the details," he told me, his voice tight.

It suddenly occurred to me what he was asking. "Did you think she went to hospital with that bruise on her face? I'd have advised it, if I'd seen her just after you struck her. The bones around the eye socket are thin. The truth is, I've just come home from France. She was waiting for me on my doorstep. Quite literally."

That stopped him. He turned to look at me and nearly ran the motorcar into a ditch.

"You're blunt."

"Yes, I am. You doubt me, you have from the moment you met me, without even waiting to find out if you were justified. I'm a guest in your house, Mr. Ellis, and I do understand that you've recently lost your only brother. It's a time of mourning, and I'm not a member of the family. I don't wish to be rude, but I think it would be better for Lydia and your mother if we could at least find a way to be civil to each other."

"I'd like to tell you my side of the story," he said after a moment. "Will you listen?"

"Of course." I took a deep breath. "But I must ask you something first. Do you trust your wife, Mr. Ellis? Or is there someone you think she might have gone to, hurt and afraid as she was, and in need of comfort?"

"Don't be ridiculous," he snapped.

"Yet you stayed here in Sussex, didn't you? She was terrified that you'd followed her to London. She even thought you'd asked the police to hunt her down. She was terrified that you'd be on our doorstep before she could face you again. And she wasn't at all sure how that meeting would be, or even how you'd receive her. Instead you never really searched for her, did you?

Even when you knew she must be somewhere in this wilderness, alone and cold and hurt—physically and emotionally. I wonder why."

"All right," he said, goaded. "There was a man she met while I was in France. He lives not far from here. I found out about him quite by accident. He's blind, you see, shrapnel fragments that scarred his face and took his sight. She went often to read to him. So I was told. It occurred to me that he was here, I was in France, and she was lonely."

I could have laughed. I hadn't anticipated jealousy. "Have you met this man?"

"Has she told you about him?" he countered.

"No. Why should she? She came to London because she was afraid. Of you. Of the future. If there had been something between your wife and this man, she would have turned to him. Instead she came to me."

He digested that for a moment, his eyes on the road. "I shouldn't have doubted her," he said finally.

"Did you think that the reason she wanted a child was to hide the fact that she was already pregnant?"

"Yes. All right. It was the first thing that crossed my mind." His voice was cold, harsh.

"Then you don't know your wife very well, do you? Or you'd recognize her need for what it is, her love for you."

"I don't want children. Now or ever. I don't want to watch them suffer and die. There's no more helpless feeling, I can tell you. I watched as my own father walked out into the heath and killed himself because the child he loved best was dead. I don't want to see my wife grieve for one dead child when she has three living children, as my mother did for many years. I see no reason to put myself or Lydia through that nightmare. I won't."

Which explained a good deal about Roger Ellis. I wondered if he and Lydia had ever really discussed having children in a quiet and reasonable fashion, or if their feelings were too shut away for them to explain to each other just how they felt.

I also found myself wondering if somewhere, sometime Roger Ellis had strayed, and if this was why he was so ready to believe his wife had been unfaithful.

He answered one of my questions. "We were married in 1913. In the autumn. It was the happiest I'd been for longer than I could remember. Barely a year later the war started, and I enlisted at once. I couldn't wait to get to France, fool that I was. Lydia begged me to wait and see whether it would last, but I promised her I'd be home again before she knew it. Instead I didn't see her for three years. We wrote, of course, but it wasn't the same. And I knew she was angry with me for lying to her. But I hadn't, I'd really believed that the war would end before I saw any of the fighting. I wouldn't have blamed her for looking elsewhere."

A silence fell between us, and then Roger Ellis said, "I never heard her mention your name before yesterday. Why hadn't she said something to me in a letter about having seen you in London—or asked me if I'd had word of you in France? She asks often enough about our neighbors' sons and brothers, you'd think she'd have been concerned about you as well. I asked Daisy, but she didn't recall mail coming for my wife with your return address on it."

I knew the anxiety of waiting for news. I'd asked about mutual friends whenever I'd run into someone I knew.

"What did you think? That she had made up our friendship, simply because you can't find a letter from me in her desk? I expect you looked last night, didn't you?" I said. "If you're trying to convince yourself that there was a conspiracy of silence involved, then perhaps I should ask you why it is that you are willing to believe the worst of me as well as your wife? If you must know, your father was once friends with mine. Or so your mother has told me."

He shot a look at me, as if trying to decide if I was telling the truth.

"Ask her," I said shortly.

And I had a feeling he would not.

We drove on without speaking, and I looked out across the barren world of the heath, at the sheep grazing where kings once hunted, and a line of cows meandering toward a distant meadow, lined up as if in a queue. The weather seemed even grimmer and colder here. It was such a cheerless place to live. Even the deserts of Rajasthan were full of life, and the vast stretches of Egypt's Western Desert for all its endless sand offered more to the eye than the stunted branches of gorse and heather and twisted scrub.

We came into Hartfield, the bustling life of its main street a welcomed sight. I saw the doctor's gate as we passed. A line of pretty cottages along the high street caught my eye. The rain was finally coming down in a fine mist. Ignoring it, women went about their marketing, pushing prams, pausing to gossip on a corner, while men, black umbrellas shielding their faces, strode purposefully toward their destinations. Roger Ellis gestured toward his right. "There's The King's Head. They have a telephone. I'll leave the motorcar in the yard, shall I, and meet you here in half an hour. Will that do?"

"Yes, thank you." The inn stood at the far end of town, on the corner of a street that led up to a church.

A tall black and white building with small-paned windows, it boasted a large sign with a crowned head that appeared to be Charles I with his narrow face, pointed beard, and long dark locks.

As Roger Ellis brought the vehicle to a stop, I noticed the small house just across from us. It was painted a very pleasing shade of blue. There was a sign hanging on the white gate in front of the tiny garden. A painted border of flowers framed the words BLUEBELL COTTAGE. A ginger cat lay curled up in the window next to the door, asleep on a cushion the same color.

Roger Ellis saw the direction of my gaze. "Pretty, isn't it?"

"Yes, very much so," I replied and was on the point of turning toward the inn.

His voice stopped me. It was flat, without emotion, but I sensed the effort he'd needed to keep it that way.

"Her blind officer lives there. In Bluebell Cottage," he said, and walked away, leaving me standing in the middle of the inn yard.

Four

I spoke to my mother, who pretended that she wasn't disappointed that I wasn't coming home directly. I explained my situation as best I could—the telephone was in a cranny without a door, and I knew that anyone passing or standing in Reception just around the corner could hear every word—and I asked if she'd forgive me for putting Lydia first.

"Yes, of course I will. But when were you invited? I didn't quite understand?"

"I ran into someone in London and came down to Sussex with her. A family member died recently, and the stone for his grave is ready to be set in place. The rest of the Ellis family is expected today for a small ceremony. They'd like me to stay."

"Darling, I didn't know you were acquainted with anyone in that part of Sussex. Are you quite sure you've told me everything, Bess, dear?"

"This telephone is in a very public place. Please, ask Simon. He can explain this far better than I, just now."

"I don't know that he's at the cottage just now. He and your father went off together, and the Colonel Sahib hasn't returned."

"I'll write," I said. I had half an hour, I could find hotel stationery and send a short note. "Will that do?" Although any letter would reach Somerset after I did.

"Darling, don't worry about it. You'll be home in a few more days. We can talk then, shall we? You sound tired and more than a little anxious. A party might be just the thing."

Depend on my mother to put the best face possible on any situation.

"Thank you," I replied, utterly sincere. "I'll still write."

I rang off.

Finding hotel stationery was simple enough, and I had a pen with me. Finding a quiet corner to sit in was another matter. It was nearly eleven, and people were coming and going as if this were the hub of activity in the town.

I sat down on a window seat overlooking the street and made an attempt to explain how and why I'd found myself in Sussex instead of Somerset. It was not my best effort, but it would have to do. I wrote my parents' direction on the envelope, and was about to ask Reception where I could find the post office, when I noticed the door of Bluebell Cottage opening and a man stepping out into the street.

He was holding a cane, using it to find his way, as if he had done this a thousand times and knew where he was. Turning to his right, he moved carefully but confidently along the pavement, and people passing him greeted him as if he were fairly well known.

In spite of the hat he wore pulled down to conceal his scars and blind eyes, I could see that he had good bones, a firm chin, and dark brows. Not precisely handsome, but what my mother would call a good face.

In front of the greengrocer's shop stood another man in a threadbare, ragged coat two sizes too large for his thin frame, and the shoes on his feet were worn almost to the point of the leather cracking open. I thought perhaps he'd been begging, because as I watched, I saw the greengrocer come out his door and angrily tell him to move on. He shuffled along to the ironmonger's shop and stopped again. Then he looked up, saw the blind man coming his way, and waited until he was close enough to speak to.

I couldn't hear the conversation of course, but it was obvious the poor man was asking for money. The blind man nodded, reached into his pocket, and took out some coins, dropping them into the grimy, outstretched hand. The beggar touched his cap in gratitude, his thanks following the blind man as he walked on.

Watching this interaction, I'd nearly forgot my letter, and made haste to walk on to speak to the desk clerk. I was halfway there when I all but collided with Roger Ellis coming out of a small parlor just off Reception. I wondered for a fraction of a second if he'd been in a position to overhear my telephone conversation.

"Going somewhere?" he asked, and I knew then that from the parlor window he must also have seen the occupant of Bluebell Cottage walking down the street.

"Yes," I told him. "I was in a hurry to mail this letter before it was time to meet you." I held up the envelope, addressed and sealed but without a stamp. "Do you suppose we could stop at the post office?"

I watched him scan the address. "Of course," he said, and we moved outside again into the chill December. He opened the door of his motorcar for me, and I noticed over his shoulder that the blind man had disappeared from view. But I saw the beggar stopping another man in front of the pub farther along the street.

We paused at the post office, I purchased a stamp, and my letter was dropped into His Majesty's red post box. We drove back to the main street and headed toward the Forest. We had nearly reached the outskirts of Hartfield when we both saw the occupant of Bluebell Cottage about to cross the street. But Roger Ellis hadn't slowed his speed, and I thought for a moment he intended to knock the man down. Someone just behind the blind man caught his arm and spoke to him, and then we were past.

"That was cruel," I snapped. "You could have hurt him."

"I doubt it. I've had a feeling his vision has improved more than he was willing to acknowledge. I've watched him walk through the town before this, and he has an uncanny ability to avoid obstacles."

"Why should he lie? It's familiarity that guides him, and remembering the number of steps to this or that place. Besides, however good his vision may be, what right do you have to test it by frightening the man?"

"Yes, all right, I'm sorry," Ellis said. "I thought when you first came through the hotel door with that letter in your hand that you were taking it across to his cottage. I was angry."

"I showed it to you. It was to my parents."

"But you just spoke to them on the telephone, did you not?"

Exasperated, I said, "I did. And I promised my mother I'd write a note as well. Do you know where that telephone is? Hardly the place for a private conversation of any kind. How could I tell her that I was worried about Lydia having a concussion, without also telling the entire village as well?"

"I apologize," he said again. "It's my shoulder. It hurts like the devil in this weather and after a while it begins to make me short-tempered."

I didn't know if that were true or an excuse for his behavior. I said only, "Where were you wounded?" Lydia had told me it had happened soon after he reached France.

"Near Mons. It's healed well enough, and I have full use of it again. But it's an excellent barometer. I'm told there are still several shards of shrapnel they couldn't reach without doing more damage."

"Yes, that's often a problem," I agreed. "Although I'm told the American Base Hospital in Rouen has an X-ray machine that allows them to locate shrapnel exactly and that makes the surgery far less invasive. I don't know whether your shoulder will improve with time or not. But you might speak to someone there if it continues to trouble you." It was a professional assessment, not meant as a personal judgment.

"I'll manage," he retorted.

"Yes, I'm sure you will," I answered, biting my tongue. Lydia was right about the fact that this man was moody and unpredictable. I let the silence between us lengthen.

I was glad to see the turning for Vixen Hill as we came down the muddy track, bouncing and shuddering in the ruts. It couldn't have helped either Roger Ellis's shoulder or his disposition.

I went directly to my room, took off my hat and coat, and sat down by the window for a moment. Trying to imagine how the knot garden must look in summer helped to take the edge off my own mood. It seemed to me that Lydia and her husband had lost the happiness that must have marked the beginning of their marriage, and I wasn't sure they could find their way back to it now. But at least now I could better understand her reluctance to come home on her own. And I pitied both of them. What troubled me was whether my presence aggravated Roger Ellis's sullenness for reasons I couldn't quite fathom, or if something else was bothering him.

With a sigh I rose from the window to look in on Lydia. But before I could open my door there was a light tap, and then Lydia stepped in.

"Roger is looking decidedly sheepish. What did you say to him?"

I thought about our conversations, about the occupant of Bluebell Cottage, and Roger Ellis's suspicious nature. Hardly something I could pass on to Lydia.

Instead I said, "I'd written a brief note to my mother, and when your husband saw it in my hand, he thought I was carrying a message from you to the occupant of Bluebell Cottage. By the time he realized his mistake, I could see that he was more than a little jealous. Have you given him cause to be?"

She threw up her hands in disgust. "That's Gran's doing. I volunteered to read to Davis Merrit. In fact, it was Mr. Harris, the rector, who asked if I had the time to come and read to him. And I'll be honest, I enjoyed it. He's an interesting man—Lieutenant Merrit—and the books he chooses interest me as well. Gran disapproves, and it was she who put the idea into Roger's head that there might be more to those weekly afternoons than meets the eye. No, I'm not in love with Davis. Nor he with me. I suppose we're both lonely, and there's comfort in companionship. Such as it is."

But sometimes loneliness led to something more. And pity could change to compassion, and compassion to love. Still, if it was true that Gran had made more of a kindness than was justified by the facts, it would have been wise for Lydia to see less of Merrit for the time being.

I said as much, and she replied, "Yes, I expect you're right. But it seemed unnecessarily cruel to Davis to punish him just because such things were very different in Gran's day. After all, we don't meet in the cottage, we sit in the Rectory or sometimes he arranges for a parlor at The King's Head. It's all very proper."

"I've seen him, Lydia. He's rather attractive. And you're vulnerable, with Roger away for so many years."

She glared at me. "If I were intending to have an affair," she said, the ring of truth in her voice, "I'd look for someone in London. Far away from Ashdown Forest. Davis is the frying pan to Roger's fire."

"You knew what the heath was like, didn't you? When you married Roger?"

"I thought I did. Roger had brought me here before we were married, and of course I was in love and this was his home. I hadn't seen it in the depths of winter." She smiled at a memory. "On my first visit, I found a nest of mice under a gorse bush. Tiny things, hardly as big as my thumb. I watched them for a quarter of an hour. It seemed magical. I'd never found mice in Bury St. Edmunds."

I laughed. "No, I expect not. Shall we go? Mrs. Ellis must be waiting for me to help with the bed in the blue room. I promised we'd see to it as soon as I returned from Hartfield."

"Yes, and I've left the silver teapot half polished." She sighed. "Alan wouldn't have cared for all this fuss, but I know how much it means to his mother. And it's given her something to keep her mind occupied." She shivered. "You'd have liked Alan, Bess. He could make you laugh at nothing, and he had the loveliest baritone voice. It was a pleasure to listen to him sing." As we walked toward the stairs, she added, "Before he went to join his ship in 1914, he put all his affairs in order. I wondered if he had a premonition that he might not be coming back."

The first of the guests were expected in time for tea. It was a little later than that when I heard a motorcar on the drive. By the time I'd looked out, I couldn't see who had arrived. I smiled to myself, thinking that it was too soon for the Colonel Sahib to appear in full dress uniform and a battalion of Household Cavalry at his back. Or at the very least prepared to deploy the full force of his charm. It could be formidable.

A few moments later, Daisy, flushed with excitement, hurried into the library where I was folding the ironed table linens on the wide desk there to tell me that someone had called to see me.

"To see me?" I repeated. The Colonel Sahib after all.

But it was Simon standing in the hall.

"I should have known. Wild horses couldn't have kept you away. I'm sorry that you've made the journey for nothing. I spoke to my mother this morning. I won't be coming home until Sunday."

"I was sent for from Sandhurst," he said, and I knew not to ask why. "I stopped at Mrs. Hennessey's when I got back to London, and read your message. Knowing you, I asked her to pack several dresses for you to wear for dinner. According to her, you'd brought only one with you."

"Did Mother tell you I was staying over?"

He laughed. "She didn't need to tell me. I had a feeling you'd succumb to pleading. All right, where shall I take your fripperies?"

"You only came to be sure this wasn't a den of iniquity," I retorted. But I was inordinately glad to see him.

We carried the valise up the stairs to my room, and as he walked into it he said, "Much more cheerful than the hall."

"Yes, I thought so as well." We deposited the valise by the wardrobe.

He glanced at the open door, then crossed the room to close it.

"Are you all right, Bess? You know nothing about these people, after all."

"Apparently Lydia's father-in-law had met the Colonel Sahib out in India. That practically makes me one of the family."

He smiled but wasn't put off by my humor.

"You can't manage all this"—his hand swept over the two valises, the one I'd taken with me and the one he'd brought—"on a train. I'll come for you. Or the Colonel will. Is there a telephone here in the house?"

"No. I put in the call from The King's Head in Hartfield. Mrs. Ellis has offered to send me home with her son. Or failing that, a family friend, George something, will take me to London."

I could tell he wasn't happy about that, but he said nothing. I explained about the concussion, and he nodded. With a final look around the room, he opened the door, and I led him back to the hall. Lydia was there, and Roger.

Simon greeted her like an old friend, although I could tell he was silently taking note of the progression of the bruise on her face. Roger flushed a little as

Simon turned to him. Lydia made the introductions and said, "We dined with Mr. Brandon while I was in London."

It had been a lunch, but I said nothing.

"Indeed," Roger Ellis replied as the two men shook hands.

"I'll be off, then," Simon said. "I'll tell your mother, shall I, that everything was to your liking?"

We hadn't opened the valises. He meant the situation. "Yes, please. And give her my love. I'll see her at the end of the weekend."

He put a comradely hand on my shoulder, a warning I thought to Roger Ellis not to lay a hand on me if he were in the mood to attack women. Then he bade us farewell and was gone out the door. As I heard the motorcar turn in the drive and head for the track through the forest, I felt alone somehow.

"How long have you known Brandon?" Captain Ellis was asking.

"Simon? All of my life, I expect. I can't recall a time when he wasn't there. He was in my father's regiment."

"A military man, is he?" I knew what he was asking: Why wasn't Simon in uniform? He was young enough to fight.

"Retired," I said simply. "He serves now at the discretion of the War Office." Turning to Lydia, I said, "I think we've done everything on Mrs. Ellis's list. Should we go up now and change?"

"Yes, that's a very good idea. It was nice of Mr. Brandon to bring what you needed. But I would have gladly let you borrow something."

Mrs. Ellis came in at that moment and said, "There you are, Roger, my dear. Would you mind running over to the Lanyon farm and asking them to deliver more wood, if they have it? Just to be sure we don't run short. And that reminds me, I need another dozen eggs. I expect I ought to take the other motorcar and beg Janet Smyth for whatever she has to spare." She turned to me. "Bess, would you and Lydia mind coming back down here and keeping an eye open for George? He should have been here three-quarters of an hour ago."

"He probably stopped at The King's Head," Roger said under his breath, but Mrs. Ellis caught the remark.

"Be a little generous, my dear," she admonished her son.

By the time we had returned to the hall, I could hear a motorcar coming up the drive.

To everyone's surprise, it was Henry, grinning from ear to ear. Margaret rushed into his arms with a cry of joy, and then clung to him, as if afraid he'd fly away if she let him go.

Henry, an artillery officer, was dark and slim, a contrast to Margaret's fairness, but I saw a nervous tic by his left eye. I found myself wondering if he had come by this leave medically, when a doctor took note of the early signs of exhaustion and stress.

Soon afterward Alan's widow arrived, accompanied by her brother, Thomas Joyner, a quiet man with a Naval beard and little to say for himself. He had lost an arm when his cruiser was torpedoed, and was now posted to the Admiralty. We had several friends in common, and he seemed to relax as we talked.

Finally, George Hughes arrived. From the flush on his face I couldn't help but think that Roger Ellis was right—he'd stopped in Hartfield for a little Dutch courage. But whatever he'd had to drink there, he was cold sober now. As he turned to greet us, his impeccable uniform was splashed with blood, and across his forehead was a bruised area that was also bleeding, as if he'd struck his head hard against something. The knuckles on one hand were badly scraped. Mrs. Ellis had returned by that time, and he apologized immediately for the delay as she broke off her greeting to stare at his face.

"But George, what on earth happened—?" she asked.

"I'm all right, although the motorcar is a little the worse for wear. That bend in the road—you know it?

After that long straightaway? I came around it and there was a dead tree toppled directly in my path."

"A tree? George, there aren't any trees just there."

"I know. All I could think of was that it had fallen from a cart carrying wood. I can tell you I was damn—very lucky. I think Roger and I ought to move it before someone else comes to grief. I tried, but I didn't have any rope in the motorcar. It would take that to budge it."

"By all means! He's just coming down. George, this is Sister Crawford, a friend of Lydia's here for the weekend. You'll allow her to look at your forehead, won't you? And what about your ribs? Did you strike the steering wheel? Did you do any damage there? I'd hate to think—they've only just begun to *heal*."

He touched his chest with his fist. "So far I can breathe without difficulty. But it was a very near thing, I can tell you. No, don't trouble, Sister," he went on as I came forward. "A little soap and water—but Daisy could have a look at my tunic, if she would. Before the blood sets."

Mrs. Ellis whisked him away to the kitchens, and on the way I heard her calling to her son. Ten minutes later, Roger and George went out to the motorcar, and I heard them drive off.

I had just gone up for a shawl to put around my shoulders when the motorcar returned. As I came into the hall, I could hear George apologizing again, this time to Roger. I caught the last words as they opened the door and came in quickly, shutting out the wind.

". . . but it was there, as certain as I am here before you."

"Yes, all right. We'll say nothing to Mother, shall we?" Roger was a little ahead of his friend, his face set. He walked on, leaving George to talk to me. I could see that the wound had been cleaned quite efficiently, but he sat down in one of the hall chairs like a man who had been shamed.

I was about to make an effort at conversation, when Henry came into the hall and said, "What's this I hear about a tree in the road? Good Lord, man, look at your face! I didn't see anything when I came through, and I couldn't have been that far ahead of you."

"I expect," George said with an effort at lightness, "I mistook a ewe for a tree. There was a scattering of fleece across the road. But no blood. I think honors go to her."

"Yes, well, how's the motorcar?"

They went off discussing the left wing, and I remembered the scraped knuckles on George's hand. He hadn't got that from charging into a flock of sheep. It looked more like trying to deal with the tree. Whatever Roger Ellis tried to tell him.

He smiled as he passed me, but it didn't reach his haunted eyes.

We gathered in the hall for drinks that evening, and I sat beside Gran, who was enjoying having her family around her, her bright eyes taking in what everyone was wearing and all that was said.

She turned to me at one point, saying, "This is a pale shadow of how we entertained in my day. My husband knew so many people. The house was always full, and we had the staff to cope with the guests. There are photographs somewhere. I'm sure we kept them."

Dinner that night was rather ordinary fare, but no one seemed to mind, and there was a good wine from the cellars.

It wasn't until we had all gathered again in the hall that George asked the question that everyone else had been too polite to bring up. "Whatever happened to your face, Lydia?"

I thought at first that he'd drunk too much port to remember his manners.

But then he added gently, "We can't help but see the bruising and the black eye. I think you'll be more comfortable if we stop trying to pretend we don't notice."

She turned beet red, and everyone stared, then looked quickly away.

Roger answered before she could. "Ran into one of the cupboard doors while looking for the wineglasses. The doctor says no harm done."

Lydia smiled gratefully at him, and I wondered if he'd been prepared for questions, because the response had seemed so natural and unforced.

I'd watched her without seeming to, and I rather thought her condition was improving. There was no sign of either a headache or dizziness, and I had the feeling that she and Roger were trying to make amends for their quarrel. She seemed more comfortable with him, and once I saw her touch his hand while laughing over a story he'd told. It was possible that I could leave with Simon the next afternoon after all.

That buoyed my spirits.

The evening was ending on a pleasant note until there was one disruptive comment from George Hughes.

"I'd have thought the drawing room would be more comfortable on a night like this," he said when a sudden gust of wind and rain roared down the chimney, sending woodsmoke billowing out of the great expanse of hearth, making us cough. "Besides, I miss the portrait. I always look forward to seeing it again."

Gran said sharply, "George, you ought to be in your bed. As we all should. It's growing late."

He took out his watch, looked at the time, and put it away. "So it is."

That was the signal for everyone to rise and murmur something about the tiring drive. I stayed in the hall until they had all gone up, and then followed. Roger passed me coming back to see to the fire, and I said good night.

He nodded, and went on his way without speaking.

I went once to the room over the hall to look for Lydia—George had been given the guest room where she'd spent last night—but she wasn't there. Smiling to myself, I slipped quietly back to my own bed.

The next day went fairly well, the sun coming out in the early morning hours and staying with us most of the afternoon before slipping again behind dark clouds.

We went to St. Mary's Church in Wych Gate in a convoy of motorcars at two o'clock in the afternoon. The track meandered and turned back on itself, and then followed a line of trees.

I could see the church now, the tower tall as the tallest tree, the red brick vivid amongst the bare branches. There was a high iron gate in the wall that surrounded the churchyard, and no sign of a Rectory. We passed the main entrance and turned into a broad grassy space just beyond. To one side I could see a smaller gate letting into the churchyard, and on the far side, I could hear the sound of water splashing over stone as the motors were cut off. A path, almost lost in the tangled growth under the trees, must lead to a nearby stream, in spate after all the rain.

As we got down and walked through the open gate, the first thing that met my eye was a grave in the shadow of the church, bordered by white marble. On the mounded earth inside the border a white marble child knelt, as if about to play with the small white marble kitten standing just in front of her. She wore a pretty frock with a lace collar, a sash at the waist, and on her feet were shoes with a square buckle, just visible at the edge of her skirts. The dress itself was incised with tiny flowers, the folds beautifully arranged. The marble face had almost the look of life, it was so finely carved, a smile just touching the parted lips and reflected in the eyes. I knew, having seen the portrait, that this was where Juliana was buried.

It was moving to see how lovingly she had been remembered. As if to keep her with the living, even if only in cold stone.

I was walking with Mrs. Ellis, and she bent to brush a leaf from her daughter's marble skirt. "My husband designed the monument," she said to me. "He couldn't bear the idea of a stone like all the rest. Not for Juliana. And I keep flowers here most of the year. Pansies in the spring, asters in the autumn." She paused for a moment by her daughter's memorial, and then moved on to a newer grave, still raw and ugly. "We wanted to bury her at Vixen Hill, but the rector at the time—Mr. Pembrey—persuaded us that here would be best. But it seems so far away. So lonely. As if we've abandoned her here and gone on with our lives. Never mind, I'm just fanciful today."

Alan Ellis's stone was plain, with his name, rank, and the dates of his birth and death. But there was a relief chiseled into the curved top of a ship in full sail.

Eleanor touched it gently. "It was what he asked for," she said to Gran. "And it's beautiful, isn't it?"

The elder Mrs. Ellis said, "Yes. Alan always had an eye for such things."

There were a number of other people present. Among others, I saw Dr. Tilton and was introduced to his wife, Mary, and then to the rector, Mr. Smyth and his sister, Janet. When we had all gathered and settled ourselves on the benches set beside the grave, Mr. Smyth conducted a very moving service, recalling Alan Ellis as he'd known him as a boy, the connection between him and the sea, and how courageously he'd faced the knowledge that he was dying.

"His faith was strong. He had made peace with God before he was rescued from the cold and turbulent sea, and he never lost that deep feeling that he was in the hands of his Lord."

He went on to speak to the family individually, to the widow first, and next to the two Mrs. Ellises, mother and grandmother, then moved on to the surviving brother and sister.

Mr. Smyth was a short, balding man, his tortoise-shell glasses catching the last of the daylight as clouds spread across the weak winter sun. His eloquence surprised me until I learned later that Eleanor had written much of it. She sat there, her face hidden by her heavy black veil, one hand holding tightly to her brother's, listening to the words and the prayers, seeming not to feel the cold.

I realized it was her farewell to her husband. That the stone on his grave was a final duty that she had taken on herself.

This was not a usual service. I couldn't recall ever having attended another dedication of a memorial stone by gathering of family and friends. But it was impressive, and I could see that to the family it was offering much needed solace.

Looking around at the faces in the half circle, I could see that Gran, shielded by the silk veil, was staring into space, her mind on the words but her eyes on what must have been her own husband's marker. Mrs.

Ellis, from behind her own veil, was lost in thought, perhaps remembering the little boy who had become a man. Margaret was weeping quietly.

The men had no such defense from the public gaze. Roger, standing closest to the stone, put his hand out to it, then quickly withdrew it, as if reluctant to touch it. George Hughes kept his eyes on Roger's face, and I was surprised to see speculation in his gaze. Henry, his arm around his wife's shoulders, looked down at the stone as if envisioning his own. The tic at the corner of his left eye had grown worse.

And then the service ended with a benediction, and we began the slow progress back to the motorcars waiting for us at the side of the churchyard.

I saw George Hughes pause briefly as he passed and put his hand on the cold marble head of Juliana's memorial. It was a lingering caress, as one might touch the head of a beloved child. Then he was offering his arm to Mrs. Ellis, and I thought that she took it gratefully. Mr. Smyth was helping Gran, while Roger held out a hand to Lydia. After a moment's hesitation, she took it.

I looked back as the gate was closing behind us and saw the last of the light touch the stone we'd just dedicated. It picked out Alan's last name for an instant and then was gone.

Janet Smyth took my arm and said, "You're a friend of Lydia's. I'm glad. She needs to have friends around her when Roger goes back to France. I hope you'll be able to stay until Christmas."

"My own family is expecting me next week," I said. "And then I must return to France."

She said, "Oh, you're a nursing sister, then."

"Yes."

"I do admire your courage! When the war began, I considered nursing, but my brother dissuaded me. He felt that I didn't have the constitution for it."

She was sturdily built, and I thought to myself that she could have made a very useful nurse, strong enough to deal with delirious men and those too ill to shift for themselves. But perhaps she meant the mental stamina. I knew all too well the cost of that.

We walked on together, arm in arm, and she was saying about the heath, "It's a dreary place, but I've come to love it."

Surprised, I said, "You weren't born here?"

"Oh, no, only the Ellises. And of course George Hughes. His family lived not far from Vixen Hill. They moved to London a few years after little Juliana died. Such a tragedy. But you must know all about that."

As we crossed the grassy dell together, Janet Smyth added, "I'll see you this evening."

I nodded and went to accompany Mrs. Ellis on the drive back to Vixen Hill. Mrs. Ellis sighed. "I think Alan would have been pleased."

"Yes," I agreed. "It was a very lovely service."

"I wasn't prepared," she said. "For the end. He seemed to be stronger. I let myself believe. And then he was gone, and there was so much I'd left unsaid. That's a terrible feeling."

"Sometimes things don't actually need to be said," I suggested.

In the front seat, Margaret said under her breath to her husband, "I don't see why he had to die."

Her husband replied, "Frostbite, and then gangrene, my love. The sea is very cold and very cruel in winter."

I saw her shake her head, but she didn't say anything more.

For dinner I wore the pale green gown that my father particularly liked, with the rope of pearls that had been given to me when I was twelve by the maharani who was a friend of my mother's. After weeks in uniforms with stiff collars and starched aprons, I felt rather underdressed.

In the hall, George Hughes sat in the shadows cast by the lamps, his face unreadable. But I thought as I watched that he was drinking more than was wise. Roger cast several glances in his direction but said nothing. Janet Smyth tried to talk to him, but his answers were terse. I heard her quietly telling her brother that he was still grieving for Alan, but somehow I thought not. I saw him look at his knuckles a time or two, as if to reassure himself that what had happened on the road wasn't merely his imagination.

I wondered if the tree he'd seen was actually just one of the logs that the Lanyon family had been delivering to Vixen Hill. And they'd come back to reclaim it.

After a lovely dinner, we took our tea in the drawing room in front of the fire, gathering under Juliana's smiling portrait. I thought, *George will be pleased.*

When the men had finished their port and come to join us, George sat down across from me. His eyes were heavy, and I thought perhaps he was half asleep. Then he turned to me and asked, "You're a nursing sister?"

"Yes."

"God bless," he said fervently. "You have no idea how much good you do."

Gran looked up at that. "What did your father have to say about your decision to go into nursing?"

I knew she'd been wanting to ask me just that. In her day, women of good families didn't nurse the ill and dying. Only the poorest of women, and even streetwalkers, were thought fit for such an occupation. Florence Nightingale had changed public opinion during the Crimean War about the role nurses could play in saving lives, but it was still not considered a proper profession until the death tolls in the present war made women of every class come forward to do what they could.

I smiled a little as I remembered my father's opinion.

"If you wash out, don't let it fret you. There are other ways to serve. Just remember that." Whether he expected me to fail to qualify I didn't know, but he was right, it was harder work than I'd ever expected it to be, and I'd had to face things that it would have been easier not to face, ever. I'd reminded myself every night when I went to bed that soldiers in the field were already enduring unspeakable conditions, and if I were truly my father's daughter, I would stick to my guns and not retreat. In the end, I qualified, and felt a surge of pride that I hadn't anticipated. This was my accomplishment. Being the Colonel's daughter hadn't smoothed my path, hadn't made it less disgusting to take away bedpans and trays of bloody cloths or mop up vomit and other bodily fluids from the floor, or clean patients who were riddled with disease or covered in pus from suppurating wounds, hadn't made the smells less nauseating, hadn't stopped the sights from invading my dreams, or taught my poor stomach to accept food again after the most harrowing of amputations. It had only steeled my determination. Now I could look back on my training with a better understanding of what it was designed to forge in those of us who survived it. And I could measure just how far I had come.

But I answered her differently. "My father knew how much it meant to me to do my duty. And to his eternal credit, he didn't stand in my way."

"Indeed." It was her only comment and could be interpreted in several ways.

Henry asked where I'd served, and I told him: *Britannic*, France, the Near East. He said, "You were on *Britannic* when she went down? Yes? That must have been harrowing."

I said, "We had a good captain and a good crew. Most of us survived."

We spoke of other things, and some little time later, I saw George lean over to say something to Roger. It was meant to be private, a quiet aside. Instead it happened to fall into one of those lulls that come at the end of an evening, when conversation is nearly at a standstill and people are about to take their leave and go home. Which meant we all heard him as clearly as if he had shouted the words from the rooftop.

"—daughter is the spitting image of Juliana. Did you realize that? For God's sake, tell me, has she been found?"

Five

We could have heard a pin drop twenty miles away, the silence that followed his words was so profound.

Roger sat as if nailed to his chair for all of several seconds. George had the grace to look embarrassed. The rest of us were sitting there with our mouths open. I shut mine smartly, prepared for anything. Out of the corner of my eye I could see Lydia's expression: shock mixed with horror. She turned toward her husband, waiting for him to reply.

Whose daughter? That was the question in everyone's mind. If she was the image of Juliana, then she must be Roger's. Or Alan's. And why was it necessary to find her?

Finally Roger said, "You're drunk and maudlin, George. You should call it a night."

Dr. Tilton stood, setting his teacup on the table beside him. "I'll see him to bed, shall I? His usual room? Good."

Roger Ellis stirred. His words to George had been clipped, the only outward sign of whatever emotion he was suppressing—anger, disgust, surprise. It was impossible to tell what he was feeling, but his eyes were so intensely blue that if they could have sparked, they would have. Turning to me, he said, "Miss Crawford, I hesitate to ask such a favor of a guest, but if you could assist Dr. Tilton, I'd be grateful."

"By all means," I answered, rising and praying that George wouldn't vomit all over my pale green dress. He looked now as if he could be sick at any moment, his face gray. Or was that shame as his careless words finally sank in and he realized what he had done?

"I can manage," he began, then nearly lost his balance as he rose from his chair.

Dr. Tilton and I each took an arm to help him to the door, but he caught us unprepared and pulled away, turning around to face everyone in the room.

"Malcolm isn't here after all. I must have imagined he was. It was to him—to my brother—that I was speaking. I do apologize if I've upset anyone." His eyes were quite sober now.

I remembered Roger mentioning earlier that Malcolm was George's late brother. And it was obvious that the others also knew who Malcolm was. But even I could see the doubt in the faces turned toward us in the doorway. It was a polite lie intended to cover the truth. And it failed.

"Forgive me," he added, and then let us lead him through the door.

As it was closing behind us, I heard Mrs. Ellis say, "Poor man. He hasn't been the same since—" The rest of what she was about to say was cut off as the door shut with a soft *click*.

We got George to his room, where the lamps were already lit and the fire burning well on the hearth, thanks to the ubiquitous Daisy, and in short order we had him in his bed, leaning against pillows.

"I feel like an idiot," he said to me as I smoothed the blanket we had pulled over his knees. Then he turned his gaze on Dr. Tilton. "I do talk to my brother sometimes, you know. A habit begun early in life and hard to break. We were close."

Dr. Tilton said, "You mentioned a child who looked like Juliana. I thought your brother was dark."

"Her mother was fair," George responded quickly. "A Frenchwoman."

But Dr. Tilton was not satisfied. "I thought most Frenchwomen were also dark."

George smiled. "I can tell you that some are as fair as any Englishwoman. Miss Crawford can attest to that, I'm sure." He looked to me for support.

I said to Dr. Tilton, "That's true. Now I think we should rejoin the other guests."

"Yes, yes, go on down. I'll be with you shortly." It was clear he would like to probe further into what Lieutenant Hughes had said. I was sure the family wouldn't care for that, and Lydia had already warned me that he was a gossip.

I could understand, then, why Roger Ellis had asked me to accompany the doctor.

"Dr. Tilton. We have put Lieutenant Hughes to bed. That was our only charge."

He looked up at me, on the point of telling me to mind my own business, when he must have realized that I was not simply a nursing sister but a friend and guest of Lydia's. He wished Lieutenant Hughes a good night and added, "Send for me tomorrow if you feel unwell."

We left then, shutting the bedroom door behind us and walking in silence back the way we'd come. The silence between us was uncomfortable, as if Dr. Tilton was clearly not accustomed to having nursing sisters or anyone else contradict him.

I wondered what had been said in the drawing room after we had taken Lieutenant Hughes away.

But the conversation when we opened the door was stilted.

Gran was saying, "—and the latest reports from France leave one to wonder—"

Every head turned toward us as we entered, and Mrs. Tilton rose, saying, "My dear, I hadn't realized how late it is."

Her husband said, "Yes, I suspect we'll meet with patches of fog on the way home."

The Smyths rose as well, and then everyone was standing, bidding one another a good night, thanking Mrs. Ellis for the lovely dinner, and five minutes later Roger was swinging the hall door closed after his guests, and turning to face us.

I realized that Lydia wasn't there.

Roger said, "It's been a long day. Perhaps we should call it an evening." And before anyone could question him, he strode through the passage door and closed it behind him.

Mrs. Ellis was running a finger around the now-empty porcelain umbrella stand, not looking at her mother-in-law as she said, "I must say I'm rather tired as well. Good night, Gran. Bess." She crossed the room to kiss Margaret on the cheek, and then Henry as well.

Margaret said hastily, "Yes, it's been a long day, hasn't it?" And with a glance at Henry, she followed her mother toward the door, Henry at her heels.

Eleanor and her brother had slipped away earlier while Roger and Mrs. Ellis were saying their last farewells to the doctor and the rector.

Gran clearly wanted to return to what had happened in the drawing room, and she looked after them with a frown between her eyes. She stared at me for a moment, as if considering whether to broach the subject with me, and then thought better of it.

"Where's Lydia?" she asked instead.

"I don't know. I thought she came down with us."

"Hmmph," Gran said, and then bade me a good night.

I was left in sole possession of the hall. I stood by the fire for a few minutes more, relishing the quiet, although I could hear the wind picking up again outside.

Tomorrow, I thought, will be a stressful day. There will be no avoiding George, and Roger will have his hands full keeping his family from demanding answers.

And Lydia? What about her?

I went looking for her then, and found her in the drawing room, staring up at the portrait of Juliana, as if she'd never seen it before.

I'd just stepped into the room when Gran came in behind me. I could tell she'd been searching for Lydia as well.

Ignoring me, Gran said directly to her grandson's wife, "He was drunk, Lydia."

She didn't answer or look away from her contemplation of the portrait. Below it a log fell in the grate as the flames ate through it, making all of us jump, and sparks flew up the chimney in a bright spiral.

"He does talk to his brother. I heard him only last evening, in his room, carrying on a conversation with Malcolm," the elder Mrs. Ellis continued.

"It wasn't Malcolm he was speaking to," Lydia said at last, her gaze dropping from Juliana's face and moving to Gran's. "Henry was coming out of George's room as I was going up."

"Nevertheless, you know as well as I do that Malcolm's death had turned his mind. Roger had even suggested that asking him to be here for Alan's memorial would be too much for him."

I'd heard that exchange. But I'd interpreted it to mean that Roger would be made uncomfortable, not George.

Lydia said, a sigh in her voice, "Gran. Thank you. But there's no way to undo what was said here tonight. George will try to put a better face on them, and Roger will deny any knowledge of what he was saying, but the words were *spoken*. None of us can pretend we didn't hear them. Or know that some sort of truth must lie behind them. The question now is, what will Roger do?"

"There couldn't have been a child, Lydia. He's been fighting in the trenches, for God's sake. There are no whores in the trenches."

"What about his wounded shoulder, Gran? He wasn't in the trenches then. There was *time*. Was it a nurse who bore him a child? Or someone else?"

"Lydia, there is no child!" Gran said, nearly angry.

"I'm Roger's wife," she answered slowly. "I know when my husband is cold to me. I know when he isn't eager to hold me or tell me he loves me. You're his grandmother. It's natural for you to feel he can do no wrong. I can't fault you for that. But something is different. I've known it since the day he arrived, while Alan was so ill. I put it down then to sorrow and impending loss. But at some point—some point in his grieving, why didn't he turn to me? And why, when I asked him for a child, did he strike me across the face? I thought it was because I'd mentioned Juliana as well. Now—now, I'm not so sure."

"You're overwrought," Gran told her. "And not making any sense."

"I'm making a great deal of sense. For the first time I see my way clearly."

"Don't do anything rash, Lydia. Don't do something you'll regret."

"There's no one else, Gran. Whatever Roger tells you, there is no one else."

"In my day, a woman knew when to look the other way. Not that I ever had to, but I knew my duty all the same."

"It isn't your day and age now, is it? When we were married, Roger promised to forsake all others—"

"Don't be naïve, Lydia. A man's needs are very different from those of a woman," Gran snapped.

"I'm not naïve," Lydia retorted. "I'm jealous. Don't you understand?"

"There's no arguing with you in this mood," the elder Mrs. Ellis said. "Perhaps you'll come to your senses in the light of day." With that she turned on her heel and walked past me and out of the room.

I think she'd even forgot I was there. For I caught a look of surprise in her eyes as they met mine, and then irritation before she'd closed the door behind her.

I said after a moment, "Perhaps I should go as well, Lydia. If you need me, you know where to find me."

"No, stay."

We hadn't heard the door open again—or perhaps Mrs. Ellis hadn't shut it firmly. Roger's voice startled both of us.

Standing there just inside the threshold, he said, "And I think it would be better if Miss Crawford left," Roger said.

"No. Whatever you have to say, she remains. What child was George talking about, Roger?"

"He told you. Malcolm's."

"We both know he was trying to cover up his gaff. What child, Roger? You might as well tell me. It's out in the open now, you can't pretend it's a secret any longer."

"I swear to you—" He cast a look in my direction.

"Is that why you don't want us to have a child? There's someone else, isn't there? Someone you met in France and love more. Why couldn't you tell me? Just—tell me."

He glanced up at the portrait over the mantel, as if looking for courage. "I don't love anyone else, Lydia. I never have."

"Then she was what? A refugee? A woman of the streets? A girl willing to sell herself for food and a place to sleep that night? Who was she?"

"Lydia, this isn't the time or place to be having this conversation."

"Why not? He said she was the image of Juliana. It couldn't be Alan's child—he's been on a cruiser in the North Atlantic. If he'd fathered a child in some faraway port, George would never have known that she looked so much like Juliana. No, this child is the reason why you didn't take leave to come to England when you were wounded, the reason you haven't had leave to return to England in three years of fighting."

"Lydia, you're letting your imagination run away with you. There was no woman. There is no child. Miss Crawford here can tell you how impossible it is to get leave, even when you're wounded."

"Leave her out of this." She was looking up at him now, such misery in her eyes that I could have wept for her. I didn't want to be a witness to this scene. But there was nothing I could do, except watch in silence, pretending I wasn't there after all.

Finally Lydia said tiredly, "I don't know what to believe. In London I'd believed that you struck me because of what I'd said about Juliana. I blamed myself for using such a vile weapon to make my point. I came home to apologize and beg your forgiveness. Well, if the truth has come out finally, it's just as well. If Bess will have me, tomorrow I'll be returning to London with her, until I can make other arrangements. Under the circumstances, I shall expect you to give me an allowance, so that I can live at least with dignity, if not comfort."

"You can't leave. We have guests. Mother and Gran—"

"Our only guests are Eleanor and members of your own family. They will understand—this time—why I need to go away and not think about anything for a while, until I'm able to decide what this has done to our marriage."

She rose, walking to the door. "What's more," she said, with an overtone of spite, "before I went to London the first time, you were all but accusing me of having an affair with Davis Merrit. And you made me feel *guilty*, when I had done nothing more than read to the poor man. And all the while, you knew what you yourself were guilty of. I think that's the most disgusting part of all this." Her voice finally broke on the last words, and she left, not bothering to shut the door behind her.

"Damn it," Roger began, but it was too late, she was gone. He turned to me then, and said, "I don't know how to reach her. It's impossible."

"Is it?" I prepared to leave as well. "We all heard what Lieutenant Hughes said. You can pretend he wasn't speaking to you. He can swear that he was drunk and talking to his dead brother. But neither will satisfy your wife."

"There is no child!" he exclaimed, angry now.

"Sadly I'm not one of the people you must convince. Good night, Captain Ellis."

"Wait!"

I stopped but didn't turn.

"I must ask you," he went on, as if the words were forced from him, "what Lieutenant Hughes said to Dr. Tilton."

"He stood by what he'd said before he left the drawing room."

"And Dr. Tilton? Did he pry?"

There was nothing for it but to tell the truth. "I'm afraid he tried. But I reminded him that we had done our duty and ought to return to the other guests, and he stopped."

"Yes, damn it, that's precisely what I was afraid he would do. Even what little he knows will be all over Ashdown Forest before tomorrow is out. That's why I asked you to go with him. I couldn't—it would look too much like I was trying to rush George away before he could say more." He hesitated. "Thank you, Miss Crawford. I appreciate your loyalty."

I turned then. "It wasn't so much a matter of loyalty," I said. "It was disliking the doctor's taking advantage of Lieutenant Hughes when he was vulnerable. And to tell you the truth, I didn't want to know any more. For Lydia's sake."

"What was the thrust of Tilton's questions?"

"Coloring. If the child was fair, like Juliana, then in theory neither George nor his brother could be the father. While you are fair, and very like your dead sister, if we can draw such a conclusion from that painting."

He took a deep breath. "Yes. I understand. Thank you all the same. Go on to bed. It's very late."

It was dismissal, and I was glad to take it.

I couldn't read Roger Ellis. Either he was a consummate liar, or he was telling the truth. And I was fairly sure he wasn't telling the whole truth.

I went slowly up the stairs, remembering that Lydia was determined to leave in the morning. I didn't know what advice to give her—to go, or to stay and get to the bottom of what if anything her husband was hiding. She had been deeply hurt for a second time, and she couldn't convince herself that this time it was largely her fault. And I couldn't imagine Lydia taking Gran's advice to look the other way. In an arranged marriage, that might be possible, but in a love match, it was the destruction of trust.

I opened the door to my room, glad to have the night to consider what to do in the morning.

Instead I found Lydia lying across my bed, crying.

For an instant I hesitated. And then I backed out as quietly as I'd come in. The wind rattled the window just as I was closing the door as gently as possible. I waited for several seconds, but Lydia didn't call to me. Turning, I walked down the passage.

Where was I to go? All the bedrooms were occupied. And Lydia was safer where she was. With luck, no one would think to look for her in my room.

The hall was too large and empty and uncomfortable. I wasn't particularly happy with the thought of sleeping in the room above the hall. Those long windows would be drafty and I'd be cold before morning. In the end I went down to the family sitting room and pulled two chairs together. There was a woolen lap rug over the back of another chair, and I pulled that round my shoulders. The fire here had died down to ashes, but there was still enough of a glow from the embers that I didn't need to light a lamp. I was just as glad, thinking that at least no one would believe anyone was in here, if the room was dark.

I'd been there for well over two hours, unable to sleep, when George Hughes, in his dressing gown, quietly opened the door. He was looking for the brandy, I thought, but found me instead. He fumbled for the lamp and struck a match, the smell of sulfur strong in the air. Just as the light bloomed, I spoke, so that he wouldn't be startled seeing me there.

"Can't sleep?" he asked, his eyebrows raised. As if the entire household had no reason to lie awake.

"Lydia is in my room. I think you'd better tell me, Lieutenant. Before this breaks up Lydia's marriage.

I won't ask you who the father is. Only, where is this child?"

He sighed. "Her mother is dead. She was put into an orphanage. No one seems to know where. That's all I can tell you."

"In France?"

"Yes. In France."

"Do you know her name?"

"No. But I saw her when she was only a year old. And she is so like Juliana it makes one's heart stop. If I'd known—if I'd had any idea—I'd have claimed her myself. Brought her to England and raised her as my own. To hell with Roger. But that's water over the dam. I remember Juliana, you see. Roger never really got over her death. Nor did I, if you want the truth. I thought when I saw Lydia for the first time that she must have reminded him of Juliana in a way. But he said not. I don't know."

"Did he have an affair?"

"I expect he did. How else do you explain the child? My God."

"And the mother? Who was she?"

"I haven't any idea."

"But you said you saw the child?"

"Quite by accident, actually. I was—" He broke off, turning toward the door. "There's someone outside."

I got up and went quietly to the door, opening it quickly. But if someone had been there, he or she was gone now. There was no one in the passage outside.

"I shouldn't have brought it up," he said as I closed the door again. He looked with longing at the brandy decanter, then sighed. "I was sitting there, staring up at Juliana's portrait, and I couldn't stop myself. I had to know what happened to that child." He took a turn about the room, fretful and angry. "I'd waited for Ellis to say something. I'd given him every opportunity. When we were alone in the motorcar. Before dinner. I even mentioned the portrait that first night, to signal that Juliana—and by extension, the child—was on my mind. Instead he avoided the subject. I began to believe there was something he didn't want to tell me. Had something happened to her? Was she dead? When he sat down near me at the end of the evening tonight, I thought, this was my chance. There might not be another. I intend to leave tomorrow. It will be less embarrassing all round."

This time he stopped by the drinks table, lifted the brandy decanter, and poured a goodly amount into a glass. But then he set it aside untasted.

"As soon as I'm back in France, I'm going to find her. See if I don't, by God. I must have been out of my mind to think Roger—" He swore under his breath, picked up the glass, and downed it in one long swallow. "She even smiles the way Juliana did. It was such a shock I stood there unable to say a word. And then they were gone, the nuns hurrying the children away. I caught up with them then, asked what the little girl's name was. I think they must have believed I had some ulterior motive, that I meant her a harm. The older nun glared at me and told me it was none of my affair. Damn it, I don't see how he could walk away from his own flesh and blood. But he has."

"But what if Captain Ellis is telling the truth? You can't be certain the child is his, just because she reminds you of Juliana. Can you? A fleeting resemblance that touched a chord of memory when you were already tired, under great stress—"

"No, I'm not mad, and I'm not mistaken. Ellis got very drunk one night, talking wildly about someone dying. He'd got a letter, he said, and he'd burned it because he didn't want to know what was in it. Now he was frantic to read it, and it was gone. I asked him how he knew someone was dying if he hadn't read the letter, and he told me it was enclosed in another letter. The next morning he was gone. I don't know how he wangled leave, or even if he did. Three days later he was back, haggard, unshaven, looking as if he hadn't slept. He asked if I had any money, and I gave him what I had. He left again, and by the time he returned that evening, I'd already lied twice to cover for him. I asked if everything was all right, and he nearly took my head off. A day or so later he told me that if anything happened to him that I was to see that money went regularly to a small convent south of Ypres. He said he was paying for perpetual prayers for someone's soul."

He broke off, and for a moment I thought he was going to the decanter again, but he only walked to the door, and as I'd done, opened it quickly and peered out. Satisfied, he closed it again and went on, as if he couldn't stop himself.

"I was curious, and months later when I found myself within a few miles of the convent, I went there. It was in ruins, and the nuns had moved to a house farther south. Some three months after that, when I was sent to Calais to expedite supplies coming through, I managed to trace the nuns. That's when I discovered that they actually had an orphanage. I hung about for an hour or more, and the nuns appeared with a crocodile of children. All ages, some of them wounded, others in a state of shock, moving like their own shadows, and a handful of very little ones holding hands. The middle one was a girl in a dress too large for her. Hardly more than a year old, at a guess, and just barely walking well. I noticed her because she kept tripping over her hems, which were dragging on the ground. One of the nuns stopped and hitched the dress up with a ribbon or something. And the child looked up and smiled at me over the nun's shoulder. I stood there, my mouth literally hanging open. The nuns marched the children several times around the house they were using as their convent, and then led them back inside. I tell you, the likeness was uncanny. Not a faulty memory or wishful thinking. It was real. I went straight to the door before they could shut it to ask about the child, but my French wasn't all that good, and I think the nuns believed I wanted to take a child away for my own purposes, and they sent me smartly about my business."

"Did you ask Roger Ellis about her? Did you go back?"

"I said nothing to him then. Well, a man generally doesn't ask another man if he's got a bastard child. I stood up with him at his wedding to Lydia, for God's sake. But I kept an ear open for news of the convent, all the same, and went back a second time. And I saw her again. I hadn't been mistaken, the likeness was even more pronounced. The third time, I was determined to speak to the nuns, to ask who she was. I'd taken care to work on my French, and I thought I could persuade them that I knew the child's father. Only this time, the house was empty. I went around the village, frantically asking what had become of them. The old priest told me they'd moved south of Angers. His housekeeper was sure that some of the nuns and a number of the children had been taken in by a convent near Caen. The next time I saw Roger, I asked him what he knew about the house. And he said he'd never heard of them. I reminded him of the perpetual prayers. He told me then that he'd lied to me about them, that it was a gambling debt he was anxious to pay. But that was a lie as well. I've never known Roger Ellis to gamble. I went on searching, but France was in chaos, and one small group of orphans was impossible to track down. And then the bottom fell out of my world. Malcolm was killed, I was wounded and sent back to England, unable to learn anything at all. It was enough to turn anyone's mind."

Lieutenant Hughes lifted the decanter again, and I said quietly, "Perhaps you've had enough for one night."

He nodded, putting it back where he'd found it. Raising his head to meet my gaze, he said, "I told Ellis outright that I knew why he'd been sending money to the nuns. He told me then that the mother had died after childbirth, and the child's father had asked him to see that the child was cared for. I called him a liar to his face, and he told me I could believe what I damned well pleased.

But I was haunted by what I'd seen, and I wouldn't let it go. I kept asking, and he refused to answer me, except to say I'd been delirious. And all this while, even from England, I've done everything I could to find the nuns. But they might as well have vanished."

The little ormolu clock on the mantelpiece chimed two, the silvery notes loud in the quiet room.

"Good God, I've kept you up all night," he said contritely.

"Can you rest now?" I asked.

"Yes. For the first time I know what to do. Thank you for listening. You won't—you won't share what I've said with Lydia, will you? Or anyone else? It would be unkind. And God knows, I've done enough damage already." He shrugged, annoyance mingled with embarrassment. "I must have drunk more than I knew, to confess like this."

"I see no reason to hurt them. If Roger wishes them to hear the truth, it's best coming from him, don't you think?"

"Thank you. Good night, then, Sister."

After he had gone, I made myself as comfortable as I could, regretting having to sleep in my pale green dress, but there was nothing I could do about it. With a sigh, I pulled a large silk cushion from one of the other chairs and wrapped my arms around it to keep me warm. And after some little time, I was finally able to sleep, although it was a fitful rest at best.

I awoke the next morning to a hubbub somewhere in the house. Smoothing my hair with my hands, I put the silk cushion and the lap rug back where I'd found them, then went to the door. The shouting seemed to be coming from the hall. I hurried in that direction, not knowing what I would find. But the urgency told me that something was wrong.

Lydia stood in the middle of the room in her traveling dress, the same coat she'd worn when first I'd encountered her in London. Her face was set, and at her feet was a large valise. A smaller one was clutched tightly in her hand.

It was Roger Ellis who was doing the shouting, telling her that he wouldn't allow her to go away again. His mother was trying to pour oil on troubled waters, and Gran, standing to one side, was saying, "Lower your voices! What will Margaret and Eleanor think?" as if they were all that mattered. But everyone was ignoring her, their eyes on Lydia's face.

She turned as I came into the hall. "There you are!" she exclaimed. "Where on earth have you been? I'd looked everywhere for you. You haven't changed from last evening. Hurry and pack, Bess. I've already sent Daisy into Hartfield for the station carriage."

"I'm sorry," I said, adding, "it will take a few minutes to collect everything," in the hope that this would give her a little time to change her mind. But I had a feeling she wouldn't. I glanced at her husband, afraid he might strike Lydia again, if he was angry enough with her. The first blow was always the hardest. And that had been struck already.

"Ask Molly to help you, then. Bess, I beg of you. I can't stay here, don't you see?" Her eyes as well as her voice pleaded with me.

There was nothing else I could do. Casting a worried glance at Mrs. Ellis, hoping she could keep her son from losing his temper completely, I hurried away. Just outside the door to my room, I encountered Molly.

"I was just about to send for you."

But she said, "Miss? Have you seen Lieutenant Hughes? He hasn't been down for his breakfast, and he's not in his room."

"He's probably gone for a walk. Mrs. Roger has asked me to hurry and pack. Will you help me?"

"I don't think he even slept in his bed. It's been turned down."

"Turned down?" But Dr. Tilton and I had put him to bed, and I'd assumed he'd gone back there after leaving the sitting room. "Show me."

She opened the door to the Lieutenant's room, and I could see that she was right. The bed had been tidily made, and then turned back, as if ready for the night. I looked in the wardrobe. It was empty. When had he dressed and taken his luggage down?

"Is his motorcar still in the yard?"

"Yes, Miss, I remember seeing it there. The wing's all dented."

"Well, then, I shouldn't worry."

"It's just that I need to be clearing away the dining room, before Mrs. Long begins preparations for the luncheon. And you've had no breakfast neither, Miss."

"I've had a little headache," I said, prevaricating. "Perhaps I'll have a little tea later."

She grinned. "I seen that you was sleeping in the sitting room when I come to make up the fires."

"Mrs. Roger was in my bed," I replied. We went back to my room, and I changed quickly into my traveling dress, and then between us we repacked my valises and set them by the door. When that was done, I said, "I've just looked at the time. It's after ten. Lieutenant Hughes may be back by now."

"Yes, Miss, I'll go and have a look. Thank you, Miss."

I went down to the hall, where Mrs. Ellis was sitting with Lydia. It was obvious that an uncomfortable silence had fallen between them while Lydia waited for me.

Mrs. Ellis said, "My dear, have you seen George this morning? I've been trying to persuade Lydia to talk to him before she leaves. Surely he can explain himself."

"Molly was just looking for him. He must have gone for a walk."

"Oh, dear, I expect he's gone to St. Mary's. Lydia, please, would you at least go with me to the church and hear what he has to say? There's more than enough time before the train leaves. For my sake."

"He'll only lie. Just as he did last night," she said, and I thought she was probably right.

Still, I said, "Lydia, I think Mrs. Ellis has a point. This is a major decision, after all. It can do no harm to hear what Lieutenant Hughes has to say. In the cold light of morning, when he's completely sober."

I could see that she wanted no part of anything that could weaken her resolve. But she said finally, "If we hurry. If it doesn't hold us up."

The first time she'd fled to London had been ill-considered. This time, she needed to be sure.

Mrs. Ellis said, "You won't regret this, Lydia. And if it takes longer than it should, I'll drive you to the railway station myself."

"I'd rather go in the carriage," Lydia said. "Thank you, but it's better if I do. And that way, Roger can't blame anyone else for my leaving."

We brought down my valises, and just then I heard the carriage wheels on the drive.

Mrs. Ellis fetched her coat, and by that time we had taken our luggage out to the carriage and stowed it.

Daisy had just finished helping us, and Mrs. Ellis said to her as she turned toward the house, "Did you by any chance see Lieutenant Hughes in Hartfield?"

"Lieutenant Hughes? No, Ma'am. Should I have been looking for him?"

"No, not at all." She turned to us. "Then it's certain that he's at St. Mary's," she said, joining us in the carriage. "Thank you, Daisy."

Lydia said to the elderly driver, "We'd like to go to Wych Gate Church first."

The carriage turned and set out for the track through the forest.

Mrs. Ellis said anxiously, "He could have walked over to his grandfather's house. I hadn't thought about that."

"If he isn't at the church, I'll speak to him in London," Lydia replied, fighting down her impatience.

I sat there, listening with only half an ear. I had a feeling that something was wrong. The way the bed had been made. The fact that the man's belongings were already taken down, the room looking as if he'd never been there. I was remembering too what Roger Ellis had said, that he was surprised, given George's moodiness, that he hadn't taken his own life. I'd thought, listening to him in the night, that he had every reason to live—to find the child he'd seen. But in the cold light of day, given the uproar over his remarks in the drawing room, George Hughes might well have decided that the search in France was hopeless. And in a flush of self-pity, he could very well have walked away from Vixen Hill and killed himself.

Pray God, not on the memorial to Juliana!

It was cold that morning, although the sun was out, colder than it had been before the storm, as often happened. In the open carriage, we felt it. We rode on in silence, listening to the jingle of the harness and the clip-clop pace of the horses over the hard ground. Finally I could see the church tower above the trees that enclosed it.

Mrs. Ellis got down as soon as the carriage had stopped. "I'll find him and bring him to you." I had expected Lydia to get down with her instead. I wouldn't have let my own mother walk into that churchyard alone. But Lydia was wrapped up in her own misery and had no room for anyone else's.

"You will hurry, won't you?" was all she said.

I quickly stepped down from the seat beside Lydia and said, "I'll go with you, shall I? In the event he's taken ill—"

Mrs. Ellis turned to wait for me, and together we approached the side gate. Mrs. Ellis was saying, keeping her voice low, "She's being so foolish, Bess. See if you can talk any sense into her before this goes too far."

"I'll try," I replied, my gaze on the wrought iron bars of the gate, almost feeling as if I ought to hold my breath. "But it will take some time before she can forgive the Captain."

"There's nothing to forgive," she answered. We were in sight now of her daughter's grave, and relief washed over me.

George wasn't lying there, his service revolver in his dead hand. I'd been able to picture it so clearly that for a moment I lost track of what my companion was saying.

"Roger told me himself this has become something of an obsession of George's. The doctors haven't diagnosed it, but Roger thinks it must have something to do with shell shock." She swung the gate open, and we walked into the churchyard. I could see frost in the shadows where the sun hadn't reached. "It apparently started with Malcolm's death. George has convinced himself that this refugee child exists. And that's something to cling to while everyone around him seems to be dying. To tell you the truth, I don't think George always remembers that Juliana wasn't his little sister too. He wants to find and save her. This imaginary child. For all we know, he may well have seen a child who reminded him of Juliana. That may be how it began."

It was a very persuasive argument. But Roger Ellis had lied to his mother. I knew that shell shock didn't work like that. What's more, George Hughes had told me chapter and verse exactly what he'd discovered about this child. And it hadn't sounded like an obsession to me. Yes, he might have seen what he wanted to see. We all do that. But if she was Roger Ellis's child, the resemblance could well have been more than passing.

We stood for a moment at Juliana's grave. Just beyond it was Alan's stone, achingly new.

"I thought he'd be here," Mrs. Ellis said, looking around her as if she'd misplaced the Lieutenant. "He comes here nearly as often as I do. Well. Perhaps we ought to look in the church. It shouldn't take long. There's still more than enough time."

As she led the way to the massive west door, I heard Lydia's voice, pitched to carry. "Is he there? Mama? We need to hurry."

The door was slightly ajar. Mrs. Ellis took a deep breath as she put her hands on the thick wooden panels. I helped to push the door wider, and we crossed the threshold side by side.

The interior felt—quite literally—as cold as the grave, and it was quite gloomy as well, despite the early attempts of the sun to break through. The stained glass on either side of the aisle and above the altar had no life, although it must have been quite glorious on a sunny day.

I couldn't imagine sitting here for any length of time, cold as it was. And at first glance the church appeared to be empty. It *felt* empty as well.

"George?" Mrs. Ellis called, her voice echoing around the walls, so that it sounded rather like "Geo-orge-orge."

Six slender pillars divided the nave, creating two narrow aisles on either side, memorials lining the walls between the windows. Before the altar was a delicate stone rood screen, setting off the choir. The pulpit was also stone, with worn steps leading up one side.

She called again, but there was no answer.

"I don't think he's here," I said. "But shall I walk as far as the altar, to be certain?"

"Yes, if you would, my dear." Mrs. Ellis's voice sounded hollow. Her face seemed pinched, uncertain.

I walked away, listening to my heels echo on the stone paving, glancing right and left as I went. But there was no one here. I reached the rood screen, paused, and then went into the choir. It too was empty, the east window behind the altar rising above me and reminding me of the oriel window above the door at Vixen Hill.

Behind me, I heard Mrs. Ellis say, "I'll just have a look in the organ loft." I turned and walked back along the opposite aisle, meeting her as she came down the stairs.

"I was so sure," she said distractedly, "that we'd find him here. It was almost a premonition."

"He went for a walk, after all," I reassured her. "He may have been here and moved on."

We went through the west door again, letting it swing shut behind us. It made a great booming sound like the gates of hell closing.

Both of us winced.

We walked right around the church, but there was still no sign of George, and I was glad to come back again to the wrought iron gate where we had entered. The empty, quiet, isolated church seemed almost to be glad to be rid of us as we went to leave. I looked again at the lovely little marble statue of the kneeling child, and marveled at how well Juliana's features and smile had been captured in stone.

Small wonder George Hughes had been captivated by the child with the nuns, and why he wanted so desperately to have her be Roger Ellis's daughter. But was she?

"Someone's moved the kitten," Mrs. Ellis said, and she stopped to set it just within reach of Juliana's marble fingers. "I expect it was George. There."

As we walked out of the churchyard and shut the small gate behind us, Lydia said, "He wasn't there? I could have told you—a wild-goose chase. Mama, if you hurry, there will just be time to take you back to Vixen Hill."

"I just want to walk a short way down the path. Roger and George used to play here sometimes. You must remember the little stream they were always talking about. I won't go any farther than that."

And without waiting for an answer, she started down the overgrown path, almost like a tunnel through the winter dead grasses leading to the unseen stream. I went with her, shutting out Lydia's protests. In gratitude, Mrs. Ellis turned and smiled at me over her shoulder.

Someone had been here before us. Even I could see that much. A deer, perhaps, if there were any left here in the Forest, or a ewe looking to drink from the stream. There were only a few bent stalks of grass here and there, and it was impossible to tell how recent it might have been.

The path turned, turned again, and then the stream lay below us, half hidden in grasses along the bank, many of them bent double with the weight of ice as the water splashed over them.

We saw his feet first, encased in his Army boots. And then his legs. One more step brought us to a sloping overlook, and from there we couldn't miss the rest of him sprawled across the bottom of the path, his face and shoulders in the clear, cold water, his dark hair moving gently with the current, his greatcoat wet across the back from the fitful eddying of the stream over its rocky bed.

Had he killed himself, after all? Not across Juliana's grave, as I'd feared, but here in this quiet place where the only sound was the water spilling over rocks.

But where was his service revolver?

Six

Mrs. Ellis gave a little cry of shock and despair, and stopped where she was, one hand outstretched, as if to comfort him somehow.

I moved around her and went down to touch the hand that lay on the marshy bank of the little stream. There was no need to feel for a pulse. George Hughes was quite dead and had been for hours. But how had he died?

We missed our train after all, Lydia and I.

Although I'd wanted to stay with the body, Mrs. Ellis wouldn't hear of it. We went back up the path, telling Lydia what we'd found.

And then the carriage took us back to the house. Roger Ellis went alone into Hartfield to bring the police.

We sat, the rest of us, in the hall, cold in spite of the fire, not knowing what to say to one another. I had let Mrs. Ellis explain what we'd found at the bottom of the path. Meanwhile, Lydia, her arms wrapped around herself for comfort, huddled in a chair to one side. I could see the effort it was taking to hold back her tears. Not for the dead man, I thought, but for her own thwarted plans.

If we'd gone directly to the station, we'd have been well on our way to London now.

It was not long before Roger Ellis returned with the local constable, Dr. Tilton, and the rector, Mr. Smyth.

To spare Mrs. Ellis, I went with them back to Wych Gate Church. I led the way down the path a second time, knowing now what was at the bottom of it, and stepped aside at the last minute so that the constable, a man named Austin, could see what Mrs. Ellis and I had seen less than an hour earlier. Roger Ellis, the doctor, and the rector had been asked to stay with the motorcar at the top of the path.

Constable Austin, square and competent, said, halting on the path, "You're quite sure he's dead?"

"Quite," I said.

"And all you touched when you went nearer was his hand, looking for signs of life?" He'd already asked me that on our way to Wych Gate. But I knew he had to be sure.

"Yes, that's right. I was careful not to disturb the body any more than necessary. You can see my tracks just there. If he'd been alive, I'd have pulled him out of the water. But there was nothing I could do."

"Then I'll go the rest of the way alone, if you please."

I stood there, telling myself not to think of what I'd seen as George Hughes. The first time, I'd been shocked, making an effort to think clearly and do what had to be done. Now, standing here, I remembered the man I'd talked to at two o'clock in the morning.

Constable Austin looked first at the body from just above it, and then squatted beside it. After a time, he scanned the bank of the stream, first this side and then the other. Getting to his feet, he scanned the scene once more, from the vantage point of height.

Finally, turning to me, he said, "Will you ask Dr. Tilton to come down, if you please, Miss?"

I went back up the path and passed Constable Austin's message to Dr. Tilton.

He went down slowly, almost reluctantly, and I followed. Stopping a little way up the path he looked down at the body and then went forward to examine it. Stepping back, he pronounced George Hughes dead, and added that while the cold water made it more difficult to judge with any certainty just how long, he believed—as I'd thought earlier—that the deceased had been dead for some hours.

"At least since five or six this morning. No later than seven, I should think. I'll know more when I've got him on the table." He glanced back at me as he said the last words. "That's to say, when I can examine him properly."

At last Mr. Smyth was allowed to come and pray for the dead man. I shivered, thinking about that cold water, and the rector said solicitously, "Would you like my coat, my dear? This is no place for you. Perhaps you would prefer to wait in the motorcar? I'm sure Constable Austin would have no objection to that."

But I shook my head, thanking him for his concern.

Finally, the constable stayed with the body while the four of us—Roger, the rector, Dr. Tilton, and I—drove back to Hartfield to arrange to have George Hughes brought up the path and into the town.

While this was being attended to, I took a moment to walk into The King's Head, out of the cold, and once more ask for the use of their telephone.

I was glad when my father answered, rather than my mother. I said, keeping my voice low although there appeared to be no one around, "There's been a death here in Ashdown Forest. One of the weekend guests.

I shan't be able to leave for a day or two. But I'm all right, there's no problem."

"What kind of death?" the Colonel Sahib wanted to know.

"A drowning. Or so it appears. I couldn't tell. Suicide? He was despondent, I'm told. And he made rather a fool of himself last evening. That may have been the catalyst. On the other hand, he may have been too drunk when he fell to pull himself out of the water."

I could hear someone coming. "I must go, this is a very public place."

"Very well. Keep in touch, will you, Bess?"

"I'll try. But it's quite some distance to the telephone, and I have no means of traveling here on my own."

He said something I couldn't quite catch. And then Roger Ellis was coming through the hotel door, saying, "We're ready to leave."

I bade my father a hasty good-bye and put up the receiver, following the Captain out to the waiting motorcar.

Dr. Tilton had gone back to oversee the removal of the body, while the rector chose to accompany us to Vixen Hill. I was grateful for his presence. Otherwise I'd have been alone in the motorcar with Roger Ellis.

I needn't have worried. He was taciturn, and after several efforts at conversation, the rector fell silent. In the rear of the motorcar, I had an opportunity to watch Captain Ellis as he drove, and he seemed to be distracted, his mind anywhere but on the twisting track. Once we almost ran into a flock of sheep moving across the road to newer pastures, and again we took a turn too fast and swayed dangerously near the ditch on the far side.

Mr. Smyth exclaimed, "Here, Ellis! Have a care."

I was reminded that just about here, George Hughes had sworn he nearly struck a tree in his path. But I couldn't see remnants that even resembled anything large enough to dent the wing of his motorcar and throw him face-first into the windscreen.

Somehow we managed to reach Vixen Hill unscathed, and everyone was waiting to hear what the police and the doctor had had to say.

But Roger Ellis shook his head. "I've not been told. I expect we won't be for some time. Dr. Tilton will sort it out." He paused, then, looking around at the circle of faces, he added, "Did anyone see George this morning? No? No idea when he might have gone for a walk? Well, the police will be here soon, asking questions. We can be sure of that. Meanwhile, we should try to go on as normally as possible. Hardly the time or place for entertainment, but we need to stay busy until the police have finished their work."

Mrs. Ellis said, "I can't quite understand why George had gone down to the stream. I'd expected to find him in the churchyard at the very least, or the church itself."

"He may have felt the need to relieve himself," Henry said. "It's one explanation, at least. It would probably be best, Roger, if we went home," he continued. "I don't see that we can contribute very much to this business, and you'll have your hands full. Meanwhile, what about George's family? Is there anyone I should contact when I reach London? George's brother is dead. Do you know who his solicitors are?"

"There's a cousin, I think. I don't know if George still dealt with Pritchett, Dailey, and Thurmond. You could ask, if you would. His things are here, and of course there's the motorcar. And arrangements to be made."

"Well, then, Margaret and I will see to our packing."

I said, "The police won't want anyone to leave until they've spoken to all of us."

Everyone turned to stare at me as if I'd suddenly grown two heads.

Lydia said, "I don't care what the police want. I'm leaving for London. If I must walk there. Margaret, if you could drive me as far as Rochester? I should be able to find a train there."

Support came from an unexpected quarter. Mr. Smyth said, "Miss Crawford's right, you know. Once the police are involved, they will wish to interview everyone who had contact with the—er—deceased. And of course we were all here last evening."

Gran said, "No one I knew was ever involved with the police. It wasn't done."

Mrs. Ellis said, "I shouldn't think it will take long. While I hate the thought of George drowning, it would be preferable to suicide. Did anyone think to see if he'd left a note in his room? It isn't like him just to walk away."

But I had already seen that room, and if there was a note—on the table by the bed or on the mantelpiece, the logical places—surely I'd have noticed it? Or Molly would have done?

"Again, that should be left for the police," Mr. Smyth told her firmly. "I think, Ellis, you and I should see that Lieutenant Hughes's room is locked until someone comes."

"Is that really necessary?" Roger Ellis asked, and then answered his own question. "Yes, I expect it's for the best. All right, come with me and we'll see to it. Gran, I'll need your keys, and yours, Mother. I'll take

Daisy's as well. We'll put them all in the bowl there on the table."

Mrs. Ellis handed over her keys without comment, but Gran said, "I have held these keys since my mother-in-law died, and I am not giving them up now."

Mr. Smyth crossed to where she was sitting. "Mrs. Ellis, I expected you to set an example for all of us."

After a moment, she gave up her keys as well. The rector and Roger Ellis went out of the room and returned some ten minutes later to report that the door was properly locked and that Daisy had also surrendered her keys.

And then it was simply a matter of waiting.

In the end, Gran played a game of patience, while Margaret and Henry went up to pack, saying, "At least we'll be prepared when the time comes."

Eleanor, Alan's widow, was upset, and her brother had taken her to her room. Mrs. Ellis went to consult with Daisy and the cook over the menu, because we suddenly realized that it was nearly one o'clock and no one had given a thought to lunch.

I sat to one side, in an effort to afford the family a little privacy. Lydia ignored me and everyone else. She was as removed from the other occupants of this house, I thought, as she would have been sitting on the train to London. Roger Ellis paced the floor until his mother ordered him to stop. Alan's widow and her brother came down again a little later and sat in the window seat, looking out across the heath, speaking in low voices, and the hands of the clock moved with ridiculous slowness.

It was nearly three o'clock, and we'd had a light luncheon for which no one had much appetite, when Constable Austin came to the door. With him was an older man by the name of Rother, the Inspector now in charge of the case. He was thin, hair thinning as well, and there was an air of resignation about him that made me think at once of bad news.

And it was.

"Lieutenant Hughes did not drown, as we'd thought earlier," he said bluntly, when he'd collected all of us in the hall. Daisy and Molly and the cook looked ill at ease seated in our midst, and Mr. Rother's words only added to their distress. "There is evidence," he went on, "to indicate that he was deliberately murdered. I'm afraid that I shall have to consider all of you as suspects until we've got this matter properly sorted out. Please give your name to Constable Austin, here, and I'll ask by and by for a statement from each of you. No one will be allowed to leave the premises until I have given them clearance to go. I'm sorry if this presents a problem for any of you, but I'm afraid I have no choice. And so neither do you."

Gran spoke up sharply. "I'll remind you, young man, who we are."

But Inspector Rother cut her short. "I'm sorry, Mrs. Ellis. We must treat everyone alike. No matter what their names may be or what their connections are."

And so we came one by one to speak to Constable Austin while Roger escorted the Inspector up the stairs to have a look at George Hughes's bedroom.

The day dragged on as we were interviewed one at a time, and the house was searched—for what I didn't know. The murder weapon? By dinner we were all out of sorts. I heard Gran say with some asperity, "If George had to get himself murdered, why couldn't he have done it somewhere else?"

When it was my turn, I admitted to my conversation in the sitting room with George Hughes after everyone else had gone to bed, although I was reluctant to tell Constable Austin why George found it difficult to sleep and I myself had chosen to spend the night in the family's sitting room rather than in my own bed. Casting about for something that would make sense, I said, finally, "He had a good deal on his mind. He spoke to me about his late brother and the fate of children in orphanages in France. I gathered that was an interest of his, how they were treated."

Constable Austin looked up at me from the notes he was making. "Why should a man who is a bachelor wish to know about French orphans?"

"You must ask Captain Ellis. Or someone else in the family. They've known—knew—Lieutenant Hughes for most of his life." The words were no sooner out of my mouth than I regretted them. It was not my intention to make an issue of the argument between the two men, or raise embarrassing questions in the minds of the police. I added, "The war is never far from any-one's thoughts."

He nodded. "Sad to say." And then he surprised me. "You didn't sleep in your bed last night, I'm told. Nor did the Lieutenant."

I could feel the color rising in my face. Who had been talking out of turn? "I have no idea how Lieuten-ant Hughes spent the remainder of the night. As for me, I've just returned from France, and sometimes I find it difficult to rest. We're accustomed to long hours and very little sleep." It was not quite true—I had learned to sleep anywhere, whenever I had the chance. But I could hardly tell this man that Lydia had been crying herself to sleep in my bed and I hadn't wished to disturb her. He would begin to wonder why she hadn't slept in her own. And that would lead to more questions that I didn't want to be the one to answer.

Changing the subject without warning, he asked, "How did Mrs. Roger Ellis come by the bruises on her face?"

"I wasn't here when that happened. However I heard her husband tell his dinner guests that she had run into a cupboard door. It takes some time for such discoloration to fade."

"It doesn't appear to be that sort of bruise. My guess is that someone struck her with the back of his hand."

"Then perhaps you should ask her."

"I did. She refused to discuss it. Her view was that it had nothing to do with Lieutenant Hughes's death."

"There you are, then," I agreed.

"When did you know that Lieutenant Hughes was missing?"

This was another minefield. "The first inkling we had was when one of the maids asked if she should continue to hold breakfast for him. We went to Wych Gate Church to look for him—apparently it was a favorite walk of his."

"Why did you go in the station carriage, when there were motorcars available?"

"Mrs. Roger Ellis wished to take the train to London. But she was in no hurry."

"It seems odd that Mrs. Ellis was so insistent on finding the Lieutenant."

"He hasn't been well. She treats him more or less the same way she treats her own son. As I understand it, she has known him all his life."

"Why did the two of you—Mrs. Ellis and you—decide to go down to the stream?"

"I don't really know," I told him. "We were just being thorough. I remember she said something about her son and the Lieutenant playing there often as boys."

"Mrs. Ellis insisted on walking as far as the stream."

"I don't remember her insisting." I had a feeling Lydia had told him that.

"It seems to me that she searched until she found the body. As if she had known it was there."

I wasn't going to be drawn into speculating. "I was there with her. I saw her shock when she realized that something had happened. It appeared to be genuine to me."

He changed direction. "Odd that you and the younger Mrs. Ellis should be returning to London with the house still full of guests."

Exasperated, I said, "The guests, as you call them, are members of her family."

"How well did you know Lieutenant Hughes?"

I couldn't hide my surprise. "To my knowledge, I've never seen him before this weekend."

"And yet he came to the sitting room to speak to you late last evening. After everyone else had gone to bed. I'm told you were still dressed in your evening clothes this morning."

"To be perfectly honest, he came into the room looking for the brandy decanter. He found me there and retreated without it. I hardly consider that a late-night assignation. He had a reputation for drinking more than he ought."

He closed his notebook. "I would advise you, Sister Crawford, not to make any new plans to return to London at this time." Rising, he walked to the door and held it open for me.

I stared at him, shut my lips on the comment I was tempted to make. But it was obvious that someone had been telling tales, and I suspected it might be Gran, whose tongue was not always guarded. She could even have pointed a finger in my direction to keep the police from asking too many questions about her grandson's relationship with George Hughes.

After all, I was the stranger here.

Was she afraid that her grandson had killed his friend?

I suddenly remembered the accident before Lieutenant Hughes had arrived.

Or was it?

It would certainly make more sense to kill George Hughes before he could mention the child in France than to murder him after he had blurted out the fact of her existence.

Still considering that, I went up to my room to change out of my traveling clothes and for a moment stood there, looking down at my luggage where it had been brought back into the house and placed in front of the wardrobe. Someone had opened the valises and gone through them, I was sure of it. I hoped it was the police. But what could they have been looking for?

A murder weapon?

Seven

The day dragged on, the hours creeping around the clock with a pace that was maddening. I had the strongest feeling that people were avoiding me. Lydia, blaming me for taking so long packing and then agreeing to help Mrs. Ellis look for George Hughes, which in the end prevented us from making it to the station in time for the train, had disappeared. I learned later that she had locked herself into the small room above the hall, the one with the long windows. According to what Margaret had told me when we were making beds together, when Juliana was alive, Gran used to read to her there in the afternoons. But she had refused to set foot in it after the child's death.

Lydia never knew Juliana, and so the room would hold no memories for her.

Thus far it appeared that the police hadn't learned of the exchange between Lieutenant Hughes and Roger Ellis. It could very well supply the motive for murder that they had spent the afternoon searching for. On the other hand, once the story about the child had come out, why kill him? Unless of course someone feared that he was planning to search for and claim that child for his own.

Once she was in England, anyone could see for himself or herself how much the child resembled the dead Juliana.

Had someone been listening at the door after all? Or had George Hughes talked to someone else after he left me?

The problem was, the family couldn't hope to keep the child a secret for very long.

The doctor and his wife as well as the rector and his sister had been present in the drawing room. How much would they confide to the police? I had a feeling that the rector would be circumspect, but Dr. Tilton was a very different matter.

Only the family had heard Roger Ellis quarrel with his mother over inviting George Hughes to Vixen Hill for the weekend.

It kept coming around to Captain Ellis. Or—his mother, if she were intent on protecting him.

I wished that someone would tell us how Lieutenant Hughes had died.

A very harassed Daisy appeared at my door. "There's a caller for you, Miss. The gentleman who brought your other valise."

Simon?

I should have known he would appear sooner rather than later.

Very likely my father had run him to earth and passed on to him what little I'd been able to say about finding the body. We hadn't known then that it was murder. But the Colonel Sahib was not one to take chances. He'd have come himself, but he was probably in Somerset, while Simon was very likely still in London and therefore closer to Sussex. I was wrong. I discovered later that it was my mother who had sent Simon post haste, when she had finally cajoled my father into telling her why he'd been frowning after his conversation with me. And if my mother asked him for help, Simon would have flown here if he could have commandeered an aircraft.

I walked into the hall to find him standing there looking as much like a regiment as one man could.

That's when I knew that somehow he'd already discovered more about this business of Lieutenant Hughes's death than I knew. And he was already aware that I was one of the suspects.

"Are you all right?" he asked at once, making no pretense that he'd come merely to collect my party dresses.

"Yes, of course I'm all right."

"You look tired."

"I am, a little. I didn't sleep well last night."

"Why?"

Until now, we'd had the hall to ourselves.

The door opened, and Margaret came in, pausing on the threshold.

"I'm interrupting," she began. I hastily made the introductions.

"Not at all," said Simon, for all the world as if we'd been discussing the weather. "I've come to drive Miss Crawford to her parents' home, but I've just been told she's not free to leave. Meanwhile, she's offered to show me the grounds."

I opened my mouth to deny it and instead said, "I'll just fetch my coat."

I was back in two minutes. Margaret pointed to the door. "Mr. Brandon has already stepped outside. Such a nice man," she added, and I knew he'd done his best to charm her. When Simon did that, it usually meant he was worried.

And I was beginning to be, myself.

I thanked her and found him waiting for me on the steps. Without a word spoken, we set out across the lawns.

"This is godforsaken country," he commented at last, looking out over the blighted landscape. "I wouldn't want to defend it."

"It's said to be much nicer in spring and summer."

"It could hardly get much worse," he replied.

We walked on, well out of hearing of anyone in the house. He stopped at the edge of the lawns, where I could see that the gorse and heather were already creeping toward this outpost of civilization. I shivered, turning my back so that I was looking at the house, not at the heath.

"Who is this man Hughes, and what is he to you?" Simon finally asked.

"You sound like my father," I said, annoyed at his tone of voice.

"In fact, it's one of the questions the Colonel instructed me to ask you."

With raised eyebrows, I studied Simon's face. "You telephoned him as soon as you realized that I could be a suspect. Even before you came to Vixen Hill."

"That was another of the instructions I was given."

"Well, yes, I'm technically a suspect, I suppose, but I had nothing to do with the poor man's death. I only met him this weekend. I had probably addressed no more than a dozen or so words to him in all of that time, until last evening. And I was there when the body was found, but that was only because I didn't feel that Mrs. Ellis—Roger Ellis's mother—ought to go exploring down that twisting, overgrown path on her own. I didn't expect her to find the Lieutenant dead. I wouldn't have been surprised if he'd been too drunk to walk. No, that's not true. I had a feeling from the start that something was wrong. That's why I went with her to the church. I know, she's lived here most of her life, still—" I shivered. "This forest is—I don't know—not haunted, but most certainly, it broods. I expect one eventually learns its moods, but that sense of—dying all around you is disturbing. I'm beginning to understand why Lydia came to dislike it so." I shrugged. "It isn't at all like Rajasthan, is it?"

"No, I agree with you there, Bess. What possessed you to come here in the first place?"

I took a deep breath. "I didn't know what else to do about Lydia. She had a concussion, Simon. I've tried to keep an eye on her." I launched into an account of the past three days, holding nothing back. I told him about Juliana, about the child in France, about the new breach between Lydia and her husband. And I told him the lies that had been circulated about my having spoken to George in the middle of the night.

Simon whistled. "Small wonder the man was killed."

"What's more, no one will tell us how he died. It might help me sort out what happened. When I saw the body, it appeared that he'd drowned."

"According to pub gossip, he was struck over the head and then dragged a little way to lie with his face in the water."

"Oh, dear God."

"Quite. It could have been a woman or a man."

"Which means I'm still a suspect."

"Which will not please your parents."

"Simon, twice last night George Hughes and I thought someone might be listening at the door. And for all I know, he encountered someone after he left me. But that was no later than three o'clock. He probably left the house somewhere around five, as far as I can decide from the questions the police are asking. It was still dark then. Where was he going? And why did he make his bed and pack his belongings before he walked away? Was he planning to leave before anyone was awake? That would have been terribly rude—and cowardly. And he didn't strike me as a coward."

He swore under his breath. "If he didn't meet someone else, then very likely you're the last person to see him alive before he left Vixen Hill. I'm not surprised that the police are looking at you as a suspect."

We turned and walked back the way we'd come.

"Why did Mrs. Ellis think he might be at Wych Gate Church?" Simon asked then.

"Juliana is buried in that churchyard, and George Hughes remembers her almost as clearly as Roger

Ellis does. I've seen the marker for her grave. It's a lovely marble figure of a kneeling child, and her face is touchingly beautiful—just like the painting of her in the drawing room. He may have wanted to say good-bye. But then why didn't he simply drive there, on his way back to London? It wouldn't have taken him far out of his way. Oh, and there's another odd thing. This morning, Captain Ellis told his mother that this story about the child is really a manifestation of shell shock. And she seemed to believe it. Then why her anxiety over Lieutenant Hughes's whereabouts?"

"Shell shock? It's hardly that." He considered what I'd told him. "Bess. Is there any possibility that the child was murdered?"

"Murdered?" I was horrified. "The one in France?"

"No. Juliana."

"Oh, no, I'm sure there isn't. There's no one—it's impossible!"

"I don't mean in cold blood. If she were suffering, someone might have taken measures to end it. Watching a child in great pain with no hope of recovery would drive anyone to end it."

"He was too young at the time to have witnessed anything like that," I replied slowly. "No, it's the living child that must be behind this murder."

"I don't like the idea of your being a suspect. The Colonel will have an apoplexy if you're arrested on charges."

"They'll let me go shortly. I do think the police will try to discover if I knew George Hughes in France. But Dr. Tilton is a gossip. He'll tell the police about the child, and when he does, they will lose all interest in me. I'm surprised he hasn't already made a statement."

"Don't count on anything, Bess. Look, I'm staying at The King's Head for now. I won't leave until you're free to go with me."

It was comforting to know that. But I protested that it wasn't necessary.

"And do you think," Simon Brandon asked, "that I could return to Somerset and tell your mother that I'd abandoned you to the tender mercies of the police and their logic?"

I had to laugh. "She'd drum you out of the regiment herself, if you weren't already retired."

"I'm serious, Bess. Don't make light of this."

"I'm not," I told him, sober again.

We were nearly back at the house.

He said, "There's something else. If someone at Vixen Hill is a killer, I want you to take this." Reaching for my hand, as if to help me over a small depression in the winter-dead grass, he put something into my palm.

I didn't need to look at it to know what it was. A small, two-shot pistol, little bigger than a derringer. Hardly deadly, but still better than no protection. I'd practiced with it occasionally when Simon or my father taught me how to shoot and care for weapons.

"Not a great deal of stopping power," he said apologetically, "but it's loaded, and it fits better into your pocket than a revolver. Keep it there. Don't leave it lying around."

"Yes, I will," I promised him. "But I think I'm safe enough."

"Unless the killer believes Hughes told you something he shouldn't have, when he found you in that sitting room."

I hadn't considered that possibility.

We were on level ground again, and he relinquished my hand. I shoved the little pistol into my pocket a few steps later, and felt the weight of it, bumping against my hip as I walked. It was suddenly comforting.

"Perhaps the police have made a mistake," I said hopefully. "I don't want to believe anyone here killed George Hughes." But I knew as I said it that it was wishful thinking on my part.

Simon didn't waste breath telling me I was foolish. Instead he warned me, "Keep your eyes open and your wits about you. If I hear anything I'll see that you know it as soon as possible. Remember this, there may be something else that George Hughes knew. And if he blurted out one secret, he was very likely to blurt out another."

We had reached Simon's motorcar. I said, "What other secret?"

"If I knew that," he said, bending to turn the crank, "I'd have told the police long before this."

And he was gone. I stood there, watching him out of sight.

Turning, I looked up at the house, and in the long windows above the great hall, I saw Lydia's face staring down at me. She was angry still, I could tell that even at this distance, and I thought it odd that her anger was directed at me, not at Roger. Even if we'd managed to catch the morning train to London, we'd have been brought back to Ashdown Forest. Surely she must know that.

But people in pain seldom think logically.

I felt a rush of sympathy for Lydia. I'd never been married, I'd never wanted a child with such desperate longing, I hadn't been faced with a truth so bitter it could very well have ended my marriage.

Gran was at the hall door, calling my name. "Your young man isn't staying?"

"He's taken a room at The King's Head," I replied. "And he's not my young man. He was sent here by my parents."

Ignoring my answer, she said, "The police wish to speak with you again."

With a sigh I followed her into the hall and was directed to the library, where the police had set up a table and were asking people to write and sign statements.

Constable Austin had been replaced by a new man, sharp faced, his hair graying, his eyes cold. I'd seen him once before. It occurred to me that Inspector Rother was changing his tactics, and that I should take this warning to heart.

"Miss Crawford," the constable said as I came through the doorway. It wasn't a question.

"Yes," I replied.

"I'm Constable Bates. Constable Austin is off duty. Who was the man who came to call on you?"

"A friend of my family's. My father was concerned about me and sent him to find out if I was all right."

"How did your father learn that you were involved in a murder inquiry?"

"He didn't. When I spoke to him, I told him that we'd found one of the houseguests dead. I didn't know then that it was murder." As I took the chair he indicated I could feel the weight of the little pistol in my pocket, and wondered suddenly if it showed to a trained eye. Constable Bates was examining me as if I were a new specimen just brought to his attention.

"And your father is . . ."

"Colonel Richard Crawford." And for good measure, I added his regiment.

"I see. All right, if you will write out a statement beginning with the arrival of the houseguests on Thursday evening, then sign it, I'll add it to the others I've collected."

He handed me paper and pen, and I sat down at a smaller table drawn up to a chair by the window and began my account.

When it was finished, Constable Bates took it from me, scanned it quickly, and then set it aside.

"Thank you, Miss Crawford," he said, dismissing me as if I were a naughty schoolgirl caught in some mischief.

I turned on my heel and left.

Roger's sister Margaret was in the passage, and she made a wry face. "I see you've met the unpleasant Constable Bates," she said. "I thought Gran would strike him with a poker for what she called his insolence." She turned to walk with me back to the hall. "I've never been involved in a police inquiry," she went on. "It's rather chilling. I have to stop and remind myself that I've done nothing wrong. But I can't help but feel guilty. And George is dead. I can't quite take that in, either."

"I'm sorry I didn't know him."

"George and his brother were in and out of the house all our lives. He lived near us—the house has since burned down—until his grandfather died. Afterward his parents moved to London. George was much younger than Malcolm—he often referred to himself as The Afterthought. But when his parents also died, it was Malcolm who took care of him, although we offered to keep him. I daresay it was because he was orphaned at a young age that he felt so concerned for that child he'd seen in France. Roger agreed with me."

Roger Ellis was being very clever. But I thought perhaps he might have a point here.

"As soon as Juliana could walk, she followed Roger and George everywhere they went. They called her the nuisance. Afterward—well, afterward they were afraid God had punished them by taking the nuisance away for good. It was rather awful, to tell you the truth. Roger and George were inconsolable." She hesitated. "I was very fond of Malcolm. My parents invited him here any number of times. I think they hoped he and I might marry one day. It was never spoken of, but my father would have been happy if we had. Malcolm was a little older than I was. Then I met Henry, and that was that." She smiled. "Malcolm went abroad for a bit."

"Mending a broken heart?"

"I doubt it. He loved France. That's why he was so quick to enlist when the war began." She sighed. "I wish now I'd done more for George—looked in on him in London, had him down to stay from time to time. It's possible I could have done something about his drinking. But I was so wrapped up in my own worry for Henry, and my volunteering, I didn't see what was under my nose." Tears filled her eyes. "I can't believe he's dead, Bess. It hasn't sunk in yet."

I had seen George's body and still I'd found it difficult to believe. But then I'd been too busy—going for Constable Austin, breaking the news to the family, dealing with all the questions, talking to my father and then to Simon. When had there been time to think of the man, rather than the murder victim?

Mrs. Ellis came just then. I thought, *She's aged in a matter of hours.* "Have you seen Lydia? That awful constable insists on taking her statement." Daisy had set a tray of tea on the small table by the fire, and Mrs. Ellis poured herself a cup, then grimaced as she tasted it, putting it down again. "I must ring for more tea." Instead she sat down, the tea forgotten. "That man Bates even asked me if George and Lydia were lovers! His mind must run in the gutter, even to suggest such a thing. Roger would be furious, if he knew."

"The police must find a motive for murder," I said gently. "A reason for the man to die, here, today. And they must look at each of us as potential suspects until they've worked out to their own satisfaction just what happened and why."

"How do you know so much about this business?" she asked, turning to stare at me.

I said, not wishing to open doors into my past, "Simon Brandon explained it to me."

That made sense to her. Men knew how the world worked. She nodded, smiling a little. "That's very reassuring, Bess. Thank you."

As if she couldn't bear to sit still, she rose again and said, "If you do see Lydia, will you pass along the message?"

We promised. After the door had closed behind her mother, Margaret said, "She can't imagine this weekend ending in this fashion. It will be the talk of the county, and she will find it hard to look anyone in the face for months. I mean, the *police*. I could almost murder George myself for bringing this down on her. On us."

She got up and walked to the hearth, her back to me, as if she was studying the fire at her feet.

"The afternoon Juliana was buried, my father came back to the house and burned everything. Her pretty clothes, her dolls, her toys, even the bedding she slept on, and the bedstead itself. Everything she'd touched, even her cup and spoon and the silver rattle he'd given her for her first Christmas. And I can remember his face, like a thundercloud, cursing God while my mother screamed, begging him to leave her something to remember her child by. We even gave her cat to the rector, for fear he would destroy it as well. My mother hid the portrait. He threatened her, but she refused to tell him where it was. He ransacked the house, looking for it. Alan and I were terrified that he would kill her, but in the end, he gave up, went out of the house, and we didn't see him for weeks. When he came home again, he was different. He never spoke Juliana's name again, nor asked for the portrait, nor even visited her grave. He stopped going to church services. He said God had forsaken him, and he intended to forsake God in his turn. And yet it was my father who ordered that lovely memorial of Juliana. Two years later, he was dead. We couldn't fill her place, you see. Not Alan, nor Roger nor Mother nor me. I think we realized then, my brothers and I, that she would always be there. George, oddly enough, said it best, that we only had to shut our eyes and we'd remember."

I thought about this traumatic event marking the childhood of the Ellis children. It would have left such terrible scars, deep and unhealed for all time. And for George as well?

"Thank you for telling me," I said quietly. "It helps to understand, a little, what this family has suffered. And why Lydia wants children so badly, and her husband doesn't."

She turned to face me, as if she needed to confess something that was on her mind. "Henry says that George wanted to believe a child he'd seen amongst the refugee children must be a second Juliana. He says George *needed* to believe that as well, because he was looking for something to cling to in the middle of this terrible war."

It was a very perceptive remark.

She took a deep breath. "I expect I ought to go up to Lydia and tell her that the police want her."

I went on to my room, wishing I could talk to Simon. With a sigh I sat down by the window and stared out at the ordered, civilized knot garden below me, such a vivid contrast to the wild and gloomy heath. And then Lydia came into my line of sight, hurrying through the intricate maze of paths, looking over her shoulder, as if she was afraid something or someone was after her. She disappeared into the stand of evergreens at the end of the knot garden, the heavy boughs closing after her like a shield, protecting her from whatever it was she feared.

Eight

Not a minute later, I saw Constable Bates step out on the narrow terrace above the knot garden and scan it. He may have seen Lydia come through the house this way, but there was no sign of her now. I watched him debate whether to go through the garden and search the stand of trees, but after looking at them carefully from his vantage point, he must have decided that she wouldn't be so foolish as to wait there for him to surprise her, and in the end he turned back into the house, and I could hear the distant slam of the door.

It was then that I noticed Roger Ellis waiting in the shadow of a tall shrub—a rhododendron, I thought, with those long, leathery evergreen leaves. When he was certain that the constable wasn't playing a game to draw Lydia out, he himself went down the path between the beds, heading for the trees.

I watched tensely, uncertain how this confrontation would end. I could hear nothing, but I saw Roger Ellis halt abruptly as he pushed aside the boughs guarding the end of the path, and then he disappeared among them.

Braced for anything, including violence, I waited. Finally, Lydia reappeared, and even from my window, I could see that she was crying. Her husband didn't follow her straightaway, but when he did step out from the sanctuary of the trees, his face was set, and he looked like a man who would like very much to break something.

Whatever had happened, I thought, the breach in the marriage had not been healed.

I was still sitting there when there was a soft tap at my door. On the heels of it, Lydia walked in. She had stopped somewhere long enough to wash her face, but her eyes were red rimmed and swollen.

"Bess?" she said tentatively, and my first thought was, *She wants something from me.*

"Are you all right, Lydia?" I asked, rising from my chair. "How is your head? Is it aching?"

"No. Yes. The police want to speak to me, and I can't let them see me like this." She wiped her eyes angrily, as if commanding them to stop betraying her. "Gran says they believe I had an affair with George. Of all people."

"Come in. I'll put a cool cloth across your eyes. It will help. As for the police, I shouldn't worry. They like to probe, hoping to find a weakness. If you don't respond, they move on to the next question."

Half reclining in the other chair, she turned her face up to allow me to set the cloth across her eyes. "How is the dizziness? And the headache?"

Ignoring me, she said, "I've just told Roger he can sue for divorce, if he chooses. I shall have to find lodgings in London until I can decide what to do, or he leaves for France. That's to say, if Mama Ellis will have me back again. I can't face the questions if I go home to Suffolk. It's too mortifying. Do you suppose your Mrs. Hennessey will know of someone who will take me in?"

"I'll most certainly ask Mrs. Hennessey," I said after a moment. "Lydia. Are you sure this is the best thing to do?"

She snatched the cloth from her face and turned to gaze at me with furious eyes.

Before she could say what was already burning the tip of her tongue, I added without inflection, "How will you live? Has your husband agreed to support you while the divorce goes forward?"

It hadn't occurred to her. She had always been someone's daughter and then someone's wife. She hadn't had
to fend for herself, and to my knowledge she had no
skills that would allow her to earn a living.

Pulling the cloth back in place she said, "I have some
money of my own. I have no idea whether it's sufficient
or not. You're right. I've never had to think about food
or clothing or a roof over my head." After a moment,
she added, "I could train as a nurse."

I changed the cloth for a fresh one. "It's very difficult in the beginning. Sometimes it's very hard to per-
severe when you're tired and there is more work to do
than you can bear to think about."

With a sigh she considered her future. The reality of
her position was beginning to sink in. She was prone, I
thought, to impetuous decisions, without regard to the
practicality of the impulse she was following. Such as
her haste to leave this morning. And fleeing to London
in the first place.

Had killing George also been an impetuous act, born
out of her hurt, her anger? No, I wasn't prepared to believe that. He hadn't betrayed her—Roger had.

But that brought me full circle to Roger Ellis, whose
motive for killing George could have been to silence
him before he'd destroyed Roger's marriage completely.
If he had acted, then it had been in vain.

After a while, Lydia sat up, handed me the cloth, and said, "I suppose I ought to get the interview over with. What did they ask you?"

"To describe the weekend. And when I'd last seen Lieutenant Hughes."

"Did you—were there any questions about the little girl in France?"

"I didn't feel it was my place to bring her up. And I rather think no one else has."

"Dr. Tilton will. Wait and see." Her voice was bitter.

I said nothing. After a moment she asked, "You'll be going back to France soon, won't you?"

"Yes, I expect I shall. But my orders haven't come through yet." I thought she might be suggesting she could stay in my flat while I was away, and I was about to tell her that there were my flatmates to consider. But I'd misread her.

"I don't think they'll let me go across to France. I'm not a nurse, I have no useful skills. But you could search for this child, couldn't you? I want to find her. I want to see her for myself. I want to be sure she's safe."

"There are my duties—I can't go wherever I like."

"No, I understand. But there must be lulls in the fighting, when you could find an excuse to search? Please? I have to *know*."

"Lieutenant Hughes might well have imagined the resemblance. Have you thought of that?" I suggested to distract her.

"I've thought of every conceivable possibility," she said tiredly. "I'm so sorry to ask this of you, after all you've done. I intended to ask George, but he's dead. And Henry will side with Roger. There's no one else, is there?"

When I didn't say anything straightaway, she added, "Where there's smoke, there's fire. If he's refused to acknowledge her, or search for her, then she's at risk. For all I know, he hopes she won't survive. A child that young? Why else would he leave her to the charity of strangers?"

"I can't believe that he could be so callous. Think about it, if she looks like Juliana—"

"All the more reason to shun her. You don't understand, he doesn't want a reminder of her. If it weren't for his mother, he'd move that portrait out of the drawing room and up to the attics where he doesn't have to see it."

"All right," I answered her reluctantly. "I'll do what I can. But I won't make any promises, Lydia. And you mustn't expect miracles."

Ignoring that, she said, "And you'll keep in touch, so that I won't make myself ill worrying about what's happening? I trust you, Bess." She crossed to the door.

"Even if I find her, Lydia, what then? You have no claim on her."

"If Roger dies," she said starkly, "this child will be all that's left of him."

Thanking me for the cool cloths, she added, "I must go while I still have the courage to face this Constable Bates. He frightens me. I saw him arrive—I thought he was going to follow me into the trees when I fled to the garden. He won't quit, Bess. He's like a terrier, digging, digging, digging, until he gets what he's after."

"He's only a man with a very unpleasant job to do. Think of him that way."

"I'll try," she answered doubtfully and was gone.

I stood where I was in the middle of the room, wondering how in God's name I was to keep my promise. Still, by the time I returned to France, she could very well have changed her mind. It wouldn't surprise me.

We were preparing to go into dinner when the constable sent Daisy to ask me to return to the library. I found Inspector Rother with my statement in his hands.

With a sense of foreboding, I sat down in the chair he indicated.

"You haven't been truthful with me," he began.

"On the contrary," I replied, refusing to let him intimidate me. "I gave you the truth as I saw it."

"Hmmm." He sat there, perusing what I'd written, as if he'd never seen it before. Which was patently not the case, if he'd already found fault with it.

I had dealt with matrons in hospital wards in England and in France. Inspector Rother held no terrors for me. But he obviously found this method useful in frightening suspects into blurting out whatever was causing them to feel guilty.

After a moment he set the sheet aside.

"You didn't tell me that Mrs. Lydia Ellis left the premises early this morning, before most of the family was awake."

"She did?" I asked, surprised. Where on earth had she gone? Not, I prayed, to the church at Wych Gate.

"She was seen as she bicycled into Hartfield. A shopkeeper was washing his windows and noticed her."

"Then you must ask her where she was going and why."

"You didn't sleep in your own bed last night."

"No. Mrs. Ellis wasn't feeling well and she slept in my room. She has a mild concussion, headaches and dizziness."

"She cried herself to sleep there, according to what I've discovered. Why?"

I remembered that someone had already been questioned about a love affair between Lydia and George Hughes. Was he suggesting that she had a broken heart, and that this was a motive for murder?

"I'm not privy to her affairs. Ask her."

"And you slept in the sitting room. After your assignation with the deceased."

"There was no meeting," I told him flatly. "The man came there in search of the brandy decanter."

"Why look in the sitting room for his brandy? Why not in the drawing room?"

Because the portrait was in the drawing room, I wanted to answer, and didn't.

"I expect only the deceased can tell you why he chose the sitting room. He was embarrassed to find me in possession of it, and retreated."

"So you say. I can't help but wonder if this—encounter—wasn't the reason Mrs. Lydia Ellis was in tears, and why in the early hours of the morning, she felt it necessary to bicycle into Hartfield, rather than take one of the family motorcars. Noisy things, motorcars."

"I think," I said, "if she had been angry with me for speaking to Lieutenant Hughes, she wouldn't have chosen my room to sleep in."

"She fell asleep there, perhaps, while waiting for you to come up to your bed. And, of course, you didn't. She must have found it distressing to face you this morning."

He had twisted events around to suit himself, using the bits he'd culled from our conversations with him to make his accusations hurtful.

Taking a deep breath, I said, "If she believed I'd taken her place with her lover, I wonder why she felt comfortable returning to London with me?"

A sour expression crossed his face. *Touché,* I thought.

"Let us return to her decision to go into Hartfield," he said after a moment.

"As I knew nothing about it," I said, "I can't be of help there."

"We believe she went to call on a Mr. Merrit, in Bluebell Cottage." Something in my face must have betrayed me. He smiled. "You know of Mr. Merrit?"

"Actually I do. When I was in Hartfield with Mr. Ellis, he almost stepped out in front of our motorcar. I believe he's blind."

"As to that, I'm told he can tell night from day."

"I wasn't aware of the extent of his blindness."

"Why would she call on him, at such an hour on a Saturday morning?"

"You're asking me to speculate," I said. "I don't know."

He dismissed me then, and all eyes were turned toward me as I returned to the dining room. Everyone was just finishing their soup, and I sat down without a word, smiling at Daisy as she brought my serving from the kitchen and set it before me.

I couldn't have said, under oath, what kind of soup it was. Parsnip pureed with apples?

Roger Ellis finally demanded, "What did Rother want?"

"He asked me several questions about my earlier statement."

Lydia looked up from her soup, then looked away again. *She knows*, I thought.

"And that was all?"

I said, "I think it was a fishing expedition."

"Fishing?" Mrs. Ellis repeated, alarm in her voice.

"He was hoping I might contradict myself."

I could almost feel what they were thinking—that I was an unknown quantity, a guest about whom almost nothing was known. Could they trust me? Or not?

What did I have to hide?

At the same time I was wondering if Inspector Rother wanted me to return to the family dinner table and blurt out all he'd discussed with me. He must have a very low regard for women! Besides, I was trained to keep patient information private, and I wasn't about to cause troubles in this already troubled family just so Inspector Rother could judge what effect my words had.

We ate in silence after that, and it wasn't until the savory had been brought in that Roger said, "You're a nurse. Surely you can tell us how George died."

"I didn't examine him," I replied. "I touched his hand, and I knew then that he was beyond my help. That was all I did. It was necessary for Dr. Tilton to pronounce him dead." I hadn't seen the blood matting his dark hair, where he'd been struck from behind. The back of his head had been turned away from me, and I'd tried not to muddle any evidence by moving the body.

"Who is the Simon Brandon who came here this afternoon to call on you?"

"A family friend," I explained once more. "He served in my father's regiment. He brought the formal dresses I needed for this weekend and has come back to take me to Somerset when I'm free to leave."

"Yes, and that's as it should be," Gran put in. "A young woman oughtn't to be traveling about the countryside alone. In my day, it simply wasn't done."

Out of the corner of my eye I saw Lydia flush with annoyance, knowing full well that the elder Mrs. Ellis was speaking to her.

We left the dining room and went our separate ways. No one seemed to be in the mood for company. I went up to my room to fetch my coat, and on the way down the stairs again, I encountered Inspector Rother. He gave me a cool nod in passing.

I ran Lydia to earth, finally, in the room above the hall.

It was very much like Aladdin's cave, mostly furnished with silk cushions scattered about the floor on a beautiful old Turkey carpet. Low tables stood here and there. I wondered if the original furnishings had been burned in Matthew Ellis's angry rampage in denial of his daughter's death.

Lydia had half started to her feet when I knocked and then opened the door. "Oh," she said and settled back amongst the cushions.

"You didn't tell me that you'd been to Hartfield early this morning."

A guilty flush rose in her cheeks. "How did you know? Did you see me leave? Have you told the police?"

"It was the police who told me. Apparently someone in Hartfield noticed you bicycling in at that ungodly hour. The police are going to ask you about it. And they'll ask the rest of the family, I'm afraid."

"Busybody," she said tartly. "I'm sure it was Dr. Tilton. All right, yes, I went to see Davis. I told him what George had said. I wanted to know what he thought. He's a man, he ought to know how men think."

"And?"

"It was his opinion that there must be a child. Otherwise it wouldn't have been preying on poor George's mind to the point that he finally spoke, there in the drawing room. And looking back, I'm convinced that Roger was avoiding him. Except when he had to go with George to remove that nonexistent tree. At that point George was probably too mortified to bring up France."

"This wasn't a very good idea," I told her. "If you'd needed advice, there was Henry."

"Yes, well, Henry is married to Margaret. There's no one Davis is likely to tell, is there? I nearly got away with it too."

"That's not the point," I said. "You compromised yourself as well as Davis Merrit."

She shook her head. "It's George's fault, when you come right down to it. I do wish I could ask Davis his opinion about this claim of murder. He knew George.

Not well, but apparently they've met before." Shivering, she added, "I've never met a murderer. I don't even know what to look for. It can't be anyone we know. George must have other enemies. Surely."

I thought it was all too likely to be someone she knew.

Night had fallen, sunset coming in late afternoon at this time of year. Outside the windows it was dark, and I could almost imagine the heath inching toward the house, eating away slowly at this pitiful attempt to keep it at bay.

I went to the windows and stood there, the lamplight at my back. Clouds were racing across the sky, hiding the stars, and there was no light to be seen anywhere. Even in the countryside in Somerset we could see a distant lamp lit in the house down the road from ours, or in another direction, from Simon's cottage. Here there was no sign of life, no hint of civilization. Only the stark blackness of a wild place.

And then I nearly cried out in alarm, for there was a face in the spill of light from these windows, illuminating the drive just below me. My heart was racing with shock even as I told myself it was another of Inspector Rother's constables, set to watch the door and prevent our leaving. And then I realized that it was Simon, looking up at me.

He must have seen me at the window before he reached the door.

Turning, I told Lydia that I ought to go, then hurried down the stairs. There was no one in the great hall as I walked through it. Opening the door as quietly as possible, I slipped through.

"I left my horse down the lane," Simon told me in a low voice that didn't carry. "I need to speak to you."

I stepped into a cold wind and shut the door softly behind me. We walked out of the circle of light from the tall windows above the hall and into the darkness. I reached out to take Simon's arm. The black shapes of the stunted bushes on the heath looked like beasts crouched there, waiting. I was learning to appreciate why Lydia found winter here so very distressful. In the daylight I'd thought I understood. But out here in the night, I knew what fear was and was grateful for the touch of another human being.

Simon didn't speak until we were well out of hearing. He seemed to be able to see in the dark, something I'd noticed before. We walked toward the lane that led from the track, and something loomed above me, catching me off guard.

It was his horse, snorting as we came within reach, and I put out a hand to touch the soft, warm muzzle. It nuzzled my hand in return, and then blew.

Simon told me, "There have been developments. Rother has brought in constables from all over Sussex to help search. One of his own men, a Constable Bates from Wych Gate, saw a beggar in Hartfield with a gold watch. He was showing it to the ironmonger at the time, like a child with a new toy. The constable stepped in and asked to look at the watch. Opening the case, he saw the name inscribed inside. It was Malcolm Hughes—apparently he was the victim's late brother."

"Yes, he was killed in the war."

"The constable asked who had given this watch to the beggar, and he answered that it was a friend."

"A friend?" I knew what was coming.

"One Davis Merrit. The police are looking for him. He wasn't at his house, and no one is certain just where he might have gone—"

"He's blind," I said. "He couldn't have gone far. Not on his own."

"The train stops nearby," he reminded me.

"Yes. I know. Do you think they'll arrest him? Merrit? When they find him?"

"It's likely. The police hadn't thought the body had been robbed. The man's purse hadn't been taken, for one thing, and there was a signet ring on one finger. It appears now that the watch was removed."

"Why? I mean, if it's so easily identified, why take it, then give it to someone who can't be relied upon to conceal where it came from?"

"A good question. Did Lydia Ellis tell Davis what had transpired last evening? There's talk that she came into Hartfield very early this morning."

"About the child? Yes. She told him about that and asked what he thought about it. He rather believed that there must be something to the story. But of course that was before anyone knew of the murder."

"And Hughes told you where to find this child."

"Yes, I told you. Apparently he'd seen her at an orphanage run by nuns."

"Which puts you in danger. Who else knew that he could have confided in you?"

"I've tried to keep that to myself, Simon, but bits are leaking out. For instance that I was still in my evening gown this morning. I think Daisy let that slip. And the fact that Lydia was asleep in my room. That could be Gran, but it could also be that Inspector Rother is very good at putting two and two together. Eleanor, Alan Ellis's widow, seems to be distancing herself from what's happening. I hardly ever see her or her brother, but they had no reason to kill Lieutenant Hughes, did they? I don't know what Dr. Tilton or his wife have told the police, nor Janet Smyth and her brother, the rector. And now this business about the watch. I really don't know what to think any longer."

"It could have nothing to do with the child. You realize that."

I was standing next to the mare, warmed by her body, and Simon was between me and the wind sweeping across the flat, featureless heath.

"Then what is it about?" I asked. "I can't imagine that Roger Ellis, for one, would kill George Hughes just to see Davis Merrit taken up for murder!"

I could glimpse his smile. "Stranger things have happened."

Shivering, I said, "I'll be glad when I can leave here. And Lydia wants to return to London—"

Simon's gloved hand covered my mouth. I heard it then, someone coming up the lane toward the house. I nodded, letting him know I had heard it as well.

He pulled the mare into the deeper darkness of stunted trees, and covered her nose. I followed him, standing close, grateful for my dark coat.

It was a constable, I could see his helmet as he bicycled furiously up toward the house, breathing hard in the cold air, little puffs visible in tempo with the energy he was expending.

He dismounted as he reached the door and lifting the knocker, gave it an almighty *whack* against the plate.

The door opened shortly thereafter, and I heard Daisy's voice, followed by the constable's.

She left him there, and very shortly Inspector Rother came to the door.

"What is it?" he asked sharply, his words carrying on the night air.

The constable leaned forward, lowering his voice.

Rother said, "Damn." Quite clearly. Then he turned on his heel and was gone for a good five minutes. When he returned, it was with his coat, and he was giving orders to the constable to lash his bicycle to the boot of the Inspector's motorcar.

It was done, and then the two men were driving toward us, the headlamps of their motorcar sweeping the lawns as they turned into the lane.

Simon swore, moving the mare deeper into the trees, turning his face away from the light, and I did the same.

The motorcar came surging down the lane, much too fast, and I heard the constable's voice earnestly answering questions that Inspector Rother flung at him almost faster than the man could make a sensible reply. And then they were out of hearing, and soon enough out of sight, even the red rear lamp no longer visible.

"I think," Simon said quietly, "the Inspector has just learned about the pocket watch."

I thought about that. "But who could have given it to the beggar? We've all been here since the police arrived. Except for Roger Ellis. And—me. When I called my father."

Had the watch been in George's pocket when he was killed? If so, the only reason for taking it was to incriminate someone.

"The question is, is the beggar telling the truth? Does he even understand what the truth is? Or remember what actually happened?" Simon paced restlessly.

I smiled. "The good Inspector is about to find out."

Suppressing an answering smile, he said, "Go back inside. The cold is making you giddy. But, Bess. Watch yourself. You have no way of knowing who can be trusted."

He walked me back to the house, and I was grateful to find that the door had not been locked. I could slip in unnoticed.

Simon waited until I was safely inside before walking away.

I had a sudden desire to see Juliana's portrait again, and went to the drawing room. I had just put my hand on the knob when I heard voices.

No, one voice. Gran's. And she must have been speaking to the portrait on the wall.

" . . . Who is that other child? I wish you could tell me. I wish the dead could speak. If only you'd lived, my darling . . ."

I didn't catch the next sentences. Gran's voice had cracked, and I thought she must be crying. And then she said more clearly, "Has he sent you back again? Dear God, I'd like to believe that. Before I die . . ."

I released the handle gingerly, trying not to make a sound, and stepped carefully away from the door. She wouldn't thank me for eavesdropping.

I went up the stairs to my room and shut the door.

It had been a very long day. I was afraid the next day, Sunday, would be even longer.

Nine

I t was raining again when I awoke and looked toward my window. Raindrops were skittering down the panes, and I could hear them whispering as the wind pushed them against the glass.

The fire had been banked for the night and the room was cold. It was too early for Daisy to make the rounds of rekindling them, and I got up to see to it myself. I soon had it beginning to take hold on the wood log that I added to the grate, and I stood there for a moment longer, rubbing my hands together.

Then I crossed to the window and looked out. It must have been raining for some time, because I could see little puddles in the knot garden where the earth was bare.

It was Sunday, but I doubted that anyone from the family would choose to attend morning service. I was just as glad. We'd be stared at, and people would whisper behind their hands.

To my surprise, when I went down to breakfast an hour later, I discovered that Roger Ellis was indeed intending to go to the early service.

"With the police badgering us at every turn," he was saying to his grandmother, "we've lost sight of the fact that a friend, a guest in our house, is dead. It isn't our fault that the police are here, and we've got nothing to be ashamed of. We're going to morning service to prove it."

"You'll merely fan the fires of curiosity."

"Every time the police come to Vixen Hill, there's gossip."

Eleanor said, "Please, Roger, I don't think I could face it."

"You're excused, then," he said shortly. "You're in mourning."

"If you insist on this foolishness, you must take Lydia with you," Gran went on. "And your mother. Miss Crawford as well, if she's willing."

He grimaced. "Lydia and I have nothing to say to each other."

"Then pretend. For the sake of the family," she answered shortly.

"And you? Will you go for the sake of the family?" Roger Ellis asked, a sour note slipping into his voice.

"I'm staying home with dearest Eleanor and her brother. No one will wonder at that."

Captain Ellis turned to me. "Good morning, Miss Crawford. Are you attending services with us this morning?"

"I shall, if you like." I could hardly say no, having heard the rest of the discussion. And I could see that it was wise, after all.

"Shall you do what?" his mother asked me as she came into the dining room.

"Attend morning services."

Her gaze moved on to her son. "Is it a good idea, do you think, Roger?"

"We'll have to face them down sometime."

"Yes, that's true. All right, I'll come. Where's Lydia? She should accompany us as well."

And so it was decided, although still Gran flatly refused to set foot outside the house. We finished our breakfast and went up to change. The rain was coming down all the harder, and our umbrellas made a bobbing black brigade to the motorcars that had been brought around.

Roger looked up as his wife stepped out to join us. I don't know who had persuaded her to come, but I suspected it was Mrs. Ellis. She was wearing a lovely black hat with a long veil she had pulled down to her chin.

"You're not to wear that veil," he told her. "You'll have people thinking you're in mourning for Hughes, for God's sake."

"What will they think when they see the bruise on my face?" she retorted.

"Yes, well, you didn't seem to mind that when you went yesterday into Hartfield."

She stared at him, and then turned to me. "Did you tell him?"

"No," I said. "I expect it was the police."

Angry, she flung back her veil.

Mrs. Ellis said, "We're getting wet through. Lydia, come with me. Miss Crawford, you will ride with Roger, if you don't mind."

We were sorted out in no time, and on our way to the church in Wych Gate.

We left the motorcars along the road and joined the rest of the congregation as it moved toward the west doors. Even so, I could see the trees that overhung the grassy dell and the path where George Hughes had been found.

The church was rather full, in spite of the rain, and those who hadn't yet taken a seat parted to let the Ellis family pass. Some greeted Roger or his mother by name, and others simply stared. Roger kept us moving, shepherding us toward the seats still vacant in front.

The choir was singing, but those who could see us were looking at us rather than at the notes on the pages of their hymnals. The organ came to a crescendo, and there was a sudden silence, which caught a few people off guard, their whispers loud behind us.

" . . . face," a woman's voice was saying, and another was commenting, " . . . the dead man's nurse." Someone else, louder than the others, as if he were slightly deaf, remarked, " . . . police have no idea," as if answering someone else's question.

Lydia, her cheeks pink, stared straight ahead while Roger's lips were set in a straight line. I saw Mrs. Ellis put her gloved hand on her son's arm, and the tension around his mouth lessened.

The church seemed a more cheerful place this morning than it had the day before, despite the rain. Candles brightened the gloom, and the congregation contributed a little warmth. Still, I couldn't help remembering walking down the aisle, into the choir, and then back again, while Mrs. Ellis's footsteps echoed in the organ loft.

The rector, mounting the steps to the pulpit, seemed not to know how to face us. I saw him glance at his sister, and then clear his throat before beginning the service.

All went well until he returned to the pulpit for his morning homily.

It was an unfortunate choice of message. Preparing for the approach of Christmas, the sermon dealt with the expected birth of a special child, and by extension the lives of children who faced the holidays without a father to care for and protect them, either because they were among the dead or still serving at the Front or on the high seas. It was well intended—I was all too aware of the long lists of casualties and the fact that each one represented a family in mourning for a father, a son, a brother, a husband. It would be a bleak Christmas for them, and Mr. Smyth was pointing to the need in his own parish to see that the widows and orphans were remembered with gifts of food and clothing and above all sympathy for their loss.

Ordinarily it would have been received in the spirit in which it was intended.

Instead the words seemed to echo around the stone walls, loud in our ears as we listened. Captain Ellis's long fingers drummed a tattoo on the knee of his trousers, and Lydia kept her eyes on the stained glass windows in the choir, their colors muted by the cloudy day. Mrs. Ellis was biting her lip to keep herself from fidgeting, and Janet Smyth, the rector's sister, looked stricken.

It was clear that the rector had not expected the Ellis family to attend morning services, and his prepared remarks and the choice of hymns must have seemed innocuous enough. But he had been there on the evening Lieutenant Hughes had brought up the missing child, and he could not pretend otherwise. "What Child Is This," sung by the choir, was the final blow.

I looked across to where the doctor and his wife were seated, and I could see that they too were feeling some distress. For themselves or for the rector or for the Ellis family, I didn't know.

Finally the ordeal was over and we could rise and walk out of the church. And standing at the main gate where the motorcars had been parked, was Inspector Rother, looking like the wrath of God. I found myself thinking that at any moment he would storm the church doors and brand us all as heathen murderers and heretics.

As it was, I was a little ahead of the family and I happened to see him first, just as the rector quickly shook my hand and murmured a few words, as if eager to get his duty over with before someone brought up his sermon. Roger Ellis simply nodded briefly, ignoring the rector's outstretched hand, which Mrs. Ellis took in her son's stead and wished Mr. Smyth a good morning. Roger had just retrieved his umbrella from the stand and was about to open it when he saw Inspector Rother.

There was the briefest of hesitations, and then he handed the opened umbrella to his mother, and picked up another to share with his wife. With that, he moved toward the gate, as if nothing had happened. Lydia, huddled under his umbrella, trying not to touch him, stumbled and then recovered her balance. He took her arm and tucked it beneath his, for all the world the loving husband. Lydia glanced at him but had the presence of mind not to pull away. Mrs. Ellis, sharing her umbrella with me, said something under her breath that sounded like a prayer as we neared the gates, her arm tense in mine as she watched to see whether the Inspector was intent on stopping her son.

But Inspector Rother let us pass without a glance. It was clear that he had someone else in mind, and looking back over my shoulder, I saw him stop Janet Smyth as she came out of the church, drawing her to one side, out of hearing of those still leaving the service.

I could also see her face turn pink and the curious stares of her brother and everyone else.

Just beyond them, in my line of sight, was the white marble statue of the kneeling child.

She looked cold and lonely in the winter rain.

Roger Ellis said as he began to turn the motorcar back toward Vixen Hill, "The fool should have had the decency to change his sermon."

"I expect he didn't have another one prepared."

Ignoring my answer, he said, "And what does Rother want with Janet Smyth? She hardly spoke two words to George that whole evening."

"Still, she was there—"

"What angers me most," he went on as he slowed to make his way through a flock of sheep barring the road, "is that he should show his face at St. Mary's, just as the service was finished. Taunting us, that's what he was doing. He could always find Janet at the Rectory."

But I thought Inspector Rother had something on his mind, and he wasn't the sort of man to stand still when he was on the scent. It made him all the more worrying, even to those of us without a guilty conscience. But why indeed had he come?

I had looked for Simon at St. Mary's, thinking he would take the chance of speaking to me. But he wasn't there, and I didn't know if it was because he didn't expect us to attend, or if something had come up.

The same something that was on Inspector Rother's mind?

We had turned into the lane that led to the house, the distances seeming shorter as I grew accustomed to them. Still, if I had been George Hughes, I wouldn't have wished to walk to the church.

Had he gone of his own volition, to avoid having to face Roger Ellis at breakfast? To see Juliana's grave? Or had he gone with someone—been asked to meet someone there?

Suddenly, in my mind's eye, I saw Mrs. Ellis pausing to set the marble kitten back in its proper place by her daughter's outstretched marble fingers.

Had that lovely bit of stone been the murder weapon that the police—so far as I knew—failed to find? The way the kitten sat on its haunches, it would fit in the hand well, and it was solid enough to knock a victim unconscious, and possibly even kill him.

We had arrived at the door, and Roger Ellis switched off the motor before going to help his mother descend from the other vehicle. I opened my umbrella, preparing to hold it over Mrs. Ellis's hat. As I did, something white fluttered past my hand, caught first by the wind and then beaten to the ground by the rain.

I stooped and picked it up, mostly my nurse's sense of tidiness. And then I realized there was writing on it.

Damp as it was, I quickly stuffed it into the glove on my left hand and took Mrs. Ellis's arm as Daisy held the door wide for us to hurry through.

We went our separate ways to change out of our wet coats, and in my room I carefully removed my gloves, setting them on the chest by the door.

The scrap of wet paper lay in my palm.

A message from Simon? I thought it might well be, but how did he know which umbrella I was using? And where had he been, because I hadn't seen him?

Unfolding the limp square of paper with care so as not to tear it, I saw that the ink had begun to run from its exposure to the rain.

I couldn't make out the handwriting, much less the two words.

eet m

Meet me?

When I held it under the bright lamplight, I thought I was probably right about that. The missing *M* and the missing *e* were so faint I had to squint to make them out.

If it wasn't Simon—then who had sent that message?

Was it for Lydia? And if it was for Lydia, what should I do now? Say nothing? Or take it to her?

The question was answered by a tap at my door, and Lydia walked in.

"I've never been so mortified in my entire life," she said, going to the fire and holding out her hands, as if chilled to the bone. But I thought it wasn't a chilling from the winter cold. "I should never have let Roger persuade me to go. Everyone—*everyone!*—stared at me as if I had two heads, wondering how I came by this bruise. And then the rector's sermon was inexcusable. And I could hardly believe it when Inspector Rother arrived."

"The sermon was probably written several days before he dined here."

"Well, then, have the good sense, and the good manners, to change it. He saw us sitting there."

"He was as uncomfortable as you were."

"It was a mistake to go. What's that in your hand?"

I was still holding the scrap of paper. "I'm not sure," I began, but she came quickly across the room to where I was standing by the lamp, holding out her hand.

"Where did it come from? Was it here, in the house? Surely not—"

"It was in the umbrella Mrs. Ellis and I were using. I don't know why it hadn't fallen out before. But as I was opening it again when we arrived at the door, it must have shaken loose."

She took it from me. "The ink has run. Can you read it?" She peered at the letters, sounding them out. "Meet me. Is that what it says? Who wrote it?"

"I don't have any idea."

"Then it must have been for me. Davis? Was he in church, do you know?"

"I didn't see him. But he could have been there," I said doubtfully. Simon had told me that the police were interested in speaking to him, and he had disappeared.

Was that why he wanted to meet Lydia? To tell her what had happened? But then why not tell her where this meeting should take place?

Unless of course she knew already.

She began to pace. "I must go into Hartfield. If this is from Davis, he must know something—heard something the police haven't told us yet. You must want to leave here as much as I do. And it's my fault, really, that you're here. Help me do something to free both of us."

She was persuasive, but I shook my head. "Um—you don't want to draw him into this inquiry. You've done enough harm already, seeing him yesterday morning." I couldn't tell her he was under suspicion without giving Simon away.

"If you asked to go in to The King's Head to speak to Simon Brandon, I could go to show you the way. You wouldn't care to be lost on the roads around the Forest, would you?"

I refused outright to be a party to such foolishness. But when she finally threatened to go alone, even in the rain and on her bicycle, I relented, against my better judgment.

And if Davis wasn't at the cottage, then she wouldn't see him anyway.

When I asked Mrs. Ellis for the use of one of the motorcars, she said, "Lunch will be served in a very few minutes. Afterward, I'll be very happy to go with you."

I couldn't argue that Lydia ought to be the one accompanying me.

Lydia, waiting in my room, turned anxiously toward the door as I came in. "What did she say?"

"She asked me to wait until after lunch."

Relief washed over her face before I could add, "Lydia. She suggested that she go with me. I didn't know what to say."

The relief vanished. "No, I was supposed to go. Why didn't you try to convince her that I should drive with you?"

"I was asking a favor. How could I press her?"

She turned and paced to the window. "We have to do something. Tell her—tell her you don't wish to put her out, that she'll want to spend the time with Margaret and Henry."

"Wait until after lunch. Then I'll see what I can do."

"I should have asked her myself," she said pacing back.

"I think," I said slowly, remembering the way Roger's mother had scanned my face, "she believes this is a ruse. That you're still intending to leave for London."

"Well, I'm not. Much as I'd be tempted to do just that. But I know the police would just find me and send me back, and that would be worse. Convince her if you can."

In the end, we ate our meal in a stiff silence, and then the problem of Mrs. Ellis accompanying me was resolved when Inspector Rother arrived and asked to speak to her.

Lydia, almost giddy with relief, said, "Oh, thank God," as she hurried out the door after me, and all but leapt into the motorcar.

I didn't tell her that I'd had to promise Mrs. Ellis to bring her back with me.

"I trust you, Bess, to see that Lydia doesn't do anything rash," she'd said, lines of worry already etched deeply around her eyes.

I drove with care, not knowing the tracks, expecting sheep to block our progress around every bend, and remembering too George Hughes's trouble with something in the road. But this time I came upon a line of cows moving stoically through the rain, as if they knew precisely where they were going and how long it would take to get there.

The rain had left deep puddles on the unmade road, and there were times when I could almost believe I was driving in France, we bounced and shuddered so ferociously.

We came into Hartfield in another shower of rain, and I made my way through the town toward the inn. I said, "You can hardly march up to Davis Merrit's door and ask him if he sent you a note."

Lydia had been quiet the last mile or so. "I don't know. It seemed so easy at Vixen Hill. Do you see him walking along the street? It would seem natural if I got down and spoke to him then."

"I haven't seen him so far."

She was craning to look first this way and then that. "If he did send a message, where do you think he meant for me to meet him?" She turned to me in alarm. "You don't suppose he was waiting near the church, or in the churchyard?"

"Hardly there, in full view of the entire congregation, not to mention Roger," I reminded her. "It would have attracted even more attention and gossip."

"Yes, of course, you're right."

We could see the inn just ahead. "Would Simon go across and ask Davis to come to the inn? If you asked him?"

"I don't know," I said. "Do you want me to knock on Davis Merrit's door?"

She bit her lip, then shook her head. "No. He doesn't know you. He might deny everything."

"He doesn't know Simon either," I pointed out.

"But Simon's a man. No one will think twice if he calls on Davis. Please, ask him, Bess."

I left the motorcar in the inn yard, and we hurried into The King's Head under our umbrellas, leaving them by the door as we stepped into Reception. I walked to the desk and asked if someone would kindly tell Mr. Brandon that Miss Crawford was here.

The young woman working on accounts looked up with a smile. "Certainly, Miss Crawford, I'll send someone to his room."

She suggested that I wait in a parlor just down a passage, and I thanked her. We opened the door to the small room. It was a little stuffy but otherwise quite pleasant, with windows overlooking the side street. It was furnished with comfortable chairs and a table for tea. I said to Lydia, "Are you sure you want to go through with this?"

"Yes. I'm here. There might not be another chance. We're so isolated at Vixen Hill. I'll go mad waiting."

The door opened and Simon walked in. "I saw you drive up," he said. "What's happened?"

"That's what we came to ask you," Lydia said at once. "Inspector Rother was at St. Mary's this morning. He wished to speak to Janet Smyth, the rector's sister. Now he's talking to my mother-in-law at Vixen Hill."

"Is he?" He glanced at me. I couldn't read the look. "I've tried to find out what the police are looking for. But even in the pubs, truth is thin on the ground, and gossip is feeding on itself."

I took the scrap of paper from my pocket. "Did you write this?" I asked.

"No. Where did it come from?"

I told him about the umbrella. "Lydia thinks it might have come from Davis Merrit. She'd like to ask him. But it isn't that easy. Could you step across to Bluebell Cottage and ask him to come to The King's Head?"

Simon hesitated. Then to my surprise, he agreed.

"I'll feel like such a fool if Davis didn't send the message. But then who else could have?" Lydia asked.

"We'll know soon enough."

We sat down, and waited. The minutes crawled by. Lydia said, "What's keeping Simon?"

"I don't know." Five more minutes passed. I was beginning to worry as well. Bluebell Cottage was just across the street from The King's Head, a walk of no more than two minutes, even if Simon had had to stop for a funeral procession to pass by. "Wait here," I said finally.

"No, don't leave me, Bess!"

"I'm just walking to the door, to look out and see if Simon is at the cottage."

Grudgingly, she let me go. But although I stepped out into the now mistng rain, there was no sign of Simon or Davis Merrit. I thought there was a lamp lit in the cottage, but I couldn't even be sure of that, for the curtains were drawn, and it wasn't yet dark enough for the lamplight to show clearly.

Simon and half the regiment could be in Bluebell Cottage and I had no way of telling. With a sigh, I turned and walked back into the inn and rejoined Lydia in the parlor.

She rose from her chair as I came through the door and shut it behind me. "Well?"

I said lightly, "If he's in the cottage, I can't tell. The curtains are drawn."

"Then Davis must be talking to him. Why didn't he come across to The King's Head and speak to me himself? If he sent me that note, there must have been a reason."

"Perhaps he doesn't want to be seen speaking to you. I'm sure after your visit with him the other morning, the police questioned him."

"I hadn't thought of that."

Another fifteen minutes passed before we heard Simon's footsteps on the wooden floor outside the parlor, and then the door opened.

He said, shutting it behind him, "I couldn't find Davis Merrit."

Lydia said, rising, "He wasn't in his house?"

Simon was choosing his words carefully. "No. I went up and down the street. The shops are closed, it's Sunday after all."

She turned to me. "I told you he could have been waiting at St. Mary's. We must go back there straight-away."

Simon quickly stepped between her and the door. "I don't believe he's at St. Mary's, Mrs. Ellis. The police are searching for him as well."

"For Davis? Dear God, just because I went to see him yesterday? No, you're just trying to frighten me away because Bess doesn't want me to see him!"

"Your visit will probably prove to be his motive for murder. But what they are curious about now is how he came by George Hughes's watch."

I was surprised by Simon's tone of voice. Cold and blunt.

"Murder?" The muscles in her face tensed, making it look more like a mask than flesh and blood. "What watch?"

"It was actually his brother's watch, I'm told. It turned up in the possession of a man the local people call Willy. He appeared in Hartfield one day, muddled and half starved. No one knows his real name or where he came from. He begs for coins, and people feed and clothe him out of kindness. No one knows where he sleeps. But during the day he's on the street, waiting for someone to put a few coins into his hand."

"Yes, yes, I've seen Willy on the streets, I know who he is."

"Someone noticed that he was carrying a watch, rather an expensive one, and mentioned that to the police. When they examined the watch, they saw the name engraved on the reverse. When asked how he'd come by the watch, Willy told them it had been given to him by a friend. I don't know how they persuaded him to identify this friend. But when they went to look for Davis Merrit, he was not in his cottage. He hasn't been seen since."

Lydia cried, "Surely they can't believe—not Davis! How would he even find George? Or kill him?"

But I could see that she remembered telling me that George Hughes and Davis Merrit had met in France. She turned frantically to me. "Do the police—does anyone think that Davis killed George—for my sake? No, he would never do that."

I said quietly, "You told me you didn't love him. But perhaps—because of your kindnesses—he was in love with you."

"I don't believe you. And even if I did, why would Davis take George's watch—and give it to Willy, of all people?"

"So that you would know what he'd done for you?"

She walked to the window, looking out at the side street. "This is Roger's doing. It couldn't be anyone else's. He's rid himself of George and of Davis as well." She put out a hand, stroking the folds of the curtains, not even aware of what she was doing. But the smooth velvet must have been soothing. "I hope they hang him!"

"You don't mean that," I said sharply. "You don't know the whole story. Neither do I. Or Simon."

"It doesn't matter. This is the only thing I can think of that would explain what has happened. Willy is lying. He has to be made to tell the truth." She turned from the window. "Take me back to Vixen Hill, Bess." There was a hardness in her face that hadn't been there before. "Thank you, Simon. I'm sorry I didn't trust you."

She walked past him and out the door. "Are you coming, Bess?" she called anxiously over her shoulder.

"Yes, yes, in a moment." I said to Simon, "Is that all you've been able to learn?"

"Inspector Rother has been busy ascertaining that Hughes had his watch at Vixen Hill. He spoke to some-one at the church today, I'm told, who remembered seeing it. That must have been the rector's sister. She has no reason to lie. Did you see it?"

"No. I don't think I did. But I had no reason to notice it. Wait, yes, he had it that first evening, I think."

"Then he must have had it with him when he was killed. It looks rather bleak for Merrit, doesn't it? As does his disappearance. Mrs. Ellis is waiting, Bess, you should go."

"Is there any possibility that Willy killed Hughes and Davis Merrit?"

"I doubt it. First of all there's no motive that I can think of. And I don't believe he has the capacity to carry out an elaborate lie. I spoke to him yesterday. He can hardly put a coherent sentence together."

"Yes, and I'd seen Davis Merrit give him money. He seemed so grateful." I remembered the marble kitten and related what I'd feared. "How could a blind man know about that—if indeed it was the murder weapon? Much less put it back almost exactly where he'd found it? I didn't notice it had been moved, but Mrs. Ellis did."

"Interesting. I'll see what I can discover about the wound. And pay a visit to the churchyard."

"Simon, I must go. Please don't go back to London just yet. I'll feel safer knowing you're here in Hartfield. Besides, the police tell us nothing."

"I won't leave until I can escort you to Somerset. You still have your pistol?"

"Yes. I even carried it to the church service this morning, I'm ashamed to say. I'd forgot it was in my pocket."

"Carry it everywhere." He walked me to the door of the inn. "This is all speculation," he warned me. "For all we know, Davis Merrit took it into his head to visit a cousin or went to London to see a specialist. He may turn up with a very solid alibi."

"Let's hope so," I said. But then that would mean that someone at Vixen Hill was a killer.

Simon asked, "Was it raining the morning that Hughes was killed?"

"It was overcast. I don't believe it had started to rain."

"But he might have taken an umbrella with him, and the note you found was one intended for him."

"He didn't have an umbrella with him when we found him."

"He could have left it in the stand at the church, before walking down the path. Are you quite sure that you took out the same umbrella that you'd brought with you this morning?"

"No," I said slowly. "It was Roger Ellis who handed it to me. His mother and I shared it on the way to the motorcar. And then it was decided that I should travel with Roger. And so I kept it, since she could share with Lydia."

"Interesting. I'd not mention the note to anyone else. It might not be wise."

I walked out to the motorcar, where Lydia was waiting, staring at Bluebell Cottage as if she could see through the very walls and into the house. As Simon turned the crank for me, she said, "He's not in there, is he? I can feel it. The cottage is empty. Well. So much for our friendship."

As we drove away, she added, "I liked him. Not as a lover or anything of that sort. As a friend. I expect part of it was pity for his blindness, and part of it was the man who loved books as much as I did. Roger isn't a great reader, did you know? Too busy for one thing. Even before the war, he had the estate to manage and all that. He worked hard. His father's early death left a void, and by the time Roger was old enough to take over, poor management had taken its toll. To his credit, he brought Vixen Hill back to where it was the day Juliana died. I expect that was partly why he did it, as well. Not just for his mother's sake."

We saw Willy as we slowed to pass children playing hoops in the street. He was standing on a corner watching them, and I thought his face was sad. And then we had moved on, and I could no longer see him.

If Lydia noticed him standing there, she made no mention of it to me.

I think Mrs. Ellis was relieved when we pulled up in front of the house. She came into the hall to greet us, and as Daisy took our coats, she said, "Do you have any idea why Inspector Rother came all this way to ask me about George's watch? It seems rather silly."

Lydia didn't reply, asking Daisy if there was any tea to be had after the cold drive from Hartfield.

I said, "What reason did the Inspector give you for asking?"

She smiled. "You know policemen. They don't explain anything."

"Do you remember seeing the watch?" I asked, curious.

"Oh yes. It was his brother's. It was sent back to him from the Front, when Malcolm was killed. It meant the world to him."

"No, I mean, did you actually see it this weekend?"

She frowned. "I'm sure I did. Thursday night, I think, just before we went to bed."

The same time I'd seen it.

"Did that please Inspector Rother? That you could answer his question for him?"

"He seemed very satisfied. Odd little man, isn't he? If he weren't an Inspector, no one would take any notice of him, would they?"

"I expect he's a good policeman."

"Yes, well, I hope we've seen the last of him. This whole business has been very trying. Especially for Roger. The last time the police came to Vixen Hill, it was to tell us that someone had found his father's body. He doesn't feel much sympathy for them. Bearers of bad tidings, he always said. And it's true, isn't it? There's never a policeman about unless he's bringing bad news."

I hadn't known the police had come about Matthew Ellis, Roger's father. I should have expected it, for it explained his animosity toward them. How old had he been then? Eight? Nine? It was an age when memories were sharp and permanent. I could picture myself at that age, seeing my first body in India. A beggar, lying along the road, wrapped against the cold night, dying in his sleep. Or at least I'd hoped he had. My father was angry that I'd seen him. The Colonel Sahib had taken me out for the day, and his men had made certain our route was safe. The subaltern who had missed the corpse got a severe dressing down. But I knew what death was. It hadn't taken a corpse on the roadside to give it a face. I'd seen the worry in my mother's eyes whenever my father was in the field. She made light of it, but the fear was there—that one day his luck would run out, and a bullet would find him. It didn't matter whether it was a bandit's shot or a Pathan warrior's or a nervous recruit's accidental discharge of his weapon. Death was not uncommon in India.

I realized much, much later that it wasn't the corpse that had disturbed the Colonel Sahib, but the fact that it could just as easily have been someone lying in wait for us. He had enemies, my father did. My mother had known that too.

Daisy brought tea to the sitting room, where it was warmer, and we all gathered there. Lydia was silent, and Roger Ellis had a grim set to his mouth. I think he must have guessed why Lydia had wanted to go into Hartfield.

That evening, just before we went in to dinner, we heard the distant clanging of the heavy knocker on the door. Daisy went to answer the summons and a few minutes later brought Inspector Rother to the drawing room, where we were finishing our sherry. He greeted Gran and Mrs. Ellis politely, then turned to Roger.

"I've come to inform you that we are satisfied that no one here is connected to the murder of George Hughes. You're free to go about your own affairs as you please."

Surprised, Mrs. Ellis thanked him. Across the room, Lydia's face lost all color.

It was Gran who demanded, "The least you can do after all we've been through is to tell us who killed poor George. He was a dear friend, you know, not a stranger who happened by. We're as relieved as the police must be that his killer is caught, of course we are. But we would appreciate a few answers."

Inspector Rother nodded. "I understand, Madam. It will come out in the inquest, which will be held on Tuesday at The King's Head. We have reason to believe it was one Davis Merrit."

Mrs. Ellis exclaimed, "Surely not! I mean to say, he's blind."

"It doesn't take sight, Madam, to strike a man on the back of his head. Or drag him toward the water."

"But how did he get to the church? How did he know that George would be there?" Lydia asked.

"He keeps a horse, I understand, and goes out riding from time to time. He's not precisely without resources. And the horse can find his way back to the stable, should it be necessary."

"What was his motive?" I asked, wanting to know what the police had discovered.

"That hasn't yet been determined, Miss Crawford," he said in a tone of voice that brooked no further questions on that subject.

Roger Ellis said, echoing his mother, "We thank you for coming to speak to us. I'll see you out."

As they left the room, Henry, Margaret's husband, said into the silence, "Well, that was quick work. I expected we might be here for several more days."

"At least it wasn't one of us," Margaret said, her voice a little unsteady. I wondered if she knew how worried her mother had been about that.

It was Eleanor who made the remark none of us had considered. "Perhaps this man Merrit was out riding and came upon George along the way, and they went on together."

Henry rested a hand on his wife's shoulder as he stood behind her chair. "It still doesn't explain why Merrit should suddenly kill someone he accidentally encounters on a track in Ashdown Forest. There must be more to this."

Lydia turned her face away, toward the window. I could almost guess what she was thinking. That she'd given Davis Merrit a reason to search out and speak to Lieutenant Hughes. But why it should lead to murder was another matter. Unless I was right about his feelings for Lydia.

Still, even if he was in love with her, what purpose could be served by killing George after he'd already told everyone about the child? I should have thought that killing Roger would have been more appropriate as an expression of devotion. If one could call murder that.

Gran had the last word. "Well, one thing to be said for Davis Merrit as the killer, you shan't be required to read to him any longer," she told Lydia. "Ah, here's Daisy. I thought that Inspector would keep us from our dinner. Henry, give me your arm. You can take me into the dining room."

Henry turned to offer her his arm, and Gran led the way with the air of a woman who was very satisfied with herself. For some reason I couldn't explain, I thought, *She's gloating.*

But what exactly did she have to gloat about?

Was it just the fact that Roger had been exonerated? Or was there something more? Watching her, I realized that in spite of her age, she was fit and a good walker. She could easily have followed George to the church and even killed him. She was tall enough. Strong enough.

And George would never have expected trouble from her.

Ten

By the time we had absorbed the fact that we were free to go, it was too late to do more than discuss whether to leave in the morning or the day after the inquest.

Lydia said to me quietly after dinner, "I've never really unpacked. If Simon would agree to take us to London, it would be easier. But I will take the train if he can't manage it. Or if he's concerned about what Roger might say or do."

I couldn't imagine Simon Brandon being afraid of anyone. But I understood that she was trying to protect him from an unpleasant scene. And Roger Ellis was likely to make one.

"We must get word to him," I said, "unless he learns of the news in Hartfield."

And where was Davis Merrit? Alive and on the run—or a dead scapegoat?

"I'll pack my own things," I told her. "Then we'll see what tomorrow brings."

But after breakfast, I happened to notice that one of the Ellis motorcars had been brought around. And I could hear Gran's voice echoing around the hall, raised in anger and fear.

I ran down the stairs, thinking that something terrible must have happened. But when I got to the hall, I found only Mrs. Ellis sitting by the hearth, tears streaming down her face while Gran was at the door, arguing vehemently with her grandson.

It was only then that I noticed that he was wearing his uniform and his greatcoat. I'd seen him in his uniform every day, but this time he wore it with a very different air. I'd been a part of a military family all my life, and I knew the look of a man on his way to war.

He turned to me as I came into the room and halted abruptly, realizing that I'd walked into the middle of a family quarrel.

"Will you please tell Lydia for me that there's no need for her to leave Vixen Hill? I'm rejoining my regiment tomorrow morning. I'll be on my way to France in a few days' time. She'll be safer here than on her own in London."

I answered, before I'd quite considered what I was saying, "Your leave isn't up. I should think your family still needs you. And this business with Lieutenant Hughes's death has surely reopened old wounds."

"She's right," Gran said, holding out a hand to me, asking me to join her at the door. "We still need you, Roger. Don't be rash. Sleep on this decision. You may feel differently tomorrow."

"Ten days or so won't make all that much difference," he said shortly. "It's better if I go and get it over with."

Mrs. Ellis said from her chair near the fire, "And if you are killed in those ten days? Do you think we will find that easy to bear?"

Gran said angrily, "Let Lydia go to London and get it out of her system. She'll come back, wait and see if she doesn't. This is her home, you're her husband. She'll come to her senses soon enough. There's no need to penalize your mother and me just to punish her."

"I'm not punishing her," he wearily answered his grandmother. "We've got off on the wrong foot. I've been away three years. I came back a very different man from the one she remembered. If I leave now, before anything else goes wrong, we might salvage something out of this muddle of a marriage."

But Gran wasn't to be put off. "You're going back for all the wrong reasons. If you're killed, should we blame Lydia for sending you away like this? I promise you we shall. It's her fault as much as yours, and your mother and I will be the ones to have to live with that."

"I'm not going to die, Gran. God willing, the war will end soon. Now the Americans have stepped in, we'll have a chance to see this business finished. When I come home again, Lydia and I may be able to mend matters and live together somehow."

Gran was inconsolable and said fiercely, "Think of your mother if you don't care about breaking my heart. You were the closest to Juliana. Losing you will be like losing her all over again. You can't do that to her. Now go back upstairs and put this foolishness behind you. We'll say no more about it."

He bent to kiss her cheek. "Good-bye, Gran." And he was off, striding to the motorcar without looking back. "I'll leave it at the station. You can pick it up any-time that suits," he called as he got behind the wheel. And then he was gone.

Gran stood there in the open doorway, the cold winter air swirling around her, blowing her gray hair free from the bun at the nape of her neck and whipping it in her eyes. She brushed it away and watched her grandson out of sight.

Then she turned and without a word stalked across the hall to the stairs and climbed them.

Mrs. Ellis, trying to stifle her sobs, had shut her eyes, as if she couldn't bear to see the motorcar disappear down the lane. Then she got to her feet and without looking at me, murmured in a voice thick with tears, "I must speak to Molly about lunch."

And she was gone, leaving me there in the hall alone.

I didn't quite know what to make of what appeared to be Roger Ellis's altruism.

It dawned on me that he was running away, more than he was running to.

Who did he really believe murdered George Hughes? Davis Merrit for Lydia's sake—Lydia herself—or someone else in his own family?

For that matter, had he himself killed his friend? I couldn't see why. Unless it was to prevent Lieutenant Hughes from bringing that child home from France.

There was nothing I could do. For any of them. And if I left, they would be free to mourn Roger's decision in their own way.

I started for the door, but Margaret came in, concern drawing her brows together in a frown.

"What on earth is wrong with Mama? She's stripping Roger's bed as if her life depended on it. And I can't get a word out of her!"

"He's just left," I told her. "To rejoin his regiment."

"No, you must be mistaken. He didn't come to say good-bye—"

I didn't know how to answer her.

"It's Lydia, isn't it? He can't bear to be in the same house with her now."

"I don't think—" I began, attempting to say that it wasn't my place to pass judgment.

But Margaret cut across my words. "Don't try to defend her. Neither one of them is blame free, I'm aware of that. They've been at odds almost since Roger came home. But Lydia leaving for London the way she did was a last straw. And her work with Davis Merrit didn't help matters. Did she tell you? She refused to give it up, even after Roger asked her to break it off. I don't condone his striking her. But you can only push someone like my brother so far."

She paced to the hearth and back. "I don't know how Mama will cope. Not to mention Gran. It's really selfish of him to do this to all of us." But as she turned back toward me, still pacing, I could see the tears in her eyes.

"Your grandmother was terribly angry with him."

"As well she might be." She stopped in the middle of the room. "I must tell Henry. We were thinking of leaving this morning, but I expect we ought to stay on for a few more days. Until Mama has come to terms with what he's done. May I ask if you're planning to leave today?"

As a hint, it was rather broad. In her eyes, I was responsible for Lydia going to London. And I could easily understand that. "Yes, I expect I shall. If someone will send a message to The King's Head, for Simon Brandon. He's driving me to Somerset."

"Someone must retrieve Roger's motorcar from the railway station. If an hour's time will be convenient for you?"

"Yes, of course," I agreed politely. Then I asked, "Do you think Lydia will still wish to go with me?"

"We'll be very angry with her, if she does," Margaret answered tightly. "She's needed here. Henry and I can't stay more than a few extra days. And what then?"

"There's Alan's wife."

"No. It needs to be Lydia. She's Roger's wife, after all, and she has duties here."

I thought it a very selfish perspective, but didn't say so.

She left to speak to her husband, and I went to stand at the door, putting off speaking to Lydia. Looking out past the holly trees to the immense stretch of heath spread out before me, I found myself thinking about Roger Ellis, still wondering why he had made such a sudden and dramatic decision. There were so many reasons.

I broke off, looking at the vehicle turning out of the track into the lane that led to Vixen Hill. My first reaction was that Roger had come to his senses, then I realized that it was Simon's motorcar.

The cavalry had returned.

I went up to find Lydia and tell her what had happened.

"He's gone?" she asked, stunned. "But why?"

"He said he thought it was the only way to save your marriage. Perhaps he's right."

She shook her head vehemently. "No. I won't believe it. There's something else."

"He hoped you'd stay here at Vixen Hill, now that he's no longer in residence."

"No, that's not it either." She took a turn around the room, thinking, then stopped suddenly and grasped my arm in a grip that hurt. "He's going to find that child, Bess. I'd be ready to wager my life that he is. But why? To bring her home? There's no other reason, is there?"

I remember what George had said to me, that he shouldn't have waited for Roger Ellis to come to a decision about the little girl. He should have gone ahead and claimed her if he could.

Lydia went on, still gripping my arm, "He wants her dead, doesn't he? He doesn't want a reminder of Juliana. Juliana never grew up, you see, she's always and forever the perfect child. But a real reminder of Juliana might have a mind of her own, and even while she looked like Juliana, she might have a very different temperament. Was it fear of disillusionment that drove Roger to abandon her? Or the fact that he couldn't replace Juliana with a bastard child?"

If the child had looked like her mother, or a great-aunt, a very different child from Juliana, would Roger have been willing to take her in?

It was an interesting thought.

Lydia was saying, "You must find that little girl before Roger does. Do you hear, Bess? For my sake, as well as hers."

"Are you sure you want any part of her?" I asked. "Think about it, Lydia, there will be reminders of her mother in many of the things she does. Are you willing to live with that?"

"I may never have a child of my own," she told me bitterly, letting my arm go. "This may be all I ever have. Please, Bess, you must promise."

"I've told you. I can't promise anything. I have duties, Lydia, remember? I can't search France for one child while so many wounded need my care."

"But you will try?" she asked, as if she hadn't heard me. "When you can?"

"Yes, all right, I'll try," I said, "but I won't promise because it will be like hunting for the proverbial needle in a haystack."

"No, it won't," she told me, the force of conviction in her voice. "You've seen the portrait. You may not know a name, but you will know her face the instant you see it. And that's what matters."

There was nothing more I could say to change her mind, and so I told her that I'd glimpsed Simon coming up the drive.

"I'm going home, Lydia. You're safe now, there's nothing to fear."

To my surprise—I was expecting an uphill battle—she said, "Yes, it's the best thing for you. I've changed my mind. I'll stay here. It won't be easy, but I really was dreading facing London on my own. I was so frightened the last time, so lost and alone. That's why I wanted so badly to stay with you."

I hadn't realized that she'd been afraid of returning to London. She had been so adamant about leaving here. That was an indication of the stress driving her that she was willing to brave a city where she knew no one with the exception of me.

"Then you're not going with me?"

"No. I'll go and unpack straightaway. Somehow I must make it up to Gran and Mama Ellis for what he's done. They'll blame me. I can't change that. But I don't want them to realize why he left so precipitously."

I didn't tell her that Mrs. Ellis had already been in Roger's room, stripping the bedding. Instead I asked, "You will see Dr. Tilton again? About your concussion?"

"I promise. But I'm much better. Truly."

I thought it could be true. But I reminded her that if she couldn't keep her promise, she would only add to the burdens Gran and Mrs. Ellis carried.

We walked together into the passage, and she said with unexpected warmth, "I really am grateful to you, Bess, more than words can say. You must know that's true."

I thought perhaps it was, and smiled at her. "You know where to find me. Anytime," I told her. "But not in the dead of winter, please."

She laughed and embraced me quickly. "Thank Simon for me too."

I went in search of Mrs. Ellis and then Gran, but I couldn't find either of them. Daisy had admitted Simon, and I hurried to the hall to greet him.

We went together to my room and soon had the motorcar packed with my belongings.

"I can't leave without a note," I said. "Mrs. Ellis will think badly of me."

"Then write it, if that makes you feel better."

I had a thought. "Come with me to the drawing room. There's paper and pen there in one of the tables, I'm sure. Meanwhile, I want you to see the portrait over the hearth."

He came with me, and I heard the low whistle as he turned to look at Juliana.

"I don't think I've ever seen a more beautiful child," he said. "Or a more beautiful painting. Did she really look like that, I wonder?"

I found what I was after in the ornate little escritoire under the window and quickly wrote a brief message, thanking Mrs. Ellis and her family for their hospitality and kindness. Sealing the note, I wrote Mrs. Ellis's name on the envelope, but I couldn't help but wish I could have thanked her in person as well.

Simon was still studying the portrait when I said, "It's finished."

I left the note on a table in the hall, where someone was sure to see it, and we went out to the motorcar together.

He was cranking the motor when I happened to look up at the room above the hall. I don't know precisely why, but possibly it was because I felt eyes watching me from there.

Gran was standing by the window, looking down on the motorcar, Simon and me.

I smiled and waved, but she gave no indication she'd even recognized us. I knew perfectly well she had.

And I realized then that from that height, looking across the flat landscape of the heath, she might just be able to see the smoke from the engine as the train pulled out of Hartfield, carrying her grandson to his regiment.

We drove away from Vixen Hill, and I didn't look back. But I did look at the heath that quickly surrounded us and wondered if I would ever see it again.

As if he'd read my mind, Simon said, "I have a feeling it isn't finished, Bess. I heard the conclusions Inspector Rother drew from the evidence. I don't know if he got it right."

I turned to look at him. "You don't think Davis Merrit killed George Hughes?"

"It's not that," he said slowly. "It's just that something isn't right. And I can't put my finger on anything to support that feeling. The motive is missing, somehow."

"Did you know Roger Ellis has left to rejoin his unit?"

"Yes, I saw him on his way to the railway station. Or I assumed that's where he was heading. His kit was in the seat beside him." He paused. "Is that why Lydia Ellis isn't traveling with us?"

"She doesn't have to face her husband now. She wasn't looking forward to London, in spite of all she said. She wasn't ready to start a new life with no friends and no prospects."

"A measure of her fear," he agreed. "When I met her in London I could sense it. I'm just glad you're out of that house. I was afraid you'd have to stay until the inquest."

"That's odd, isn't it? That I haven't been asked to give evidence."

"It will probably be adjourned until they've found Merrit. And you may yet receive a summons. Much will depend on what motive Inspector Rother discovers. But the watch and the fact that Merrit left without warning or a word will count heavily against him."

"But did he pack up and leave? Or walk out of the house and never come home again?"

"Gossip says he left tea on the table. And that morning his horse came back to the stable without him."

I hadn't heard that.

"Well," I said. "It's over. But she wants me to search for that child, Simon."

"I don't think that would be wise. Didn't you say that Hughes told you she was in the care of nuns? She should be looked after well enough. What would you do if you found her?"

What, indeed. "Heaven knows there are enough orphans, thanks to this war."

"Sadly," he replied.

We had reached Hartfield and I saw the man Willy just stepping into the road, crossing it just beyond the shops. He looked up then, and his eyes met mine as he stopped, waiting for us to pass.

I had expected the vacant expression of a man whose wits were impaired.

But I could have sworn, in that brief contact, that he knew who I was. And I would have sworn as well that beneath the recognition was another expression.

I couldn't quite be sure of what it was. But the word that came to mind was *sly*.

If Simon noticed, he said nothing, busy driving through the early Monday morning traffic.

I spent a very happy Christmas with my family. It was good to be home, and I knew my parents were almost beside themselves with joy.

A letter arrived the day before Christmas Eve, forwarded by Mrs. Hennessey from London. It was from Lydia, and very brief.

Life here at Vixen Hill has settled into an armed truce. I don't think Gran has forgiven me, but even she can't hold a grudge for very long. Mama Ellis has heard from Roger, telling her that he'd

*arrived safely in France. But he hasn't written to
me. I'm glad I stayed. I never expected to say that,
but it's true.*

*There is no news about the inquiry into the
murder. The inquest was held on the Tuesday after
you left. After Dr. Tilton had established that poor
George was indeed murdered, Inspector Rother
asked that the inquest be adjourned until such
time as the whereabouts of a crucial witness, Davis
Merrit, could be determined and his statement be
entered into evidence. He was asked if the search
was limited to Sussex, and Inspector Rother
replied that the Chief Constable had asked that
Scotland Yard be brought into the case. Then
Inspector Rother was asked if he believed he knew
the identity of the murderer, and he answered that
he did, but was not prepared to make an arrest
until Davis was found. No motive was presented.
Nor were any of us required to give evidence,
except for Dr. Tilton, and no statements were
read. It was all very odd, according to Henry, who
knows more about such things. But I think it may
come out in the trial that after my visit to Davis,
he went in search of George. I still don't know why
he should have killed him. I imagine that's what
Inspector Rother must find out before he can*

proceed any further. But I dread being asked to give evidence in court, if it is Davis after all. Henry says it will be necessary and I must be prepared to brave it out. Meanwhile, we have been locking our doors at night. Vixen Hill was never locked before this. But with Roger away I think we all feel terribly vulnerable.

I must wish you back in France soonest. Roger has had a head start in the search. And that worries me even more than what Inspector Rother is up to.

A happy Christmas. I wish I could tell you it comes from all of us, but Gran refuses to be included. I don't quite understand why. But Mama Ellis believes that Gran blames you for insisting on looking for poor George, that if you'd left well enough alone that Saturday morning, he would never have been found and none of this terrible business would ever have happened. But it was Mama who insisted, wasn't it? And someone would have stumbled over the body, sooner or later. I hope you'll find it in your heart to forgive her.

I found it interesting that still no motive had been brought forward. More surprising was the fact that Dr. Tilton hadn't said a word about the events of that evening in the drawing room. Why? It was prime gossip, and he would surely have relished passing it on. But the Ellis family was a force in Ashdown Forest, and Dr. Tilton must have very wisely decided that telling this particular secret could see him ruined.

But perhaps, with the inquest out of the way, the hue and cry for Davis Merrit could commence in earnest. If he could be found, the police would do their best to find him now.

I would have given much to know what had become of him. That expression in Willy's eyes had disturbed me, and I couldn't quite put it out of my thoughts. After all, it was his possession of the watch that had made the case against Davis Merrit. Not just his disappearance.

Christmas Day passed, and the day after Boxing Day, Simon and the Colonel Sahib drove me to London to meet my train.

I said good-bye to my mother, as I always did, at the door of the house. I said good-bye to my father and to Simon at the door of the compartment of my train.

My father said, "I know you've had Ashdown on your mind, Bess. I've said nothing, because it takes time to put something like that behind you."

I didn't deny it. Instead I said, "It was very unpleasant, being a suspect in a murder inquiry. Even for so brief a time."

"I doubt that's what's been on your mind. Let it go. There's nothing more you can do."

I smiled and kissed him, then said good-bye to Simon.

As the train pulled out, I turned to wave, and saw both men staring after me with nearly the same expression on their faces.

Worry. As if they knew me too well to be taken in.

In truth, I was too busy the first weeks after my return to think about a child in an orphanage, but when there was a lull in the fighting, I was given a few days in the rear to rest.

And there I encountered two nuns with five small children who had been injured in the shelling, their parents killed. Soldiers had brought them to safety and seen to it that they were treated, but it was time to look at the wounds again to see how they were healing. It was work the nuns could do, but I saw their tired faces and worn hands, proof that they were overburdened as it was, and suppurating wounds were nasty to deal with.

I crossed to the tent where they were waiting in a long line with their charges, and I said to a nursing sister, "Shall I take a look at these for you?"

"Sister Crawford, would you mind?"

I took the nuns and the children aside, found a seat for them, and unwrapped the bandages around small arms and legs. Thank God the wounds had begun to close, and the nuns had kept them meticulously clean. I talked to the children as I worked, telling them as they watched me warily that all was well, and to mind the nuns about keeping their bandages tidy and in place.

A little girl clung to me, her eyes still shadowed. Sister Agnes, the younger nun, said to me in heavily accented English, "She lost her mother and younger brother. It has been very difficult. For a long time, she would not eat."

I turned to the child, and in my best schoolgirl French, asked her name.

"Marie Thérèse," she answered softly, hardly loud enough for me to hear her.

"What a pretty name! How old are you, Marie Thérèse?"

"Six," she replied after a moment. "My brother was only four."

"What was his name?"

"Henri. After our father."

"Ah. A good name, Henri. Did he have blue eyes like yours?"

"No, they were not blue. There was brown in them."

"Did you and Henri play games together?"

This time she nodded vigorously and began to list their games. I had finished examining her broken arm, which was healing well. It had been a compound fracture, and surgery had been necessary to reset it.

"My arm was broken too. Almost a year ago," I told her as I helped her put hers back in its sling. Pushing up my sleeve, I showed her where my break had occurred. Her eyes grew large, and she touched it with a small finger.

"There is no scar," she said, wonderingly.

"And the scar on your arm will also disappear. If you mind the Sisters and take good care of it."

"Henri's neck was broken," she told me then. "There was no way to heal it."

I could have taken her in my arms and held her close, but I smiled and said, "It didn't hurt, you know. Necks are not like arms."

She nodded.

At that moment, an Australian soldier strode by, a tall man, broad shouldered and fair. I stopped him and indicated the children. "Do you by any chance have chocolates, Sergeant?"

He grinned down at me. "I believe I do." The children were staring at him, round-eyed, and watching as he dug into his kit. He came up with a very flat chocolate bar and handed it to me. I thanked him, knowing well that chocolates were treats even for the men. Hadn't Princess Mary's Christmas Gift in 1914 included sweets for those who didn't smoke?

I handed the bar to the Sisters, to be shared with the children on the journey back to their convent.

As they prepared to take their leave, effusive in their gratitude, I hugged the children, then said to the younger nun before she turned away, "As a matter of fact, I'm looking for a child. She's half English, and her father has been searching for her since her mother died." I described her, using Juliana's portrait as my guide. "Have you seen her? Do you know where I could find her?"

But they hadn't seen her, had no idea where I might begin to look.

"Convents from the north have been taken in by other houses wherever possible," she told me. "And a few have been given shelter by benefactors. With so many children displaced by the war, it is difficult to keep proper records. Some are too young to know how they are called. And for others, like this little one"— she touched the head of a boy who must have been close to two years old—"there is no village name or family name." She shrugged, that very Gallic shrug that said, *What can one do?*

I thanked them, and watched them go.

"That's a bonny lass, that little one."

I jumped, unaware that the Australian was still there just behind me.

"Yes, she is," I said, wondering what life held in store for such children.

"If you ask me," he replied, echoing my own thoughts, "those are the real victims in this bloody war—begging your pardon, Sister. I sometimes wonder what's ahead of them. And what sort of men and women they'll grow up to become."

"At least these have found shelter," I said. "That counts for something."

"Does it? My best friend's mother came out from England when she was seven. Taken from a poor house where her own mother had just died and consigned to a convict ship filled with thieves and whores and the scum of the prisons. She was raped before she reached Australia, and then served as an indentured servant to a family who nearly worked her to death. My friend's great-aunt took pity on her and rescued her. She turned out to be a fine woman. She never spoke of her trials. She said she had put them behind her. She was the bravest woman I ever knew." There was pride mixed with an old anger in his voice.

"She must have been, to survive."

"My friend was set on going to England after the war is finished and finding the men who put her on that ship. But of course they must all be dead now. What's more, my friend is dead. Killed last week. So, with any luck, he's caught up with them at last."

He touched his hat to me and was gone. I stood there, looking after him. And then the nursing sisters were calling to me, asking my help with a delirious patient who had taken a turn for the worse. From what I saw of his leg, swollen around the ankle and purple with gangrene, I knew it would have to come off, and soon. He wouldn't make it alive to England otherwise.

Half an hour later a surgeon's assistant came for him.

I spent my few days of respite asking if anyone knew of other convents in the vicinity that had taken in orphan children, but no one seemed to be aware of any.

One doctor, his apron dark with other men's blood, said, "Why do you want to know?"

"Curiosity," I replied. "I treated those five children who were here on Tuesday."

"Hmmmph," he answered. "Thought you might be one of those wanting us to take on the care of the civilian population. Leave that to the French doctors. We've got enough on our hands as it is, trying to save the men who get this far."

"What happened to the Corporal with the gangrenous foot?" I asked.

"Didn't survive. Bled to death, in spite of all we could do. Just as well. When I got in there I could see it wasn't just his foot we'd have to take, but the entire leg, if he was to have any chance at living. Too little too late."

He nodded and walked away, leaving me standing there. I went back to my assigned quarters and bathed before lying down on my bed.

It was hopeless, trying to find that child. I couldn't imagine that Roger Ellis would have had any better luck. Even though he had come back to France while he still had nearly ten days of leave. Had he looked then, or gone directly to his regiment? She was lost in a sea of humanity. Perhaps after the war—but that could be years away, in spite of what was being said about the Americans soon turning the tide. With their ships being destroyed by German torpedoes, how could they resupply themselves, or bring in fresh troops? It would, I thought wearily, be more likely that the Germans and their allies and the British and their allies would simply fight each other to a standstill, until there were no more men, no more shells, and no more bullets left on either side.

I fell asleep for a few hours, and then went back again to see if I could help. But there had been a lull in the long line of wounded being convoyed back to us, some of them on omnibuses painted khaki, and I finally had an evening to write letters home and indulge myself in a long, hot bath. If I could find someone to heat the water and haul it to my quarters.

I returned to the Front when my relief was up. On the third day, while bandaging the head of a young private who came from Sussex, I asked if he'd ever been to Ashdown Forest.

"No, Sister. I'd never left Eastbourne, until I joined the Army."

"Do you by any chance know Captain Roger Ellis, of Vixen Hill, near Hartfield?"

His eyes brightened. "That I do. I served under him for a time. Took good care of us, he did. He said Sussex men must stand up for each other."

It was a side of Roger I hadn't seen before. "He's liked by his men?"

"Trusted is the word. You always knew where you stood with him."

Noting the past tense, I said, "Knew?"

He grinned. "Sorry. What was left of our company was sent along to another regiment to make up their numbers."

"Then he's still alive."

"Oh, yes. There's a rumor that he got to Paris one day. Bluffed his way onto a convoy. Went to see the dancing girls, someone said. Perhaps he did. Perhaps not. But he came back from Paris with a bottle of champagne. It was the most expensive he'd ever paid for, he said, and gave each of his men a taste."

A very different Roger Ellis from the man I'd encountered in Ashdown Forest. I wondered if Lydia had seen this side of him before the war. If so, I could understand why she had found the man who came home on compassionate leave almost a stranger.

I moved on to the next patient, and then it was another day, and the fighting was fierce in one sector. We began seeing the casualties around noon. It was in a brief lull that I was reminded of what the young private had said. That Roger Ellis had gone to Paris to see the dancing girls.

It occurred to me that it was a story certain to please his men. And that wherever he went, it was to find a small child who had reminded a dead man of Juliana.

Eleven

One morning we were brought a dozen Australian wounded, men there was no room for in the crowded forward aid station but who were not severe enough cases to be sent back for major surgery. They were, for the most part, shrapnel victims where bursting shells tore through flesh and bone and sinew.

We had been warned to prepare for them, and the first inkling we had that they were arriving was an assortment of whistles and jeers and general catcalls, from the English Tommies lying on stretchers or sitting on whatever they could find. It was all good-natured, a rivalry of long standing. And then I heard the most maniacal laughter, so wild and crazed that I went to see what was wrong, expecting some sort of head wound. A burst of laughter followed the sound, and at that moment a tall Aussie Sergeant was limping toward me.

He greeted me just as I recognized him as the soldier I'd asked for chocolate when the nuns had brought in the five wounded children a few weeks earlier.

"Still searching for that little girl?" he asked, one hand gripping his other arm at the shoulder. I could see beneath the hasty field dressings that it was lacerated, deep wounds still bleeding.

There was no time to answer—the other sisters were there, and we got the Australian soldiers inside and began evaluating their wounds.

The Sergeant insisted that we look at his men before he would allow us to touch him, and as I worked on a leg wound, cleaning it and removing bits of shell, he sauntered over, clapped the young private on the back, and said, "Good lad."

The boy—for he hardly seemed more than that—grinned weakly. He was pale, his teeth clenched against the pain, but his Sergeant's praise saw him through his ordeal.

The Sergeant then turned to me. "Ever find that lass you were looking for?" he asked again.

I was surprised he'd remembered our conversation.

"No luck so far."

"You're not going about it the right way," he told me. "Put the word out, let others be on the lookout for her."

I hesitated, for I realized that word could easily get back to Roger Ellis that an English nursing sister was searching for a fair-haired orphan. But even if it did, there wasn't much he could do about it, was there?

"I'd like to find her," I said over my shoulder as I bandaged another soldier's back. "Someone I knew was set on finding her and bringing her back to England. He wasn't the father, but he knew the father didn't care enough to rescue her. Only he was killed before he could return to France."

"Killed?" the Sergeant asked, frowning. "In England, you mean?"

"He was murdered," I admitted. "It's a long story, but never mind. I just want to find her, and then perhaps her family can be persuaded to bring her home. She'll have a better life than she could have here in this war-torn country."

"I'll put the word out," he told me. "Describe her again."

I did. "It must seem quite fantastical, but she ought to be just that pretty."

"If you've never set eyes on the lass, how do you know so clearly what she looks like?"

A perceptive question. I smiled.

"There's a portrait of another child—a—a relative of this one. I was told she bears a strong family resemblance to Juliana. That's how I know what to look for."

"A needle in a haystack," he said cheerfully, "but we'll do what we can."

One of his men began to scream as Sister Bedford probed for an elusive bit of shrapnel.

The Sergeant was there, saying, "Buck up, my lad, you don't want those Tommies out there laughing up their sleeves at us."

The soldier grinned sheepishly. "No, Sergeant. But it damned well *hurts.*"

"You can scream at the Hun when we get back to our lines."

That brought a shout of laughter from the others.

While I appreciated the Sergeant's willingness to help—I was grateful, in fact—I rather thought he was enjoying flirting with me, and as soon as he and his company were back in the line, my orphan child would be forgotten.

The Sergeant himself took the painful digging in his shoulder stoically, tight lipped and teeth clenched. I could see the muscle in his jaw clearly.

When we'd finished, he ordered his men to follow him, and "stop cluttering up the sisters' ward."

I said, "Wait, where is the man with the head wound?"

He looked at me, then scanned his company. "The only one with the head wound didn't make it, Sister," he said, frowning. "Unless you're counting Teddy, there, of course."

He gestured to the private who had had bits of shrapnel in his scalp.

"I'm sorry," I said, thinking that the man must have died outside the station. I added, "But I daresay your man Teddy will survive."

"You'd better believe he will," the Sergeant said, grinning. "I promised his mother special."

And they were gone.

One of the sisters working on a stretcher case watched them walk away. "I do like tall men," she commented. "And that one in particular."

My next encounter with the Australian Sergeant was nearly a fortnight later, in the form of a message brought to me by a Scottish Corporal who had met him on a muddy road outside Ypres. The Corporal's arm was in a makeshift sling, and I could tell before I had cut away his sleeve that it was badly broken. He said, his face pale with pain, "Is there a Sister here called Crawford?"

"I'm Sister Crawford," I said as I finished with the scissors and laid bare the broken limb.

"I'm to gie ye this, then," he answered, and with his good hand, he fished a slip of dirty paper from his blouse. "There's a Sergeant Larimore fra' Australia who's been sending messages back by any wounded laddie he meets."

"Ah, the Australian," I said, smiling, taking the sheet and opening it. I found it was a list of orphanages that he'd somehow come up with by questioning everyone in sight, or so it appeared. I could never have collected such a list on my own, not without weeks of intense searching.

"Bless him," I said, after scanning it.

The Corporal replied, "If it's only a list that will make ye smile, I'll draw up one masel'."

Shaking my head, I said, "It's not any list. I'm searching for a convent that used to be in a house on the road south of Ypres. They took in a number of orphans, but with the fighting had to move south to Calais. After that I've lost touch with them. There's a child in that group of orphans that I'm trying to find, for a—a friend."

"Ye'll niver find one child in the hotch potch of religious houses," he said earnestly. "Ye ken, there's likely one on ivery corner."

Spoken like a true Scots Covenanter, I thought, *scandalized by Catholic France.*

The doctor had come to have a look at his arm, and I prepared to move away.

"Is it important, Sister?" the Corporal asked. "Yon list."

"Very."

"Aye, well, I'll pass the word back," he told me, and I thanked him.

It was another week before I could take the few days coming to me and find a lift to Calais. An officer, a Major Fielding, was carrying dispatches to be sent on to London, something to do with ordnance, and as I got down near the harbor, he said, "Do you drive, Sister Crawford?"

"Yes, sir, I do."

"Then keep the motorcar, will you? I'll be back from London in three days and I'd like to find it here whole, not commandeered or stripped of parts badly needed elsewhere. It's my own motorcar, you see."

"Thank you, sir! I'll take good care of it."

"See that you do. And meet me here on the dot of noon in three days' time."

I saw him off and gratefully turned the motorcar to go in search of the house where the nuns had taken shelter after leaving their convent on the road to Ypres.

Easier said than done. When I stopped a French priest and asked him where to look, he shrugged in that Gallic expression of ignorance.

"What can I say, Sister. There are so many houses dispossessed by this war. But if you go to the church two streets over, the one whose tower is visible from here, they may be able to help you."

And so I found myself in the office of the monsignor of St. Catherine's Church.

He was a thin man, prematurely aged by war and responsibility, but he took time to listen to me.

I showed him my list, courtesy of the Australian Sergeant, and he scanned it quickly.

"You permit?" he asked, pen poised over the sheet of paper. When I nodded, he began to make notes. "This house had only six elderly nuns," he said, "And this one is now in Rouen, but I don't know if they have orphans in their care. Their duty before the war was to the sick, much like yourself, and in particular, the care of the elderly and aged, many of whom have nowhere else to go. This next house is also in Rouen, and it may be the one you seek. But I make no promises. This and this and this house are now scattered." He shrugged again. "Alas, I have no way of knowing where the rest may be. We are endeavoring to keep up with the displacement of religious houses, but there are so many, and I am one man."

As I thanked him for his assistance, he asked, "What is your business with this child you seek?"

"I don't know," I told him truthfully. "But it's a charge I was given, to find her and make certain that she is safe."

"Is the child's mother French?"

"I was told that she was. Which is why the child is in an orphanage. The father, we believe he is an English officer, didn't know that the mother of the child died, and by the time he discovered that, she was already in this orphanage or another like it."

"And why is he not seeking this child himself?"

"I have reason to believe that he is. But France is wide, and one child is hard to find."

"And you do not know how this child is called?"

"If I did," I said, "it would make my task easier. But I do know what she looks like, and if I see her, it's possible that I will recognize her."

He considered me for a moment. "There was someone here also searching for a small child. I was not in Calais, you understand, and my housekeeper told this Englishman, an officer, that we could not help him. She was suspicious, you see. She did not think he was"—he looked for the right word—"'so frantic as a father should be, if his child was missing.'"

"Does she remember when this Englishman came—and what he looked like?"

"It was three weeks ago. I know, because I was in Lille at the time."

Then it wasn't George Hughes, trying to discover where the nuns at the convent on the Ypres road had gone. It had to be Roger Ellis.

. . . so frantic as a father should be, if his child was missing.

"Why then was he searching for the little girl?" I asked, curious.

"I have no idea." He smiled. "She is afraid, Madame Buvet, that he would take the child to England and rear her as a heretic."

"Is that so terrible, if she is loved and given a proper home?"

"In the mind of my housekeeper, better an orphan than a heretic."

"But you have helped me."

"You are a nursing sister. I believe that you are concerned for the welfare of this little girl."

"And if the English officer comes again?"

"I shall judge him for myself. And then I shall decide what is best to do."

I thanked him again, and went out to the motorcar. Three private soldiers from a Yorkshire regiment had lifted the bonnet, and when I appeared, they quickly lowered it again. "Sister," they said, almost in unison, coming smartly to attention. "May we turn the crank for you?" one of them asked.

I could see then why Major Fielding had feared for the safety of his transport. I was pleased to find that the motor did turn over and nothing appeared to be missing as I drove on.

It was not far to Rouen, as a French crow might fly. But given the heavy traffic of military vehicles and the condition of the roads, I didn't arrive in the city until well after midnight. For a mercy the town was quiet. The Base Hospital in the old race course was brightly lit, but the motor ambulance convoys, lorries, and omnibuses bringing in the wounded were thin on the ground with the lull in the fighting. Even the trains that brought in many of the wounded were idle. The raw recruits had already marched up from the River Seine and found their billets for the night. No one had the energy to fill the bistros and the corner wine shops at this hour.

This English Base Hospital for the wounded was manned by American doctors and nurses, filling in the decimated ranks of English medical men. Indeed, the shortage had become acute. I'd sent patients to them from the advanced dressing stations and knew that they did good work. But I never quite understood why the permanent buildings at the course had been turned into offices and the wounded were housed in tents.

Ever mindful of the fact that I must return to meet Major Fielding in one more day's time, I knocked at the door of a house on Rue des Champignons that an elderly gendarme had directed me to in the maze of half-timbered housing in an older quarter near the river.

The sleepy nun acting as porter opened the small peephole in the door and peered out at me. "What do you want of us at this hour, Mademoiselle?" she asked in French heavily accented by the Breton tongue.

"I'm an English nursing sister," I said, for that she could see for herself. "I've come to ask if you have children here, orphans. We treated several children some time ago, and I wish to be certain that they are no longer in need of care."

"You are from the Base Hospital? But we have no children here, Sister. There is no space for the little ones. We have only the aged and the dying."

Disappointed, I asked, "But did you have children at one time? There was a very young nun who brought them to me. I'm sorry I don't remember her name."

"We have no young nuns here. You must be mistaken. But we did have thirteen children at one time."

"And where are they now?"

"Here in Rouen." And she gave me the direction of another house, this one on the Rue St. Jean.

I thanked her and drove on. In the dark, it was very difficult to find this particular house. It was south of the cathedral, and as I crossed the Place in front of it, I looked up at the great west front, the lacey stonework and niches so heavily shadowed in the starlight that they were almost sinister, the faces of the saints dark and unreadable. Above my head, the three great towers were stark against the night sky, the iron tower at the center almost lost in the blackness of the night.

The house I was looking for was on a back street in a quarter that a century ago had been prosperous, the buildings huddled cheek by jowl with their neighbors, as if for comfort and support. Still, it was large enough to accommodate several nuns and their charges.

I knocked on the door, but no one answered my summons, and so I sat in the motorcar until a murky dawn began to break. By that time I was so cold and stiff I could hardly get out and walk to the door.

An elderly nun answered my summons, although she had taken her time about it. And I saw why, when the door swung open, for beneath her woolen robes, one foot was encased in a heavy boot with a thick sole, designed to make the left leg the same length as the right.

She asked my business, and I again used the ploy that I had come to see if the children that had been treated at the English aid station were in need of further care.

To my utter relief, she invited me into the foyer. It was a blessed reprieve from the morning cold outside, although still hardly what I would consider warm.

"We have fifteen orphans here," she was saying. "None of them to my knowledge treated by the English."

She made it sound as if they would have been treated by the devil and his cohorts, but I smiled and asked if I could see the other children, since I was here.

"Yes, it is hard to find medicines for the little ones. Do you have medicines? Come with me."

She led me through a labyrinth of rooms to a large kitchen, where a small fire had been built on a hearth large enough to roast an ox. A kettle of what appeared to be something like porridge was bubbling on the hob, and I could feel my mouth water.

At a long table sat the children, who fell silent and looked up from their bowls to stare at me with wide dark eyes, wary and uncertain. I was sure that strangers seldom brought good tidings to this house. Another nun, older than the first, was also staring at me, pausing as she stirred the contents of the black iron pot.

My heart plummeted when I realized that the youngest of the fifteen was nearly five. And I had never seen any of them before.

"Are there by any chance younger children here?" I asked the nun.

"Younger?" she asked sharply, straightening up.

"Yes. In particular a little girl of perhaps two years of age. Very fair, very sweet smile."

"There is a little boy upstairs, badly burned from falling into the fire. But no little girl."

"Then I will see the little boy, if you like."

"He has been treated by the local doctor," the nun said, returning to her pot. I could see that she didn't care for my coming here. I wondered what her experience of the war had been, for I could see that she had a long scar, healed but still raw and red, down one side of her face.

"Then he's in good hands," I assured her. "Do you know where I might find this little girl? Is there another orphanage in Rouen?"

I was prepared to hear that there was not. It was the first nun who answered me, after a quick glance at her companion.

"Three streets away, in Rue St. Catherine, there is another house, not of our order. But they have some nine children there, I believe. Mostly infants younger than these."

"Thank you," I said, then asked, "Is there anything I can do for you?"

"There's no money for anything. The church does what it can. But there are so many refugees. It's very difficult."

I thought at first she was asking me for money, for a donation for the children. And then I realized she was saying something else, that the war had disrupted her quiet life in a convent devoted to prayer and contemplation. Instead she was struggling to feed and dress and care for children in a dilapidated house in a town that was within hearing of the guns that had changed all their lives. I had to wonder if her faith had been tested almost beyond her ability to cope.

I nodded and made my way back through the warren of rooms that couldn't be kept warm or made more comfortable. And growing children needed more than just porridge. But there were shortages in England as well. What was happening in Germany? Were they suffering too?

I drove on to the house the nun had described.

It too was old and tired, and the smoke coming from its chimneys was thin and discouraging. I lifted the weather-etched iron anchor and let it drop against the iron plate.

This time the nun who came to the door was frail, her face lined, but her eyes were a vivid blue that was in sharp contrast to the soft, sagging skin of age. "Sister," she said, "how may we help you?"

"I'm looking for a child," I said, giving her the same account that I had used before.

She smiled. "That would be Sophie. Yes, come in. I'm Sister Marie Joseph."

The carpet was threadbare, the furniture in desperate need of polish, the walls in dire need of paint, patches of the ornate ceiling stained by water from a roof that most probably should have been replaced even before the war.

"Tell me how you knew about Sophie?" she asked, offering me a chair. I could understand that she was reluctant to let me, a stranger, see Sophie, and what I was about to say would determine whether or not I would be allowed beyond this parlor.

I tried to explain that someone in England had begged me to find her.

She nodded. "Her mother told me that the father was English."

"And she is dead?"

"Oh, yes, of a raging fever a week after childbirth. We had taken her in, she had nowhere else to go. She had gone to market the day that a shell landed squarely on the kitchen of her house. She came to us, then, already in her fifth month of pregnancy. A lovely young woman, I must tell you. She was an enormous help to us for as long as her health was good. But we lacked the food she needed. Not enough milk or meat, but still, she would have lived but for the fever."

"May I see the child?" I asked. "I have come a long way."

"She's asleep, but yes, you may look in on her. You will carry the lamp for me, please."

She climbed the stairs with an effort, holding on to the banister and almost pulling herself up the narrow steps.

In a bedroom on the first floor were two cribs, and in one of them, wrapped in a blue blanket with a ragged fringe was a little girl with golden hair that shimmered in the dark like a halo as the lamplight struck it. She lay asleep with her thumb in her mouth, the edge of a night dress just visible at her throat.

I moved quietly into the room to see her better. In the next crib was another little girl, perhaps a year or so older, but small framed for her age.

The elderly nun said softly, "Is she the child?"

I couldn't see her eyes or her smile, I couldn't see her face fully.

But I had no doubt that this was the little girl George Hughes had seen.

"Has she always been in your care?" I asked softly.

The elderly nun said, "Our house was larger and we had more children. But of necessity we have had to separate, some to the Loire, near Angers, and others to Caen. Wherever we could be taken in. The children too have been separated. This house was given to us by a family that was moving to Marseilles, away from the war altogether. They feared another German break-through. And we've been fearful ourselves. But there is nowhere to go."

And the family had been clever, leaving these nuns in charge of their home. It wouldn't be vandalized or, worse, filled with refugees desperate for a roof over their heads.

I crossed the room and put a hand on the child's silky hair.

And realized that she was feverish.

I said something to the nun, and she nodded. "It's been a trial for all of us. She sleeps now, because we have given her a drop of something to help her. But we can find no cause for this fever. The doctor has been called to her. He says she is teething."

But teething was not the problem, I was sure of it. "How long has it been going on?"

"It rose the night before this last."

I reached into the bed and unfolded the blanket that had been a barrier against the cold in this room. Then I lifted the little nightdress that was too large by half.

What I saw made me draw back quickly.

"She has chicken pox. It has finally erupted. I must wash my hands at once, for I work with wounded men. But I will tell you how to treat her. And you must remove this other child quickly. She and the others may have been exposed already. But if you keep Sophie quarantined, you may escape a general outbreak."

"But when I bathed her last evening, there were no spots," she said, leaning over the crib to examine Sophie's back.

"No, possibly not. But warm water would have hastened the eruption. Please cover her again. I dare not touch her."

The nun gently drew the nightdress together again and then tucked the blanket around the child.

Between us we moved the other crib into another room where one of the nuns slept. And then I was shown to a kitchen where I could wash my hands with a scrap of carbolic soap and dried them on a towel that had seen better days.

"Soap is hard to come by," the nun said, apologizing.

"I understand," I said, wishing I had a cake to give her.

The problem was, if Sophie was ill, leaving here with her was out of the question. Even if I could persuade Sister Marie Joseph to allow me to take her. For that matter, where could I take her? A dressing station was no place for a child. And I had no more leave coming to me for the foreseeable future. Was Lydia even of the same mind about wanting her? I could try to find Roger Ellis, but was that wise? I hadn't been able to read his intentions toward this child. Still, she must be his. She couldn't look so much like Juliana if she weren't.

After that one letter from Lydia reporting the inquest, there had been no others. I didn't know whether they had failed to reach me or she hadn't written.

I said to Sister Marie Joseph after I'd washed my hands and accepted the offer of a little coffee from their precious store, "I know this child's family. I wish to ask them what they would have me do, now that Sophie has been found. Will you keep her here, until I've learned what is expected of me?"

"I would like to see this child—indeed all the children—safe. But we have been charged with her care, and I cannot simply hand her over to you or anyone else, without some proof that you have the authority to take her."

"I understand," I said. "You must be assured that this is not a frivolous request."

"I permitted you to see her, because you are a nursing sister," she went on. "A woman I could trust with the knowledge that she is here. And to reassure her

English father that she has not been abandoned. But beyond that, there is nothing I can do until it is decided that she belongs in your charge. There is an *avocat*—a lawyer," she added in English when I frowned over the term, "here in Rouen who arranged for this house to be left in our care. You must speak with him, and if he agrees to represent this child, we will abide by whatever decision he makes for her future. There could be the question too of any inheritance. It's possible that her mother's husband provided for her."

"That's very fair," I said. I hadn't considered a French husband.

She rose in a swirl of black wool, and I knew she was pleased with my answer. Crossing to the small desk behind where I was sitting, she found paper and pen and wrote out the name and the direction of the French solicitor. Bringing it to me, she said, "Sophie is very pretty—it will not serve her well, this beauty, in the future. We cannot protect her always. You understand?"

"I do understand. Completely. Has anyone else come in search of her?"

"No. We were certain that the father must be dead. To abandon such a young child seemed cruel. Unless of course he has a wife in England. These things happen, you know."

Sadly, I did.

Thanking her, I left the house and went out to the Major's motorcar. Turning it, I drove back the way I had come to prevent getting lost in the twisting streets. It had started to rain, the cobblestones slippery and grimy under a darkening sky.

I had just passed the cathedral for the second time, searching for the Street of Fishes, where the *avocat* lived, when I saw that another motorcar was coming toward me. I pulled over as far as I dared in the narrow, medieval street, to allow it to pass me. The wings were dented and the paint was scratched but I recognized it as English, then looked up to see who was driving it.

He must have turned to look in my direction because I was conspicuous in my blue coat and hat. Anyone in this part of France could identify my uniform at a glance.

Our eyes met, and I recognized Captain Ellis in the same instant he recognized me.

Twelve

What was Roger Ellis doing in Rouen? Was he this close to finding little Sophie too?

His reflexes were faster than mine. He spun the wheel, and before I could grasp what he was intending, he'd turned his motorcar across the path of mine, and it was all I could do to grip the brake hard enough to prevent the Major's motorcar from crashing into his.

He was already out of his vehicle, and before I could reverse, he had opened the near passenger-side door and slid into the seat beside me.

"Are you following me?" he demanded, flushed with anger.

Quickly rethinking the situation, I said, "No. I'm on leave. What are you doing here?"

"Whose motorcar is this?"

"It's none of your business."

"Pull over."

"No. Why?"

"Because the middle of the road is nowhere to talk."

My first reaction was to tell him I would do nothing of the sort, and then I thought about Sophie, and I decided that agreeing with him might make more sense than refusing and driving away, leaving him to do as he pleased after I was gone.

"All right."

He was instantly suspicious. "I'll stay here until you do."

I reversed, found a place to leave the motorcar, then got out and walked with the Captain to his, waiting while he pulled it out of the middle of the road and brought it around behind the Major's vehicle.

Then, taking my arm, he guided me to a small bistro that was still open just down the street. It was narrow, grimy, and filled with the smoke of those French cigarettes that caught at the back of the throat. I coughed as he led me to a small table. The top was ringed with circles from the glasses of previous occupants, and I felt like taking out a handkerchief and wiping it clean. The proprietor came over, nodding, and swiped at the circles with a cloth that might once have been white.

I had expected to be the only woman present, but while I was the only one in uniform, there were a number of others, mostly middle-aged and in black. In the provinces, French women wore black as a rule, but I had a feeling from their long, joyless faces that this was mourning, not fashion. There were no young men present, only those past the age of military service, or even elderly. There was very little conversation, as if everyone was sunk in his or her own thoughts.

Roger Ellis ordered wine and asked if I preferred a coffee. I nodded, wanting to keep a clear head.

"Why are you in Rouen?" he asked a second time.

"I told you, I'm on leave."

"Sister Crawford. You are driving a motorcar that isn't your own, and you'd hardly take an excursion to Rouen, which is crowded with refugees and new recruits, just to have a look at the cathedral. Where are you staying?"

"I'm not. As you say, I came to see the cathedral. I was driving back to Calais when you saw me."

"You're here to find that child."

I was tempted to tell him her name was Sophie, and she'd just been diagnosed with chicken pox, to see if he cared at all.

Instead I said, "Why are you so certain that I have any interest in your child?"

"She's not my child."

"Lieutenant Hughes told you that night in the drawing room that she was the image of Juliana."

"He was drunk and confused."

The waiter came with a glass of wine and a cup of coffee on a tray, setting them down before us.

"Where were you then, when you told your men you'd been in Paris?"

That shocked him.

"Who told you about that?"

"I don't precisely remember. Perhaps it was an Australian Sergeant with shrapnel in his shoulder."

Anger flared in his face. "Don't deliberately annoy me."

"I'm not. I'm simply treating you with the same courtesy you've shown to me."

The flush faded, and he grinned in spite of himself. "Yes, I'm sorry. But you see, you're a friend of Lydia's, not mine. And I wouldn't put it past her to take it into her head to want this child, whether it's mine or not. Which I must say surprises me, because she gave the impression once or twice that she was jealous of Juliana."

"I don't think either of you really knows the other. Three years of war can be a very long time in a marriage. Whether they want to or not, people change, and especially with the strain of war. She'd hardly got to know you when you went off to France. And when you did come home, you didn't appear to be overjoyed to see her. And you were violent."

"Yes, all right, I deserved that. I didn't intend to hit her. It was just that—well, never mind, you weren't there. I needn't bore you with my worries."

"It might help me to understand why you are so adamant that this child isn't yours, and yet here you are in Rouen for the same reason you claim I've come here. That's why you were so displeased when you saw me. To put it mildly. You almost wrecked my motorcar."

Roger Ellis took a deep breath. His wine remained untouched, while the one sip I'd taken of my coffee made me wonder what had been substituted for coffee beans.

"May I call you Bess?" he asked, catching me off guard. "It seems ridiculous to stand on social ceremony at this stage."

"Please do."

"Thank you. When I was wounded, I was in great pain and frightened because I overheard the doctors debating whether or not to take my arm. At least I thought they were discussing me. Apparently I was mistaken, because when I woke up, too terrified to look at my right side for fear I'd see an empty sleeve, I lay there with my eyes shut. Very cowardly of me, I realize that. But the thought of going home to Lydia half a man was something I couldn't contemplate. The nursing sister who tended me was a young woman, much like you, who finally said to me that if I didn't sit up and eat, they would have to send me to England to recover. That was the only threat that would have worked, because the last thing I could face was that. I hated her with all my heart, but I opened my eyes, and when she handed me the fork, I was so busy being angry that from habit I reached for it—and a pain shot through my shoulder so fierce, I turned to look at the hand. And it was there. I was so weak with relief she took pity on me and fed me, thinking I was about to pass out from lack of food. I never told her what was going through my mind. I was too ashamed. There were other men in the ward with horrendous injuries, and I had been too wrapped up in myself to notice. I made up for it, helping feed some of the patients once they allowed me out of bed."

I said, "You haven't been the only man who feared amputation. I've had to hold them afterward, when they cried."

"A doctor asked me if I wished to go to England to recover, and I couldn't accept when there were so many others in worse shape. So they found me a house in a little village behind the lines. Chalfleur, it was.

And the woman in that house was much like Lydia. Her husband was at the Front, she hadn't heard from him in weeks. While I was there, he came home on a twenty-four-hour pass, which meant he had less than twelve hours with her. And two weeks after he left, she got me drunk one night and slept with me. That was the only time, and I left the next day."

He drank a little of his wine and made a face. I thought it must be as bad as my coffee.

"At any rate, some months later I received a letter from Claudette, telling me that her husband had been killed, and that she was expecting his child. I was glad for her and wrote to let her know I was. The next message I had was that she had given birth to a little girl, and that she wanted me to know that the child must be mine, not her husband's. I didn't want to believe it. For my sins, I didn't answer the letter, and then word came that she'd died. I sent what money I could scrape together to the convent where she'd been taken, for her burial and to ask the nuns to look after her child. After that I sent money regularly. But then the fighting drove the nuns and their charges south, and by the time I'd learned of it, I was in the middle of the Somme fighting and there was no way to trace them. Afterward I was too tired to try, and I told myself that I'd done all I could. But George got it into his head that I was hiding something and started his own search. And apparently he found the nuns and saw this child." He shrugged. "You know the rest, I think."

"He was going to adopt her himself. With Malcolm dead, I think he wanted to believe he had someone at home. A tie to life, as it were."

"Yes, and I begrudged him even that. Because I knew if the child did look like Juliana, my family would hear of it soon enough. And Lydia would know who the father was. But by law, the child is not mine. Since Claudette's husband didn't disown it—in fact died before he knew she'd borne it—it carries his name, and not mine. It is—was—legally his." He shook his head. "God knows, there are enough orphans in France. Why did George insist on saving that particular one?"

"Because he loved Juliana, just as you did. And he wanted in some fashion to bring her back again. In war, these things seem important. Because life is important."

"I know. And because George is dead, I realized that I had to shoulder my own responsibility. I've looked, when I could. The question is, have you had any better luck? Is she here in Rouen, is that why you've come here?"

I didn't know what to say. Could I trust him? Could I believe anything he'd told me? It had the ring of truth. Watching him, watching his eyes as he spoke, I thought it was probably the truth. But he had changed stripes so many times that I wondered whether to tell him or not.

The thought occurred to me that he could be killed in the next action, and then what would I do about Sophie?

I said, buying a little time, "What will you do if you find the little girl? You've talked to me about responsibility, about George and his foolishness over her, about the fact that she doesn't bear your name. You seem to have no feeling at all for the mother, even though you slept with her."

"I liked her very well, Bess. She had a very appealing laugh. Her eyes crinkled at the corners when she was amused. And she was well read. Don't mistake me, she wasn't a loose woman, she was quite respectable. And rather pretty. But I didn't fall in love with her. It wasn't even lust. That night when she got into my bed, I'd had enough to drink and the guns were loud in the room, reminding me that I was going back to my regiment very soon, and it happened. Damn it, I oughtn't to be telling you this."

"I give you my word I won't repeat any of this to Lydia or anyone else. You haven't told me about the child."

He rubbed his face with both hands. "God knows. She ought to be brought up in a French family that will love her as she ought to be loved. I've never seen her. And men don't have the same feeling for babies that women do. We don't know what to do with them. Women seem to have a natural knack for that. I'd see that she was well taken care of. I've money enough to do well by her, whether she's mine or not. But I love Lydia, Bess, and I won't break her heart."

"You came close enough to that when you were on leave. Did you know I found her huddled in my doorway, chilled to the bone, crying and lost and without enough money to find a decent hotel for the night? If I hadn't returned from France that evening, I don't know what would have become of her."

I thought he would throw the glass of wine across the room. His fingers clenched around it with such force that it was a wonder the glass didn't crack. And then he said, "Do you know where she is, Bess? If you did would you tell me?"

"I don't know," I said, answering the last question rather than the first. "I've been given no reason to trust you. And there's still the matter of George Hughes's murder. I don't even know whether they've found his murderer."

"My mother says the police have not located Davis Merrit. Someone in London thought they'd seen him. And there was another report in Wales. Wild goose chases, on both accounts. The police are still looking. Mother says that the frightful—her word—Constable Bates has come back a time or two to interview one or the other of the family. And Inspector Rother has been scouring the Forest. I think he believes Merrit is dead. That he killed himself after killing Hughes."

"But that's unlikely," I replied.

"Did you know the man?" he asked me sharply.

"I saw him in Hartfield at the same time you did," I replied with some asperity. "It's just that I can't find a reason for him to kill Hughes. I don't think he was in love with Lydia, or she with him, whatever you chose to believe. And I can't accept that he was trying to save her grief. If he meant to do that, he'd have murdered you."

Roger Ellis opened his mouth, and then shut it again smartly. Finally he said, "The police may know more than you do."

"That's true," I agreed.

He toyed with the glass. "If I tell you something, will you swear never to reveal it to anyone?"

"If you're confessing to murder—" I began, for it was a secret I didn't want to have on my conscience.

"Damn it, no."

"Then I'll promise."

"No. Swear."

I did, with some trepidation, uncertain what I was getting myself into.

And Roger Ellis surprised me.

Ever after, I knew I would remember that little bistro, the small table between us, and the face of the man across from me, the smoke burning both our eyes, making them red.

"I had a feeling that someone killed my brother. Or I should say, shortened his suffering. I don't know who it was. I thought for a time that it was either Eleanor, unable to watch him die so slowly, or her brother, because he knew how hard it was for her. I even suspected George, because they were in the room alone for some time, and it was possible that Alan asked him to help him die."

"Dear God," I said, and could think of nothing else to add.

"I know. I said nothing. There would have been no point in involving the police. I looked at it as a kindness. Something I myself should have thought to ask my brother. But I loved him and I didn't want him to die. Selfish of me, but there it is."

"But you should have said something after George was killed. It could have been important. Instead you let Davis Merrit take the blame because you didn't like him."

"No, that's not true. I was jealous of him. What's more, I was trying to shield my mother. I couldn't let her know what I suspected."

"Be that as it may, we've strayed from the subject," I said, not wanting to take this any farther. "I can't tell you where to find this child—" I'd nearly slipped up and called her Sophie.

"Can't—or won't."

"I expect we came to Rouen on the same errand," I said. "There is a house of nuns here with no children in their care, and another on a street not far from here where there are children. I've spoken to both of them. I've seen the children in their care. She isn't one of them. You can go there yourself, if you like. Or I'll take you there."

"Is this the truth?"

"The absolute truth," I answered.

He swore. "All right. I believe you. I should have done this a year ago. It's my fault. And now she's somewhere in France, and we may never find her."

"Then all your problems will be solved."

"No, not all of them," he said wearily and pulled some coins from his pocket, tossing them on the table. "I'll see you to your motorcar."

I rose as well and walked with him to the door. Outside the rain was coming down in earnest, and over its noisy patter I could hear the guns at the Front, and from the river, the sounds of a boat coming up the Seine to the dock, its whistle carrying on the damp air.

Roger Ellis took my arm and led me across to the Major's motorcar. He turned the crank and then came to my door.

"I didn't kill George. Either to keep my secret or to avenge Alan." The rain was cascading off the brim of his cap now.

The shelling to the north of us was getting heavier. In the flashes of light, the Butter Tower was spectral against the sheets of rain falling from the black sky.

"Oddly enough, I think I believe you," I said.

But even if I did, I still wasn't sure I trusted Roger Ellis.

I think he must have read the shadow of doubt in my eyes. His hand on the door clenched, and then he said, "All right. Go on." He gestured to the gun flashes. "They'll be needing you soon."

"Yes. Good-bye, Captain Ellis."

And I drove away, leaving him there, wondering if I'd done the right thing.

Thirteen

I reached Calais in time to meet the Major as he came out of the port and strode down the busy street, looking this way and that. He smiled as he saw me, and hurried over to where I'd put the motorcar.

"On time," he said approvingly. "Thank you, Sister." He ran his eye over the bonnet and the wings, as if searching for dents or scrapes. Then he laughed as he saw me watching him. "I brought this motorcar over to France in the summer of 1914, and I was in Paris when the war began. I stored her in a house in Neuilly, and came home to enlist. She was still there when I got back three months later. I'd heard that the French Army used even the Paris taxis to ferry men to the Marne, when the Germans first broke through. God knows they could have used her too."

I laughed too, and thanked him as well. We drove back through the shattered landscape and the rutted, rain-soaked roads to report to my sector. As Roger Ellis had predicted and the shelling had foretold, they needed me desperately.

After quickly changing into a fresh uniform, I hurried to take my place, sorting the long line of wounded into manageable units—the walking wounded, the seriously wounded, those needing immediate attention, and those who were dying, for whom nothing could be done. The sounds of machine-gun fire, rifles, and the booms of the shells were deafening.

Yet from the surgical ward behind me I heard a burst of the same maniacal laughter I'd heard once before, only this time cut short with a curse.

Ten minutes later, directing the stretcher bearers, stalwart Scots with grim faces, to follow me with the chest wound they'd brought in, I saw another stretcher being brought out of the surgical ward. Even though he was pale and groggy, I recognized the Australian Sergeant.

He saw me as well, blinking to clear his vision as he peered in my direction. The morphine was taking effect. He grinned and did a very poor imitation of that same laugh.

He must have noticed the surprise on my face.

"Kookaburra," he said. "It's a bird, love." And then he closed his eyes and lay back.

I took his hand. "I found her," I said, leaning down to whisper in his ear. "Thank you. You made it possible."

I couldn't be sure whether he'd heard me or not. And my chest wound was in need of urgent care. I walked away from the Sergeant and found the tired, overworked doctor waiting for me.

My chest wound survived and was sent down the line for further treatment. I had very little time to think about anything after that as the level of severe wounds rose. It was another ten hours before I was relieved, and I walked wearily back to my quarters, falling into my cot to sleep heavily.

The next morning I was back at work, and the next. And finally, as the flow of wounded slowed with the desultory sounds of firing from the Front, I could take a deep breath and massage my aching shoulders and the small of my back.

I found one of the ambulance drivers who had taken patients back to the main dressing station. He smiled, his eyes bloodshot and strained, as weary as I was.

I asked if my chest wound and several other very difficult cases had survived, and he told me they had reached the next station alive. That spoke well for the immediate care they had received here. "And the Aussie Sergeant?"

"He wasn't doing well. I'm sorry, Sister, we did our best. But his breathing was ragged when we got him there."

I thanked him and let him go to a well-deserved rest.

A day later when I ran into an Australian officer in consultation with an English Major as they stood in the entrance of a tent out of the fierce wind that had begun to blow across the flat, decimated landscape of war, I walked up and begged their pardon for the interruption. Then I turned to the Australian officer and asked, "Sir, what is a kookaburra?"

He glanced at the English Major and smiled. "It's a very large kingfisher. Very striking bird. When half a dozen of them gather in the trees, you can't hear yourself think. Its call is something you won't forget, once you've heard it." The smile faded. "You haven't treated Sergeant Larimore, have you? It's his signature, so to speak."

"Yes, sir, I have. He was brought in a few days ago. I was just speaking to the ambulance driver. He said the Sergeant wasn't doing well when he arrived at the main dressing station."

"A pity, that. He's a good man, one of the best."

I thanked him and walked on.

There was no time to return to Rouen. The next fortnight was busy, and besides, I'd just been given leave. I couldn't ask for more so soon.

I found three soldiers from my father's old regiment and put out the word that I was concerned about an Australian Sergeant named Larimore who had been under my care.

Word came back that he'd been taken to Rouen and sent on to Boulogne for transport to England. And then someone else reported that he had died before he reached Rouen.

I could feel the tears in the back of my eyes. *Such a waste,* I thought.

I was still feeling low from the shock of that, when I received a visit from Matron. She came in with a frown between her gray eyes, and I did a hasty review of my sins, for I thought she was angry about something.

Instead she asked, almost with distaste, "Sister Crawford, have you been involved in a murder inquiry in Sussex?"

"Yes. Before Christmas. A guest in the house where I was staying was found dead."

"I see. It appears that your presence is required at an inquest being held next week. We've been asked to approve leave for you to give testimony."

"I was with Mrs. Ellis when we were searching for the missing man, and we were the ones who found his body."

"Yes, I see. Then I shall approve this request for leave. Five days should be sufficient? We're really short staffed, and you are one of our most experienced nurses."

"I don't know what is sufficient, Matron. I've had no news since the first inquest was adjourned while the police proceeded with their inquiries."

"Very well. I shall ask for five days, with the understanding that if more time is required, the police can give you a chit explaining why it was necessary to remain longer than that."

"Thank you, Matron."

And she was gone. Official word of my leave came down the next day, and I asked if I could be sent home via Rouen, as I'd like to look in on patients there.

To my surprise, the request was granted. And then I learned why when I was given orders to accompany a train of severely wounded men to Rouen for further care.

It proved to be an arduous journey, and I lost one patient before we pulled into the station in Rouen. Stretcher bearers and orderlies and ambulance drivers helped us take the wounded out of the train and ferry them to the race course.

There I found a very orderly receiving station, although what had been a five-hundred-bed hospital had soon expanded to thirteen hundred or more. The American nurses were quiet and efficient, and soon my charges were dealt with.

I had just signed the paperwork when I heard off in the distance that wild laughter. Cracked and weak, but undeniably Sergeant Larimore's kookaburra.

I said, "I know that sound."

An American nurse rolled her eyes. "I declare, he's the most impossible man." She wore pince-nez glasses and had a soft voice that reminded me a little of Devon.

"It's a bird. Like a kingfisher. An Australian bird."

She considered me, doubt clear in her face. "I live by a river. I've seen kingfishers most of my life. They don't make any sounds like that."

"No. May I see him? I'm so glad to know the Sergeant is still alive."

She weighed the possibility that I had a romantic interest in an attractive man. I could see the thought passing through her mind as she debated whether to allow a visit.

"I was the sister who took the shrapnel out of his shoulder the first time he was wounded," I added helpfully.

"Ah. Sister Crawford. He's done nothing but compare everything we do to your skill and dedication. I'm delighted to meet this paragon at long last."

I could feel the warm blood rush into my face. "I'm so sorry! I expect he was being cheeky."

"Indeed." She looked in the direction the sound had come from. "I must tell you, he's not out of the woods yet. He had such a fever when he was brought to us— that was almost three weeks ago—and he was out of his mind the first few days. You will find him much changed. There's still the possibility of pneumonia. But he insists on getting out of bed and walking about. He even disappeared into Rouen two days ago. When he was brought back, he claimed he'd been delirious and didn't know what he was going. It's difficult to keep him quiet. Perhaps you can persuade him to be more sensible."

She pointed to a tent in the third row, the first one in the tidy white line. The contrast with the forward dressing station where I'd been working was very evident. And I even caught a glimpse of the X-ray machine that had saved so many lives.

I went down to the race course and located the tent in which Sergeant Larimore was once more making his raucous call.

Walking through the flap, I said in my best imitation of Matron's voice, "That will do, young man. There are other wounded in this Base Hospital, you know. Show a little consideration for them."

He turned his head to argue with me, recognized me, and grinned. "So they finally brought you here," he said. "I was on them about you often enough."

"So I heard," I said. "Nurse Barlow was disappointed that I didn't walk on water." I nodded to the nurse who had just completed his bath and waited while she took the used water out to dump. It also gave me an opportunity to come to terms with the change in the man I remembered as tall, vigorous, and healthy.

His face had been pared down to the bone, and his body seemed thinner under the sheet and blanket. A ravaging fever could do that. He was wearing the blue hospital suit the Americans issued to all patients, and it appeared to fit well enough. I thought perhaps his own determination was healing him faster than medical care at this stage.

The Sergeant tried to stand up, and I pushed him back down again. "I shall be sent home in disgrace if you take a turn for the worse on my account," I told him firmly.

"Yes, well, I'd heal faster if I could move about. Lying here day after day, I can't regain my strength. I walk when they aren't looking, and that's helping.

I thought in the beginning they were sending me home—I heard them talking about Boulogne when I was awake enough to understand what was going on. That's where the ships leave for Down Under. I'm damned if I'll let them do that. My men need me more than Australia does."

I thought perhaps that was where his determination sprang from. And I'd seen, more than once, how the resolve to go back into the line had worked miraculous cures.

"Have you been assigned here?" he asked hopefully, changing the subject.

"No, actually I have a brief leave coming to me. I asked to be sent home by way of Rouen because of the child."

"I didn't dream it then. Your voice, thanking me."

"Your list helped enormously, and the house is here, in Rouen. It's an almost unbelievable stroke of good luck." I told him how I'd found Sophie and what I'd learned from Sister Marie Joseph. "I intended to speak to the solicitor here in Rouen to learn what was necessary to take her to England, but I ran into her real father—almost literally ran into him. And I had to put it off, for fear he might try to follow me. Besides, Sophie had just broken out with chicken pox, and she shouldn't have been moved."

"Do you want me to pose as her real father? If that would help?"

I smiled. "You don't sound much like a British officer."

"But I can do just that, my dear," he retorted in perfect imitation of one.

I should have realized that if he could imitate the bird's call so well he was a natural mimic.

The nurse returned to retrieve her towels, soaps, shaving gear, and scissors, telling Sergeant Larimore not to tire himself. Turning to me, she said, "A torn lung."

"A torn lung," he mimicked as soon as the tent flap fell behind her, then in his normal baritone voice, he added, "As if I didn't know. The surgery nearly killed me. It was a close-run thing. But I'm mending now. Tell me more about the child. I need something to think about besides the Base Hospital's bloody routine. Sorry, Sister."

And so I related the entire story. "My ship leaves at three o'clock this afternoon. I just have time to go back to the house and see how she is."

"I hope you find her recovering. She's young for that, isn't she?"

"Not really. Chicken pox can sweep through an entire family in a matter of days, from the youngest to the eldest. In fact, the earlier you have it, the better. Older children often have more trouble, and scarring can be a problem. Although those scars often fade with the years."

"If I'm ever allowed to leave this place, I'll go along to this Rue St. Catherine and see her for myself."

"You must be very careful," I warned. "The nuns are not very happy with visitors."

"I understand that. A great lug of a soldier frightening the little ones won't do. I won't go empty-handed. I've been collecting what I could. Soap, a little sugar and some coffee." He smiled. "Will you be coming back through Rouen, then?"

"I hope to. I don't know."

"Don't forget to look me up." We were interrupted by a thermometer put in his mouth by an older woman with a severe face. When she had gone, he asked me about myself. "My neighbor for the first week was an English Corporal. I must have been calling for you when I was off my head. He told me about your father. They're rather proud of you, you know—his old regiment. Word got around you were out here."

I didn't know, and was rather pleased. And so I told him about growing up in India and other corners of the Empire, and about Somerset and even about Mrs. Hennessey.

He laughed at that. "You're better than a tonic," he told me when I'd finished. "Stay in Rouen, and I'll be back on my feet before the week's out."

Smiling, I said, "Nurse Barlow means well. I think you gave her a fright when you went missing."

"I told her I was on walkabout. It's what the Aborigines do when they get tired of one place. She thought I'd gone off my head again. I'm used to the spaces of the Out Back. I can't bear being cooped up here like a fish in a bowl."

"If you want to rejoin your men, try showing her you're healing."

I left a few minutes after that, mindful not to tire him. He took my hand and thanked me for coming.

I turned as I was leaving and asked, "What did you do in civilian life?"

"My father owns a large sheep station. I breed dogs for herding sheep. There's a large market for them in New Zealand. I never cared for sheep, much to my father's chagrin."

I left him then and made my way out of the race course. Outside in the street I found a man willing to drive me to the Rue St. Catherine, and then take me to the port.

No one came to the door of the house where I'd left Sophie. My spirits plummeted at the thought of missing this opportunity to see her. But where were they?

I stepped away from the door to the edge of the street and looked up. The nuns could be in the kitchen—upstairs—somewhere that the sound of the knocker couldn't reach.

But I could see nothing, no light on this gray, grim afternoon, no small faces at the windows looking down on the street. Nothing.

I was about to turn away when the woman in the neighboring house came out her door with a market basket over her arm. I turned to her and asked in French, "Is anyone at home? Where are the nuns?"

Her accent was very heavy, but I thought she said, "*Elles sont va au cimetière.*"

They have gone to the cemetery.

As if she saw my confusion she added, "St. Sever."

"Who is dead?" I asked. "*Un enfant? Une soeur?*" A child? A nun?

She shrugged. "I don't know who is dead."

"But someone must have stayed behind to watch the children."

"I do not know," she repeated, and with a nod, she walked on toward the shops some streets away.

I went back to the door and banged the knocker vigorously, and in the end I was rewarded. The door opened a crack and a middle-aged nun peered through it at me. "We have no one ill at this house," she said, looking at my uniform. "You must be mistaken in your directions."

"Please. I have come to see if Sophie is well again. When I saw her last, she had chicken pox and was very feverish."

"No one visits the children except for the doctor in the next street. We have no need for the care of an English nursing sister."

"But Sister Marie Joseph allowed me to see her. I am leaving for England today, and I would like very much to know that all was well with Sophie. I—I know her father. The English officer. He would like to be sure, since he sends money, that it is properly used."

"He has sent no money for a very long time."

"Because he couldn't find you. Please, let me be certain she is alive and well, and he will begin to pay again for her care." I did a swift inventory of the money I had with me, remembering how Roger Ellis had had to borrow sums from George Hughes. There was no one I could borrow money from—unless it was Sergeant Larimore. "I have some money with me. I can leave it with you to show his good faith."

She relented finally. "Very well. But you will not speak to her. Only observe. This is the only home she has known. Do not alter that in any way."

"I promise."

I was taken to a small parlor heated by a coal fire in the grate. The rest of the house was damp and cold. The children were sitting on the floor, and I could see that the nun had been reading to them from a French children's book. They looked up as I entered, their faces bright with curiosity. Visitors were a rarity.

I greeted them, and my gaze swept the circle, stopping on the fair, blue-eyed child nearest the hearth. Although pale from her recent illness, I could see that the remaining scabs were dry and healing.

She smiled at me in that way that some children have when meeting a stranger, and now I could see what George Hughes had seen, a likeness perhaps not as strong as he had wished to believe it was, but so pronounced that this child and Juliana could have been sisters. I wanted very much to speak to her, to hear her voice, to hold her on my lap and watch the play of emotions on her face.

I'd never known Juliana, but now I understood why she had left such a void in her family. The portrait had done her justice, and even the memorial stone had captured something of the living child. But here was the warmth and the smile and the tilt of the head and the lovely blue eyes under fair lashes that gave life to the static reflections of her.

I couldn't understand how Roger Ellis could abandon her.

And would Lydia be able to love her, when she was the image of Juliana?

The nun touched my elbow, reminding me that I had had my brief glimpse and must be satisfied. I allowed her to escort me from the room, and I gave her what money I could, not nearly enough, but I needed sufficient funds to reach England and travel on to Ashdown Forest.

"When I return," I said, "there will be more. Keep her safe."

She thanked me gravely, and I could tell that even that meager amount was appreciated.

Just as I was about to walk out the door, I asked, "What will become of her, if there is no family to take her and educate her?"

"We have already spoken of this, Sister Marie Joseph and I. We will find her work out in the world, if that is what she chooses. Our girls learn to sew beautifully. They will be in demand for fine work. If she has a vocation, and we shall pray that God will be so kind," she said, "we will welcome her into our house. Surely when the Germans have gone, we will be able to rebuild."

It was a very different point of view from Sister Marie Joseph's, that Sophie's beauty could be a curse. What's more, I couldn't imagine Sophie as a seamstress at someone else's beck and call, or a nun, shut away from the world for the rest of her life. I wanted to argue vehemently against either possibility. But I had to remember that without the care of the nuns, Sophie might not have survived at all.

I left then, and went back to my waiting taxi. We reached the harbor to find my ship already at the quay. I waited for the wounded to be taken aboard and then followed them.

"There is no cabin for you, Sister," one of the officers told me. "But there's a chair in what used to be the lounge, if you care to sit there."

"That will do very well," I said and went to the rail to watch our departure. The gangway was brought in, the ropes cast off, and we were free of the land, swinging with the tide, the engines rumbling under my feet.

I was about to walk on to the lounge, when across the water soared the call of that Australian kingfisher. Loud and clear, heads turning to see what it was and where it was coming from.

And there, behind the barriers on the quay was a tall man waving his distinctive hat, his face a blur, but I thought it was surely split from ear to ear by that cocky grin.

He'd escaped Nurse Barlow again and come down to see me off. She would be exasperated with him, and he would blandly tell her he was feverish again and off his head.

Still, I waved back, distinctly cheered.

It wasn't until the ship moved slowly out into the current, heading downstream toward the sea, that I finally went below.

My orders were to report directly to Inspector Rother in Wych Gate. But they didn't forbid finding a telephone as soon as we landed in Portsmouth, before I went on to meet my train.

I put in a call to my parents.

They were delighted to hear my voice and know that I was in England. But I had to tell them the reason why I wouldn't be coming home.

My father said, "I must be away tomorrow morning. But Simon is in London. Shall I send him to Sussex?"

"Please, would you? I shall need a means of getting about." And it would be a touch of home for me.

We talked for a few minutes more, as I assured my mother that I was well and hoped to have leave again soon. A little white lie for her comfort, I told myself.

The train to London met with the usual delays, and when I arrived at Waterloo Station, I collected my things and prepared to go in search of the next available connection to Hartfield.

Instead I found Simon Brandon waiting to help me descend from the carriage, and then he reached inside to take up my valise.

"The motorcar is this way."

A cold rain was falling, but as we handed in my ticket and went out into the fading light, he studied my face and said, "Your mother wished to know how you looked. Tired, but well enough. That sums it up, I should think."

I smiled. "Yes, very well. Simon, I've seen the little French child. Her name is Sophie." And I went on to tell him how I'd managed to find her, and what I'd discovered.

We had reached the outskirts of London as I finished the account. Simon nodded, "I was fairly sure you would search. Against all advice."

"There was so little opportunity to look for her. I despaired of finding her. But an Australian sergeant, his name is Larimore, put the word out, compiled a list of convents from the responses he received, and had it delivered to me by way of a wounded Scot. It made all the difference."

"And you say Ellis knows nothing about this?"

"I don't think he does. But running into him prevented me from speaking to the solicitor to ask how the child might be returned to her natural father."

"Hardly your place, Bess."

"Yes, I'm aware of that. But I'd have liked to know if it was even possible. That would guide me in deciding what to do about telling Roger Ellis—or Lydia, for that matter—that I know where Sophie is. Which reminds me, I shall need some money before I return to France. I gave the sister at the orphanage all that I could spare. They have so little, and the children need so much. French law may be very different from English law in these matters. And there's the fact that Roger was never officially registered at Sophie's father."

"Leave it, Bess. You're unwise to grow attached to this child."

"I'm not attached. But I have become aware of another side of this war, Simon. It's difficult enough for us to make sense of it. Think what a child who has lost everything must feel, when the future appears to be so bleak and comfortless."

We drove on in silence, covering the miles of winter-bare England, and I wished we were heading in the direction of Somerset, on the other side of London.

We stopped briefly for tea and sandwiches in a small shop in Sevenoaks, then drove on to Ashdown Forest. This time as we approached, I recognized the first signs of it now.

"I don't think I shall be invited to stay with the Ellis family this time," I said ruefully.

"No. I expect not."

"I can't think of why I should be summoned from France for the inquest. After all, the police have my statement. Have you heard anything about the case since we left?"

"Only what you already know, that the inquest was adjourned."

We drove through Hartfield, the street deserted, the houses already dark. I glanced toward Bluebell Cottage and saw that it looked closed and somehow forlorn. I was suddenly reminded of the cat I'd seen on a blue cushion asleep in the window.

"Simon. What's become of Davis Merrit's cat? Surely it wasn't abandoned, when he didn't come back!"

"You must ask the police."

We left Hartfield behind and soon came to the turning where the left-hand track went to Wych Cross and the right to Wych Gate.

In the far distance, across the barren landscape, I could just see the lights of Vixen Hill as we passed the place where the lane ran into the darkness under the trees where Simon had left his horse one night.

I'd been to St. Mary's Church, but not into the village of Wych Gate itself. It lay on the far side of the trees that stood to the west of the church, over an ancient bridge that crossed the little stream where George Hughes had died. There was a cluster of houses that clung to the road in defiance of the heath that all but surrounded them. Half the size of Hartfield, it was neither bustling nor busy, and most of the inhabitants worked elsewhere in the Forest or just outside it. But once it had been a very wealthy village based on the wool trade, when sheep had replaced the deer and other game that had drawn kings and their courts to hunt. The church was a mark of its past, and of a time when a village could afford to build it.

Inspector Rother lived on the corner of one of the two side streets in Wych Gate. We found him there after going to the police station, once a gaol for poachers and other village miscreants, that stood foursquare between the bakery and a solicitor's chambers. He had left a note on the door directing me to his house.

He must have been watching for me. He came out of his door almost as soon as we pulled up, and said, peering into the vehicle, "Sister Crawford?"

"Yes, Inspector?"

Reaching for the handle to the rear door, he said, "I'd rather speak to you in the police station, so as not to wake my family."

He wasn't the sort of man I'd associated with having a family, a home life. He had seemed to be wedded to

his work. I'd never quite pictured him at the breakfast table, his children around him, as I could Inspector
Herbert, whom I'd known in London.

Simon turned the motorcar and drove back to the
station. We hurried through the rain in Inspector
Rother's wake and waited for him to light a lamp.

In his office the furnishings were plain, with a
narrow desk, a chair, and two others in front of it. Over
Inspector Rother's head as he took his seat was a pho-
tograph of the King in his naval uniform, staring at the
opposite wall.

I made the introductions.

"I expected the station carriage," he said sourly,
"from Hartfield."

"My family sent Mr. Brandon to see me safely here,"
I answered. "It's rather late, after all."

"Yes, yes, I recall seeing Mr. Brandon in Hartfield
before Christmas. You must be tired, Miss Crawford.
I've taken a room for you at The King's Head."

"Thank you." I hesitated. It seemed very odd to
have made the long trip here only to be told that he'd
taken a room for me. Was there more? I added, "Have
you found Lieutenant Merrit? The last news I had was
that the inquest had been adjourned while the police
continued to look for him."

He considered me, then glanced at Simon, standing behind my chair, leaning his shoulders against the

corner of a tall bookcase. "There were questions that only the Lieutenant could answer. For example, why was a watch removed from the body of the deceased when other valuable items were not taken? What became of the murder weapon?"

"You haven't found it?" I asked, feeling a frisson of guilt when I remembered the marble kitten slightly out of its accustomed place.

Although I had listened, I hadn't heard the slightest sound from behind the cell door I'd glimpsed at the end of the passage some ten feet beyond Inspector Rother's office. If Lieutenant Merrit had been taken into custody, he must not be held here.

"So far we've been unable to account for it."

When he didn't immediately go on, I asked, "When I was at The King's Head using the telephone—this was before Lieutenant Hughes was murdered—I noticed a cat asleep in the window of Bluebell Cottage. Has anything been done about it?"

"We brought Mrs. Roger Ellis to Hartfield and asked her to look through Bluebell Cottage. She was there very early on the morning of the murder, and we wished to know if the cottage appeared to be the same as when she saw it then. She found the cat and insisted on taking charge of it. We had no objection to that."

Lydia hadn't told me that in her letter. "This was before the inquest?"

"Yes, in fact, later in the afternoon of the day you left for London."

"And was the cottage the same?" Simon asked.

"It was, as far as she could tell. There was no sign of a hasty departure. Lieutenant Merrit had changed into his riding clothes and gone out. He had a habit of riding out early in the morning. We believe that he had either intentionally gone in search of George Hughes or encountered him by accident. Constable Bates found signs of someone standing by a horse for several minutes. And then the two went on together. Where they went from there was lost when a flock of sheep moved through the same ground. A clever piece of police work, that. It placed Lieutenant Merrit not far from Wych Gate Church."

Suddenly I knew why I had been sent for. "I was told in France," I began, "that I was required to testify at an inquest. But you haven't caught Lieutenant Merrit, have you? And you haven't taken anyone else into custody. Does this mean that Davis Merrit is dead?"

I felt Simon stir behind my chair.

Inspector Rother held my gaze for a long moment, then said, "Either you are quite perceptive or you have heard something in spite of our efforts to keep the discovery from the public." He went on slowly. "Five days ago, we found the remains of Davis Merrit's body. On the heath, in a dell that the locals call The Pitch. It appears that he died by his own hand, after returning to Hartfield long enough to pass the watch to the man we call Willy. He had taken great care to make us believe that he had then left the Forest."

I was shocked, in spite of my premonition. "But if he's dead, why is it necessary for me to come back from France to give evidence? Surely my statement would be sufficient, if the case is already closed?"

"I don't care for loose ends, Miss Crawford. Why did Merrit feel it necessary to come back to Hartfield long enough to give that watch to Willy, when no one suspected him at that time and probably would not have done. If he intended to tell us that he was the killer, then why do away with himself here in the Forest? It would be more useful if he went to Devon, or Northumberland, where he could conceivably remain unidentified."

"I don't know. Described that way, it seems rather odd."

"Yes. And so we find ourselves back to the beginning of the case. It's late, and you must be tired. I hadn't intended to speak of this tonight."

But I thought he had. Otherwise, instead of coming to the police station, he would have sent me directly back to Hartfield and asked me to return tomorrow. Today, it was now.

And then he said meditatively, "Four men. Davis Merrit, George Hughes, Roger Ellis, and William Pryor. And now two of them are dead."

"Who is William Pryor?"

"I don't like murder on my patch, Miss Crawford. That's why I have to wonder why you never told me about the quarrel Roger Ellis had with George Hughes the night before he was killed. Or the jealousy that Ellis had expressed concerning his wife's volunteering to read to the blind man. Oh, yes, the doctor has suddenly become very eager to help us in our inquiries. As has his wife. Now I think it's time we all went to bed, and continued this discussion tomorrow."

With that he rose and ushered us out the door, bidding us a good night as he walked through the driving rain back to his house.

Simon and I began the long dark drive back to The King's Head. I was grateful for his quiet presence in the motorcar beside me. I didn't believe in ghosts, I never had, but two deaths in this Forest had somehow left a haunting presence behind.

I said, after we'd passed St. Mary's Church, "An unexpected turn of events."

"I told you in the beginning, Bess, that I had a bad feeling about this business. From the start. From the time you found Lydia Ellis outside your door that December night and took her in."

"I could hardly have turned her away. But who is William Pryor? The Inspector never answered me when I asked."

"I should think it's the man you know as Willy."

"Yes, of course." I shook my head. "I must be more tired than I thought. But how did the police find out his real name? I was given the impression that no one knew who he was. And now Inspector Rother is adding Captain Ellis to his list of suspects."

"Or he wants you to believe he has."

"It would make sense. A clever way to rid himself of both men. Even Lydia wondered about that." I considered what I had just said. "Simon, if that is true—and I'm not convinced that it is, mind you—why is Roger Ellis searching for Sophie? Is she in peril too?"

We drove on in silence. And then the track through the Forest ended in what would shortly become the High Street of Hartfield. Ahead of us, the inn loomed out of the dark, and across from it Bluebell Cottage, standing empty.

"I'm glad Lydia took the cat," I said as we turned into the yard beside The King's Head. "I wouldn't have liked for it to be turned out into the winter cold. It had a cushion the same color as the cottage was painted. He liked that cat, Simon, and it was cosseted."

We hurried out of the rain into The King's Head to hear snoring coming from the small room behind Reception. Simon went to tap on the door, and a very sleepy man came out to greet us, smoothing his hair as he asked our business.

Ten minutes later we were climbing the stairs to our rooms, and Simon saw me to my door.

After he'd gone to his own room, I went to sit by the window and look out into the night, unwilling to undress and go to bed. My mind was too busy, and as I looked across the street toward Bluebell Cottage, I felt discouraged.

I'd been sitting there ten minutes, possibly fifteen, when I saw someone coming down the street, a shambling walk that made me think at once of the man Willy.

And as he drew nearer, I saw that it was indeed he. I watched him come through the shadows cast on the road by the houses across the way, and stop near Bluebell Cottage's door.

I drew back a little from the window. I didn't think he could see me sitting there. But I wanted very much to know what he intended to do next.

After hesitating, as if waiting to see who might be about, he finally crossed the road and came into the yard of the inn.

I could just see where he was going, and I thought at first he was hoping to find somewhere dry to sleep. Instead he walked up to Simon Brandon's motorcar and looked it over, as if it could tell him who owned the vehicle. Or perhaps he'd seen it before and was making sure that it was the same motorcar.

I was reminded of a fox, sniffing for danger.

Finally, satisfied, he turned and walked quietly back the way he'd come.

I sat there by the window for almost another hour, but he never came back, and the road in front of the inn remained deserted, only the rain whipping through the village disturbing the peace of the night.

The next morning at breakfast, I told Simon what I'd seen.

"He didn't interfere in any way with the motorcar, did he?" he asked sharply.

"No. He never lifted the bonnet nor touched the tires. He must have felt he recognized the motorcar from your last stay here but wasn't quite sure it was the same. Once he was satisfied, he went on his way."

"Hmmmm" was all Simon had to say in response. Still, I could tell the incident had made him uncomfortable. I remembered that his years in the Army had given him a finely tuned sense of danger.

"Why should he worry you?"

"Because Rother is of two minds. Either Ellis is the murderer, or Willy killed both Hughes and Merrit."

"Davis Merrit was very generous with Willy. It's rather terrible, to think Willy turned on him."

After breakfast we drove back to Wych Gate. We had just reached the turning to Vixen Hill when a motorcar came down the drive and stopped to let us pass. I was surprised to see that it was Mrs. Ellis at the wheel. I waved in greeting when I saw that she had recognized me.

"Bess," she called, and then frowned. "Has that Inspector sent for you as well? I'm just off to the railway station to meet Roger. He's been called home too."

"I know you'll be happy to see him," I said. But would Lydia feel the same?

"Yes, but what is this about? Do you know? We've been waiting for weeks to learn what's happening. Have the police found Davis, do you think?"

I wanted to warn her, to tell her that Roger was now a suspect—we all were—but I hadn't the heart.

"I expect he'll tell us soon enough," I replied, then before I could think it through, I said, "Did you know that Dr. Tilton and his wife have told the police about the quarrel between George and Roger?"

"It was hardly a quarrel," she said tartly. "Poor George was drunk, and his mind was wandering. But it's just like Dr. Tilton to make more of it than it was. He's a very good doctor, but I sometimes think he enjoys making trouble."

Leaving it at that, I asked, "How is Lydia? And Gran?"

"Very well. Lydia is nervous about Roger coming home, but I told her there was nothing to fear. Will you come and see her? I know she'd like that."

"Yes, I'll try."

"Good. Now I must hurry. I have a list of things I must buy before the train arrives. Good-bye, Bess, Mr. Brandon."

And she was gone.

"Why did you tell her about the doctor?" Simon asked as we drove on.

"I thought she ought to be warned. None of the family had said anything. But it was bound to come out. And now that it has, it makes us look as if we were concealing something."

"But aren't you?" Simon asked.

I had no answer for that. I still believed it wasn't my place to reveal the family's secrets. I had left it to Dr. Tilton . . . had that been cowardly of me?

"Nor have you told them about the message you found in that umbrella."

"That was different. It's not the sort of thing a man would do—to leave a message like that in an umbrella, on the off chance it would reach the right person. It's too uncertain. But I thought perhaps Davis Merrit might have hoped Lydia would find it and come to Hartfield. Then I discovered that she'd already been to Bluebell Cottage the morning of the murder. But perhaps it had never been left in the umbrella. Perhaps someone put it there to throw the police off the scent."

"That's an interesting theory."

At first I thought Simon was being facetious, but when I glanced up at his face, I saw that he was in fact agreeing with me.

"Since we're confessing, there's the marble kitten as well."

Inspector Rother was expecting us. He said as we walked into the police station, "Thank you for coming so early. I'd like you to tell me again about finding the body of Lieutenant Hughes," he said. "I know what's in your statement, but perhaps you've forgot a detail."

I didn't think I had. But I repeated my account of our search for George, and how I'd come to follow Mrs. Ellis into the church and then down the overgrown path.

He listened, then asked me, "You heard nothing— rooks calling? Birds flying up?—to indicate that someone else was nearby, while you were searching for the Lieutenant?"

"No, the wood around us was quiet. Besides, I touched the Lieutenant's hand. He had been killed some time before we found his body. Even accounting for the cold morning and the cold water in the stream."

"You weren't aware that there's a shortcut from St. Mary's Church to Vixen Hill?"

Surprised, I said, "No. I didn't know that."

"It isn't suitable for motorcars, of course. But anyone from Vixen Hill could walk to Wych Gate and back again inside half an hour. Less, on horseback." He drew a rough map on the sheet of paper in front of him, and I could see that he was right. The house was set to connect with the track from Hartfield, but if one knew the way, from the knot garden there was another, smaller track that cut cross-country. Had George taken it? Had his killer?

"We can turn it another way," the Inspector went on, holding up his hand, ticking off the points on his fingers.

"Mrs. Roger Ellis is struck by someone, and has already run away once to London—the stationmaster and the woman who gave her a lift there have confirmed this. She returns home with a friend, and shortly afterward, her husband has words with the victim about a child he fathered while in France, and early the next morning, Mrs. Roger Ellis goes into Hartfield to speak to Davis Merrit. Afterward she packs her cases and prepares to leave again. According to the driver of the station carriage, she was very anxious not to miss that train. So much so that she was short with her mother-in-law. And with you. Was she expecting to meet Lieutenant Merrit at the station? After he'd killed George Hughes? Why didn't she want you to go down that narrow path to the stream? Did she already know that a dead man lay at the end of it?"

"If she had intended to run away with Lieutenant Merrit, why had she asked me to accompany her to London?"

"For the sake of propriety, I should think," he countered.

"I can't think why Lydia Ellis would wish to kill George Hughes."

"In the expectation that her husband would be blamed, and she would be free to remarry."

"Yes, well, Davis Merrit should have thought of that before he handed Lieutenant Hughes's watch to that man Willy."

"I expect our friend Willy was supposed to tell the police that Roger Ellis had given him the watch."

That was an interesting supposition. It was clear that the police *had* put the last five days to good use, coming up with the ramifications of finding Davis Merrit's body.

Simon had put two and two together as well. "Are you saying that Merrit killed himself when everything went wrong?"

Distracted, I was thinking of the message in the umbrella. *Meet me . . . .*

Perhaps I'd been wrong. Perhaps it *had* been a last desperate attempt by the Lieutenant to reach Lydia. Only I found it instead, and then the Inspector was waiting in the churchyard when services ended. And Merrit had to leave quickly.

I nearly shook my head, answering my own question. I hadn't been wrong. But who had sent it?

Inspector Rother was already replying to Simon. "It's likely."

All his conclusions had a ring of truth—but I knew Mrs. Ellis and Lydia and even Davis Merrit better than the Inspector could do. Why would Mrs. Ellis put her own son in jeopardy by killing George Hughes less than twelve hours from the time he'd confronted Roger in the drawing room? Wouldn't she have been glad of the child, rather than angry? And Lydia was too impulsive to be included in any convoluted plot to make the police believe her husband had killed his friend. Even the little I'd seen and heard about Davis Merrit didn't match the picture of an obsessed lover who killed himself when his plans went awry. But that left Roger himself, didn't it?

I was trying to order my thoughts, to make certain that what I was about to say made sense.

"Inspector, I don't think you've brought me here to speculate about the Ellis family's motives for murder. I think what you really want to know is if you can clear them, and open the inquiry in an entirely different direction. For instance, in the direction of William Pryor—Willy."

"There's still Roger Ellis. Who could have killed both men, to rid himself of the erstwhile friend who knew too much about his affair in France and the blind man his wife had been seeing too much of in his absence."

"But George had already told everyone about the affair. Captain Ellis had no right to be jealous, did he?"

He gave me a sour smile. "In for a penny, in for a pound."

"Was the body of Davis Merrit too decomposed for you to be completely satisfied that he'd killed himself?" Simon asked.

He looked up at Simon. "You have a most inconvenient mind," he said. "I have a dead man with a spent bullet under his remains, his service revolver in what is left of his hand, but no marks on the skeleton to tell me where the bullet entered, and where it came out. I can find no one who has heard a single gunshot out on the heath. And there is some small indication that the man was throttled, but we can't be certain of that because foxes and rooks were at the body."

"And no way of knowing precisely when the Lieutenant died," I added to the list.

"You and Captain Ellis left the Forest on the same day. Merrit must have been dead by then."

And Mrs. Ellis was already on her way to the station to meet her returning son.

"So it isn't Willy you're looking at, but Roger Ellis," I said. "You used us."

He could hear the disgust in my voice, and answered coldly, "I have a murder case to solve, Sister Crawford, and my best suspect is dead. If he killed himself, all well and good, but if he did not, then our murderer has two deaths on his conscience."

"If he has a conscience," I replied. "Have you finished with me? Am I allowed to return to France? I'm needed there."

"You are needed here as well. Would you be willing to return to Vixen Hill?"

"No," Simon answered for me. "The Colonel would be furious if you put his daughter in harm's way."

"Besides which," I added, "Roger Ellis may not want me there." In spite of the time we had spent together in that little bistro in Rouen, he wouldn't want me to tell Lydia he was also searching for Sophie.

"I think," Inspector Rother said dryly, "the person who would most dislike having you there is the senior Mrs. Ellis."

"Gran?" I repeated.

"Quite," he answered. "She has been throwing sand in my eyes since the moment I arrived at Vixen Hill, busily protecting her grandson. And you see far too clearly for her comfort. I have just verified that myself."

I remembered Lydia's letter to me in France. Everyone had sent me Christmas wishes—except for Gran.

Fourteen

I had no intention of returning to Vixen Hill. I didn't want to spy for the police. What's more, on our way back to Hartfield, I had all but promised Simon that I wouldn't consider it.

But in the afternoon, Lydia Ellis came knocking at my door in The King's Head, and when I answered, she said, "Mama Ellis was telling the truth. You are here."

"Did you doubt her?"

"Roger swore you were still in France. That he'd run into you at one of the hospitals."

That was close enough to the truth for his purposes.

"Yes, not surprisingly."

I asked her to come in, and she did, looking around at my room with interest. "I've been to The King's Head I don't know how many times," she said, "but

I've never been in one of the rooms. It's rather nice, isn't it?"

For the polished wood of the floorboards was set off with a dark blue carpet and paler blue curtains accenting the chintz covering the chairs. Framed prints of hunting scenes hung on walls papered with morning glories. Nothing to compare with Vixen Hill, but quite comfortable.

"As you already know, Roger is back from France too," she said, walking to the window to look out and then turning to face me. "He's different, somehow. I don't know what it is."

"This time he hasn't come home to watch his brother die," I pointed out gently.

"Yes. But I'm wary, I don't know if it's a real difference or feigned. Or my wishful thinking." She was pacing again, back and forth, back and forth.

"Are you asking me whether you should stay here with me for the duration of his leave?"

"Will you come back to Vixen Hill? Margaret has been asked to return as well, and she's hoping the police will even summon Henry home from France. But they've dispensed with Eleanor and her brother. That's odd, isn't it?"

"The police have their own way of judging these matters," I replied, unwilling to go farther.

"I expect they talked to her in Portsmouth, and don't want us to know what was discussed." She stopped by the door and touched a picture frame, straightening it. "The police asked me over and over again—even though I'd given them a statement, just as you'd done—about finding George's body." She toyed with another frame. "I thought they were convinced after he went missing that Davis Merrit had killed George. That was the conclusion of the inquest, for heaven's sake. So why are they intending to look at Roger now? Because they are, aren't they? Do you believe Roger is a murderer, Bess?"

There was fear in her eyes when finally she turned to face me. All I could do was shake my head. "I'm not the right person to ask," I answered.

"I don't want him to be guilty," she said quietly. "I've had a lot of time to think after you left. Have you found that little girl?"

"I looked for her," I countered. "Do you have any idea how many orphans there are in France?"

"I wonder what Roger would say, if he'd come home to find that you'd brought her with you."

"Lydia, it's not as simple as that. There are legal issues. She's a citizen of France, because her mother was. Rules. Even if Roger wanted her, he would have to go through a solicitor, to find out what he was required to do. You and I would have no claim on her."

"Yes, but I don't see why that should stop you from looking for her."

"No, of course not."

She sighed. "You'd think, wouldn't you, that everyone would be glad to find that she has a good home."

"Lydia. You do realize that if George knew what he was saying, that this child is the image of Juliana, will you be comfortable bringing her into your home? Mrs. Ellis will see her dead daughter in yours, and so will Gran. And Roger, of course, if he survives the war."

"I don't care who she looks like. I'd be grateful to have her."

But that was easy to say now. When she hadn't seen Sophie, as I had.

"What would you say if Roger came home with her?" I asked, curious.

She laughed, but not in amusement. "He never will. You know that. He's ashamed of what he did, and he won't want a constant reminder underfoot. He couldn't have loved her mother very much, could he, or he'd have moved heaven and earth to find her."

I couldn't judge whether that was a consolation to Lydia or if she was seeing the relationship between her husband and the French mother of his child as she would like it to be. Not love, but lust. She could live with lust. Or so she thought now.

Yet from what Roger had told me in Rouen, it hadn't been either love or lust, but loneliness and fear and the knowledge that for this moment, at least, they were both alive. If Roger had spoken the truth, it was never an affair.

"You'll keep trying all the same?"

"I'll keep trying." I'd seen Sophie. I knew I had to.

She nodded and turned from the fire. "I have Davis's cat. I couldn't bear to see it put out, and of course it couldn't stay in the cottage. He had nowhere to go, did he? Merrit? And so he couldn't have taken his cat."

"What did Roger have to say about that?"

She smiled sadly. "He doesn't know. I've put Blue-bell in the room above the hall, and she seems quite happy there. No one goes to that room, except for me. I'm not haunted by Juliana, like the others."

And yet she had been, by her own account, when she fled to London that first time.

"Will you come back with me?" she asked. "Please?"

"I don't know that it's wise, Lydia."

"Please?"

"How did you get to Hartfield? On your bicycle?"

"I learned to drive," she told me. "I never want to feel dependent on someone else again."

"That was clever of you," I told her sincerely. "Lydia, let me think about it. I don't know just what I should do."

"I'll bring Mrs. Ellis back with me. To help convince you."

And with that she was gone.

I sat there by the window, watching the street below.

I'd all but promised Simon. But if I were at Vixen Hill, I could better judge the situation there. And what to do about Sophie.

Would she be better off with the nuns after all? What would it do to a child to be brought up not as herself but as the child everyone had so tragically lost?

After a while, I went to find Simon. He'd been out, he said, when I ran him to earth in the telephone closet.

"Have you learned anything about"—I remembered how public this telephone room was—"about our friends?"

"No news yet."

He came out of the shallow closet and considered me.

"You look distinctly guilty."

I laughed and pulled him around the corner to the small parlor. When we were out of hearing of the rest of the world, I said, "Lydia came to see me. She wants me to come back to Vixen Hill."

"And you told her . . . ?"

"That I didn't think it was wise. She is bringing Mrs. Ellis back to Hartfield, to tell me that I'm welcomed there."

"And now you're having second thoughts?"

I bit my lip, trying to think how to put my reasoning into words. But of course I knew that it would have been easier if my reasoning had been sound.

Simon waited patiently. Finally I said, "It's the little girl. Sophie. I don't quite know what should be done about her. If her father is taken up for murder, Lydia may marry again. Would she want Sophie then? And if Sophie is left with Mrs. Ellis and Gran, will she live out her life in Juliana's shadow?" I shrugged. "That's very muddled."

"In the first place," he answered, "the child isn't your worry. If you let her into your heart, Bess, you'll never have any peace."

"But you haven't seen her," I told him. "And I have."

"Which makes it all the harder. I know." He sighed. "Kittens and puppies. And now someone else's child. What are we to do with you?"

"At least I didn't insist on rescuing Bluebell," I retorted. Then I realized he didn't know who Bluebell was. "Davis Merrit's cat."

He laughed in spite of himself, touching my face with his hand, then he said, serious once more, "Yes, all right. But there's another problem. I just spoke to the Colonel. I'm needed in London straightaway. It will only be for twenty-four hours. At the most a day and a half. I can't take you with me, Rother won't allow it, I'm sure, and yet he's in Wych Gate, not Hartfield. Much as I dislike saying it, you might be safer in Vixen Hill than staying here in the hotel alone. What's more, I need the motorcar. If Rother wants to speak to you, he'll have to come to you. I wish you had that little pistol I'd given you once before."

"I couldn't take it to France with me," I reminded him.

Actually, I didn't know whether I was pleased or not to be going to Vixen Hill. And I disliked losing Simon. Still, if my father had summoned him, even in these circumstances, it must be very important indeed.

"Yes, all right. I'll go."

His hand dropped to my shoulder. "Be careful, Bess. Promise me you'll take every care."

"I shall."

With that he was gone, and I stood there in the parlor where I had waited once before with Lydia and listened for Simon's footsteps as he returned with his valise and then strode out the door.

I was in my room, still undecided about whether to pack or not, when there was a knock at the door. Expecting Lydia, I opened it, saying, "I've decided—"

But it was one of the hotel maids. She bobbed her head, then said, "There's someone to see you in Reception, Miss. Could you please come down?"

Which sounded very much like Inspector Rother, commanding my presence.

"Yes, all right. Thank you."

After she had gone, I stood there in my room and counted slowly to one hundred. It wouldn't do to appear to be anxious.

But when I came down to Reception, there was no sign of Inspector Rother, and when I asked at the desk for my visitor, the woman smiled and said, "I believe he just stepped outside."

I went to the door and opened it. To my surprise, Roger Ellis was standing there, not Inspector Rother, and even from the back I could tell that he was not in the best of moods. His shoulders were stiff with annoyance.

"Captain?" I said.

He turned. "We can't talk here. The parlor."

And so I found myself back in the small parlor facing an angry man.

I thought it was my fault that he was angry. For keeping him waiting, even for making it necessary for him to drive in to Hartfield to beg me to come to Vixen Hill—or perhaps even to tell me not to darken his door.

But I was wrong on all counts.

Shutting the door behind him, Roger Ellis said, "The police, damn them, are talking to my mother again. I thought this business had been settled, that it was Merrit who'd killed George and taken his watch to prove it."

"I'd thought the same thing—" I began.

But he cut across my words, adding, "It would explain why they sent for you. You were there with her when George was found."

"I'm not sure why Inspector Rother wished to speak to me. But yes, he asked me to go over the same ground."

"If Merrit is dead, the case would be wide open again."

"I suspect you're right," I said. "I don't know whether or not I should tell you this, but Dr. Tilton and his wife informed the police about the exchange between you and George on that last evening. He'll be wanting to speak to you next."

Roger swore under his breath. "I sent you upstairs with George and the doctor to prevent just this sort of thing."

"I've told you, George wouldn't talk to him. It was what was said in the drawing room before he went up that Dr. Tilton and his wife reported to the police. It probably didn't seem relevant to the police when Davis Merrit was under suspicion, but now—it must loom large."

"And that will be all over Ashdown before very long. I told my mother we shouldn't invite George. But he knew Alan, there was really no choice in the matter."

"You don't think the police suspect your mother?" I asked, putting it all together. "That makes no sense whatsoever." Unless it was an effort to make her son confess.

"No, it doesn't. But who knows which way the wind will blow before this is finished." He hesitated. "Did you tell Lydia about Rouen? I need to know."

"I didn't think it was my place."

"Thank you. I'd just as soon she didn't know. Are you coming with me to Vixen Hill?"

"I—didn't know how you would feel about that."

"As long as you don't tell her about the child, or what I said to you that night in France, there should be no problem."

"Very well then. I haven't begun my packing. Give me ten minutes, if you will?"

"There's someone I want to talk to. I'll be back. My motorcar is just outside."

I had finished packing and went to the window to see if Captain Ellis had returned. Instead I saw him speaking to someone outside the greengrocer's shop. And the other man was Willy. They were in earnest conversation as far as I could tell, and just then Willy broke it off and walked away.

Captain Ellis turned back toward The King's Head, his face like a thundercloud.

I carried my own valise down to Reception and was waiting there when Captain Ellis came striding inside, as if walking off his black mood. He saw me and without a word took my valise and went out to the motorcar. I followed, and he handed me into the seat before turning the crank.

When we had reversed and were heading in the direction of the Forest, I said, "From my window I saw you speaking to the man they call Willy. What sort of person is he?"

I thought at first he would take my head off for asking.

I added, "Once when I was passing by, he looked up, and there was an odd expression in his eyes. I couldn't quite put my finger on what it was. But surely not that of a half-witted vagabond. Slyness? Calculation?"

"I've only spoken to him once or twice before this," Captain Ellis said, driving far too fast for the condition of the roads after so much rain. "But I think you're right. He's not quite what he seems. I was asking him if he was sure that Davis Merrit had given him that watch. And he was unshakable on that subject."

"Do you know the Lieutenant? From the war, I mean? Could he have been one of your men? Or someone you saw in a dressing station?"

"No. I'd have remembered. Merrit was wounded about the same time I was. Or so my mother has told me. But we weren't in the same sector, apparently. He was with the Buffs, I think. The Kent regiment. So far I've never served with them."

"Did Lieutenant Hughes know Merrit? Or Willy?"

"If he did, he never mentioned it. Why?"

"I'm not sure. I expect I'm looking for some connection that might explain what happened. As in an old quarrel resurfacing."

"Ridiculous." And then he said slowly, "Yes, I see what you mean. If there was bad blood, encountering each other again might have meant trouble. Trouble that had nothing to do with the Ellis family. I wish I knew. It might help take attention away from Vixen Hill."

We drove on in silence then, and finally ahead of us was the turning for the house. But Roger Ellis didn't turn. He drove straight on, and I said, "Where are we going?"

"To St. Mary's. I want you to tell me precisely what you've told Rother. Will you do that?"

I was suddenly wary. "I don't know if that's wise."

"What harm can it do?" he asked shortly, and a silence fell again. He broke it this time.

"Will you continue to search for this child? Or will you give it up?"

"I'm not always free to come and go," I told him honestly. "But if I can, yes."

"I don't see why. There's nothing you can do about her even if you find her."

"That's true. I just have a feeling I ought to do this."

He grunted wordlessly in answer.

When we came to St. Mary's, Roger left the motorcar by the verge, and we walked through the tall wrought iron gate. I looked at the marble kitten, but it seemed to be in exactly the same place. Had Mrs. Ellis really noticed a change? I was no judge.

"I brought you here to help you remember. Was there anything unusual about the churchyard that morning?"

"It was quiet. I didn't notice that anything had changed since we were here the day before. But when I came to the path down to the stream, I could tell that someone—something—had come that way earlier.

Stems bent or broken. That was George Hughes going down, surely, and whoever had followed him."

But he wasn't satisfied. "There must have been something. A man had been killed here just hours before. For God's sake, help me!"

"I wasn't prepared to find a dead man. I wasn't looking for signs, evidence." Was he trying to find out whether or not I knew about the kitten? I was beginning to regret coming with him. Simon had been right, I needed to be careful.

"They took all the walking sticks at Vixen Hill. Did the police tell you what sort of weapon was used?"

I hadn't heard that. "No. And I couldn't see the back of his head from where I stood. Nor when I bent over him to feel for a pulse. His hair was wet, what I could see of it, and I didn't move him."

I think he'd forgot that I was a nurse and had seen many dead bodies before this. He glanced quickly at me, and then away.

I remembered something. "Yesterday he asked me— Inspector Rother—if your mother and I had seen birds fly up, or heard them calling, as if disturbed. But we hadn't. And I couldn't think why we should have done. Surely the killer wasn't still here after all that time."

"Not if he was wise." Roger Ellis sighed. "All right. It was worth trying. They'll be wondering at

Vixen Hill what has kept us." He took my elbow as we turned back across the rough grass toward the motorcar.

We were halfway there when I stopped short. "Captain Ellis."

"I told you in France. Roger. What is it?"

"Roger. It wasn't *birds* he was asking me to remember. He just used them as an example, to nudge my memory. What he wanted to know was if we'd heard a horse neighing or moving about. There are horses here and there in the Forest. But he didn't want to put that idea into my head. Because Davis Merrit had been out riding that morning, and the horse came back without him. What if he hadn't encountered George and killed him, as Inspector Rother wanted to believe—what if instead, quite by accident, he'd met someone else out here, and that person had not wanted to be remembered so close to where the body would eventually be found?"

"Then Merrit is dead, isn't he? It would explain everything—sending for you and for the rest of us, having to begin the inquiry from the very start."

"But how did the watch come into Willy's possession? Who gave it to him? Unless Willy himself is the killer, and he was trying to throw suspicion in Davis Merrit's direction?"

"Why would Willy kill George Hughes?" Roger Ellis asked as he closed the tall iron gates and then held my door for me. "I didn't think they even knew each other."

"What if they did? Inspector Rother has asked me several times if I knew any of you from France. What if the connection was there? Did George ever mention Willy to you? Did you ever see him speak to Willy?"

"No." He cranked the motorcar and then stepped in beside me. "It's more likely that George knew him from here, in the Forest. He lived here, remember, for much of his life. He and Malcolm."

"But you didn't know Willy, did you?"

He smiled grimly. "There are many people here in the Forest that I don't know. And I'm not even certain that that's Willy's true name."

"Inspector Rother called him William Pryor."

"Pryor? I don't know of any family in the Forest by that name. But it proves nothing. Still, you'd think if Pryor came from here, Inspector Rother would know all about him by now."

"That's true. Inspector Rother has told me that he suspects everyone. Even me."

"He's found Merrit's body, then. I wonder where it was?"

I knew. At a place called The Pitch. But I was still wary of telling anyone too much about my conversation with the Inspector. I had a feeling he was laying a trap.

When I said nothing, Roger went on, anger in his face. "I don't like any of this. Damn it, I left my men to come home, and they've been fighting. Someone told me on the ship that the Germans had tried to break through again. And I wasn't there. I wasn't *there*."

I knew what he was feeling. Men at the Front were bound by ties that had nothing to do with blood or class or county. And a good officer wanted to be there when his men were in jeopardy. Whether he could protect them or not, he would try his best. And he was never satisfied that anyone else could fill his shoes. I'd seen badly wounded men get up and try to walk, to convince us that they were able to return to duty.

I put out a hand, before I could change my mind. "Wait. Will you go back to the churchyard with me? There's something I want to show you."

He stopped the motorcar. I thought he would argue with me, but he didn't. He got down and came around to open my door.

We walked back in silence, opened the gate, and after closing it, he followed me across the cold, winter-brown grass. I stopped at his sister's gravestone.

"Do you notice anything different here?" I asked.

Frowning, he looked carefully at the figure of the marble child, and then dropped to his haunches, squatting on an eye level with the grave.

"No. All seems as it should be."

Watching his face carefully, I said, "Then I was wrong. I—it's just that I thought the kitten was not in its usual place."

He studied the kitten, almost as realistic as the little girl it kept company through all these years.

"It's exactly where it ought to be—almost touching her fingers."

"I'm sorry," I said. "But you did ask me to consider everything."

"Yes, well done." We went back to the motorcar after closing the gate a second time.

I had seen Roger Ellis's expression. If that marble kitten had been used as the murder weapon, it wasn't the Captain who had employed it.

And I realized all at once that he wouldn't have. If he'd intended murder, he'd have come prepared. He wouldn't have desecrated his sister's grave.

We drove to Vixen Hill in silence. Roger Ellis had been pleasant enough so far, but then he'd wanted my cooperation. Time would tell whether his mood lasted or not.

Mrs. Ellis looked tired when I saw her as I walked into the hall. Inspector Rother had gone, and although she smiled and told her son that he'd just made her give the same account over and over again until she was confused and felt a headache coming on, he looked sharply at her.

"There's more. What did he tell you?"

"Very little. Except at the end. Roger, I think the police have found Davis Merrit's body. Something—I didn't know quite what it was—distracted him the entire two hours. I could tell, because sometimes I had to repeat what I'd just said. Finally I asked him if there was any news of Davis Merrit's whereabouts. If that was why he'd come back here to question me. And he said he was unable to question the Lieutenant at this time. Not that he hadn't found him, mind you, but that he was unable to question him."

Roger turned to me and said, "I told you!" Then he said to his mother, "Where? Where did they find him? Not here, not in the Forest. You wrote that the police had searched the Forest from one end to the other."

"In The Pitch," I said before I could stop myself. "I think that's where."

"Good God."

Mrs. Ellis turned to me. "I don't think you've been there. It's a low saucer of land that has become quite boggy over the years, particularly in winter, with the rains. I remember Roger's grandfather showing it to me and telling me that when the King was too old to ride, he and his men would stand in that dip of ground and wait for the deer to be driven past them."

"Perhaps half a mile from the church. From St. Mary's," Roger said. "Only it's rough going there. Still, I don't see how—do they know how he died?"

"They never admitted he was dead. I told you," his mother answered.

Lydia had walked into the hall. She must have seen or heard the motorcar arrive and had come down to meet me.

She stopped. "Who is dead?"

"We think it's Davis Merrit, my dear," Mrs. Ellis told her. "We think they've found him at last."

Her face lost its color. "Oh, I'm so sorry. He had handled his blindness so well. It was amazing to me how he got about. I never believed he killed George." She turned to Roger. "Is this why they've reopened the inquiry?"

Roger Ellis had been watching his wife closely. "You must ask the police that." He turned away, his mouth tight, and went up the stairs.

Lydia closed her eyes for a moment, then said to me with a forced smile. "I'm so glad you could come. Mama Ellis was closeted with the Inspector, and Roger volunteered to go to Hartfield in her place."

Because he needed to be sure he could count on my silence about Rouen. But I said, "That was kind of him."

"Yes, I told you he'd changed. Well. Let me take you up to your room. It's the same one."

She caught up my valise and was holding the door as I thanked Mrs. Ellis for letting me stay.

She said, a sadness in her eyes, "We're all in this together, aren't we? I can't help but wonder where it will end."

With the arrest of her son? Or was she fearful for herself?

I followed Lydia up the stairs. On the landing, we encountered Gran. She looked at me with surprise and displeasure. I could guess that no one had told her I was coming back to Vixen Hill.

"Mrs. Ellis," I said, smiling politely, and walked on.

"I can't think why Gran is so cold to me," I said, when we were in my room and the door had shut behind us. "What have I done to upset her?"

"I expect she feels you've let down your sex and your class by taking up nursing. She's very old-fashioned, is Gran."

"Many of the nursing sisters in Queen Alexandra's Imperial Military Nursing Service are women of the middle and upper classes. We're said to look down on the Australian nurses, who sometimes aren't. Although I haven't seen any of that. We're far too grateful for help to quibble. Australian, American, English, we all save lives."

"Yes, well, Gran gave Inspector Rother an earful this morning." Lydia grinned, remembering. "He was asking her how well she knew Davis, and she told him he could take his suspicious mind elsewhere, that she had not known Davis either in the biblical sense or the literal sense of the word."

I had to laugh, picturing their faces as the Inspector and the indomitable Gran squared off.

"What was his reply?"

"He turned as red as a sugar beet and stalked off." Her smile faded. "But he came to see me after that and wanted to know what my relationship with Davis had been. I told him I counted myself a friend, which is exactly what I'd said before."

Daisy summoned us to our luncheon soon after that, and we were all, I was surprised to see, gathered at the table. But we ate our meal in silence, and afterward I was taken up to the room above the hall to meet Bluebell, Davis Merrit's cat.

Bluebell was wary of me—I think she still missed her former life, and I was another stranger in her eyes, bent on taking her away from where she belonged. But Lydia had thought to bring the cat's favorite cushion, and soon Bluebell curled up on that and ignored us.

Lydia said, "I can't believe Davis is dead. I wish the police would tell us—did he take his own life because of his eyes, or did he really murder George? Will they clear his name? If they've been wrong about him?"

"To clear his name, they must arrest someone else."

"Oh."

An hour later Margaret arrived, her face drawn with worry. "I haven't heard from Henry in three weeks," she said as she greeted her mother and grandmother. "And there were two soldiers from his sector who came through London last night in the train of wounded. One of the women bringing the men coffee and fresh bandages told me. They couldn't ask either man for news of Henry. They were too heavily sedated. I should have stayed at home, where I can be reached. Has anyone contacted you, Mama?"

"Henry is all right, my dear," Mrs. Ellis answered her. "I'm sure of it. Now come in and have some tea. I'm so glad you're here with us."

For the next three days Inspector Rother was in and out of the house, taking one or the other of us aside and either going over and over old ground or asking new questions based on whatever he had learned. Sparing no one, not even the distraught Margaret.

I had my share of the Inspector's attention. I was asked if I knew where everyone in the house was that morning when Mrs. Ellis and I set out to search for George Hughes.

I thought I had seen everyone. But after another round of questioning, probing, trying to trick me, I began to doubt my own memory.

Gran took to her room, angry and refusing to have anything more to do with the police. Daisy took to leaving trays of food outside her door. Sometimes they remained untouched.

And I had another worry on my mind. Simon hadn't returned, although he'd told me he would be a day, two at the most. I wondered where he was and what was keeping him. I'd have liked to know too what if anything he'd been able to discover about William Pryor.

Tensions were running high in the house. Roger Ellis lost his temper twice to my knowledge, sending Lydia to her room over the hall in tears the first time, and upsetting his mother the second time. Word from the Front, what we were able to hear of it, was not good, and Roger chafed at being here when he was sorely needed in France. To his credit, he did make some telephone calls from Hartfield to see what he could discover about Henry, but there was no news at all.

"Which is reassuring," Mrs. Ellis told her daughter. "Take it as a good thing, my dear."

But Margaret shook her head and went to her room "for a lie down" she said, but it was to cry. At dinner that night her eyes were red-rimmed and puffy, her voice husky.

The morning of the fourth day, Inspector Rother arrived at Vixen Hill and after an hour's discussion with Roger's mother, took her away to Wych Gate. Roger was livid when he came home and heard what had transpired in his absence. He set out for Wych Gate straightaway, and when I asked if I could go with him, he was curt.

"No."

Neither of them had returned in time for lunch, and there was still no news when our tea was brought in at four o'clock. It was already dark as pitch outside when there was a knock at the hall door. We could hear it from the sitting room, as if whoever it was had used his fist.

Lydia went with Molly to answer it, and then came back to where we all waited in anxious silence.

"The hotel clerk from The King's Head," she said to me. "There's a telephone message from your mother. You're to call her back at once."

"I'll go and see—"

"He came on his bicycle, Bess, and the wind is fearsome," Lydia said. "Take Mama's motorcar. It will be quicker as well as warmer."

Margaret sat up straight. "But what if there's news of Henry? And I can't get to Hartfield?"

"I can take a bicycle," I began, but Lydia wouldn't hear of it.

"If there's a message from Henry, Bess can come back for you," she told her sister-in-law.

And so I set out for Hartfield, the silent clerk in the motorcar beside me, his bicycle strapped to the boot. He could tell me no more about the telephone call, but I asked all the same if my mother sounded upset.

"I wasn't the one who answered," he said. "I'm sorry."

When we got to Hartfield, there was a flurry of activity in the normally quiet streets, and I said, "What's happened?"

The clerk, peering out the windscreen, said, "I don't know. There was no one in the street when I left. Silent as the tomb, it was."

It would have taken him well over half an hour to bicycle to Vixen Hill.

Slowing, I said, "Is that Inspector Rother with the torch? There, just across from the inn. Look, he's going to Bluebell Cottage!"

He disappeared inside the door, closing it after him. The small circle of onlookers was being kept back by a constable, and I recognized Constable Bates. There was someone else just coming up the road, hurrying to speak to Constable Bates, and as he was allowed to proceed, I recognized the rector, Mr. Smyth.

I drove slowly, cautiously, edging past the gawking crowd, and then I heard Constable Bates shout, "You there. Where do you think you're going?"

I was saved from answering by the inn's clerk, who leaned out his window and called, "I need to reach The King's Head. Is that all right?"

"I thought it was one of the Ellises, pushing their way through. Yes, go on."

I crept slowly past, but just as I drew even with him, there was a shout from the cottage, and Constable Bates turned toward it, not toward me.

"Can you drive? Take this motorcar, turn around, and go to Vixen Hill. Find Captain Ellis and bring him back," I told the clerk quietly. "I'll get down here."

I slipped out into the shadowy darkness beyond range of the torches and was out of sight by the time Constable Bates had crossed to the cottage door to speak to Inspector Rother. Behind me, I could just hear Mrs. Ellis's motorcar reverse as far as Dr. Tilton's house, the headlamps dimmed. I walked into The King's Head and sought out the woman behind Reception's desk.

She smiled as I approached. "Yes?" And then as she recognized me, she added, "Ah, Sister Crawford. What's happening out there? I hear people shouting."

"I don't know, I think the police must be after someone," I answered quickly. "The telephone?"

"I'm afraid it's in use at the moment. It was your mother who telephoned. Mrs. Crawford. She said it was urgent. I hope it isn't bad news."

Fifteen

Well out of sight of the police outside, I stood there in Reception, trying to contain my impatience and my worry. My mother wouldn't have telephoned me unless it was a dire emergency.

Was it Simon, who hadn't come back as he'd promised in "a day—a day and a half at most"?

Or my father. Had something happened to the Colonel Sahib?

I was trying to think what to say to Inspector Rother if I had to leave for London straightaway, or even Somerset.

I decided then that if it was necessary, I would take the Ellis motorcar and drive to London without telling anyone. The same hotel clerk could carry a note to the family in the morning, when it would be too late to stop me. I'd find someone in London who could ferry the motorcar back to Sussex. One of my flatmates, if anyone was there. Someone. I was willing to pay handsomely, it wouldn't be impossible.

Finally the artillery officer who had been using the telephone stepped away from it, and as I hurried forward, I heard him say to the woman behind the desk, "I shall need to put through another call to London shortly. Will you keep the line clear?"

My heart plummeted. As far as I knew there was no other telephone in Hartfield.

She saw me hesitate. "This young woman has missed a call from her family. She looks very worried. Would you mind if she used the instrument meanwhile? I'm sure it won't take very long."

He turned, on the point of saying no, I could read it in his face. And then he saw that I was a nursing sister, and his expression changed.

"Yes, go ahead, Sister."

I thanked him and after some difficulty with the lines, I put through the call to Somerset.

The phone rang and rang, my anxiety growing with each ring.

And then my mother's voice came down the line.

"Bess, dear?"

"I'm here, Mother. Is the Colonel all right? Simon?"

"Yes, my dear, they've been delayed. I have a feeling they're in Scotland. Or else training Scottish troops. Your father murmured something about haggis as he left."

I was so relieved I couldn't stop my lower lip from trembling, and it was a moment before I said, "That's wonderful."

"Not the haggis, Bess, he abominates it."

I swallowed a bubble of hysterical laughter.

She went on, "Are you all right? Simon was quite worried about having to abandon you. Richard wasn't very happy about it either."

"Yes, I'm very well, Mother. It's been rather trying, but I hope the police will be satisfied soon." Was this the reason she'd called? Because she was worried about me?

But then she said, "I had a telephone call earlier this evening. An hour or so ago. Someone trying to reach you. Apparently he was in Dover, in some difficulties with the authorities there, and needed to speak to you urgently. He wouldn't give me his name, and I rather thought there must be others listening in to his side of the conversation. But he said you would remember the kingfisher. Do you have any idea what on earth he was talking about?"

I drew a blank for all of ten seconds. And then I did laugh. "Did he sound Australian to you?"

"I'm not sure, Bess. His voice was very strained, and he coughed every other breath. In fact, he seemed to have some trouble breathing."

"How on earth did he find you in Somerset?"

"I've no idea. He begged me to reach you, and he said he'd be waiting in Dover for you, and if you could come there straightaway, he would be very grateful. He said it was most urgent, or he'd be clapped in irons and everything would be lost."

I couldn't imagine why Sergeant Larimore should be telephoning me from Dover, or even how he got there.

"Was he—do you think he'd been drinking?" I asked, for the Australians had a reputation for putting away large quantities of beer. And he might have taken a dare and tried to come to England.

"I couldn't tell, not with the coughing. He wouldn't leave a number. He said you must come as quickly as you could."

"I'm not supposed to leave here," I began, and then I had one of those feelings we all get at one time or another, that I ought to go. After all, Dover was closer than London or Somerset. If I was prepared to risk Inspector Rother's ire by leaving to go to either place, why not risk it and go to Dover? If the Sergeant was a deserter—and somehow I couldn't picture him abandoning his men—he'd be in a great deal of trouble. I wasn't sure what I could do, but I would try to help.

"I've changed my mind. Mother, if he should telephone you again, tell him I'm on my way."

"Yes, I'd feel very much better if you did go. But it's late to be starting out for Dover, my dear, and you must be very careful. Promise?"

"I promise." Out of the corner of my eye I could see the officer hovering, wanting his telephone back. "I must go, someone else needs to use the telephone. I'll give you a shout as soon as I can."

"I'll send Simon to you as soon as he returns."

"Thank you. Good night. And don't worry."

"And you'll tell me all about this kingfisher, won't you?"

She put up the receiver on that note, and I turned to thank the officer trying to hide his impatience.

As I turned away, I said to the woman at Reception, "What happened across the street?"

"I don't know," she said. "I looked out the door just now and saw one of the constables speaking to Inspector Rother. I didn't know he was in Hartfield this evening—he often dines with us when he's here, and I hadn't seen him. Someone who came in just after you said something about a fire. But I haven't seen the fire brigade."

I thanked her and was about to wait outside for Roger Ellis to come, when the officer using the telephone came striding out and said to the woman behind the desk, "I'm off, then. Thank you for your help."

Off?

I stepped forward and asked, "Major? May I ask where you're going—and if you have a motorcar?"

"Yes, I do. I'm reporting to Dover tonight. They've canceled my leave."

"Please? Would you mind if I go with you? I—I've had a summons from Dover as well, and I'm not sure how to get there." Holding out my hand, I said, "My name is Elizabeth Crawford. I'm Colonel Crawford's daughter."

"By all means, I'll be happy to escort you to Dover."

Turning to the woman behind the desk, I said, "Please, if Captain Ellis comes, will you tell him I will be back as quickly as possible?"

We went out to his motorcar and drove out of Hartfield, crossing the railroad tracks outside the town before turning toward Kent, and Dover, on the English Channel. He reached in the back and brought out a rug, which I pulled around my shoulders.

The night had turned cold, the stars overhead bright in the blackness of the sky, and I could feel my feet beginning to go numb from the frigid air. The heater was barely sufficient for one of them, and I kept alternating them close by the vent. Once or twice we stopped on the verge of the road and stamped some circulation back into our limbs. Major Hutton asked me at one point where I lived, and when I told him London, he said, "Then you've been to see the bear?"

My mind was on Dover. "The bear?" I repeated, then remembered.

A Canadian officer of the Fort Garry Horse, one Lieutenant Colebourn, had smuggled a small female black bear into England. Her name was Winnipeg, after the town where he lived. When he and his unit sailed for France, he left her in the care of the London zoo. She was enormously popular. Diana, Mary, and I had gone to see her one afternoon, and I told the Major this.

He grinned as we walked together in the glare of the headlamps, his teeth very white in the shadow of his military mustache. "I took my future wife there the first time we went out to dine. Two years ago. She's expecting our child now, and she's threatened to name it Winnipeg, if it's a son."

"Be very glad, sir, that you didn't take her to see one of those Australian kingfishes, a kookabura."

We laughed together, and then, blowing on our fingers, we walked back to the motorcar. I was glad of the Major's company on this dark and twisting road.

Outside Chatham we stopped again, and later drove through the silent streets of Canterbury. It was nearly dawn when we drove down from the cliffs and into the seaside town of Dover.

It had grown with the influx of people coming from and going to France, and even at this early hour there were men lining up for roll call before being marched on board. Their faces pinched with the cold and anxiety for what lay ahead, they looked dreadfully young to me. The days when men lined up in their dozens to be the first to enlist had long since passed. Now the reality of the trenches had scoured away that bravado, and in its place were these recruits, afraid of shaming themselves in front of their mates but probably wishing themselves anywhere but here.

The Major asked me to drop him near a cluster of officers standing some distance away from the Sergeants barking orders.

"If you will, take the motorcar to HQ. Someone there will see to it. Do you have time?"

"Yes, sir." I took the wheel and went first to the police station. But they knew nothing about an Australian Sergeant, and so I went to find the officer in charge of the port.

He was sitting in a cramped office that overlooked the sea. It was filled with paperwork, with ships' manifests, lists of supplies destined for France and no doubt roll after roll of names, and all the other paraphernalia of getting men and materiel across the sea to France.

He looked up as I was admitted, rising tiredly from his chair. "Sister," he said.

"Good morning, sir. Sister Crawford, sir. I'm sorry to disturb you, but I understand there's an Australian Sergeant who is in Dover, possibly without his proper papers." I'd had the long dark ride across Kent to think about what I should say.

I'd expected a blank stare. But he said, "Ah, yes. I think he's being held in one of the huts under guard. Number seventeen. He says he has a head wound and can't remember much after the forward dressing station. It's likely he came from the Base Hospital in Rouen, judging from his blue uniform. He can't remember how he got aboard a ship. He claims you'll be looking for him."

"Yes, sir, he's been quite troublesome, wandering off," I said, feeling my way. "Er, how does he look?"

"His hair is singed, he has no eyebrows, and his hands are badly burned. I had someone take a look at him."

He hadn't been burned when last I saw him. "He's not accountable," I said.

"I should think not. When he's questioned, he breaks out in crazed laughter. It gave me quite a start the first time I heard it. He was brought here because he was stopped on the street and couldn't account for himself."

More bewildered than anything else, I said, "I think I ought to have a look at him. We need to return him to France as soon as possible. He'll have been reported missing by now."

"You'll be careful? I'll send one of my men with you."

"I'll be all right," I told him, not wishing to have an audience when I found Sergeant Larimore. Gesturing to the cluttered desk in front of him, I said, "You have enough on your hands this morning. I saw the recruits preparing to report."

"Yes, poor devils. Thank you, Sister Crawford. Any relation to Colonel Crawford and his family?"

"He's my father."

"Is he, by God!" His attitude warmed considerably. "Tell me what you need, Sister, and I'll see that you get it."

I thanked him and went out. The port was cluttered and crowded. I managed to find the line of huts. They turned out to be temporary housing for any number of offices associated with the smooth running of the port. Number seventeen, set to one side of the rest, had a soldier on guard by the door.

With a sinking heart, I walked up to the soldier, a grizzled veteran with a decided limp, and told him I'd been asked to take a look at his charge.

"I don't think it's safe, Sister," he warned me. "He's right barmy, is that one."

"I've handled worse cases. They seem to respond to the uniform," I said pleasantly.

With some reluctance, he stood aside. "I'll stay within call," he promised.

I went to the door. It was, to my surprise, unlocked. I walked in as the first late rays of winter sun rose over the horizon and sent a shaft of light across the gray Channel to wash the drab, salt-stained huts a pale gold.

At first I couldn't see anyone in the dark interior. And then as my eyes grew accustomed to the shadows, I saw that there were two cots in the room, and a bucket on the floor between them. Nothing else.

"Sergeant? Sergeant Larimore?" I said, and immediately the prone figure on one of the cots shot up with an oath.

"Sister," he answered in a low, hoarse voice. "Great God, woman, I'd given you up." He stood, and the light of the rising sun caught him full in the face.

I gasped. He was burned, just as the Captain had said, his face raw, his eyebrows all but gone, his hair shorter in front than in the back. His blue hospital uniform was torn, stained with God knew what, and scorched.

"What happened to you?" I asked, appalled.

"We haven't time to talk. You must get me out of here, it's—just trust me, and I'll tell you everything," he pleaded in a hoarse whisper.

"But you're in Dover—how did you get here? What have you done?"

"Never mind that. I've told them I had a head wound, I'm out of my mind. Just play along, Sister, and help me. For God's sake."

I had two choices: to go along with whatever it was he wanted to do or to turn him over to the authorities as a deserter. And if I did that, he would be shot.

I said, exasperation clear in my voice as I spoke loud enough to reach the sentry outside, "Sergeant. I told you I must go to England. Not you. Didn't you understand? I can't help you here, you should have stayed with Sister Barlow. She's a good nurse. And none of this would have happened."

A grin split his thin, tired face. But his voice was humble as he answered, "Sister, please help me. My head hurts something terrible, I can't think straight. You told me you'd see me right. That's why I came looking for you."

"It's a wonder you haven't fallen ill of pneumonia. Oh, very well, Sergeant. Come along and I'll do what I can. But give me any trouble and I'll turn you in to the nearest soldier."

I pushed at the door, and the guard took two quick steps out of its way as it swung open. I could tell he'd been listening. But he asked, "Everything all right, Sister?"

"Yes, he's not clear in his mind. I'll find a doctor and see about returning him to France."

"Shall I go with you? He don't appear dangerous to me, but you never know." He looked Sergeant Larimore up and down. The Sergeant managed a lunatic grin. "He's a big 'un, and it's the quiet ones that go off their heads when you least expect it."

"He's too ill to hurt a fly," I scoffed. "You may report that I take full responsibility." Then turning to Sergeant Larimore at my heels, I said, "See what you've got me into. And don't make that ridiculous noise again. This way."

"Yes, Sister," he replied meekly.

In single file we walked back down the row of huts, and then out through the port gates, no one stopping us, although I saw several faces turned our way, curiosity writ large. I couldn't help but think that it would take all the Colonel Sahib's authority to save me if this went wrong.

But the Sergeant loped behind me, head hung in contrition, looking like a lost soul in need of resurrection.

When we'd cleared the gates and were some one hundred paces farther along, he caught me up, saying in a very different tone of voice, "You must come with me. Quickly."

"Where?"

"Not here." We walked on into the town, avoiding the foot traffic and all the lorries that had finished unloading their cargo on the ships, their drivers looking now for breakfast before making the long drive back to London. We passed half a dozen officers who nodded to me and then looked askance at the man trailing me.

"Sergeant. We ought to get off the streets. I have a motorcar—"

"That hotel on the far corner. Do you see it?"

I did. A seedy hotel favored by ships' crews and with something of an unsavory reputation.

"That's where we're heading."

We covered the distance without mishap, and he led me in the door.

The woman behind the desk, her eyes sharp and knowing, said, "Hold on, I'll have none of that here."

I said in my best imitation of Matron, "We've come to fetch the Sergeant's things. He's ill, he ought to be in hospital."

She turned her gaze to his face. "Anything catching?"

"I don't know. The sooner he's examined, the better. Now will you let us pass?"

She nodded, adding, "Just get him out of my hotel quick as may be."

We climbed stairs tracked with muddy footprints.

"It was the best I could do," he said softly. "They wouldn't let me through the door of a decent place. Not like this."

"I understand."

We walked down a passage with bare floorboards and ill-painted doors to either side. Sergeant Larimore stopped at one of them, dug in his pocket for the key, and unlocked the door. "I'll go first," he said, and I let him, not knowing what lay ahead.

But it was only an empty room, the bedclothes a-tumble.

"There was a fire," he said, turning to look at me. "Half the houses went up in flames. After you left, I'd been keeping an eye on Rue St. Catherine whenever I could slip out of hospital, and I was one of the first on the scene. I rescued as many people as I could before the roofs started to come down. Dry as tinder, those old houses, in spite of the rain we've had."

I was watching his face, dawning horror drying up my throat.

"The nuns—did you see the nuns?" I couldn't say anything else.

"They got out safely. I saw the elderly one. Her robes were singed about as bad as my uniform, but she was looking after her charges."

"They made it out safely?" I asked. "All of them?"

"All of them. Only I got away with one of them." He walked to the tumble of bedclothes, and I realized with something like shock that a small child was asleep in the cocoon of sheets.

I went to the bedside myself, gently pulled a corner of a coverlet away, and a strand of fair hair, bright as sunlight in the dingy room, caught in my fingers.

"Sergeant—you didn't—you kidnapped her! The nuns will think she burned in the fire. They—they'll be distraught!"

"It was the only chance to get her out of there," he said, his voice still hoarse. "The house is rubble. What was I to do? Leave her to the French authorities to decide her future? Not likely! You would never find her again."

It was so like Sergeant Larimore to have acted on the spur of the moment, when the opportunity came his way, knowing I was gravely concerned about this child's fate. I couldn't fault him—and yet I was horrified by the decision he'd made. What on earth was I to do about this?

He'd listened to every word I'd said about her, that was clear enough, and he remembered everything I'd told him about myself, or he'd never have known how to contact my mother. I couldn't help but be amazed as well as shocked. He was the most extraordinary man.

He stood there while I took it all in, giving me time to come to terms with all that he'd just related to me.

I sighed. "What are we to do now?"

"I see it this way, Sister. You get me aboard a ship soon as may be, telling them I was out of my mind from a fire in an empty house where I'd wandered, and that I must be returned to the Base Hospital. And you take the little girl home. We both come out of this without any trouble. You still have leave, don't you?"

"Yes, but—" I pictured Inspector Rother's furious face. "Yes," I said firmly.

He was right about his own situation. I had to get him safely back to France, I couldn't let him be disciplined or put in any further jeopardy on my account.

"How did you smuggle her out of Rouen? She doesn't know you."

"I was clever. I took her to an American nurse, told her the child was frightened out of her wits—and that was true, as God is my witness!—and could she sedate her until I could find her family. Everyone knew about the fire. You could see the flames and then the smoke. It was dark, everything at sixes and sevens. I think she's a little sweet on me, that nurse, and she gave the child something to calm her. She's been sleeping like this ever since. Exhaustion as well as the drug. I went out to get some milk for her last night, and that's when I was picked up. I was frantic something would happen to her while I was in custody." He gestured to the door. "I had a key, for what it's worth. But I had to take the chance, Sister. There wasn't much choice."

"But how did you get her aboard ship?"

"That was the easiest part. It was late, very dark, and there were a great many wounded being loaded. I slipped aboard when no one was looking and found a rope locker down below. When we landed I picked up a mop and a pail, and walked off with it in one hand and the little one wrapped up in an Army blanket and slung over my shoulder. We'd only just arrived when I telephoned your mother, and I found this hotel straightaway. I couldn't help but think I might have been a German spy. There's a frightening thought for you."

"Yes, and you could well have been mistaken for one. And shot. It was a terrible risk. And what would they have said, if they'd found you with Sophie?"

"I'd have told them she was mine. That I'd taken her from her dead French mother and was carrying her to my English fiancée." He grinned. "That's you. Besides, I'm fair enough to make that believable."

And he was.

"Sister Marie Joseph will be mourning her. They will all mourn her. I must take her back."

"No such thing, Sister. She belongs here. And she's young enough to settle in now. Wait until the war is over and the lawyers are finished, and it will be twice as hard for her. She'll be right as rain, wait and see."

But Roger Ellis *was* in England just now, and that complicated matters no end. I'd let him think I hadn't found her. What would he say when I walked into Vixen Hill with her?

The Sergeant said gently, almost as if he realized the quandary I was in, "You can always take her back, if it doesn't work out."

And he was right, I could. But with what explanation?

"They don't have to know she left France. Someone could have rescued her and kept her. She's that pretty."

And that was true too.

"All right."

He pulled back the bedclothes, lifted Sophie like a bundle of old clothes, although his hands were gentle and he held her with care.

"Do you have children of your own?" I asked, watching him.

"God, no, Sister. I haven't found the right wife yet."

We went out the door, down the passage, and out into the street. I made a point of leaving the key on the desk at Reception.

Outside, he said, "You'd better hurry. She's waking up."

"Let me have her."

"Not yet. She's heavier than you'd think."

But he gave her to me when we reached the port again, and I walked along the water until I found a ship bound for Rouen. There was a nursing sister mopping up blood from the deck as we came aboard, and I said, "Sister, I've got a patient here. He's not right in his mind. Somehow he got sent to England with the latest casualties because of his burns, but he belongs at the Base Hospital in Rouen. Can you see him safely back there? My leave is just starting, I'd hate to lose it."

She straightened up, massaging her back. I knew how it must hurt after a night voyage from France.

"Base Hospital, you said? Rouen? Is he an American?"

"No, he was there being treated. He was collected with the other casualties by mistake. He's safe enough, he just has no idea where he is or how he got here. He'll sit quietly until you tell him to disembark."

It took some persuasion. I didn't think she wanted to be encumbered by a patient on the return crossing, when she could spend the time catching up on her sleep. But Sergeant Larimore was a tall, attractive man, and that was in his favor. I could read that in her face too.

I said, "He's no trouble. Just confused and uncertain. Will you see him safely back?"

"Just starting your leave, you said? Where did you find him?"

"Walking the streets of Dover. Fortunately I recognized him. A pathetic case, really, I don't know if he'll ever be entirely right. But he's gentle. I've had no trouble with him."

Sophie stirred in her bundle of wraps.

"Who's that?" the sister said, peering into the little face that was emerging.

"My goddaughter. I really must go. Her mother will be frantic by now. I was just taking Sophie for a walk when I ran into the Sergeant here."

"All right, I'll see him safely back to base." She looked him up and down. "Was he in a fire?"

I shrugged. "How should I know? When I left him, he was clean, shaven, and quiet."

"Not shell shock, is it?"

"No. I swear to you it isn't shell shock." That I could state with complete truthfulness.

She must have believed me. Ordering Sergeant Larimore below, she told him, "I'll sort you out in a few minutes."

"He'll need something to eat," I reminded her. "I don't know when he last had a meal. He can't remember."

I followed him to the companionway, as if making sure he went below, saying to him in a low voice, "If there's any trouble, send for me."

"I'll do that, Sister. Although I think I've earned the right to call you Bess now." He grinned, cast a quick look around the empty deck, and then before I could stop him, he stooped and kissed me on the lips. Then he was gone.

I looked after him, hoping he'd be all right, and then carried the wriggling bundle in my arms off the ship and out of the port. Sophie was beginning to whimper, and I hurried to the Major's motorcar, making what soothing sounds I could. The sun was well over the horizon by that time, winter bright and blinding as it created a golden path across the water.

What was I to do now? I asked myself as I turned the crank.

Where was I to take her? To my mother? To Vixen Hill?

I'd have been happy to pass the problem to my mother, who had the reputation of being able to cope no matter what was happening all around her. But this was, in a sense, my doing, for having unwittingly involved Sergeant Larimore.

The first order of business was to get as far from Dover as I could.

By the time I'd reached Canterbury, Sophie was wide eyed and staring around. I'd handled and looked after babies and small children during my training, and so I began to talk to her in French, smiling and asking her name, telling her mine. We counted to ten, and sang a little song. She bounced in time with the ruts of the road. When that palled, she made the sound of the motor, pretending there was a wheel in front of her and turning it this way and that, mimicking me. I don't think she'd ever been in a motorcar before, and it fascinated her.

I stopped in a village not far from Chillingham and bought milk for her as well as a few biscuits. She drank the milk with an appetite, but I didn't think she'd ever had biscuits, for she turned them this way and that,

before I could persuade her to taste one of them. Then she was so enthralled she hummed to herself as she ate them.

Beyond Canterbury, the warmth of the sun in the motorcar made her eyes heavy, and her head flopped to one side as she fell asleep on the rug I'd wrapped around my shoulders the night before.

I knew better than to try to make her more comfortable. Instead I let her sleep.

And what in God's name was I to do about the Major's motorcar?

By the time we'd reached the Sussex border later in the afternoon, she was awake again, and complaining, more a whimper than a cry. Her mouth turned down, and her eyes looked so sad I could have picked her up and held her. Pulling to the verge, I turned to her.

The nuns and the other children were the only family this child had ever known, and she had been taken unceremoniously from them. But the fire must have frightened her and made the initial separation much easier.

Now she wanted familiar faces and familiar surroundings, and she began to cry in earnest, great tears rolling down her cheeks.

I lifted her into my lap and held her, feeling such guilt I could hardly bear it.

The last of the biscuits stopped the tears, and she looked at me with large, bewildered eyes before falling asleep on my shoulder. I put her carefully into the seat beside me before driving on.

Even with the best of intentions, there was no way to carry her back to France now. By this time Sergeant Larimore had already sailed, and I was already long overdue in Sussex.

I bought more milk for her just before crossing the Kent border into Sussex, and turned toward Ashdown Forest.

And I still didn't know what I was to do with Sophie.

I didn't even know the child's last name.

Sophie was crying again, a forlorn little creature huddled in her blankets by the time we'd reached Hartfield, and my level of guilt had spun out of control. Night had fallen, and I was wondering how I could find my way through the heath.

I couldn't go to The King's Head. Arriving with a very young child would cause comment that would get back to the Ellis family almost overnight. And the explanations I would have to make would only add to the gossip.

I had no choice but to continue to Vixen Hill.

I was halfway there when Sophie fell into a restless sleep. It was just as well, because suddenly a motorcar coming out of a side track nearly cut me off.

I stopped quickly, throwing out an arm to keep the sleeping child from sliding off the seat.

By that time Inspector Rother was out of the motorcar and stalking toward me in my headlamps.

My heart sank.

"You do realize," he said, "that you can be taken into custody after what you've done?"

"I'm so sorry, Inspector. I was under orders."

"I doubt that. Where have you been, Miss Crawford?"

"To Dover," I told him truthfully. "I'm a nurse, Inspector. I was needed, and I went. Now I've come back to Ashdown Forest to continue answering your questions."

"I told you not to leave."

"So you did. But this was a military matter, and not for my own pleasure. If you will telephone the port, the officer in charge, a Captain Wilson, will tell you that it was a matter of a man with a head injury who had to be identified and processed."

That gave him pause, and it was still the absolute truth.

"And when did this summons come? Were you the only nursing sister available for this task?"

"I was the only one who could recognize him. As for how the summons came, a clerk from the inn came to Vixen Hill to tell me that there was an urgent message for me. He and I drove back to The King's Head, I put through my telephone call—there are witnesses to that as well. I set out for Dover immediately with an Army officer. The woman at Reception can verify that."

"At what time?"

"I don't know the time. But I did see you walking toward Bluebell Cottage, and your constable, Constable Bates, even spoke to the clerk as we drove into Hartfield. I left some ten minutes later."

"The Ellis family was not aware that you had left. They have been concerned. I have spoken to them."

"Sadly, there was no way I could send a message to them." But I'd left word at the inn. Had no one gotten it? "I would have spoken to you, but you were occupied with Bluebell Cottage. Did you find something significant there?"

"We went there to search for another body. See that you don't take such liberties again," he said gruffly, and turned back to his vehicle, leaving me to stare after him.

Sixteen

I drove with great care the rest of the way to the turning for Vixen Hill, and in spite of that, the tires swerved in a rut, and Sophie woke up and started to cry again. She was hungry and very, very tired. I was so grateful that Inspector Rother hadn't seen her in the darkness.

Sergeant Larimore had had her best interests at heart, but he hadn't thought it through any more than I had when I began to search for Sophie.

We pulled up in front of the door to the hall, and I turned off the motor.

In the quiet that followed, Sophie sniffed and looked at me as if to ask why we were stopping. "*C'est votre maison, maintenant, chérie. Votre nouvelle maison.*"

This is your home now, dear one. Your new home.

She turned to look up at the imposing house before her, tears still streaking her cheeks, and then held up her arms to me to take her out of the motorcar.

Keeping her well wrapped against the cold, I carried her to the door and lifted the knocker. But Daisy must have heard the motorcar arrive, because she opened the door at once.

"Oh, Miss, we was so worried!"

"I'm sorry, Daisy. It's a long story. Is—everyone all right?"

"Yes, Miss. It was you we was worried about." She peered into the shadows at the bundle I was carrying. "Is that a baby?"

"A child," I said, "hungry and tired and frightened."

"I've looked after my brothers and sisters," she said. "I can manage. But where did she come from?" She reached for Sophie, who pulled away.

"I'll take her down to the kitchens, Daisy. Will you lead the way?"

There was no one in the hall as we entered. Daisy had been building up the fire when I knocked, her tongs lying on the carpet, an extra log in the wood box for the evening. She hastily put the tongs back where she'd found them, and, dusting her hands, she went through the door into the passage.

"The family is dressing for dinner," she said. "Should I send for Mrs. Matthew?"

"Later, perhaps."

We made it to the kitchen without meeting anyone. Around me sat the array of dishes that would be taken to the sitting room in another quarter of an hour. Onions baked in a cream sauce, a side dish of greens, a small platter of roasted chicken and potatoes. I felt my own empty stomach growl at the sight.

We put Sophie down in one of the wooden chairs, and Daisy found milk for her in the pantry, as well as a scone that had been left over from tea.

Sophie sat on my lap and drank the milk, then nibbled at the scone, her gaze sweeping the kitchen and then scanning Daisy's face. I expect she had never seen so much food or been in a room quite so warm. After a moment she got down and held out the cup to be filled again, and still nibbling at the scone, she considered me.

I smiled. "*Je m'appelle Bess*," I said softly. I call myself Bess.

Daisy stared. "What was that you said, Miss?"

"It's French—" I could have bitten my tongue. But I was tired, it had been over twenty-four hours since I'd slept, and I'd driven miles.

Daisy's eyes grew wide. "This isn't the little girl that was spoken of in the drawing room before the

Lieutenant was killed?" She studied the small, tear-streaked face. "My good lord, she does look like Miss Juliana, in that portrait."

"How did you hear about her?" I asked sharply. "You weren't in the drawing room that night."

"No, Miss, but the lad who brings our order from the greengrocer's is brother to the cook at Dr. Tilton's house, and she overheard them talking about the child. They said it was Mr. Roger's. Is that true?"

"You'll have to ask him," I said. "Will you make up a little porridge, or a pudding?"

"Yes, Miss, and there's an extra potato left in the pot. I can make up a little soup with the broth from the chicken."

"Yes, that will do well." I held out my arms to Sophie, and after a moment she came to them, wary and uncertain. "I'll take her to my room for now. And I'd rather you didn't say anything until after—"

The door to the kitchen swung open, and Lydia came in. "Was there someone at the door—" She too broke off in midsentence.

"Bess! Where on earth have you been? "And then she saw Sophie, whose face had crumpled at the sight of the newcomer, and I remembered that the nuns had said that there were few visitors who saw the children.

"Is that—oh, Bess, where did you find her? How?" She came around to the other side of the table. "Dear God," she whispered as she saw Sophie clearly. "She's Roger's daughter. She must be."

"I don't know whose child she is," I said quickly. "And she's here only for a very short time. The nuns in France—"

"I don't care about the nuns," Lydia said, and dropped to her knees before Sophie. "Can she understand us?"

"She speaks only French," I said.

To my surprise, Lydia began to speak to Sophie in French that was far better than mine. I hadn't known she'd studied the language, much less spoke it so well.

For a moment Sophie leaned back against me, staring at Lydia. But the accent was familiar enough that after a moment Sophie began to reply. Tentative at first, and then more readily.

Lydia asked her name and where she was from, how old she was—the sort of questions an adult usually puts to a child.

I said, "Where did you learn to speak French?"

She answered, never taking her eyes from Sophie, "When I was fourteen, we had a French mistress at our school. I won a prize for the best accent."

"She's very tired," I told Lydia. "I was just about to take her to my room. She isn't used to so many strangers at once."

"No, I want her in my room. There's Davis's cat, she'll like Bluebell, and I can get to know her." She got up from her knees and flung her arms around me. "Bess, you're wonderful. I'm so grateful. You can't know how grateful."

"She isn't yours," I insisted. "She must go back to France as soon as I can return her to the convent. The nuns will be frantic, there was a fire—"

Lydia's face hardened. "She's not going anywhere. She's mine. I won't let her be taken back to France."

I said wearily, "You don't have any choice, Lydia. She's not yours. Nor is she mine. There are laws, papers, arrangements to be made."

"Then we'll make them. Why should she live out a life of drudgery in a convent? Look at her, she's the image of Juliana. Roger is her father, he can tell the French authorities that he's adopting her. Or whatever they call it in France."

"He doesn't know she's here. He may not want to keep her."

"Yes, he will. She's his flesh and blood. And I'm his wife."

There was no reasoning with her. Before I could say anything else, make any stronger arguments, she had lifted Sophie into her arms, asking the child if she wanted to see the cat.

Sophie's tired face brightened, and she nodded.

"See?" Lydia said to me over her shoulder. "She's happy with me."

"She's hungry, Lydia. I've asked Daisy to make her a light supper after the family has dined."

"That's a lovely idea. Daisy, ask Molly to bring a tray to my room." She corrected herself. "The room I'm using. And some bedding, please. Pillows, a quilt or two."

"We'll see to it," Daisy promised her. "But isn't she the dearest little thing?"

And Lydia was out the door, calling over her shoulder, "Bess, please, will you tell the family I have a headache? I won't be dining tonight."

And she was gone.

I didn't know how I was to get through the dinner ahead. I debated going after Lydia and taking Sophie away from her. But that would only serve to frighten Sophie and make her cry.

"I must hurry and change," I said and left the room before Daisy or the cook, Mrs. Long, could ask any more questions.

I bathed my face and hands, changed out of the uniform I had worn for nearly two days straight, and put on the only evening dress I had with me, a dark blue one that was more practical than it was stylish.

When I came down to the drawing room ten minutes later, everyone turned to stare as I crossed the threshold.

"I'm so sorry, Mrs. Ellis. When I went to Hartfield to take the call, I was asked to proceed at once to Dover. There was no one I could ask to carry a message to you."

"Why Dover?" Roger Ellis asked, suspicion darkening his eyes.

"There was a problem with one of my patients. Daisy said you'd been worried, and I apologize for that as well." I looked from Mrs. Ellis to Margaret and then to Gran. "As Captain Ellis can tell you, duty is not a matter of choice."

"We were quite concerned, especially after the situation in Hartfield. We were afraid something had happened to you." She went to the table by the window. "There's a little sherry left of our trove. You look as if you could use something to lift your spirits. Was it very bad in Dover?"

I took the sherry gratefully, feeling its burn as I swallowed it. "I drove straight there with a Major on his way to join his regiment, and I returned, without sleep. Yes, Dover was quite trying." While I still held the floor, I asked, "But what were the police doing in Hartfield? I had to leave before I could discover what their interest was in Bluebell Cottage. The constables were holding everyone back. Tonight, when I encountered Inspector Rother on the road, he told me that they were searching for another body. But he refused to tell me any more than that."

"A body?" Mrs. Ellis turned to her son. "You didn't say anything about a body."

"It was mostly over by the time I got there," he replied. "I told you, I asked Mr. Smyth what was going on, and he said he wasn't at liberty to tell me." He turned to me. "Just where did you run into Rother?"

"There's a track coming in from the left that meets the main track running past Vixen Hill. A mile or two from where your lane turns to the right. He was coming from that direction."

Roger said, "There's the ruin of a windmill that way. Not much else."

"And you're sure he said a body?" Margaret asked, a frown between her eyes.

"Yes, I'm sure. I was asking him about the excitement in Hartfield. And that's when he told me. I think he was too angry with me for leaving to say any more than he had. My—punishment—for disappearing."

"He's incompetent," Gran said. "I'd complain to the Chief Constable if I thought it would do any good."

"It can't be easy for him," Margaret pointed out. "He hounds us because he doesn't know where else to turn and George was our houseguest."

Before I could make Lydia's excuses, Daisy came to the door to announce dinner. Mrs. Ellis said, "We're waiting for Lydia. She hasn't come down."

Daisy flicked a glance in my direction then said, "She has a headache, ma'am, and doesn't feel up to having dinner."

"Then I should go up to her," Mrs. Ellis said.

Daisy hastily improvised. "I think she's sleeping. She's asked for a tray later."

"Well, then," Gran said, "there's no reason to let our own dinner spoil."

She led the way into the dining room, and as we were taking our places, I saw Roger Ellis watching me with wary eyes.

We didn't linger over dinner. And when everyone went to the hall to have our tea, Roger Ellis caught my arm and held me back.

We stood there in the dining room, the remains of dinner on the table behind us, and waited until the others were out of earshot.

"What took you to Dover?" he asked in a low voice. "It wasn't duty. They wouldn't summon a nursing sister from Sussex to deal with a patient in Kent."

"I actually did meet a former patient and got him transferred back to the Base Hospital in Rouen." I pulled my arm from his grasp.

"Rouen? What was he doing in Dover?"

"He'd been badly burned in a fire, and was out of his head. They put him on the ship by mistake."

"The devil they did! Why did you go to Dover?"

I took a deep breath. He would learn about Sophie soon enough.

"It's true. As far as it goes. But the fire was in Rouen, a street of houses burning. In one of them lived a handful of dispossessed nuns caring for a number of French orphans. Your daughter was among them. Thank God the children were rescued, and the man who brought her out of the fire knew I'd been searching for such a child. He brought her to me. Only I didn't know that when I drove to Kent. I only knew that a man I'd treated in France was in Dover without proper papers and in a great deal of trouble. It wasn't until I'd got there that he told me the rest of the story."

"You knew when I met you in Rouen where she was. I suspected it then. I know it now. Why did you lie to me?" He was very angry.

"I didn't lie. I didn't feel it was the right time to tell you the whole truth. What could you have done? Nothing. Which is all I was able to do. And—to be perfectly honest—I didn't know what you intended to do when you found Sophie."

"Did you believe I would harm her? I only wanted to pay for her upkeep, to give her a chance at a decent life."

"But not to bring her to England."

"Where is this child now?"

I hesitated. "Here. At Vixen Hill. I didn't know where else to take her, and I'd already been away from Sussex too long. But I must find a way to return her to France as soon as possible. The nuns will think she's dead in the fire. Or worse. That's not right. The Sergeant meant well, he thought he was doing what was best. But he shouldn't have taken her away. The nuns are the only family she's ever known. And the other children are her family—"

He cut me short, his voice harsh. "Is she in your room?"

"No. Lydia came into the kitchen when I was trying to feed her and comfort her. She took her to the room above the hall."

He swore then, and started for the stairs. I went quickly after him, and said, "Whatever you want to say to me or to your wife, you will not frighten that child. Do you hear me?"

"I don't frighten children."

But I thought in the mood he was in, he might not remember Sophie. And so I followed him.

When we came to the room Lydia had taken over, he knocked, and then without waiting for an invitation to enter, he opened the door and walked in.

Lydia, startled, looked at him and then her gaze slid to me. "You told him," she accused.

Beside her on the cushions spread about the floor, the cat and the child were curled up asleep. She moved away from them and stood up to face her husband.

He didn't look at Sophie. His eyes were on his wife. "Her father's name is Hebert. She is not my child."

"You've only to look at her to know she is," Lydia retorted. "Whatever name you used."

"He was a French officer. He died in the fighting six months before she was born. Her mother died of childbed fever."

Lydia shook her head. "You can't deny her, Roger. It would be cruel to try."

"You can't keep her," he said doggedly. "Ask Bess, if you don't believe me."

"She's here. And she'll stay with me. I don't care about French law or the nuns or anything else."

"Lydia," I began, but she shook her head a second time.

"No, I don't want to hear it. Roger made his choice. I've made mine. I'll have a child now. It's what I wanted from the beginning. And you needn't worry about me anymore."

"How will you explain her to the world, Lydia?" I asked. "You must think about this practically, not emotionally. Will you let everyone in Ashdown Forest point her out as Roger's love child? She'll be under that cloud for the rest of her life, if you aren't careful. She's not yours. She must go back to France. If Roger wants her, he can go through the proper procedures. I'll take her back as soon as possible."

"You won't. I won't let you. Now go away, both of you. I've nothing more to say." And she turned her back on us, walking to the window and looking out into the darkness.

Roger tried to argue with her, to no avail. And then she said, suddenly turning toward us, "There's a motor-car coming up the lane. I expect it must be the police."

She turned toward the bed, intent on taking up the sleeping child and going somewhere with her.

I said, "Lydia, stop! The police don't know anything about this. They've come because there was another murder, not for Sophie."

She hesitated. "You're lying to me."

"No. There's no way they could have discovered anything about her. Even if the French police are searching everywhere, there's nothing to lead them to Sussex."

Roger looked at me. "You have more explaining to do," he said, and then turned and went out of the room. I could hear his steps on the stairs.

Lydia hovered protectively over Sophie, daring me to take her away.

I said, "Are you sure you want a child who looks so much like Juliana?"

"I don't care what she looks like. It won't matter."

"But it might to your husband. Did you see? He never looked in Sophie's direction. He doesn't want to know how much she looks like his sister. He doesn't want to be reminded."

"He'll change his mind in time. You don't know him, Bess."

I was getting nowhere, and I could just hear the knock at the hall door.

I said, "We'll have to deal with this later," and followed Roger Ellis down the stairs.

When I walked into the hall, I saw that Lydia was right. Inspector Rother had just been admitted. He crossed to the hearth and put out his hands to the blaze, saw that I had joined the others, and nodded. "You're all here then. Except for Mrs. Roger Ellis," he said. "Will you please bring her down to hear what I have to say."

"She has a headache. I hope you will allow her to rest now," I answered him.

"Very well. We've come to search Vixen Hill."

Captain Ellis moved a little from where he stood. "I'll know the reason why before I allow you to search my house and upset my family."

Inspector Rother said, "We've searched the Forest in every direction. The windmill, the church, the villages, everywhere. This is the only place we haven't been."

Roger flicked a glance in my direction. I knew what he was thinking: Had the hue and cry gone up for Sophie Hebert after all? Or was this police business of another sort?

But Sergeant Larimore would never have given us away, even if somehow he'd been connected to her disappearance. I moved my head just a fraction, and Captain Ellis saw it.

He said, "That's all well and good, Inspector. But you've yet to tell me why you must invade my privacy."

"Very well," he said grudgingly. "Dr. Tilton went out on his rounds yesterday afternoon. His last patient was Mrs. Jenkins, who lives in Wych Cross and suffers from sciatica. He saw her, and as he was leaving, she offered him tea, but he told her he was expected home for his own. But he never arrived. Someone suggested he might have gone into Bluebell Cottage, which is of course empty now. And so we went there to look for him. There was no sign that he'd been in the cottage. That's when we began searching the Forest."

"He's not here. I can give you my word on that."

"That may well be. But this is a large house, you don't use all the rooms these days. And the grounds are extensive."

Roger Ellis considered the request. "I shall give my consent with one reservation. I was just in to see my wife, and asked Sister Crawford to give her something for her headache. She's in the room above the hall, here. You will not disturb her."

"Agreed," the Inspector said with poor grace.

He went to the door and admitted his men. Among them was Constable Bates, whom none of us could abide. As they spread out to search, I said, "Who told you that the doctor had gone into Bluebell Cottage?"

"It was his wife," the Inspector answered. "Mary Tilton. His mother is coming up from Eastbourne to live closer to him, and if Bluebell Cottage was to her liking, he was prepared to make an offer for it." He turned and followed his men from the room.

We sat there in silence, the tea that Daisy had brought in while I was upstairs with Lydia and Roger growing cold.

After a moment Mrs. Ellis said, "I do hope they'll be careful and not break anything."

"Or pocket anything," Gran added sourly. "I don't trust the police."

"Why should Dr. Tilton have gone missing?" Margaret asked. "I can see that he might have been summoned to see another patient in an emergency. But if that were true, surely he'd have sent word to his wife?"

"One would think so," Mrs. Ellis replied distractedly, listening to any sound from the search.

"I wish Henry was here," Margaret said. "I'm afraid."

"There's no need to be frightened," her brother told her. But I thought she'd been away from the Forest long enough to feel differently about it.

After what seemed to be hours, the police returned. Roger, standing by the fire, came forward to meet the Inspector.

"Are you finished?"

"All but searching the grounds."

They left, and we could see their torches flashing as they spread out across the grounds.

Gran said, "If they were as clever as they think they are, they'd have come here before dark. Those torches will do them no good, and we shall have them back tomorrow. Wait and see."

And as she had prophesized, they returned at first light in the morning.

I was first down to breakfast, judging by the dishes that Daisy had set out.

When Roger Ellis came in just minutes after me, I said, "What will you do about Sophie? Have you told the rest of your family that she's here?"

"If I do," he said tiredly, "there will be no hope of taking her back to France. You have put me—and that child—in an untenable situation."

"I realized that, the instant I saw her in Dover. But I couldn't leave England. And there was no safe way to return her."

"The fool who brought her to you deserves to be taken out and shot."

Before I could answer that, Mrs. Ellis came in. She had passed a sleepless night, her eyes dark-ringed, her face drawn.

"They're out there, just as Gran predicted," she said. "The police. Surely they don't believe we could have harmed Dr. Tilton. It's ridiculous."

"They have their duty to perform," her son told her. "I expect they rather enjoyed this one."

"Yes, it's so different since the war, isn't it?" She filled her plate, then set it aside. "I don't feel like eating after all. How is Lydia feeling this morning?"

"I haven't disturbed her," he answered.

She glanced at me. After a moment she asked him, "You and Lydia will make up this quarrel, won't you? Whatever was said or not said, done or not done when she fled to London, surely it isn't as important as your marriage. God knows your father and I didn't always see eye to eye. About many things. But we loved each other."

"Not enough to prevent him from killing himself over Juliana," he retorted, then said at once, "No, I'm sorry, that was cruel and uncalled for."

She bit her lip. "But so true, I'm afraid. We were all devastated, my dear. You as well as the rest of us. I don't quite know how any of us survived. Well. I hope you and Lydia can find common ground to mend matters."

"I'm willing to try," he told her, but I didn't think he meant it.

Just then Daisy came into the dining room. "That Inspector Rother is in the hall, and he wants to see the family."

Mrs. Ellis rose. "I don't think Gran is awake yet. Will you look, Daisy? And see if Miss Margaret has come down, as well."

Roger was already heading for the door, passing Daisy and striding down the passage toward the hall. I waited for Mrs. Ellis and walked with her.

"I have a bad feeling about this," she said, speaking to herself as much as to me.

"I expect he's come to say that the second search was no more successful than the first."

"Pray God you're right, Bess, dear. I don't think any of us can endure much more."

But as soon as I saw Inspector Rother's face, I knew she was right.

Roger Ellis was already speaking to him as we came into the room. "You will not disturb my grandmother or my wife. What you have to say you can say to me." He looked around as his mother came in. "I'll deal with this, my dear. Don't let it distress you."

"But I'm afraid my news will distress all of you," the Inspector said, looking from one to the other of us. "We have found Dr. Tilton's body. It was lying in that culvert that runs past the barn. It's overgrown, that's why we didn't find it last night."

Mrs. Ellis grasped the back of a chair to steady herself. "Our barn? But how did he come to be here?" she said. "I don't understand."

"What happened to him?" her son was asking at the same time, his words cutting across hers.

"He was struck over the head. Murdered." As Gran came into the room, followed by Margaret, he added with intense anger, "One of you in this household is a murderer. Three dead men at your doorstep, for all intents and purposes. Now what do you have to say for yourselves?"

There was a long silence as we digested his words. Then Roger Ellis said coldly, "Until you can prove that, I shall ask you to leave my house. Do what you must do to remove the doctor's body, and then I'll thank you to leave my land as well."

Inspector Rother smiled. "I'm afraid that's not possible. I shall require statements from each of you regarding your whereabouts night before last. We're waiting for Dr. Ledbetter from Groombridge. He will tell us the hours of interest. Until then we ask that you not leave the premises. I'll be posting a constable at the door, meanwhile. At the moment I must go and break the news to Mrs. Tilton. You might spare a thought for her in her loss—"

He'd been standing with his back to the door. It opened, and I heard Margaret cry out. I turned in time to see her husband, Henry, walk through the door.

"What the hell is going on?" Henry demanded, looking from one to the other of us.

Inspector Rother said, "You were summoned days ago."

"I know. There's a war on, you see. I was rather busy." He went directly to his wife, who held him as if he were the anchor she'd been waiting for.

"Where were you these last two nights?" Inspector Rother demanded.

"In London," Henry replied shortly. "I couldn't leave France, and when I did, I was seconded to carry dispatches to the War Office. My commanding officer doesn't hold with provincial policemen disrupting his war."

It was said to irritate, and it hit its mark. Inspector Rother flushed.

"Nevertheless, you will give your statement to one of my constables," he said, and then turned to the rest of us.

"In your earlier statements, none of you reported the conversation in the drawing room that led to Lieutenant Hughes retiring early. No one, that is, save Dr. Tilton and his wife. Even the rector and his sister professed not to recall what led to the Lieutenant going up to his room. And by the next morning, Hughes was dead and Davis Merrit was accused of his murder. But Davis Merrit must have known something about that conversation. After all, Mrs. Lydia Ellis had rushed into Hartfield to speak to him on that fatal Saturday morning, and the only conclusion to be drawn is that she was upset by events and confided in him rather than her husband. Merrit disappeared, and again the only conclusion was that Merrit, in a fit of misplaced gallantry, rid Mrs. Lydia Ellis of this man who had upset her. But Merrit turned up dead, and not by his own hand, as we'd begun to suspect might be the case. And now Dr. Tilton, who might have appeared to be the tattler to the police, is dead." He swung around toward me. "Indeed, Dr. Tilton had mentioned that you refused to allow him to question the Lieutenant more fully, and that you'd been ordered to accompany him to help put Hughes to bed by Roger Ellis himself."

"I was sent because he was too unsteady to walk alone to his room. Captain Ellis gave me no instructions. The rector and his sister can verify that. I was acting in my capacity as a nurse, not a spy," I replied shortly. "And if you question Mrs. Tilton on this subject, she will tell you that that's the truth."

"Nevertheless, Dr. Tilton is dead. On your property, Captain. Because he failed to keep your family's secrets. Now I ask you to consider who among you had the greatest need to do murder."

Mrs. Ellis stood up. Her face was pale, but her voice was steady. "It wasn't my son," she said. "I killed these men."

Gran crossed the room and stood beside her. "Don't believe her. I did it. I can even tell you how."

We were all shocked into silence. Then Roger Ellis said sharply, "There's no need to defend me. I can speak for myself." He turned to Inspector Rother. "You're telling us that these murders were done to keep the world from discovering that I possibly had a love child in France. This 'love child' of mine, however, is the daughter of Claudette and Gerard Hebert, both of whom are dead—the mother in childbirth, for which there are witnesses, and the father fighting in the French Army."

There was the ring of truth in his voice, and it was the truth. As far as it went. As he finished, he flicked a glance in my direction, as if defying me to contradict him.

I had no intention of betraying his confidence. It would only hurt Lydia and stain Sophie's reputation for all time.

"What do you know about this business, Sister Crawford?"

"I have seen this child." I heard Mrs. Ellis and Gran gasp. "And no one has tried to kill me. What's more, the nuns into whose care she was given called her Sophie Hebert."

"Are you defending this man for personal reasons, Sister Crawford?"

"I am not. But if he has committed murder, it was not because of Sophie Hebert."

He considered Roger Ellis, then said, "Thank you for being frank, sir. But it's clear your family is not a party to this information. That leaves them as suspects in these murders."

"I tell you, neither my mother nor my grandmother is capable of killing anyone."

"How much strength does it take, Captain, to slip up behind a man and strike him hard on the back of the head, hard enough to break his skull? One blow was not sufficient for Lieutenant Hughes—he was left to drown while he was unconscious. But practice makes perfect, does it not? A single blow dispatched the other two victims."

He hadn't told us any of that. "What was the weapon?" I asked. "I thought a revolver was found by Merrit's head?"

"A walking stick? One might carry that without suspicion. As for the revolver, it was window dressing."

"But you've taken all the walking sticks in this house. Did you find that one of them had been used as a murder weapon?" Captain Ellis asked.

"You're right. None of the sticks showed signs of use. But were these all the sticks that were here to start with? I questioned the staff, and they either can't or refuse to help me."

"What about William Pryor?" I asked him. "At one time you thought he might know more about the death of Lieutenant Hughes and even Davis Merrit than he was willing to admit."

"I haven't forgot Mr. Pryor," he told me, and then said, "Mrs. Ellis, I'd like you to come with me."

Roger stepped between his mother and Inspector Rother. "No. She's had nothing to do with this business."

Mrs. Ellis put her hand on her son's arm. "Let me go with him, let him question me. The sooner we cooperate, the sooner this will be finished."

"He'll do his best to confuse you. I won't have it. If he has questions, he can ask them here, in my presence."

Gran said, "I have told you. I killed these men. You can decide, Inspector, which of us to believe."

The door opened and Lydia walked in. I thought perhaps she'd been listening at the door, because she didn't appear to be surprised to see the Inspector or to feel the tension in the room.

"Inspector, do I understand you to say that one of my family has killed three times to keep my husband's secret love affair out of the public eye?"

"Indeed, Mrs. Ellis. That's how it appears."

"Well, you're wrong. Why should any of us kill poor George or Davis, or even Dr. Tilton, when the child is here in this house, for all the world to see."

I felt cold. This was Lydia's attempt to make certain that Roger couldn't send Sophie back to France. I couldn't believe how misguided it was.

Inspector Rother stood there with his mouth open.

"I don't believe you," he said bluntly.

"Then I'll prove it." She turned back into the passage and held out her hand. Sophie Hebert reached for her fingers, and in front of all of us, Lydia led her into the hall.

She stood there, looking around with large, uncertain eyes. And then she saw me, turned Lydia's hand loose, and rushed across the room to cling to my skirts, smiling up at me.

Lydia's face froze.

Gran stopped stock-still, with such an expression of pain in her eyes that I took a step backward. Margaret sat down suddenly, as if her limbs could no longer hold her. And Mrs. Ellis's knees buckled. If Roger hadn't been quick enough to catch her, she would have fallen to the floor in a dead faint.

Holding his unconscious mother in his arms, Roger Ellis turned his back on the child, as if she were not in the room.

I lifted Sophie into my arms, and she leaned into me. "I think it best for me to take Sophie back upstairs." Turning to Inspector Rother, I went on, "You have ruined a surprise, Inspector. I hope you are satisfied."

But he didn't hear me. Lydia started to follow me from the room, but Roger's voice stopped her in midstride. I left them there and carried Sophie back to the room where Gran had once played with another small, fair-haired child, long ago.

She said, an arm around my shoulders, *"Le chat?"*

"Yes, we are going to see the cat. Will you stay there with it for a little bit? And I'll bring you soup, perhaps a little cheese, and more biscuits."

As I opened the door, she got down from my arms and went to the low bed of cushions, climbing into them and rousing Bluebell from her sleep. Giggling, she pulled a bit of green ribbon from her pocket and began to drag it over the bedclothes. I thought Lydia must have given her that.

Shutting the door, I went back to the hall, where Lydia was standing over the still-unconscious form of her mother-in-law while Gran was searching around the hearth for feathers to burn under Amelia Ellis's nose. Lydia looked tearful now, and I thought that her grand entrance at the wrong time had suddenly dawned on her.

Gran found part of a feather from a duster caught in a length of wood sitting by the hearth, and held it to the flames for an instant. The nauseating odor of burning feathers filled the room, and she blew out the small spurt of fire on the tip before hurrying to Mrs. Ellis's side to wave it under her nose.

Mrs. Ellis moaned a little, brushing weakly at the feather to push it away, and then opened her eyes. Looking around, she said, "Did I dream that Juliana was here?"

No one quite knew how to answer her.

Inspector Rother drew me to one side. "What happened? How long has that child been here? Why didn't the others know she was here?"

"Mrs. Roger Ellis wanted to—to make sure Sophie was comfortable here before introducing her to everyone else. Sophie speaks only French, you see. And she doesn't know these people."

"Is Mrs. Lydia adopting her? The Captain didn't appear to be keen on the idea."

"She would like to, very much. There are procedures to be followed—" I let my voice fade away.

"So it's not all that certain that the child will stay?"

I sighed. "She's an orphan, Inspector. I'm not entirely sure what must be done."

"They could still have killed Hughes, Merrit, and Dr. Tilton. Those women. Not knowing."

"They could have," I agreed. "But Mrs. Roger Ellis knew from the start that a search was being made. First by Lieutenant Hughes, and then by her husband." I was praying he wouldn't ask me how Sophie came to be here in the first place.

He cleared his throat, trying to attract the attention of a family who had all but forgot that he was even here.

Mrs. Ellis was crying, Gran was gripping her shoulder so tightly I could see that her fingertips were white from the pressure, and Lydia was staring up at her husband, silently pleading with him.

Roger Ellis was very angry. The back of his neck was red above the collar of his tunic. He turned, saw me, and came toward me, catching my arm and leading me to the outer door.

Inspector Rother shouted, "Here!" But Captain Ellis ignored him, slamming the door behind him.

If there was a guard posted, I didn't see him, although a constable sat in Inspector Rother's motorcar, staring out across the emptiness of the heath.

I pulled free and said, "Blame me if you like. Then go back to your family. They need you."

"This is why I didn't want anyone to know about that child. By bringing her here you've ripped open scars that had finally healed. You've given my wife the means to blackmail me for the rest of my days.

You've caused irreparable harm by interfering. Are you satisfied?"

I held my ground before his onslaught. "Captain Ellis. You never wanted to see that child because you knew that if she looked as much like Juliana as George Hughes insisted that she did, you were more likely to be her father, not Hebert. And you couldn't face that."

He put his hands over his face and brought them down again, as if to scour the very flesh from the bones.

"God help me" was all he said.

I reached up and touched him, then let my hand drop. "There is nothing you can do about the past," I said. "And there will be nothing you can do about the future. Your mother won't let that child go now, and Gran will support her in that. She will become a little Juliana, with all the promise that was taken away when the real Juliana died. You must try to prevent that from happening. Lydia will help."

"Lydia will want to keep her from them. For herself." There was agony in his eyes. "What if Lydia dies? Just as Alan did? What then?"

"You think—you believe that your mother or your grandmother could be a murderer?"

He shook his head, but I could tell he didn't know how to answer me.

"Do you believe they could have killed the others—George, and Davis Merrit, and even Dr. Tilton?"

"I don't know. Damn it, *I don't know.* Why did you do this to me? To us?"

"I never intended to bring Sophie to England without your permission, without the arrangements only you could make. The fire in the Rue St. Catherine changed that. I can only say I'm sorry. But in the end you would have had to face up to Sophie. Thanks to George Hughes, too many people knew she existed, and that was the end of secrecy for you."

"Then why the killings?

"Perhaps," I said wearily, "they have nothing to do with Sophie. And we're just too blind to see it."

Seventeen

Ne went back into the hall. Nothing had changed. Lydia had asked Daisy to bring tea, and now she was coaxing her mother-in-law to drink a little. Gran stood behind Mrs. Ellis's chair, a frown on her face, and something in her eyes that disturbed me. Margaret and Henry sat in a corner talking in low voices. I could see that she'd been crying.

But the cause of this, Inspector Rother, was standing by the window, where I was sure he'd been watching Roger Ellis talking to me. He turned as we came in.

"I have to close this inquiry," he said doggedly.

Gran spoke, and I hardly recognized her voice. "I think you will agree with me that my daughter-in-law is not well enough to be interrogated. But I suggest that you consider the fact that if a body was found on our property, it doesn't follow that one of us is the murderer. Be very careful about accusations that you will not be able to support when the Chief Constable of Sussex sends for you."

"There are three men dead in Ashdown Forest, Mrs. Ellis. How do I explain them?"

"I'm not a policeman," she answered him. "I'm not required to explain anything."

Inspector Rother took a deep breath. "I must meet the doctor from Groombridge. As soon as I have taken care of that, I'll be back at Vixen Hill, and I expect Mrs. Ellis to be well enough to answer questions."

And he was gone.

I stood there, looking at this shattered family. They stared back at me.

Gran said, "Why does that child know you better than her own father?"

I answered, "She's been told she was an orphan. The reason she clings to me is that she knows me. I must take her back to France, and then proceedings may begin to bring her here legally, if that's your decision. She—" I looked for a way to say it gently. "The nuns who have cared for her will wish to say good-bye."

"No," Mrs. Ellis said before Lydia could speak. "I don't care how she has come to us. She's here. Roger, tell her that we don't want Sophie to return to France."

Caught on the horns of a dilemma, Roger Ellis said, "She's not my child. Wherever her birth was recorded, her father is listed as Gerard Hebert. I shall have to declare her illegitimate in order to claim her."

Mrs. Ellis began to cry. Gran said, a hand on her daughter-in-law's shoulder, "There must be a way."

Lydia said, "What does it really matter? She's here. We'll simply keep her."

I wanted to tell them that they couldn't, that the nuns were grieving for a child they believed to have been burned to death.

But before I could speak, we heard another motor-car pull up in the lane outside the door.

"See who it is. Tell them to go away," Roger said to me, since I was nearest the door.

"It's probably the doctor from Groombridge searching for the Inspector," I replied as I went to the door and opened it.

I stood there transfixed.

Simon Brandon was just stepping out of the motor-car, and his face was bruised, a cut ran from close to his eye to the corner of his mouth, and one arm was in a sling.

"You're still here," he said. "I'm so sorry, Bess, but it has been a very long four-and-twenty hours."

I found my voice. "What happened to you?"

There was a distinctly pleased note behind his words. "I had a small task to perform. Don't ask, I can't tell you. But it ended very satisfactorily."

He'd been in France. It was something he'd been eager to do since the day war was declared. But he'd been set on the sidelines, an adviser, his experience consulted again and again, but his vast talents never put to their full use.

"I'm very glad," I said faintly. "Are you all right?"

"I will be in a day or two. More important, are you?"

"It's been a very long four-and-twenty hours," I answered in my turn, and he was instantly alert.

Roger Ellis was at the door. "Who is it? I told you to send them—" He broke off. "Brandon," he said in acknowledgment. And then he looked over his shoulder, before adding, "I think it would be for the best if you took Sister Crawford back to The King's Head. We've had a difficult time here, and she may feel more comfortable in other surroundings."

I turned to him. "I'm not leaving without Sophie. She's my charge, not yours."

"Sister—Bess. Give them a few days to get used to the fact she must leave."

"If I give them a few days, they will have grown so attached to her—and she to them—that it will be impossible to take her away. If you will ask Daisy to pack my things, I'll go up and fetch Sophie."

"For God's sake," Roger began.

But I said, "You didn't want her."

"Dear God, Bess—"

"There's a solicitor in the Street of Fishes. Go and speak to him, if you want her."

I walked past him and into the hall. It was going to be very difficult, even for me. But if I left her, for the Ellis family it would be like losing Juliana all over again. And I didn't know what else to do.

To my surprise it was Henry who came to my aid.

He stood up for me, saying, "It can't be any other way for now. You must see that. She's not yours. This child. But if you insist on having her, there's a proper way to go about it."

When I came down with Sophie in my arms, there was no one in the hall but Simon Brandon and Roger Ellis.

As Simon escorted me to the motorcar, Roger Ellis brought the valise that Daisy or someone had hastily packed.

I suddenly remembered the Major's motorcar, but before I could mention it to Simon, Roger Ellis came to shut my door, saying to me, desperation in his voice, "Both Claudette and Gerard Hebert were fair."

I knew at that moment that he couldn't accept Sophie until Lydia believed that. And I thought she could be brought around to it, given time. She too would prefer not to dwell on that night with Claudette Hebert. It would be Mrs. Ellis and Gran who would fight hardest to hold on to the knowledge that Sophie was Roger's child.

And then Simon was turning the motorcar, and we were heading toward Hartfield, leaving Vixen Hill and Roger Ellis behind us.

After we had reached the track, Simon spoke. "You'd better tell me everything."

I did, ending with what, next to Sophie's welfare, worried me most. "Who is the murderer, Simon? And is it finished, all this killing?"

"Go back to the facts you know, Bess. Leave everything else out of the equation."

I smiled. "Easier said than done."

We were just coming into Hartfield. "What am I to do about Sophie?" I asked as she reached up to touch my face.

"If you really want to return her to the nuns in Rouen, I'll see to it for you."

He had the means, I was sure of that. I wished with all my heart that I could leave Sophie's future in Simon's capable hands. But the more contact I had with her, the harder it was to be objective.

"Let me think about it. Please?"

"You'll have children of your own one day, Bess. She isn't yours. She never can be."

"It isn't that, Simon. It's what I've done to hurt so many people. I don't want to make the wrong decision about Sophie too."

We had reached the inn, and when Simon had seen to the arrangements, I took Sophie up to my room and settled her. She asked two or three times for *le chat*, and I told her that Bluebell hadn't come to The King's Head.

After she'd been fed and put down to sleep, I went next door to Simon's room and sat disconsolately on the chair by the window.

"If I could fix it, I would," he said gently.

I smiled. "Would it were as easy as that."

Taking a deep breath, I began with the facts.

"George Hughes came here when Alan Ellis was dying. And nothing happened to him. He came again when the memorial stone was to be set in place. And this time he was murdered. It's possible that he went to meet someone—the note I discovered—or that he encountered someone when he went for a walk that last morning. He often went to Juliana's grave."

"All right. Let's look at that. If he'd prepared to leave first thing—his valise in his motorcar, nothing left but to say his farewells—why did he take the time to walk?"

"Everyone thought to say good-bye to Juliana. And then Davis Merrit, a blind man, went for a ride on the heath after Lydia came to see him and told him what George had said. He often went riding. His horse could find its way back to Hartfield, if the Lieutenant got lost. This time it did just that—but without its rider."

"I'll just look in on the child," he told me and was back quickly. "Asleep. Go on."

"The police believe Lieutenant Merrit rode out to find George and kill him. But how did he, a blind man as I said, know where in all the heath to find George Hughes? Or that he was walking at all?"

"Had Lydia seen him on her way to Hartfield?"

"She never mentioned it. Nor did the police. So I must assume she didn't."

"And it wouldn't be helpful to Merrit, if she spotted Hughes as she returned home."

"True. Which must mean that somehow Lieutenant Merrit knew where and when to find George Hughes. And that would explain why George went for such an early walk, even though he was in something of a hurry to leave Vixen Hill and all the embarrassment he'd caused."

"So far so good."

I took a deep breath. "Simon. That message I found in the umbrella. What if it was dropped in there *after* the meeting took place. A good many people were at Alan's memorial service in the churchyard. Anyone could have passed it to George Hughes then. But that leaves us with another quandary. Why would those two men wish to meet? The police haven't been able to come up with any connection between them so far. Except Lydia."

"They didn't know where to look."

"Good God, are you telling me that you've found a link?"

He nodded. "Actually it took your father's connections to uncover it. There was a general court-martial two years ago. Merrit and Hughes were asked to sit on it."

"A court-martial? I would never—but what was the case?"

"A Sergeant, one Albert Halloran, was accused of shooting an officer in the back during an attack across No Man's Land. It could have been accidental, God knows there's chaos in a charge, and no one can be sure when he fires who will suddenly step in the path of the shot. But in this case, the Sergeant had had words with the officer, and he was still angry when he went over the top. This was reported, and it was decided to try the man to get to the bottom of it. The court decided, unanimously, that the shooting had been intentional because the slain officer had warned the Sergeant that he was in danger of being sent back for dereliction of duty. He was sentenced to be hanged, but before it could be carried out, he overpowered his guards and escaped. It was thought that he managed to reach Boulogne and sail aboard a hospital ship bound for New Zealand, but when the ship was searched in New Zealand, he couldn't be found."

"He's back in England looking for revenge?"

"It's possible. Bess, what was unique about Merrit?"

"He was blind."

"That's right. He couldn't recognize faces."

I remembered Lieutenant Merrit stepping out the door of Bluebell Cottage and tapping his way down the street here in Hartfield. "But the blind often compensate by developing acute hearing. He could recognize a voice. And when he learned that George Hughes was coming to spend the weekend with the Ellis family, he wanted him to see the owner of the voice he'd heard."

"Men who have served on courts-martial seldom meet to share a glass of beer in the local pub and talk over the trial," he agreed.

"William Pryor. Willy," I said, getting up and walking across to the hearth to warm my hands.

"You can't be sure of that. Only that someone here in Ashdown Forest could be Halloran."

"Do you have any idea what this man Halloran looks like?"

"The description could fit half the men serving in the British Army. No distinguishing characteristics. Medium height, medium coloring."

"I'll never be able to convince Inspector Rother to look into this. I wonder if George and Davis Merrit actually did meet? Or if the killer got to each of them first?"

"Or if Merrit accidentally got the message into the wrong pocket."

I shivered. "How awful! But George went to the churchyard that morning, didn't he?"

"To meet Merrit—or to say good-bye to Juliana? We'll never know."

"Simon. There's George Hughes's accident. As he drove to Vixen Hill. He swore there was something in the road. But when he and Roger Ellis went back, there wasn't."

"Halloran couldn't have known when he was coming to Vixen Hill."

"But he could. George stopped here, at The King's Head, to brace himself for talking with Roger about Sophie. He could have been seen in time to prepare the accident. If George was here in Sussex, Davis Merrit would be able to have any suspicions confirmed. And so both had to die."

"It's too late to do anything about this tonight, Bess. But I think tomorrow we ought to speak to Roger Ellis before talking to Inspector Rother or one of his constables. Meanwhile, I should lock my door, if I were you."

I was halfway to the door when I stopped. "It all makes perfect sense. Except for the death of Dr. Tilton."

"To throw us off the scent? It might raise eyebrows if the only victims had a link with Halloran."

"Yes. Of course. He was found on the grounds of Vixen Hall. A case could be made for his learning something in the postmortems, and coming to speak to the family. Or to blackmail them. Who can say?"

He touched the wound on his cheek. I thought it must be hurting. But Simon would never tell me if it did. "I'll walk you to your door. Don't forget to lock it."

"I'll be all right. Good night, Simon."

I opened Simon's door and turned to walk down the passage to my room. And saw Gran standing in front of my door, staring in my direction.

"Gran? Mrs. Ellis?" I said.

"Can we talk, Sister? Isn't there a parlor down-stairs?"

"I should look in on Sophie. It's nearly time for her to wake up."

"It will take no more than five minutes."

I hesitated, then said, "Yes, all right."

We went down the stairs and found the little parlor empty. Gran closed the door after her, saying, "I don't want to be interrupted."

Sitting in the nearest chair, I reminded her, "You said no more than five minutes."

"I've come to ask you if you thought that the nuns who had charge of Sophie could be persuaded to accept a large sum of money in exchange for allowing us to keep her. I should think, given the situation in France at the moment, money could buy many necessities for the children in their care. Medical treatment, food, soap, clothing. Shoes. Children grow so quickly."

"It's not a question of money. Sophie is a citizen of France. There are laws. The nuns would be guilty of breaking them."

"At least you could ask, my dear. It could do no harm. And possibly a great deal of good. The other children would benefit, and Sophie would have a new life with people who care very deeply for her."

"She isn't Juliana," I said.

"I'm an old woman, Elizabeth Crawford. I know this child isn't Juliana. But we could watch Sophie grow into womanhood, which we were denied when Juliana died so tragically, and it would make up, a little, for all we've lost."

"I will speak to the nuns on your behalf," I said. "But I can make no promises." I'd said that once before. To Lydia. Promising that I would at least look for the child.

"I can ask no more." She nodded to me and opened the door.

"Have they taken Mrs. Ellis away?" I asked.

"They have. That idiot Rother wouldn't allow Roger to accompany her. She insisted that she would be all right. God help Rother if she isn't."

She left then, striding out the door with the support of anger to keep her strong.

I went back up the stairs to my room. When I opened the door I called softly to Sophie, so as not to startle her, then crossed to the bed. The little nest of bedclothes that I'd made for her was empty. I looked around the room, thinking that she might have crawled out of it and fallen asleep behind a chair or under the bed.

She wasn't there. I opened the door and went down the passage to Simon's room.

Even before I got there, I knew what must have happened.

While Gran had kept me busy in the parlor, Lydia must have slipped up the stairs and carried Sophie away.

Simon answered my knock at once, saying as soon as he saw my face, "What is it?"

"Sophie is gone. I think Lydia took her. The elder Mrs. Ellis was just here—I think to distract me while it was done. We'll have to go after them."

"Yes, get your coat. I'll meet you at the motorcar."

I ran back to my room for coat and scarf and hat, then raced down the stairs. Simon had already cranked the motor and was behind the wheel. We were rolling almost as I shut my door.

"They couldn't have too much of a head start," I said.

"We'll find them," he said grimly.

Ahead of us, crossing the main street in Hartfield, was Willy. He paused in the middle of the street, staring straight at us, then moved to the verge. I looked at him as we passed and saw that same expression in his eyes. Sly, knowing that he was tricking us, enjoying the joke on us.

"He's a healthy man, why isn't he in the Army?" Simon asked with interest.

"He's unfit mentally. Or so they say. He couldn't take orders, follow instructions, be trusted in the field."

"A very good disguise for a man who doesn't want to fight."

We were beyond Hartfield now, and there was still no sign of the Ellis motorcar ahead of us on the track. "They're driving too fast," I said. "The sheep—"

Simon said nothing, his eyes on the road.

We had turned into the lane that led to Vixen Hill before we'd caught up. To my surprise, I saw that Gran was driving I hadn't known that she could. But then the war had taught women to do many things, and driving a motorcar was the least of them.

We caught her up before she'd even opened the driver's door. She turned and stared at us over her shoulder, her face startled.

"Lydia isn't with her," I said sharply. "Look!"

Simon pulled up behind her motorcar.

"What is it?" Gran called. Stiff from the drive, she waited until Simon had come round to open her door and help her out.

"Sophie is gone," I said, reaching her as she stepped down and quickly scanning the empty seats. "I thought Lydia had taken her—while you were speaking to me."

"But Lydia didn't come in with me," she said. "She's sulking in her room."

"Are you certain?" I asked, looking up at the long window above our heads.

"Did you think I was tricking you with my offer? Of course I wasn't. Go on, then, see for yourself."

I opened the door to the hall and hurried up the stairs that led to the room above. I tapped lightly at the door, then opened it without waiting for an invitation.

"Lydia?" I said, looking for her. But the room was empty, and I turned to run back the way I'd come. She wasn't in the sitting room, nor in the little room that Mrs. Ellis used, nor in the library. I opened the door to the drawing room, and there she was, staring up at the portrait of Juliana, her face swollen from crying.

"Where is Sophie?" I demanded. "Did you come and take her?"

"What do you mean, take her? Don't be stupid, Bess, Roger would never let me keep her."

I told her what had happened. Sitting up, she said, "Are you quite certain she didn't simply wander down the hall? Bess! Oh, my God—Roger!"

She was already out the door, shouting her husband's name. I went after her.

We reached the hall to find Simon standing there, Gran beside him, her face anxious, her hands hanging at her side. "Anything?" he asked.

"She's not here."

"What is it?" Roger demanded, striding into the room. "I heard motorcars in the drive—is it my mother?"

"It's Sophie—she's missing."

Roger wasted no time on words. He caught Lydia by the arm, took her out to the motorcar. Gran followed. Simon was already turning the crank.

We drove back to Hartfield and searched the hotel, the environs, all the way up to the small church and down to encompass Bluebell Cottage.

She was small, and distances would tire her. So where had she gone?

Simon, meeting me again in front of Bluebell Cottage, said, "Someone took her. Why?"

"The police? No, they wouldn't do such a thing. Simon—"

"Don't panic, Bess. She'll be all right, wherever she is."

"No, she won't, Simon. I've got to find her."

But half an hour later even I admitted defeat. Sophie hadn't wandered off. She'd been taken. Just as Simon had said.

We collected, the five of us, in my room, and we searched that again. Simon brought his torch, and we looked under the bed again. But I knew it was useless.

Gran said, "How long were you in Mr. Brandon's room?"

"Half an hour? At most."

"I don't understand," Lydia said.

"Where do we look next?" Simon was asking Roger Ellis.

"God knows. All right, let's find the police and report this. The sooner we cast a wider net, the sooner we'll have her."

And so we looked for Constable Bates and reported the child as missing. He took down the details and suggested we drive to Wych Gate to tell Inspector Rother ourselves.

Three hours later we'd made no progress. Simon and Roger Ellis had taken it upon themselves to search the Forest, while Lydia and Gran took the Major's borrowed motorcar and went to search Wych Gate Church. Margaret and Henry were waiting at the house to coordinate the search.

By the time I had come back to the village of Wych Gate with the rector, Mr. Smyth, driving, Mrs. Ellis was just leaving the police station there. She appeared to be dazed as Inspector Rother put her into his motorcar. But she looked up as we pulled in front of the Inspector's vehicle.

"What is it?" she asked.

"Sophie is missing," I told her. Turning to Inspector Rother, I asked, "Any news?"

Mrs. Ellis, collecting herself, asked, "Are you sure you looked everywhere? The kitchen, the attics, the public rooms? Was it Lydia? Surely—"

"She says she didn't. I believe her. But who could have done this?" Desperate, I asked the Inspector, "Is there any family in the Forest by the name of Halloran?"

"It's not a local name," he replied. "Why?"

"There isn't time to explain," I told him. "But if I'm right, if we find Sophie, we'll have your murderer as well."

"That's what Ellis told me. Grasping at straws, that's all it is. But I promised to help, and I'll keep my word."

Mrs. Ellis asked to come with us, and I decided that even as tired as she was, she would worry less if she were with us.

Rother drove away in the direction of Hartfield. Mrs. Ellis said, "Quickly. Where have you looked?"

I told her, and she nodded. At the rector's suggestion we decided to stop at the churchyard, and we searched that again, torches flashing in every direction, then the church itself, and Mr. Smyth even went up into the tower. I walked partway down the path to the little stream, and then turned back.

If Sophie lay at the bottom of the path, I didn't want to know.

And then we went back to Hartfield. It had occurred to me that we'd seen Willy in the street there, Simon and I, before the search had begun in earnest. If he'd taken Sophie, she had to be somewhere in the village.

It took me a quarter of an hour to find the man who called himself Willy.

He was squatting by a horse trough, washing a pair of gloves, his hands red from the cold water, a frown between his eyes as he concentrated on what he was doing.

When I approached, he stood up and faced me. For an instant I had the urge to back away. There was something about him that was repellent. But I stood my ground and said, "I've come to ask you if you saw anyone with a little girl—about two years of age, very fair. She was in the hotel until earlier in the evening. We don't know if she wandered away or if she was taken away."

He stared at me, and at first I wondered if he'd even understood my questions.

Then he said, "I don't want any trouble with the police."

"They won't trouble you. Just tell me what you saw."

"I didn't see anything. I've already had trouble with the police over the watch. I'm afraid of them."

"But you must tell me—if the little girl will be harmed, I need to know. I need to find her."

"The police are already looking." He gestured toward the inn. I could see that Simon had just returned and was getting out of his motorcar, crossing to speak to the rector and Mrs. Ellis. "But it won't do any good, will it?"

"Please, Albert. Try to remember. Were you near the inn earlier in the evening?"

But he shook his head and turned to wring out the tattered gloves and hang them over a nearby bush. A cold wind was starting up, and he shivered. "My name isn't Albert," he said with an odd dignity. He started to walk on, his bare hands buried in the armpits of his coat.

"I'm sorry. Willy. I'll buy you a new pair of gloves," I said. "If you will try to remember."

That got his attention and he turned around. "Will the police take the gloves away as they did the watch?" he asked. "He said it was mine to keep. Always."

"Who said?" I asked. "And why won't it do any good for the police to look?"

He ignored my questions. "Will they take the gloves?" he pressed.

"No. The gloves will be yours."

"For always?" That sly look was there again. This time I recognized it for what it was, the craftiness of a man who had lived by his wits for so long he was forever looking to find an advantage. Someone who would give him coins, as Davis Merrit had done, who would promise him a watch in return for a lie, or offer him a pair of gloves in return for the truth. His only loyalty was to opportunity.

"For always," I promised.

He considered the bribe and finally said, "My hands are cold. Bring me the gloves, and I'll tell you what I saw."

There was a dry goods shop near the greengrocer's. They were just closing, but I went in to look at men's gloves, resenting the wasted time. But it was necessary, and I waited my turn with the clerk, counting the seconds as she finished wrapping a scarf for the woman ahead of me, assuring her that it was pure Welsh wool and would last a lifetime.

I bought the gloves and asked that a scarf be added to my purchase, then hurried back to the street to find Willy.

But he'd vanished, just as Sophie had done.

Eighteen

I hurried back toward the inn with my purchases and met Simon coming to find me.

"No one seems to know the name Halloran. He's changed it. He must have done."

I told him about my conversation with Willy. "He knows something. He must. He wanders through the village at will, and people are so accustomed to seeing him that they almost overlook him. Or else he's our killer."

"Keep looking. I'll go with you. Mrs. Ellis is exhausted. I asked the rector to take her home with him."

"He's been so clever thus far, Simon. Why take Sophie? What earthly good will it do him?"

"Something frightened him. And there was no time to plan."

The rector's motorcar was passing us, on the way to the Rectory. I smiled at Mrs. Ellis and waved.

"Simon. Remember the night when Willy came into the inn yard to inspect your motorcar?"

"I do."

"You're Army. One has only to look at you. Is that why Willy was anxious to find out about you? Was he once Army too?"

"There's Margaret's husband. And that Major of yours."

"Henry is artillery. So, come to think of it, was the Major. And he isn't mine."

Just ahead of me I could see Constable Bates coming out of the inn. I called to him and hurried to catch him up.

"We're looking for Willy, Constable. Have you seen him?"

"I have not, Sister. Is it important? I'll carry a message for you."

"Just tell him that I need urgently to speak to him. Thank you, Constable."

As he walked off, I said, "Did you search everywhere, Simon?"

"As well as I could. Ellis told me what to look for."

We began again, knocking on every door, taking people from their dinners, rattling the doors of closed shops until someone came to let us in.

No one had seen Willy.

"Where does he sleep?" I asked.

But no one knew.

When anyone asked, I told them I'd bought gloves and a scarf for him.

"You'll spoil him," the baker's wife told me flatly. "I don't hold with beggars."

Willy's wet gloves were still dripping on the bush where he'd hung them. He hadn't come for them when my back was turned.

When we asked the stationer where Willy slept, he replied, "In the old livery stable, that's now a garage. There's a shed out back he's allowed to use. Keeps him out of doorways. Not good for business, having to step over a beggar on the stoop."

The livery stable cum garage was close by the railway station, where the carriage was kept. I thanked him as Simon touched my arm and said, "We'll drive. It saves time."

His motorcar was still in the inn yard. In the glow of the headlamps as we drove to the station, I saw a hare zigzagging across in front of us before darting into the dry brush at the side of the road.

A little farther on, Constable Bates was coming toward us, and Simon pulled over. "Any word?" he asked.

"No, sir. I was just coming from the station. He sometimes sleeps in the ticket office."

And we went on our way, the livery stable already clear in our headlamps. As we neared, I could hear the stamp of horses' hooves, and once the sound of one blowing. Simon and I left the motorcar ticking over and went around back to where the shed stood at the end of the yard, ramshackle and bare of paint, the boards a silvery gray in Simon's torchlight. The door hinges were rusty and squeaked loudly as he dragged the door open.

I shone the torch into the black interior, glad of the shelter of the door as the wind blew hard across the bare fields beyond.

The shed was barely large enough to hold the battered old mattress on the floor. A peg for clothing was on one side, and on the other, a spirit lamp for making tea. A tin stood on the shelf above, and a cracked jar that held a little honey.

And it was only marginally warmer than the outside. I shivered at the thought of living here through the winter.

"No wonder the man begs," I said.

Shutting the door again, we turned back toward the motorcar. In the darkness I tripped over something underfoot, nearly sprawling on my face in the torn grass of the yard.

Simon put his torch on whatever it was, saying, "Careful. These old stables are a minefield. Horseshoes, wire—" He broke off as the light caught the side of a torn shoe, and then came back again to pin it squarely in its beam.

"Willy was wearing that shoe when I met him. Just over an hour ago."

"No one said anything about the man sleeping in the railway station. Except Constable Bates."

He flashed the light around, but there were no other signs that anyone had been here before us. Then he walked to the barn where the carriage horses were kept, shifting the door to walk inside. "Stay here," he said to me, and I stopped in the doorway. He disappeared for a minute or more, then came back to where I was standing. "One of the horses is sweating. Someone rode him recently."

"And there's no train at this hour of the night." I could just see his face in the faint light of the stars as we made our way back to the motorcar. "What's more, I don't remember the carriage in Hartfield. Not tonight."

"No. But there must be a way to reach the heath without going through the village, if you are leading a horse. I think we've found our killer."

"Constable Bates?" I felt a surge of relief that it wasn't anyone from Vixen Hill. "Do you think he's

Sergeant Halloran? Yes, it would explain— Simon, I told him I was searching for Willy. I'm responsible."

"You had no way of guessing."

As we drove back to Hartfield, I said, "It was Constable Bates who found the tracks where George Hughes and Davis Merrit met and then walked on together. Inspector Rother praised him for that bit of excellent police work. But he must have been following Merrit and saw them together. He was already suspicious of Merrit, surely. Who did he kill first, do you think? George or Davis Merrit?"

"Merrit. Before he could ride back to Hartfield. And then Hughes."

"Yes, of course. He could have hidden Merrit's body until George was dead, then arranged his supposed suicide. Simon, he was right under our noses. At the heart of the inquiry. Able to cover his tracks. But why take Sophie? I can understand about Willy. I'd wanted to question him, and that was too dangerous. Men like Willy *can* remember, sometimes."

We had reached Hartfield, and I scanned every face, searching for Constable Bates. Instead I saw Roger Ellis, just pulling into the inn yard as we came up. In the glare from his headlamps, his face looked haggard.

"Anything?" he asked, hailing us as we slowed.

I said quickly, "We've been searching for Willy. He's missing— I think we've just found his shoe." I was about to add that we feared that Constable Bates was involved, but for some reason I stopped myself. This was hardly the place. . . .

"Good God—why Willy?"

"It's possible he saw who took Sophie."

Just then Lydia and Gran drove up. Gran's face told me that they'd had no more luck than Roger had. Her usually stiff back was hunched with fatigue.

"Any news?" Lydia asked quickly. But I shook my head.

"Lydia, why don't you take your grandmother home?" I asked. "Henry would be glad to take her place, I'm sure."

Gran protested, but Roger said to her, "No, really, you must rest a little."

Lydia was saying, "I won't stop searching." Anxiety was plain in her voice. "And there's the old mill. We haven't gotten there yet. And I must ask the hotel for the use of a blanket. I don't know if whoever took Sophie thought about wrapping her well."

Roger hesitated, then said, "I'll take Gran home. Lydia, go with Bess. I'll bring Henry back with me."

"I thought you were to look at the windmill?" Simon asked, turning to him.

Lydia said, "He asked me to. He was going to The Pitch. Where Davis Merrit's body was found. But I stopped at Vixen Hill for a blanket for Gran's knees, and it wasn't until we left there that Gran said we should have taken another for Sophie." She shivered. "They used to claim the mill was haunted. Some tragedy or other, years ago. And it's hardly more than a ruin. I thought it was a waste of time."

Simon glanced at Roger. "Is that true?"

"True enough. I haven't been there in three years."

I said, "Still—it's the only place we haven't looked. Simon—we ought to hurry."

Lydia said, "Wait for me!" Leaving the motorcar by the inn, she came quickly over to ours.

Roger, visibly torn between going with us and his concern for his grandmother, said, "I'll follow as quickly as I can."

"Search the grounds at Vixen Hill. It's where the doctor's body was left," Simon told him, and then we were away, keeping to a steady pace through the rest of Hartfield, and then driving fast as we reached the heath, holding the heavy motorcar on the track.

I said to Simon, "It's possible we will find both of them there. If he's hurt that child—!"

"I don't know why he took her," he said grimly. "He has nothing to gain by harming her."

"Don't even think it," Lydia said from the rear seat, her voice frightened.

"Tell us where to find the turning," I said to her over my shoulder. "I can't be sure I'll recognize it in the dark."

"And I don't understand why anyone would want to harm Willy. He's not very bright, and he muddles things. Whoever is doing this must be mad."

The motorcar rocked, as if shaken by a giant hand, then steadied as we bounced high over a deeper rut. I could see sheep, ghostly white, staring at us as we passed, as if we were the ones who were mad.

"We think it must be Constable Bates." I explained to her what had happened. "I'd made the mistake of telling him that I was searching for Willy. Constable Bates must have gone to look for him straightaway."

"But where is Willy now? Surely not the mill—how would Bates get him there?"

Simon told her about the horse. "And I saw him earlier, before all this began, driving the Inspector's motorcar."

She leaned forward. "He's the one who always frightened me. The one with the cold eyes. But he's a policeman. Why would he murder someone? I know, I know. The court-martial. Still, this man Halloran could be someone else, quietly living in another part of the Forest."

"There's that," Simon agreed, but I could tell he didn't believe it.

"Has he lived here for very long? Does his family come from here?" I asked.

"I know almost nothing about him. Constable Austin could probably tell you more. I think something was said about Constable Bates coming from Cornwall, but I don't know if that's true or not. At a guess, he's been here two years? I know Constable Freeman died of cancer the first year of the war, and it was hard to find a replacement. Oh—there's the turning!"

We nearly missed it. Simon stopped as quickly as he could, then reversed. I could see as the headlamps swept it that our way was going to be much rougher here. A horse made sense.

About three miles down the track we were now traveling, I thought I could see the windmill ahead against the night sky, blotting out the stars. The top was misshapen, as if it had rotted through, and the arms were mere skeletons. I pointed it out to Simon.

"That's it," Lydia said, from just behind my shoulder. "I don't think it's been used since Roger's grandfather's day. There's a new mill on the road to Groombridge."

Simon switched off the headlamps, pulling over to the edge of the track.

"We ought to walk from here," he said quietly. "Sounds carry in the night."

He got out, and I followed him, asking Lydia to wait in the motorcar.

"I'd rather come with you," she said in a small voice, and I remembered that she had not cared for the heath at night.

"You'll be all right. Use the horn if anyone comes near you. Anyone. We dare not leave the motorcar empty."

"Yes, all right," she said, climbing into the driver's seat. I saw her rest her hand on the horn.

And then Simon and I were off across the heath. It was rough going, although the stark black shapes of the wind-twisted heather and gorse were easy enough to see. It was the roots sprawling out between them that caught at our feet. Simon had taken my hand to guide me, and together we made fairly good time.

The windmill grew larger. Bare of sails, it looked ominous against the night sky. The black weathered wood looked as if it had come from the gorse under our feet.

"There must be an opening," I said and nearly went flat on my face as the toe of my shoe snagged a root.

"The other side."

We reached the mill, and it was easier going, a cleared space around it not yet swallowed up by the heath. There was a window higher up, but I didn't think anyone was there. Still, we were more easily spotted than someone inside the shadowed interior.

"He's not here."

Simon leaned over to whisper against my hair. "Don't be too sure. There must be another way in."

Making our way silently around the rough wooden sides, we found a door. It was merely a blacker rectangle, standing half open, as if it had been left that way so long ago that the door had petrified in that position. A torch gave too much light. I reached into my pocket for matches, and pressed several into Simon's palm.

It was then I heard the whimpering, like a puppy left alone in the dark.

I would have dashed inside without thinking but for Simon's hand clamping down on my shoulder. I winced and stood still.

We waited, straining to hear the smallest sounds from inside. But there was nothing, not even the scurrying of a rat.

Simon struck a match and held it just inside.

Shadows danced about the walls, but we could see very little. Part of the upper floor had come down, half filling the ground floor.

"All right," he said. "I'll go first." And lighting a second match, he stepped inside as quickly as if he were entering the tent of a suspected tribesman. I tried to see around him, but he was blocking my view. A third match, and then he said, "All clear. Watch out. There are timbers everywhere, and Willy's body is just beyond the door."

"And Sophie?"

"She's on the stone. I think she's well enough. I could see eyes peering at me."

He flicked on his torch, the light blinding both of us, and we had to stand still until our eyes adjusted to it. As soon as I could pick out her shape, I walked over to Sophie. She opened her arms to me, and I picked her up.

"I don't like it," she said to me in French. "Dark."

"Yes, darling, we'll have you out of here quickly. Simon, she's all right. How is Willy?"

He was bending over the man. "There's blood on the back of his head. But he's still breathing."

"There's the scarf in the motorcar. I meant it for him. We can bind his head with that. But how do we get him there?"

Simon was rummaging around now and discovered some sacks in a corner, but they were filthy and rotting.

"Lydia can take Sophie, and then I'll be free to help you." I stepped outside and called to her.

She refused to come at first, then stepped down from the motorcar and whimpering almost in imitation of Sophie, she made her way through the dark. When she finally reached me, she gripped my arm with anxious fingers. "Why would anyone do this to a child? I find it hard to believe." Taking Sophie from me, she shivered as she looked down at Willy. "How did anyone manage to bring him here?"

"The station carriage horses, at a guess," Simon answered her. "Or the motorcar."

She started back the way she'd come, picking her footing carefully.

I watched until she reached the motorcar, and then went back to Simon. I found that he'd brought Willy around. The man was sitting up, holding his head, moaning.

"Can you walk, if we help you?" Simon asked him.

"Dizzy," Willy said. "Sick."

Shining Simon's torch on the back of Willy's head, I could see bone shining through the bloody tear in his scalp, pinkish white in the light.

"Gently. His skull may be fractured," I warned Simon, and then bent to take Willy's arm. "Will you try?" I asked him.

He smelled. And I wondered if there might be lice in the folds of his clothing as we supported him between us.

It took us nearly ten minutes to persuade him that he could walk. Even so, he gagged twice as we got him to his feet.

"Close your eyes," I told him. "Let us guide you."

And so we got him moving, slowly taking him through the gorse, stumbling and begging us to stop, once falling to his knees and refusing to stand again.

When we reached the motorcar, he put out a hand to touch it, as if uncertain that it was really there. Then he half stepped, half relapsed into the rear seat.

Five minutes later, we were on our way back to Hartfield.

I was questioning Willy, but he couldn't remember being attacked or who had taken him to the mill. Groaning, he held his head in his hands, motion sick from the blow.

In the seat next to Simon, Lydia was asking Sophie what had happened to her, but all she would say was that the man had told her he had a cat.

I said to Simon, "How are we to prove any of this?"

"I'll call London straightaway and get someone down here. Meanwhile, the doctor is dead. Someone ought to take Willy to the one you mentioned from Groombridge."

I could see that Willy's wound was bleeding profusely, already soaking through the wool scarf I'd used to bandage it.

When we came to the turning, Simon suggested taking Lydia and the child to Vixen Hill, where Margaret and Henry were waiting for news. "She'll be safe there."

We did that, making certain that Henry and his wife knew what to expect, and then Willy, Simon, and I headed toward Hartfield.

We stopped at the Rectory, and Mr. Smyth agreed to convey Willy to Groombridge, and his sister went with him. Mrs. Ellis had fallen into a restless sleep, and I agreed to sit with her. We managed to move Willy to the Smyth motorcar, and then Simon and I were alone, standing there in the windy High Street.

"I must put in a call to London," he said. "They'll send someone."

And he was gone. I stood there in the darkness, feeling the weight of exhaustion overwhelming me. Where was Constable Bates?

Ten minutes later, Simon came back out to where I was waiting. "Bates was Halloran's mother's name. Her nephew, one Thomas Bates, was a constable in Cornwall before the war. Apparently he was among the missing on the Somme. Halloran must have assumed his identity, claiming a medical discharge. I expect no one here in Sussex doubted his credentials. If he conducted himself properly, there would be no reason to question them."

"And who would look for a deserter in a village constable? The police are so shorthanded, thanks to the war. I remember Inspector Herbert complaining about that in London."

"At any rate, the Army is sending men posthaste to help us find him and take him in charge."

I went back to the Rectory and found Mrs. Ellis awake and in the parlor, looking for the rector or his sister.

"What's happened?" she asked, her face white with fear. "Don't keep it from me!"

I took her into the kitchen and set about making tea, all the while giving her a brief account of what we had discovered.

"Oh, thank God," she said when I'd finished. "I thought the rector might have gone because—because someone was dead." After a moment, she went on. "You don't know—I thought—I thought God was punishing me. Taking her from me a second time. I didn't want her to pay for my sins." Then, without warning, she began to cry.

"She's safe, Mrs. Ellis," I said. "And no harm came to her. She was a little frightened in the dark, but that was all. There's nothing to fear."

"I killed them, you know." She raised her head to look at me. Tears were streaming down her face. "And when I saw Sophie, I thought God had forgiven me. But he hadn't. I don't deserve Sophie."

I felt cold. "Killed whom?"

"Juliana. And then Alan. They were suffering so, and there was nothing to be done. I couldn't watch it any longer. The doctor had told me it would be a matter of hours. He gave me laudanum to help me through the end. But I gave a little to Juliana, and she simply went to sleep. It was so quiet, so peaceful. I was so grateful. And I asked for laudanum again when Alan was dying. And I helped him through the end. You're a nurse, have you never wished for something, anything, to end the pain of those in your charge?"

Swallowing my shock, I said, "It was wrong. You know that."

"God forgive me, I do. That's why I was willing to take the blame for the other deaths, I thought I could make amends."

What to do? Did I call the police and hand this woman over to them? She had lost her husband and buried two children as well. Could it be proved that the amount of laudanum she gave her dying daughter and her dying son had speeded up their deaths? Or changed the manner of their deaths? I wasn't a doctor, I didn't know. Perhaps it only eased her to think so.

"Mrs. Ellis."

"I know. I've told you. A nursing sister. I want a little peace, you see. I want to be punished, so that the rest of my family will be safe. Please. Help me."

"Your family needs you. I can't give you absolution for what you did. Nor can I hold you accountable, because I wasn't there. I have only your word, not that of a doctor. You must make your peace in another way. Perhaps Mr. Smyth can help you."

She broke down again, too tired to stop the tears. And I did what I could to comfort her. When she was quieter, I told her I must find Simon, to see if he or Roger had had any success explaining the situation to Inspector Rother.

"Yes, go see to it," she said, taking my hand for a moment. "Thank you, Bess."

I knelt by her chair. "You won't do anything foolish?"

"No. Sadly, I don't have the courage. But I think it helped to confess. I've held it in so long."

I left her there to finish her tea, the pot beside her, and walked back to the hotel.

The first person I saw as I came through the door into Reception was Constable Bates. He was walking down the main stairs, as if he were coming from one of the rooms on the floor above. It was an ideal place to stay out of sight, with windows overlooking the street.

My first thought was, *Where is Simon?* He'd been here when I left only half an hour ago.

Nineteen

Bates read my face even before I could speak.

Moving quickly down the remaining stairs, he was coming across Reception directly toward me. And I was all that was between him and the door. And escape.

I stayed where I was, wishing that I still had that small pistol that Simon had once given me.

The hotel clerk stepped out of the inner office, saying, "Miss Crawford?" and for an instant distracted my attention. And in that same moment, Constable Bates walked straight into me and spun me toward the desk. My ribs took the brunt of the blow, and I caught my breath with the pain. And then, with both hands gripping the edge of the desk, ignoring my ribs, I pushed myself away and turned as quickly as I could to go after him, well aware that he had nothing to lose.

Behind me the desk clerk cried, "Miss? Constable?"

I ignored him. Bates was moving briskly toward the motorcar standing in the corner of the inn yard. I thought it was Mrs. Ellis's vehicle.

He bent to turn the crank, his eyes on me, gauging my approach. The motor caught, and he was behind the wheel in a flash. Without warning he spun it and turned toward me, gunning the motor, heading straight for me at speed.

I stood there for an instant, uncertain which way to move. And then at the last second, ignoring my ribs again, I flung myself toward the inn's door.

He veered just in time to avoid hanging up the front wheels on the inn's steps and kept going out the Groombridge road, toward the north.

I ran for Simon's motorcar, just beyond where Mrs. Ellis's vehicle had been left, and turned the crank like a madwoman. It was late enough that the road was empty, and I gave the big motorcar its head, the headlamps sweeping the road.

Someone darted out in front of me, waving, and I spun the wheel to miss hitting him, seeing Simon's face at the last minute.

I pulled on the brake with all my strength, and the vehicle slithered to a sputtering stop, spraying stones and earth in almost a bow wave.

Simon swung himself into the vehicle, and I was able to keep the motor from stalling. Straightening us up, I went after Constable Bates as fast as I dared.

"Where were you?" I asked, not turning my head.

Simon, out of breath, said, "Arguing with Rother. I saw what happened. You shouldn't have taken on Bates alone. He's dangerous. He's killed four men, counting that officer in France, and he did his best to kill Willy. He won't stop at you."

"He's already tried," I told him, and heard the low growl in his throat.

"We'll see about friend Bates," he said and leaned forward to watch the road. In a straightaway I could just pick out the round red rear lamp ahead of us. But I was closing the gap quickly.

"Why did Bates have to kill Dr. Tilton?" I asked. "He wasn't at the court-martial."

"Dr. Tilton conducted Merrit's postmortem. He tied the two deaths together. That's why Inspector Rother abandoned the idea of suicide, even though at first it appeared to be one. The question is, what else did Tilton find? Or what was Constable Bates afraid he'd found?"

"Inspector Rother wouldn't tell us anything. Simon—what if he didn't *know*? What if Dr. Tilton had told Constable Bates what he'd discovered, but Bates never passed it on because it would change the whole investigation? Yes, of course. That's why Inspector Rother was going around in circles. If he was getting impatient—if he was on the point of speaking to the doctor himself—" The wheel jerked in my hands as we hit a deeper rut this time.

"Keep your attention on the road!"

I set my teeth, concentrating on driving. The rear lamp was brighter, sharper now.

"Should I try to stop him? Or just keep up with him for now?"

"For God's sake, don't use my motorcar as a battering ram. Try to run him off the road if you can."

"Yes, all right."

I caught up with Constable Bates finally and began to torment him. I'd seen my male friends play this game with each other—making an effort to pass, rushing up and then pulling back a little, flashing the headlamps. It was a dangerous business, but it was the only weapon I had.

And then I realized that I was making Constable Bates jittery. He could drive, but he wasn't an experienced driver. The constant threat of us passing him on this narrow road was requiring all his coping skills, and when he veered the wrong way, trying to second-guess me, I took advantage of the small space he'd given me and sped up.

Beside me, Simon swore in Urdu, but I ignored him.

The verge of the road was only a little rougher than the unmade center with its winter ruts and holes. I bounced over low-growing gorse, gave the motor more power to deal with it, and forged ahead.

For a second I thought that Constable Bates was going to sideswipe us in his fright. But trying to watch me and manage the motorcar at the same time was too much. Suddenly he lost complete control, and the vehicle thundered wildly across a field lumpy with last summer's crops toward a copse of trees that marked a bend in the road.

Simon yelled, "Watch yourself," but I had the motorcar under control and began to slow for the bend, even as Constable Bates came to a grinding halt. And I thought, *That's how George Hughes must have felt when he nearly collided with that length of tree trunk.*

Simon was out the door almost before I had slowed enough to make it safe for him to find his footing. Then he was sprinting across the rough field, and I watched, holding my breath, for fear he would twist an ankle as he leapt over obstacles and dealt with the deeper rows between the remnants of the crop.

Constable Bates, stunned by his abrupt contact with the steering wheel and the windscreen, was not as quick. But he was running before Simon could reach him, heading for the deep shadows of the trees. They were just disappearing from my sight in the darkness when I saw Simon hurl himself after Bates, and then they both went down.

I swung the motorcar so that the great headlamps pointed in their direction, and it was like watching a shadow show, one minute seeing only silhouettes and the next, a shoulder or an arm raised high, a head flung back.

I scrabbled in the floor of the motorcar, looking for a torch or any other weapon that I could use.

Just under the other seat, my fingers closed over a sheet of crumpled paper. I brought it up and tried to read it in the glow of the headlamps.

Get out of Forest, or child dies.

It was intended for Simon, the Army man. And in the dark we hadn't seen it where the wind must have tossed it off the seat.

Furious, I pulled on the brake, leaving the motor running, and was out of my door, running through the long bright beams of the headlamps, my shadow looming ahead of me like some black, disembodied thing with a will of its own. I nearly tripped over a length of fallen branch, and reaching down to retrieve it, I kept going.

I could hear them clearly, the grunts and blows of two men who were well matched, and I knew fear of capture must be driving the constable. There was nothing left to him but the rope. Simon nearly had him subdued when Bates's hand came up and raked the long wound that ran down Simon's face. As Simon arched back, out of reach, Bates ducked and plowed his head straight toward Simon's chest.

Simon had seen the move coming, and as nimble as a bullfighter, he sidestepped before bringing both fists down in a single blow to the unprotected back of the other man's head.

Constable Bates went down as if he had been poleaxed, and Simon, stepping clear of the man's body, turned to me, breathing hard.

"And what the hell did you think you were going to do with that tree limb?" He pointed to the length of wood I was holding like a cricket bat. "That's rotten. Didn't you see?"

I looked down at my unlikely weapon. The part in my hand felt solid enough.

"I was coming to your rescue," I said. "I wasn't going to let him get away."

"Did he *look* as if he was going to get away?"

We glared at each other. And then we both began to laugh. He reached down and took the offending branch from my hand, tossed it aside, and put his arms around me. "My dearest girl," he said gently, "your father is right, you are afraid of nothing. And that can be very dangerous, has anyone told you that?"

His embrace was comforting. It had been a long day, and I had carried enough burdens.

And then without a word, I handed him the slip of paper I'd found in his motorcar, telling him what was written on it.

"Bastard," he said under his breath, and then to me he added, "Where was it? I never saw it."

"It had fallen under a seat."

"All right, as Hamlet said, shall we lug the guts into another room? At least as far as my motorcar. Then we'll try to get the Ellis vehicle back on the road. Or not, as the case may be. Can you manage his feet?"

We put the still unconscious Constable Bates/Sergeant Halloran into Simon's motorcar, then managed after several attempts to get the Ellis motorcar out of the field. Soon we were driving sedately back to Hart-field, in tandem.

Alone in the motorcar, following Simon, I could hear Mrs. Ellis's voice in the darkness around me. I didn't know what to do about it. I didn't know what to do about Sophie, except to hand her over to Simon and my father to return her to the nuns in Rouen.

It was a long night. Simon stayed with me as we made our explanations to a very angry Inspector Rother.

He refused to believe me at first, just as he'd refused to believe Simon and Roger Ellis, accusing us of trying to distract him from the Ellis family. Constable Bates had served the Forest well for nearly two years, responsible and capable. He couldn't be a deserter under the sentence of death. He'd been invaluable to the inquiry. And so on.

Close to dawn, when Army officials arrived from London, Inspector Rother was finally satisfied that Sergeant Halloran and Constable Bates were one and the same.

And when Constable Austin was sent to search the small cottage where Constable Bates had lived, he found a broken walking stick, the length of an officer's swagger stick, with the blunt end still sticky with Willy's hair and blood. I was so grateful that it hadn't been the marble kitten after all.

I went to see how Willy was faring. Mr. Smyth had taken him in. The doctor from Groombridge told me that with care, Willy would survive with no ill effects. The scarf was a loss, but I laid the new gloves on his pillow. He didn't seem to remember what had become of his own.

Gran, her face gray with fatigue, was finally allowed to take Mrs. Ellis home. Roger was coming to drive them, after a few final words with the rector.

She and I had only a few seconds together as I held her door and Simon bent to turn the crank. Gran was speaking to Inspector Rother, giving him her views of overly keen policemen harassing peaceful citizens.

I said to Mrs. Ellis, "I told you earlier that I can't give you absolution for what you did. But for your family's sake, you must find the courage to put it behind you. It will hurt them terribly if they knew. Your penance must be their happiness."

She put up a hand and touched my face. "You are a dear girl, Bess. I was haunted ever after by what I'd done. I thought my husband's suicide was my punishment. But when George was killed and I saw his lifeless body there in the water, I realized that I was no better than a murderer myself. And that there is no punishment that befits taking another's life. Under any circumstances." She swallowed her tears. "I loved them so dearly."

"I know. Sometimes love tries to do too much."

And then they were driving away.

Simon came to me and said, "What about the child?"

"I'm too weary to think. I'm overdue in France. But Inspector Rother can deal with that. I must get word to Sister Marie Joseph—but I don't know where to find them after the fire!" The realization was like a blow. "It's all to do over again, searching for them. And what shall I do with Sophie, meanwhile? I can't take her to Somerset. I can't change her world a third time."

He pulled me into his arms and held me until I was calmer.

"You need sleep, Bess. Tomorrow we'll deal with Sophie and the nuns."

"I should go back to France tonight. And what about that poor Major's motorcar?"

"The war will keep. So will the motorcar."

I laughed, and he let me go.

"The war might wait," I said ruefully, "but Matron is likely to kill me."

He drove me to Dover the next afternoon, after I'd given the police my statement, and I'd said good-bye to Roger Ellis, who had come into town to speak to me.

He too was on his way back to France, his orders sending him through Portsmouth.

He stood before me, trying to find the words he wanted to say.

I shook my head. "I don't like leaving Sophie in Vixen Hill any more than you do. But I have no choice until I find Sister Marie Joseph."

"I don't know what to do about her," he told me truthfully. "She's probably mine, isn't she?"

"She's legally Sophie Hebert. You told me. I'd leave it at that. Even if you adopt her."

"Yes. You can't know how many times I've regretted that night."

"I don't think Claudette did. She gave her husband a child, even though he didn't live to see it. Did you ever think that Sophie might, one day, inherit his property? She deserves it. When the war is over, you could see that her interests are protected."

"I shall." He took my hand, then leaned forward and kissed me on the cheek. "I hated you when I first met you. God keep you safe."

"And you as well."

He was gone, and Simon was ready to leave. He had already arranged for someone to transport the Major's vehicle safely back to Dover. I stepped into the motor-car and leaned back against the seat.

"I would so much like to go home to Somerset." I'd spoken to my mother and the Colonel Sahib on the inn's telephone. Their voices had sounded so near, I felt the distance sharply.

"I know. Next time."

When I landed in France, it was the darkness before dawn, and the streets of Rouen seemed empty, even the new recruits gone up toward the fighting.

But across the water as we had moved toward the quay and set about docking came the call of an Australian kingfisher, and I stood by the rail, waving a white handkerchief in response.

Sergeant Larimore was there to greet me when we were allowed to disembark. He looked better than I'd seen him since he'd been wounded, though still a little singed around the edges.

"You got back safely, I see," I said.

"It's the saintly life I lead," he assured me. "They fussed over the burns and my bravery, and the fact that I'd passed out from the pain and couldn't report back to the Base Hospital."

And I was sure there was a hint of canary feathers around his mouth as he added, "I told the nuns, Bess.

I traced them and I confessed to what I'd done. And I told them Sophie was safe, that she'd be brought back to France if they wished."

"Dear God. What did they say?" I stopped stock-still, waiting for another blow to fall.

"They were that grateful. I had a long and very serious lecture from Sister Marie Joseph about the dire effects of impulsive behavior. They're being moved to a house in Lille, the nuns and the children with them. She gave me the direction. And the direction of that lawyer on Fish Street."

"The Street of Fishes."

"Aye, well, I'm a sheep farmer, I can't speak the language."

I laughed. "You're the canniest sheep farmer I know."

"I should hope so. At any rate, the good Sister told me she would consider a proper request for Sophie to live in England, as long as she is taught about her parents and the nuns who protected her."

We walked on. "I must write to Roger Ellis. He's on his way back to France. He'll have to see to it, and contact the solicitor."

"As to that," Sergeant Larimore said, more canary feathers drifting around his cheeky head, "I paid that gentleman a friendly call. Said I was best mates with this Ellis chap, and he's willing to represent him."

"Sergeant Larimore, you're incorrigible!"

"Aren't I just?" He shifted my valise to the other arm, and said, "Do you know the French think there's a German spy in the bulrushes down along the river? I've been here for every ship landing, waiting for you. Only yesterday they sent another detachment of soldiers to scour the banks. If you hadn't come soon, I was likely to be shot as a spy."

I laughed.

But I had also noticed that he was wearing not the blue serge of the Base Hospital but his uniform.

"Are you healed?"

"Not completely," he informed me. "But if you're going back to the forward dressing station, I don't see any point in lingering here. I'll just get myself wounded again and you can save me this time. The Aborigines have a saying, you know. That if you save a man's life, he's yours as long as he lives."

"I don't believe a word of it. Besides, if it were true, you already belong to another nursing sister."

He chuckled complacently, shortening his stride to match mine. "Ah, but it was the doctor who saved me that time. And he doesn't count."